there's a DAGGER *in your* BACK

STACEY WILLIS

it is our DUTY; we the chosen and sharpened TOOLS, to cleanse the land of the dripping red sun of traitors, liars, the greedy, the bigoted, and the wicked. only with the SACRIFICE of blood is the underbelly of the city made righteous. dare not to feel PITY based on the feign of repentance. always pull out the ROOT. the stain of sin will forever remain. our BLADES will cut them from the cloth of time. and I vow to be a BEACON.

THE KEY HARVESTER

There's A Dagger In Your Back

†

OTHER BOOKS IN THE SERIES

Dot Dot, Line Line

OTHER WORKS BY STACEY WILLIS

THE DAUGHTER OF FIRE SAGA

Daughter of Fire
Son of Death
Mark of Kóri
Heir of Bones

OTHER BOOKS IN THE SERIES

Flake of Snow: A Novella
Reaper of Gods
Tempting of Fate

STAND-ALONE BOOKS AND NOVELLAS

Ear to the Serpent

To the Family Flat,
who thought that being put in a
book would be a good thing.

Enjoy.

the city of idun

translated from an old Seelie tongue, '*land of the dripping red sun*'
from blood, by blood, in blood

LOEGON : THE CAPITAL

Imans (those never born with majik blood)
Seelie (Faery kind with majik blood, or majik-less descendants)
Favoured (other creatures born with majik blood, or majik-less descendants)
Maji (those who practise acquired majik)
The Court (Her Excellency, the rich and invited, and Officials)
The Guard of Madir (law enforcement of the city)

FRANQ : THE HARBOUR

Mer (those who reside in the sea)
Syrens (ruthless and carnivorous Mer)
Kraken (rogue sea serpents and cephalopods)
The Central Blades assassin rings (an unlikely ally and
irritation to The Court, tasked with [redacted] *)*

GEHMAN : THE UNSEELIE COURT

Unfavoured (other creatures born with majik blood
who practise forbidden majik and follow His Holiness)
Unseelie (ill-meaning Faery kind with majik blood.
Governed by His Holiness)

pronunciations

Lorrin Raffe: *Lauren Rah-feh*

Loegon: *Low-gone*

Zemir: *Zeh-m-ear*

Gehman: *Jeh-men*

Imannity: *Ee-man-ity*

Fayth: *Fay-th*

Char: *Sh-ar*

Lei Baiwen: *Lay Bye-when*

Mingxiao: *Ming-zhu'ow*

Petre: *Pet-reh*

Sedar: *See-der (Cedar)*

Hehl: *Hell*

Ixor: *Icks-ore*

Horjen: *Hore-jin*

Libbesh: *Li-beh-sh*

Ciaran: *Sigh-ren*

Franq: *Frank*

Idun: *Ee-doon*

Lois: *Low-iss*

Nadune: *Nay-doon*

Madir: *Mah-deer*

Iman: *Ee-man*

Maji: *Mah-j'eye*

Sythe: *Sigh-th*

Pense: *Pen-suh*

Moore: *Moor*

Verdia: *Ver-dee-ah*

Tianyu: *T'yan-you*

Huhmar: *Huh-mar*

Leifsdotter: *Lay-f-s'dot-er*

Euradon: *You-rah-don*

Kiilla: *Kee-lah*

Note: *this story takes place in a modern universe both like and unlike our own. It has advanced at a similar rate with similar conflicts, though intermingled with 'majik' and the creatures which come with it.*

PRAISE FOR
there's a dagger in your back

"I do very much respect and admire the scale and the details of her world building. A lot of love and attention was put into it and it's visible from page one. I do agree that fans of *Crescent City* and other urban fantasy will enjoy this!"
Lauren Dedroog, author of *A Curse of Crows*

"*There's a Dagger in Your Back* jumps into the world of Majik and assassins, with a plot filled with teeth biting and book throwing moments, it is one for fans of *Crescent City*. Stacey has taken her own twist to fantasy, with beautiful world building with the City of Idun, of different species such as Mer, the Seelie and Favoured, and the Imans. Her story is complex and keeps you guessing! I can't wait to see where book two will lead!"
Shyanne Taylor, author of *The Triumph Series*

"The story was very much at the forefront of this book beginning to end with the romance happening alongside it, which worked really well. The build-up was steady and very cleverly written. It set the main event up perfectly. The last half was so full of action, you can't help but keep turning the page!"
sophslilbookcorner, Goodreads

"This book honestly had one of the best world buildings I've ever read. On top of that, the very start had the guides to everything you needed rather than leave those to the end. In this book, it was one of the rare times I wasn't left with questions about the world and the systems in place."
Alys Milton, Goodreads

content warning

THE FOLLOWING IS A LIST OF TRIGGERS AND TOPICS OF WHICH THE READER SHOULD BE AWARE:

violence, murder and gore

alcohol use and abuse

panic attacks

mention of psychological abuse

mention of family death

mention of suicide

suicide ideation

mention of physical child abuse

non-consensual majik use

consensual and on-page sexual content

UNSEELIE
COURT

GEHMAN

THE CITY OF

IDUN LO

hall of
legacy
museums

gu
i.
tra

mine now

hemmingway
estate

N
W E
S

IMAN DISTRICT

h
sa
me

MAJIK
DISTRICT

hall of
excellence
academy

sythe river

THE COURT

*madir
manor*

*as if.
éllency.
madir's
ffice*

ON

FRANQ

X X

*ir
d
my*

X

*Wyche
hangout
spots*

IRIS DISTRICT

*where the
Syrens
frolic*

FENCE
STRICT

*madam G
493-593345*

*frangon
watch
tower*

LOIS SEA

CHAPTER 1

lorrin

Loegon and Franq never slept.

And frankly, neither did she.

The blinking streetlights dazzled stumbling partygoers in their stupor. The sky was hazy with it —that fog of pollution; it shadowed the moons and stars. One could only ever see them on a clear night on the outskirts of the entire city. It was not quite permitted to wander freely beyond the safety of the Wall, but Lorrin Raffe had never been one to adhere to the Guard of Madir's rules. The Unseelie Court was looser —but it traded fairness for debauchery and unhinged delights. Though it was entertaining to see the Guard recruits squirm at the idea of what offenders truly went outside of provincial limits to engage in.

The velvet against her skin was cold and slippery.

This shawl and short gown, like all of the decent clothes she came to possess, would be a pile of ashes in but a few hours. It felt strange to have stark mulberry lipstick upon her mouth as well, but it was not about her discomfort. It was not about her displeasure with the disguise worked on so diligently by Madam G.

Lorrin was only walking through the Loegon-bordered streets of the Iris District in order to carry out an order. The only differing condition about this mission, was that it was the iman herself who had decided to draw her blade.

Favoured ring leader Jerrek Money-Bags Burr was on an excursion in the far-off northern province of Gehman. *Complete Unseelie territory.*

1

Lorrin decided that he had some rather large balls to go there unaccompanied by Madam G or any other Wyche —in the sole hope of seeking out spies. Lorrin lived for the twisted underworld of Idun, but she understood something that he did not. Mortality was a precious thing, and she wanted to remain alive.

That was why the Favoured and Seelie had given up the city to an iman ruler. Natural death fascinated them. The fluidity of self-preservation was alien to most, even though they understood that flesh and bone were fragile. If she was honest, Lorrin had an inkling that the former Seelie King had relinquished his land simply to sit back and watch the show: the self-inflicted extinction of all imannity.

Ill-meaning or not, every ancient being born with majik had the same ambition; the same prejudice; and the same naivety. Lorrin had learned from a very young age that the world would not embrace her and offer her a place in it. She had not struggled in the slums —but she knew of the hardship. It had been a losing battle to earn something in Idun. She had no particular pursuits or yearns when faced with the available work in the city. Going beyond the borders to the greater continent was out of the question. Not without significant savings.

Lorrin glanced at the rose-amber twilight water of the port, noting the splash of mischievous Mer. Their sinister cousins, Syrens, typically emerged at night when visibility was low. Kraken were even rarer. Even though classified as wicked, the biggest reason those eldritch monstrosities didn't reside by Gehman was that they were useless on land. The Harbour was simply one's own risk.

A Mer suddenly swam up beside the iman along the wooden docks. She clicked her tongue; the sound resembling the high-pitched mating call of some marine animal, and giggled before diving back down. Her hair was a shimmering curtain of silver fire, extinguished by the uncharacteristically choppy waves.

Lorrin fought off a chill. That meant Syrens were coming, and in their hordes.

Her feet hesitated. She didn't have to deal with this. She could pack up and move to the distant Moore Country, where all manner of beasts roamed free.

The Mer popped up again, her head inclined in invitation as where there once had been a bra fashioned out of shells and coral, was now bare. Lorrin paused. What a treat it was to be desired by a Mer. The iman then blew a discreet kiss and winked, before turning on her short heel. Perhaps she would find her later.

Oh, how had she ever have considered leaving?

Lorrin liked her job —mostly. Killing was rewarded because it was difficult to walk away with a Favoured head. She kind of enjoyed watching the life drain from those distinctive eyes, and she had gotten a taste for immorality.

Long gone were the fair, golden years of childhood where fairies were the size of her pinkie finger; Mer were simply friendly folk who wasted time braiding hair; and princes and stableboys were suitors of virtue. The only consistency was that many stepmothers were indeed shallow and wicked.

At the end of the day, fairytales were blossoming flowers for sensible and privileged children to pick apart at their fancy; to admire and regather into whatever should suit them. On their every whim.

But once upon a time, a girl grew thorns. She stopped planting and picking, and became a thing of lore herself.

The people called her occupation a hoax spun and run by Her Excellency and the Guard themselves to control the city and protect certain reserves of interest.

Lorrin didn't care nor mind. She might never have, and she never would. Fairytales no longer harboured her hope —reality had weaponised it. It had weaponised *her*. No dashing stranger had come to her rescue. She had clawed from that Hehl herself. And no one would ever peel back her shrivelled petals.

There was a very wealthy iman by the name of Jon De Polis, who had a bony finger in every reserve in Idun. His late wife, Sera, had had pale hair like sunslight and fair skin —with a thin nose and narrow hips. Lorrin knew this because they had shared a likeness in their appearance. She was wearing this little, hideous, green velvet frock to twist the knife into De Polis further.

Further than she had driven it into Sera's chest, a few years prior.

What a fitting end: to be laid side by side with his love after being slain by the same hand. Sera De Polis had been the initial target due to her ringleader-ship of the family operations. Now that Jon was left a widower, he was squandering and gambling the funds. Jerrek Ego-To-Big-For-His-Shoulders Burr had been strict in his brief: the Ivory Blade did not tolerate such indulgent, pathetic behaviour.

That, and Burr had his eyes on the lack of a De Polis heir.

For this mission's sabotage, Lorrin had decided that she couldn't allow her boss to claim the spoils. In fact, there would be no claiming of anything —apart from Jon's life. The nasty repercussions were the furthest thing from her mind. No punishment would await her. Because if there was one thing on which she could count, it was that Jerrek Burr was a greedy Drakon descendant —and that His Holiness did not possess a merciful or empathetic bone in his body. Burr's corpse would arrive at the Central Blades by the end of the week.

When the Drakon is away, the business burns and goes to shit.

She was going to be his ruination.

The assassin had finally had enough of being passed back and forth all over Idun for every measly errand and inconvenience. She was not getting any younger. Not that twenty-four years old was exactly an age to consider herself elderly —though for an iman, it was around the average midpoint of life. It was simply time for her to become the only person to whom she answered.

Lorrin's shoulders then tensed.

A shadow moved within the corner of her vision; toying with the knowledge that they were too quick for her proper observation. It wasn't an officer. They didn't move like that. So she swallowed and kept walking, so as not to draw attention to herself. The real Sera De Polis; whether living, undead or spirit, would not have been rattled by such an instance.

It was precisely that irrational, inflated sense of irreplaceability and arrogance that had gotten her killed. But Lorrin was not so foolish. She searched for the nearest crowd of people, and disappeared amongst them. Her satin gloved hand stayed glued to the gilded handle of her dagger beneath the shawl. If she was being followed, then she would provide a show.

Jon De Polis would be leaving one of the popular casino and gala palaces now —*The Silver Reef*—having dined with members of The Court.

The plan hinged on an intoxicated Jon to recognise her better from behind than directly from her face.

She weaved through the already departing throngs of imans, Seelie and Favoured; spotting a few wheelchair-bound Mer who possessed the ability to trade gills for lungs. Despite the heels she loathed, Lorrin danced swiftly towards the giant metallic filigree doors. Unlike most of the attractions in the Iris District, this establishment was far too classy for neon, and had opted for vintage bulbs lining the inside of the frames of each letter instead. Patrons were encouraged to dress in casual suits and flapper dresses —and not to be stingy with the fake jewels.

Lorrin sneered at most of the pieces, even the real ones, and deemed them not worth her time. Besides —she couldn't afford any distractions.

Jon De Polis had to die.

Her gaze then shifted to a small sea of black and gold —Court and city colours. There he was. A tall, lanky male in a well-tailored white and silver suit. It must have cost him a fortune, but he was flaunting it with a false air of humility. The Court members around him feigned smiles and polite conversation —coughing into fists and fanning feathered fans to hide their gossip and whispered opinions.

They would no longer matter.

Or perhaps...when De Polis was gone, they might matter all the more.

Lorrin ducked back behind the wall and in an alcove near the entrance, a careful eye on both her target and her surroundings. There was no doubt that this kill would be a coveted prize; most of the rings would find satisfaction in the demise. The Ivory Blade was the most feared and respected of all of them.

And Lorrin was *their* most intimidating and revered.

More streams of people moseyed along by her, unconcerned with a figure in the shadows. And then Jon De Polis strode closer, his teeth gleaming in the street lights. The assassin didn't do much to get his attention —all she did was slacken her expression and incline her head in mimic of an apparition.

In the moonlight, her powdered skin was almost ghostly white. Her eyes did not match Sera De Polis', so an irritating pair of luminous golden brown contact lenses covered her cool marbled green-grey. But the wide-brimmed hat would conceal the minor imperfections. Excessive amounts of alcohol aided, too.

And it worked.

Jon paused; that stupid grin fell, and his eyes widened.

And as unprofessional as it was, Lorrin almost smirked. Though the real Sera might have done the same if she knew how her pense was being spent.

From the mildly bewildered look which then cemented Jon De Polis' features, Lorrin took her signal to turn away leisurely. His gaze followed.

She turned into a secluded alley a few streets away; to isolate him from witnesses. The drunkards and patrons around them would be far too preoccupied with their own affairs to concern themselves with an iman wandering off deeper into the Iris District. If she was fortunate, he may last long enough to be led through a maze before tasting the cold ivory and gold of her blade.

She could hear his sluggish footsteps tailing her sharp ones.

She allowed the smile to slip now.

The assassin led Jon further through the district; to the quiet and cheap apartment blocks, and brothels. Where no one would hear the violence —or care. There would be no report to the Guard, because no one here would dare. Every civilian knew it: if you want to stay alive, keep your mouth shut.

Jon De Polis' steps hastened; becoming shorter and quicker despite the few grunts and stumbles in between. Then he found the courage to speak.

"…Sera?"

Lorrin did not waver.

"Sera, is…that you?" he slurred, before walking into a lamppost.

It was almost…sad. That was the word she would use. It was pathetic that she had to lure him in this way —to resurface memories drowned by drink and pense. It wasn't that she thought it problematic to psychologically fuck with someone; on the contrary, she enjoyed mind games and intellectual torture. No —what dispirited Lorrin was how *this* was how low she had to stoop.

She could have slithered in with swords and shadows, before quietly plunging in a blade or slashing a jugular. She could have done it *professionally*. Now she was dolled up like a dead female and scaring her husband to death.

6

But it was certainly the most intriguing way.

A slow, methodical downfall.

The assassin's hand tightened on her dagger's handle.

"Sera!"

De Polis' cry was desperate now. It was that of a lost child, suddenly separated from the familiar. A part of him ought to have known it then —that it couldn't possibly be his wife. That this was a fabrication. But the alcohol was telling him it was real, and that she had come to carry out his reckoning.

He bumbled on, his steps nearing again with renewed urgency.

Lorrin was far enough from public view. She could turn and stab him now. Though her gaze kept snagging to the figure half there and not there; always a few metres behind or ahead. She was indeed being followed.

"Sera, please," Jon pleaded. "I...I'm sorry."

The assassin ignored his attempt to spark conversation. She knew not to engage to such a degree. Besides —if she were the real Sera, a mere apology was not going to cut it. But her dagger certainly would.

The figure of shadow had melted away for a moment. Lorrin wondered for a few seconds if it had actually been there. Though she was not one to hallucinate due to nerves. She wasn't intoxicated either.

"This is about —*hic* —the money, isn't it?" Jon hiccupped halfway through.

Lorrin stopped.

The sound of De Polis' footsteps faded as well.

She slowly turned around. Jon was squinting in the darkness, which worked in her favour. She walked back to him; her stance telling of her rage. She took hold of his tie, before pulling it sharply. De Polis trembled with terror.

"Jon, dear," a poisonous voice she had spent hours fabricating in front of a vanity came from her freezing lips. "You've been a very bad male."

He let out a sob. "How...how did you...how are you..."

"I never left, Jon," she told him. "I watched your every move. How much you gambled. All of those young females you acquired. How you disregarded my advice and rubbed shoulders with The Court. You're really quite stupid, dear."

De Polis' shoulders shook in another guilty whimper.

"But it is mostly about the pense," the blonde said truthfully. She abruptly let go of the tie and he toppled backwards before her onto the tar.

"You…you *died*," Jon then blurted, trying to rationalise the situation.

"Did you really think that a little death was going to rid you of me, Jon?" She then tutted, like a scolding parent, and produced her dagger from her shawl. His eyes went comically wide and he started shuffling along the road.

"What —Sera, please…be reason —*hic* —able!"

Lorrin couldn't control the dark laughter that erupted in response to his hiccups. This was utterly ridiculous. And equally hilarious. "Don't run away," she then chuckled, effortlessly closing the distance between them each time he got far enough to feel a shred of safety.

"Please spare me," he begged, hands shooting upwards in surrender.

Lorrin did not feel for him. She did not feel anything at all.

Her amusement died as she realised that her mission had now reached its lacklustre peak, and that the only thing now which would give her satisfaction was the gurgled scream on which he was about to choke. The assassin finally discarded her guise, tossing it aside as if it were a mere overcoat, and moved with the speed and efficiency she had come to hone. The dagger's ivory blade was a slither of moon parting the curtains of indigo darkness.

Jon was now shaking more violently. "You —you are not truly —"

The accusation died as abruptly as Lorrin's patience snapped. She slashed a clean line across his Adam's apple, and not as easily cut into his fingers when he instinctively reached upwards to his neck. Ruby blood burst from the wounds as though from an old unused fountain —directly onto the front of her gown.

It was fine. She'd burn the monstrosity after this, anyway.

She idly wiped the droplets on her cheek with green satin, still holding his gaze. His terrified bark-brown eyes rolled. De Polis knew it in his final moments of life: the assassin who had killed his wife had finally gotten him, too.

CHAPTER 2

lorrin

DEATH TASTED SWEET. Like ripe cherries or chocolate. Lorrin had read in several novels that the lingering tang of murder —whether accidental or purposeful —was usually bitter and unsatisfying. But the assassin had never felt more aware of every breath in her lungs; every pump of her heart; every muscle which protested with overwork. She had never felt more *alive*.

"You made a bit of a mess, Raffe," a deep, gruff voice said from the alleyway nearby. A voice belonging to someone who knew her methods well. Therefore, at least, they were not one of her supposed rivals.

"Did you enjoy the show?" Lorrin scoffed, wiping her blade between two folds of her gown. "Why didn't you try to stop me?"

"That wouldn't be as fun as watching you panic, thinking that there was a second ghost," the voice chuckled.

"And now?" said the blonde, sheathing her dagger. "Still playing coward?"

"Spectator," came the correction. A figure emerged into the pool of light from overhead. A dirty blond Elf around her height, cloaked in a robe of emerald over an Academy uniform with a ruby sun strung on gold around their neck. Their stubbled face was rough —maybe they had gone about a week without sleep. "I wasn't following you because I wanted to kill that iman," they went on to explain. "I need to speak with you." The gold rings in their large, drooping ears jingled with every movement of their head. Then they muttered, "…Lavender."

Lorrin squinted. "…Rye?"

She didn't have to kill again after all. There was only one person who knew the operation passwords. As an Arch Favoured, Rye was closely associated with The Court and the infamous Hall of Excellence Academy. The scholars and Maji avoided involving themselves with people so far outside of their social standing, but Rye had always established himself as a Court Favoured *'for the people'*. He was…personal. And he would turn a blind eye to Lorrin's crimes.

"Why were you so conspicuous in your tailing?" the assassin huffed, gingerly stepping away from Jon De Polis' limp and leaking corpse.

"Of course I was hoping that you would end up doing the right thing," the Elf sighed, glancing at the body. "I'm always hoping for that, Raffe."

That sun pendant glinted. Lorrin's expression soured. There it was —the self-righteous hypocrisy of The Court. What gave them the impression that they were so lofty and wise, to judge and sneer at the citizens who struggled daily?

"Do you even know me at all if you cling to that hope? Besides —you're not a priest of fayth. Merely a patron," Lorrin then reminded him as she turned to walk down the quiet street. The lights were not alight here either, but it was not unusual. Neglecting such jobs was commonplace in the Iris District. The sparce shrubbery and flora were also testament to a lack of respect for the Harbour. "But even if you were," she sighed, "my afterlife is not your concern."

"I am not trying to preach to you," Rye insisted, moving to accompany her. "That is simply my general empathy and worry."

"Don't need it," Lorrin clipped. "I like my life exactly the way it is."

There was a white yet overbearing lie weaved in there somewhere; one which she did not ever intend to unravel.

"Fine, fine," the Favoured finally relented, waving his hand dismissively. "While I don't approve of your occupation nor hobbies, you're usually an iman of reason. Which is why I sought you out in person."

The assassin paused, giving him a withering look. "Now that you've finished dishing your propaganda, I need to know. How did you know where to find me?"

Rye shrugged. "Simple majik."

"Bull. Normal people drop a call."

He cleared his throat. "…A strand of your hair."

Lorrin veered away from him, towards the park coming up on their right. "What the Hehl? How did you —when did…Oh my Goddess —Rye! And somehow *I'm* the psychotic creepy one?"

"No need to take the Daughter's name in vain," the Elf huffed. "I did not take it without your knowledge. Do you not recall when I asked for one when I was practising a location spell? It was from then."

She didn't look convinced, but she offered no further argument as she ducked behind a tree to change into stashed clean clothing, before gesturing for the Favoured to look aside. "…Hm. By the way —I can't take Her name in vain if I don't follow the fayth," she carried on while peeling off the splattered dress.

Lorrin had always scorned the idea of an all-powerful being hidden in the clouds further and more obscure than any airplane or rocket could go. The followers called Her the Daughter because as the scientists and scholars had established, there were multiple mirrors of their world and others; all akin to strange shards which reflected and fit together. Therefore, there was possibly not one God, but many —and since this world was not a primordial one, it made some sense that other Gods could be the Parents' Children.

It was the Seelie and Unseelie who had come at the dawn of their time before imannity who believed that their omnipotent being to be a daughter.

"You most certainly can," Rye still said with surprising adamant. His back was respectfully turned towards the iman. "You still acknowledge the Daughter, do you not? Especially when you speak of Her that way."

"I don't, so I can say whatever I want."

He grumbled, but understood that the topic had now been exhausted. And he waited to speak again until Lorrin had changed into dark jeans, a grey milkmaid top and her favourite oversized blue denim jacket. The contact lenses had been discarded, but a hat remained. This one, was a white diveball cap. On her shoulder sat a large duffle bag, stuffed full of the soiled disguise.

"I wish that you would take this more seriously," sighed the Favoured as the two then continued on into the adjoined public parking lot.

"I take everything seriously," Lorrin insisted, before stopping beside her car. It was a small, compact model —a midnight blue hatchback with two doors and a decent trunk. "You getting in?" she asked.

"We're still talking. Do I have much of a choice?" Rye chuckled, walking around to the passenger's side. "And I couldn't have just '*dropped you a call*'— you're still using those absolutely ancient burner phones."

"Hm," Lorrin huffed. "You could at least then give me a heads up." She stuck the key into the ignition and turned it after he had closed the door. The engine spluttered to life, before the car jerked slightly as she pulled the handbrake.

The Favoured clutched at the seat beneath him. "Why don't you upgrade to an alchemic car, at least?" he complained. "You can afford it."

Lorrin snorted. "And make it easier for The Court and Guard officers to track down my every move? I don't think so."

Rye glanced down into his lap. "…Why *were* you so sloppy this time, Raffe? You are usually far more methodical. It's as if it was spontaneous —"

The tyres skidded on the road.

The assassin sighed irritably. "It might have seemed unplanned to you, but I have my reasons as to why I made it look hasty. After this long in the industry, you would think I've picked up on that sort of thing. I can't have the Guard or ring leaders thinking it was one of the established *sophisticated* rings. I needed it, at best, to look like a beginner's attempt."

"Ah."

The Elf tried not to look too uncomfortable. But he had to understand what the title of '*friend*' meant in her case. A friend to Lorrin Raffe was complicit. They resided in the cloak of shadow and ensured that there was always a dagger in her hand; never to her back. They did not lecture, and they certainly didn't snitch.

The assassin knew that Rye was far more self-righteous. He voiced all of his judgemental opinions, even if they ended up wafting out of the other ear. One particular area in which she couldn't tolerate criticism, was her driving.

Lorrin liked to drive fast.

That rush of wind in her hair; the suns beating down on her face…it was the only time when she felt truly free. If she could, she would drive all the way out of the city gates; out of the continent and then ferry to the setting suns beyond. Alone, in her car, she almost recalled a semblance of the blind hope of happiness.

"Is that all?" then asked the blonde. "Did you corner me just to interrogate?"

"No," Rye said gravely. "I came to warn you before you could do something rash in the coming weeks. It is best that you hear it from me."

"What?"

"After my prayers today, I visited the Seeyer. She was in mild distress, and in hindsight, I am relieved that I was first to see her. She had just had a vision —one which had utterly shaken her."

Lorrin tilted her head to the side. "What does it have to do with my rashness?"

The Elf turned grave. "Because I believe that it was about you, Lorrin."

She flinched, and the car swerved again. He had said her first name. He never did that unless it was absolutely serious. But no —it couldn't be. A prophecy about someone as secretive and nonchalant as herself? Prophecies should be about valiant heroes —about the ends of worlds and the majik needed to stop it. An iman like Lorrin, especially such a traitor to the basic concept of right and wrong, had no business with fate. She also thought majik to be a thing of frivolity and nonsense —a thing so out of depth and reach of the realm of imans. After all, there had to be a reason why her kind had been made without it.

"…Are you fucking with me?" she eventually hissed. "Because I swear by the stars, Rye, this isn't something to joke about —"

"I am not that cruel," he assured, his expression dark.

Lorrin pressed her lips into a thin line and gripped the steering wheel even tighter. "Then are you absolutely sure that it's about me and not someone else? I don't want to be scared shitless for nothing."

"Oh it's definitely you," the Arch Favoured sighed wearily. "I cannot think of any other female who would want to ascend the throne of the Central Blades. No one else is more capable, and no one else is that reckless."

Lorrin drew a sharp breath. There were very few females in the assassin rings

13

as it stood, let alone one to rival her position.

"What does this prophecy say exactly?"

"I cannot recite it word for word, but I can try to prevent it if you hear me out. Many things are going to happen should you choose to take the path which you are considering right now. Things which not only affect you, but the whole city, Raffe. An ancient grudge is awakening; one resonant from generations of quiet, and festering from building resentment. It takes the shape of a beating heart. The old kings want their kingdom. And at the centre of carnage, is a blonde female with a bone-white dagger and a crown of thorns."

The iman paused. "…What old kings?"

"The Unseelie."

She hit the steering wheel.

Rye drew a weary breath. "Perhaps if you lay low and possibly quit your job altogether, there would be no reason to —"

"Quit my job?" Lorrin cut him off. "Do you honestly believe that assassins can just *quit* their job? Especially if they don't plan on vanishing afterwards."

Rye frowned. "But if you pursue a role within the Idun underworld, you will become that bloody queen —"

"Are you just trying to discourage me from taking over my ring? Or from taking the head seat of the Central Blades. You think I'm not good enough?"

"No. That is precisely the problem, Lorrin," he insisted, his expression then growing more and more pained. "You *are* good enough. Too good. And the wrong person is going to see it, too."

His Holiness might be that person.

He was the only Unseelie with that power; with that title of an old king.
An ice frosted her muscles. Could Jerrek Burr have known that?

Lorrin scoffed. If he was remotely smart, the Drakon would not have even set foot in Gehman. However…she began to wonder if Burr had gone to beg for his life to be spared. If he knew about the Unseelie King's possible ambition, then he would know that the Idun Seelie weren't safe.

That no one was.

14

"*Shit*," Lorrin cursed again, but refrained from swerving. Instead, she tried to concentrate on the road ahead. She thought that she had taken all of it into account. She had adequate forethought. Apparently, not when it came to the affairs of The Court and the fayth.

Her plans needed re-evaluating. She couldn't afford to give up a single inch to an entitled bastard who had every intention to break the ancient treaty.

But why her, she questioned. Why someone who cared nought for tradition or the olden times? Lorrin hoped that fate did not deem her the next ruler. She would settle for the role of a saviour, maybe; in addition to a sum large enough on which she could retire, as a handsome reward.

"Please, reconsider my advice," Rye spoke up. He shifted in his seat as though there was something else that he wasn't saying.

"But...what difference would it make if I remove me, the variable, from the prophecy? Will the King still not rise?"

The Elf hesitated in giving an answer.

"At best," Lorrin sighed as she turned by the dock, "the conflict might be postponed. And yet...I somehow don't see that happening. I have a worrying suspicion that my boss has already sealed the outcome."

"I'd like to say that surprises me."

Burr's reputation truly preceded him.

The assassin glanced out of the window as the car ground to a halt. The water lapping against the algae covered brick walls and wooden planks was frothy and cold. Rye was about to ask why she had parked, when a silvery head popped up from the surface. He yelped and grabbed the hand grip at the roof, thinking it was a Syren, but Lorrin simply chuckled.

"I'm going to need you to get off here," said the iman. "I'll think about what you've said, though. I just need some time."

"What? Here. Why are you leaving me *here*?"

"Well I can't have you tagging along on my date," she explained, making shooing motion. "Unless you want to watch me make out with —"

"No, no! But you —you're going out with a *Mer*?" he spluttered, gawking between her and the Favoured in the water. "Assuming that it actually is one."

"She is," Lorrin assured. "I met her earlier this evening."

The Elf frowned. "What —"

"I just…I need a distraction, Rye," she cut in. Her face softened and she wouldn't meet his gaze. Those pale eyes almost brimmed with tears.

This was too much. For someone who did not usually participate in society, the last five minutes had been an unwelcome and overwhelming slap in the face. Rye pressed his lips into a tight line. It was moments like these which reminded him how iman she was under the surface.

"All right," he said quietly. He unfastened his seatbelt and opened the door. He lingered for a moment, evidently struggling with something. "…No one will force you to stand against the Unseelie Court," he reminded her. "The Guard exists for a reason. And we have tall walls."

"None of it will matter," Lorrin countered. "They'll find a way in. That's the scariest part. That it's inevitable. And, I think…my role might be to aggravate him. Everyone knows what he thinks of females. How they are lower in his eyes. If he sees me on a throne, he will use it to justify a war that no one wants."

Lorrin wasn't quite so foolish.

She saw sense in staying out of His Holiness' way. But she also realised that her own ambition need not be so self-serving. She could lower collateral. If she wore that crown, she could do the worst thing that anyone —especially one born without majik —could do. She could bargain with him.

The Elf still dithered. "You must decide whether you wish to be a bystander, or the catalyst."

A sly and deadly smile spread across Lorrin's face. Her pride and freedom were worth far more than the consequences of not obediently melting into the shadows. "You know me, Rye," she said. "It's go big or go home."

CHAPTER 3

lorrin

LORRIN WOKE TO a dull headache and the blare of the television. Had she then drank late into the night before? Indeed —there was a lingering bad taste of alcohol. She glanced down to the thing beside her as the sheets rustled. A familiar shimmer of silver hair curling around soft, milky skin.

Right —the Mer she had brought to her on-site apartment.

Lorrin rose and swung her legs over the edge of the bed as she tried to recall what her name was. Glimmer? Glitter…?

A soft giggle turned her attention back to the Favoured. Her eyes were large pools of stark violet; deeply pulling and mesmerising. Paired with her unnerving smile, the assassin wondered why she had ever felt comfortable in her presence.

"There's a murder on the News," said the Mer.

"Hm."

Glisten then leaned up on her forearms, revealing a lightly scaly body that had flashes of the night before reeling through Lorrin's mind. The creature's smile impossibly widened as though she knew exactly what she had just done. "You wouldn't happen to have anything to do with it, would you?"

Lorrin, still naked, inched towards the adjoined bathroom. "What?"

"I saw the knives you had to discard before climbing into bed with me," the Mer elaborated. "You're one of those…assassins, aren't you?"

Lorrin went still. She had a few choices. She could gut her right there and then. She could scare her to a slower, more painful decline with a thorough threatening and possibly a few severed fingers. She could even be honest. But she could not get angry. Lashing out would only serve as an indication that the Favoured had any sort of upper hand.

She raised a brow. "I would think that you of all creatures would sympathise about being profiled. Yes, I kill for a living. Does that mean that I am the only one? Does that mean that I am always the perpetrator?"

Glammer blinked. That expression didn't change —the grin was fixed and her gaze was an unwavering magnet.

"...No," she answered. "You're right. I shouldn't have been so careless. Sometimes the fishermen throw harpoons at us too, because they can't be bothered to learn the difference between a Mer and a Syren."

"I'm sorry to hear that," Lorrin said flatly.

She didn't actually care. But she would feign sympathy in order to deflect any suspicion. The assassin then clicked her tongue as she spotted a red envelope on the mat by the front door. A small, gilt dagger was embossed on the front. After bending to retrieve it, she tore it open with one nail. It was a summons letter from the Central Blades —one reserved for official and urgent matters among the higher-up ring leaders. Lorrin wondered why she was receiving one —but considering her position and Burr's absence, it made sense.

And she couldn't dare to ignore it.

THE IVORY BLADE

If you watched the News, you would know that the
predicted Court member Jon De Polis has been killed.
Alongside our investigation, we order all ring leaders
to attend a meeting at 16:00, today, 23 Juno.
This incident will have unsavoury consequences should we
find that a fool felled the wrong target. Even more
so if it comes to light that this fumble was PLANNED.

There is no warning.
Turn yourself in, and your ring might live.

S I G N E D , *the central blades*

The timepiece on the wall showed it was already past three. "…Will you be all right making it back?" Lorrin asked the Favoured. "Got a friend to call?"

The bed shook as the Mer moved. "Are you in that much of a hurry?"

"Evidently," Lorrin sneered, holding up the tattered envelope. She didn't wait for a response as she headed back towards the bathroom.

Gloria swung her temporarily iman legs over the edge of the mattress and sighed. "Well. It was fun. But would it be too much trouble to drop me off by the south-side harbour at least?"

Lorrin grabbed a pair of jeans, underwear, a t-shirt and a towel hanging from the door. "Only if you can be ready in ten minutes."

The Mer clapped her hands. "Goody!" she exclaimed. "But…I do need some help with getting out of bed and into the shower."

†

"So how long have you been coming up onto the shore?"

Lorrin wasn't one to spend time with a partner after the suns had risen, but she felt minimal shame for not remembering her name nor what had really transpired. It must have been satisfactory though, since the Favoured had not said otherwise.

Gleamer turned from looking out of the car window, her silver hair billowing in the breeze. Lorrin had been itching to ask, but it seemed as though all Mer carried clothes with them for going ashore; she had returned from their touchy shower to find a flowy cotton skirt edged with shells and beads to match her bra. "Two years back," she then answered. "You were my first lay in *months*."

"I'm honoured," Lorrin smirked, tipping her diveball cap.

"But, I don't usually have to be so drunk," the Mer grinned, eyeing the iman

19

with mischievous curiosity. "Was this your first time with a female?"

"No," Lorrin scoffed.

"Then…why did you suggest drinks?"

"Why did you agree?"

The Mer laughed with unbridled glee. "Because you were paying. That, and I thought it would be best to stick to what you wanted to do."

"Did you do that in bed, too?"

"Yes."

Lorrin raised an eyebrow. While she would like to think that she was the dominant type who held the reins, more often than not, she surrendered and took it on her hands and knees. To think that she had topped this over eager Mer…

Gleeful giggled sweetly, her cheeks flushing.

No, Lorrin realised. Upon second thought, it was highly believable.

She then slowed down by the quiet intersection at the harbour, before parking on the pavement. It was hot today. It had been yesterday as well, and all that week. The iman squinted in the sunlight as she got out and headed for the passenger door. The Mer eagerly outstretched her arms, then wrapped them around Lorrin's shoulders as she lifted her up for the second time.

This would have been far easier with a wheelchair.

It was not that Glossy was particularly heavy —the assassin simply came to the conclusion that her arms could use more muscle, and that she did not like carrying people in her arms. It made walking and other basic functions awkward —and it was the furthest thing from romantic. Yet the Favoured stared at her with such fragile affection that it was difficult not to grimace.

Lorrin sighed in relief as she lowered her into the harbour, slowly and carefully. She wouldn't hide her own stare here. She had seen it in person only a handful of times before —the change between legs and a tail. The Mer held onto the dock and moved her legs up and down as the sparkle of light pierced through the dark water. The smooth skin grew blue and scaly and merged together, until the splash coming from Glow was as a result of fins.

She flashed another smile. "Thanks for the good time."

"Sure."

And then she was gone; the chilly surf spraying the iman's face as the sound of gurgled laughter echoed through the afternoon air. Lorrin smiled. At least she didn't have to worry about a clingy new problem.

She promptly returned to her car, turned on the ignition, and set off for the Central Blades Hall a few blocks away.

The assassin had to admit that the higher-ups were efficient busybodies if Jon De Polis' death had been discovered so soon. Perhaps the News stations and media, too. Or...someone had failed to keep what they had seen to themselves. That made her grit her teeth. Clearly they had a death wish.

But Lorrin resisted the urge to panic. No one would actually recognise her for her —not in the darkness, and certainly not in costume. She was safe, for now. That was what she would count upon as she pulled up to the compound.

The Hall couldn't get away with being anything too fancy from the outside. Opulence attracted Court attention. The building was a proud, temple-like structure all the same; with fillagree pillars at the entrance. It was as weathered and unassuming as the Central Blades would permit their pride to tolerate. And inside...Lorrin recalled the horrors with which she had had to grow. She could palette the removal of a finger or an eye; the slicing of an ear.

But a part of her would always flinch at gunshots and lashings. The screams which were relentless —and only ceased with death. What a small, stupid mercy to be as hidden from internal affairs for as long as she had managed. Now she had to gather the courage to tear that façade down. To make those males kneel.

Even though it was a little faster than she had anticipated, it was time to put some rather convoluted plans into motion. This meeting would be unlike any the greater Harbour Blades had ever sat through. Because in this meeting, a female would be vying for queen-pin. As slowly as the twist of a dagger.

The iman waltzed into the Hall as though her presence had been anticipated. It was somewhat expected, granted, but not that welcome. She returned their sneers; at slightly greying bastards she had worked under for years. No one was quite what she would go so far as to call 'old' or out of regular shape, though.

21

There was a variety of assassins whose prized skills ranged from quick and nimble, to brutal strength and power.

Then she paused at Burr's chair.

There were new faces.

She could see the fear in their already hollow, glassy eyes. She noted every tremble of muscle and nervous swallow. New recruits and replacements were common enough, but it was always troublesome to train them and deal with the disposal of the ones who would still inevitably come to quit.

Lorrin didn't bother to eye them too closely and engrain their appearances into her memory. She sank down into the velvet chair and swivelled around once, before clasping her hands and propping her elbows on the long table.

A mountain of a Troll cleared his throat as he passed her a brief glare. Verdia Kon liked to think himself as the absolute kingpin, but he was merely the master of his own ring: the Carved Bone. Everything about him was severe and cutting —sizable tusks, deep scars etched his grey-blue visage, while his suits curiously resembled the Guard of Madir's uniform. No one questioned it or him, and Lorrin had personally concluded that it was his way of blending when in public.

As usual, she tried not to stare at his one broken cerulean horn.

"Thank you for your promptness," Verdia began, lowering to his seat. "We all know of the distaste I harbour for these unforeseen emergencies."

"Aside from the inconvenience," quipped Ron Duncan, the leader of the Diamond Knife, "do you have a perpetrator yet?"

"Unfortunately, no," Verdia grumbled. "Considering the newness of the case, we haven't been able to procure adequate evidence. Even the Guard hasn't."

The other leaders frowned and clenched their fists. Lorrin was careful not to move too suddenly or smile. She levelled a dark look in the off direction she was facing, and then slowly tapped a finger up and down.

Markus Arrium from the Ash Blade then shifted forward. He was particularly irritating for a Jackal Seelie. "So…do we have any information at all?"

"All we know is that it was an amateur's kill," sighed the Troll. "Otherwise it was deliberately made to appear so. Which would beg the question, why De Polis?

Everyone knew that he was a candidate being watched. This had to be a planned attack. Extremely foolish and against what we had concluded in our last meeting."

"What if it wasn't any of us here?" Lorrin raised her hand slightly, in an off-hand manner. "Or even an assassin? We shouldn't assume."

"What?" Verdia clipped.

She leaned forward in all seriousness, as though she truly possessed a seat here. "Besides. I don't think it was a secret that Burr had his eyes on Jon De Polis."

The other ring leaders shared looks. Knowing looks.

Verdia's jaw clenched. "But he isn't here."

"Exactly," said the blonde.

Markus eyed her from the corner of his slitted silver-grey vision, as his long unravelling amber curls fell forward over his dark face. "You were here, Raffe," he said lowly. "And everyone knows that you're in charge when Burr is absent."

Lorrin then shifted back. It was easier to pin the suspicion on Jerrek Too-Big-For-His-Boots Burr, but she had not anticipated that accusation reflecting back on her for this reason —simply because she was a substitute in place of a reckless leader who could have just as easily given her orders.

The assassin thought on her feet. "I cannot give actual orders to the ring," she reminded him. "And you all know that I don't exactly take them, either."

Verdia grunted, irked.

Markus' gaze narrowed. "All the more reason to suspect y —"

"She wasn't near the central Iris District at the time," someone then spoke up. Lorrin glanced at one of those new faces. A short Syren who commanded more space than she actually occupied; with wispy coppery hair and a strange glint of life in her moldavite eyes, stared back at her. Her worn and fraying clothing was telling of the sort of treatment she had received since leaving the water. What marked her as distinct from a Mer were her longer pointed ears, sharpened teeth, and visible olive green fins along her forearms and spine.

Lorrin blinked. The two had never met. Yet the small female inclined her head as though the two shared some sort of secret.

Every creature in the Hall shifted slightly. It wasn't completely unusual to

23

recruit Syrens —they were efficient male-killing machines. But they made the rings wary all the same.

"She was training me until the morning," explained the Syren.

The iman almost snorted. What an ambitious lie.

"*She* was?" Hordor Fore —the Elf who had recruited Lorrin —spluttered.

"Little Lorrin Raffe," Markus chuckled, his lupine ears twitching, "the very same girl who never wants anything to do with the new recruits?"

"I'm more than twenty, Markus," she cut back.

He huffed and leaned against the wood in a taunt. "And *somehow* still single."

Lorrin smiled and raised one middle finger.

"*Raffe*; Arrium," Verdia barked in warning.

Both assassins dithered, before sitting upright.

"It's true," the Syren nodded vigorously as she then offered a timely interruption. "We started in the Iris District, but that was only from the afternoon. Around six-thirty, long before the casinos there close momentarily before the night shift, we moved to the Franq side of the River Sythe."

A good lie required enough detail to be irrefutable, but it needed to be just as vague to avoid constantly spinning a tale which could unravel into a mess of endless strings. This Syren was clearly well versed in the art, though Lorrin could not understand why she was fabricating an alibi for her. She could not have the naïve thought that this was an act of kindness.

Nothing in Idun was ever given without expectation.

Her dark brows furrowed as she considered her options. Could the creature possibly know of her crime? That might make this an inadvertent threat in order to secure a repayment which would be just as risky and beneficial.

Lorrin didn't like being indebted.

"Hm," Verdia grunted, his forest eyes narrowing on the slight and hardened Syren. "Thank you for your account, uh…?"

"Char," she answered. "Char Gilligan."

"Well, there you have it," Lorrin quipped, leaning back against the rest. She thought it a shut case, but her gaze was met with contemplating frowns.

"One witness does not an alibi make," Ron spoke calmly.

"Are you doubting her?" Lorrin accused.

"No," the ash haired iman assured. "If anything, I'm doubting *you*. And I am simply bringing light to the fact that no one else can back that up."

"Who else would be able to?" she then countered. "The Iris District is the pinnacle of seduction, blinding lights, strong drinks and good times. Everyone is either unconscious or preoccupied. But do humour me and track down every single citizen who was present in order to question whether they saw a blonde iman and redheaded Syren sparring at the docks."

Her temper was itching to get the best of her —she knew it.

Tentative silence followed the assassin's outburst as the snooty ring leaders digested her point. They moved slightly in their chairs and glanced down at their hands or their laps; none willing to be the one to speak first.

It was a subtle and relenting acknowledgement; a quiet victory.

Verdia looked unimpressed, as usual, but he swallowed a scowl and sighed as he rose to his heavy feet. He offered only one line in the way of a dismissal. "...This discussion has grown tiresome."

And just like that, the meeting was adjourned.

Creatures obediently filtered out with grumblings or mutterings, but Lorrin hung back until it was her and the Carved Bone leader. She caught Char's eye as the Syren left, with a wordless invitation to find her later.

Lorrin flanked Verdia's side; her stiff stance that of a soldier.

"Kon..." she began.

The Troll rolled his eyes and straightened his tie as they fell in step. There was precisely a minute between them and the exit. "Your flattery is as always, useless, Raffe. State your business. You have recruits to orientate, at least."

They both knew that she wasn't ever going to do that.

The iman cleared her throat. "Burr has gone to Unseelie territory."

"And?" Verdia quipped. "I trust he is aware of what he is doing."

"He may not make it back," she bit. "My point being, I want to be put forward for the next Ivory Blade ring leader."

25

Verdia actually halted. His giant feet skidded the polished wooden floor and he slowly turned to face her. He had never paid her that much attention. And she thought that he might show a little more of his own temper and spit a quick refusal. Instead he stared; those wide green eyes expressing surprise for the first time.

"...Are you quite sure of what you are saying?"

"I want more than second fiddle," Lorrin begged in earnest. "And Burr has always been known for having a lack of forethought."

His brows furrowed in disgust. "You want power."

"I want respect. A legacy."

Lorrin's spine straightened, before the Troll tilted his great head to the side and assessed her. She could not decipher about what it was he thought so deeply, but it was not with mockery. He was considering her on a close to equal platform.

The fact that he would consider making her an ally at all was a good sign.

"...First, you will have to do something for me," he laid out a bargain. "You are among the best assassins in here, Raffe. I know that. I...will support your acting leadership if you assist me with this."

"With what?" Lorrin said carefully.

"This De Polis case is vexing me. Dig into it alongside the Guard. Report back to me all which you find, no matter its significance. And should the need for a permanent replacement arise, then I will be sure to appoint you."

It was an offer for which she had accounted in order to gain Kon's favour.

"You want me to play at law enforcement?" she still snorted.

"I want you," he corrected, reaching into his pocket to produce a small gold rectangle embossed with the Idun coat of arms, and then huffing, "to spy."

CHAPTER 4

lorrin

SHE FELT THE full weight of that slither of gilded card.

Simply burdened with the looming need of making a decision, the sensation resembled something closer to lead. And it rattled with every step she took in pursuit of the strange Syren from the meeting. Printed on it was the Guard of Madir pledge and an unidentified phone number. Kon had instructed her to ask after Detective Zemir Kal if she chose to accept the mission.

'*I want you to spy.*'

Did Lorrin even dare? It would be easy. Forging information and evidence was not difficult. But working with officers proved to be a daunting obstacle. Lorrin didn't even work well with other assassins. As much as she wanted the Troll's allegiance and endorsement, would this sort of undercover work not mean spreading herself too thin and ensuring a knife at her own back?

Because if there was one thing which had been drummed into her from birth by her parents; caretakers; and especially Burr, it was that no one deserved that much trust. She should never find herself betrayed.

If the iman played her hand correctly, she could fool Kon and still hold his assumably flimsy support. Though he had pick of willing subordinates. Any one of them would happily walk into a lions' den for the chance of leading their own ring. They'd likely cut off their own hands for it, too.

Lorrin Raffe had a lot more at stake than just her life.

She pinned everything that she was and could be, on sitting at the head of that table. And she was sure that no one else was that desperate.

Char Gilligan was waiting for her outside of the entrance, on the pavement. The Syren jumped to her feet and offered an unnerving curl of her wide mouth. The recognisable ivory dagger sheathed at her side gleamed like those teeth.

Lorrin wasted no time as she halted before the shorter female. "Who told you to defend me?" she demanded.

The creature was undeterred. "My friend Giselle told me the most interesting story this morning," she began. "She had spent the night with an assassin, and she was pretty sure that they had killed the rich male from the News. Ordinarily, she would have reported them, but it was simply the best sex she had ever had. So she urged me to keep the culprit out of trouble."

Aha —Giselle. That was the elusive name.

Lorrin had been a little off.

She tried not to feel bad for not having the slightest interest in the Mer's name or identity, and it was only made worse by this revelation.

The more people who knew the truth, the tighter the noose pulled around the iman's neck. Both creatures of the sea were risks she was beginning to question whether or not she could afford. Neither had shown that they could keep a secret. And Char was easily the less careful one. The Syren would no doubt lord it over her for as long as possible.

She still smiled, waiting for Lorrin's response.

"I have my reasons," she clipped, folding her arms. Her shoulders squared and her spine lengthened in an effort to appear threatening.

"Oh I'm sure," purred Char. The effect was lost on her.

Lorrin's nose wrinkled. The Syren would prove to be an indecipherable annoyance. "So…you're helping me because your friend asked you to?"

The creature tilted her head and stopped smiling. It was somehow more unnerving than that grin. Her eyes burned with a very recognisable flame. The desire for something bigger than herself. "I bailed you out because I can see what you're trying to achieve. I have eyes, see. There are a lot of self-important older males who feel the need to command and instruct. I believe that I share in your vision, Raffe. To see a female on that throne."

Lorrin raised an eyebrow. This was rather unexpected. Although, upon further thought, gathering the forces of females in the rings would strengthen her cause and provide a bit of weight to her influence.

"Yes," the iman conformed. "I do want that head seat. But it will take a fight to get it. Possibly some blackmail, too."

"Then let me be the first to aid you in your venture," Char offered. "I can be of use. I'm small and majik runs through my veins. I can disappear."

I can be your spy, was essentially the proposal.

Lorrin blinked. Were all assassins so easily inclined to espionage? There must be something thrilling about deceiving and operating in plain sight. And the temptation of spinning an elaborate web of double agency was certainly delicious. However, the girl had to wonder if it was worth taking on the responsibility of protecting another creature.

"What if I work alone?" Lorrin hedged.

The Syren's eyes gleamed with unrestrained hunger. "It wouldn't be too difficult to confess the truth and rat you out."

The blonde stiffened. This female was volatile.

"I don't want to keep tabs on you," Lorrin reiterated. "And I'm sure you can understand why I would need to do that."

Char beamed again. "You don't trust me."

"I have no reason to."

"But I defended you back there," she quipped, leaning in and rising on her toes so her height came to something a little closer to the assassin's. Her teeth grated together in a mesh of razored white. "I could have kept quiet. Or worse."

"So you *are* threatening me?"

Char studied the iman's expression. It wasn't one of offence —it was sheer surprise at her audacity, and cold amusement. She certainly didn't look as though she *felt* threatened. The Syren must have been nothing to her. She then paused and tentatively lowered back to the ground; arms crossing. "...No."

Perhaps she now realised the imperative need to keep in Lorrin's good graces. As fast as she could tattle, the iman could as easily dispose of her. Hardly anyone would think twice. It would be easy, too —the sea hid everything.

And the creature knew what made Lorrin so notorious. How ruthlessly and meticulously she killed; how terrified she rendered her prey; and how she left no traces. She could erase Char Gilligan from existence.

Not that she possessed that much significance to begin with.

The assassin spied a trail of bruises and burns fading underneath the Syren's t-shirt, scattered amongst the cluster of scales and edging her fins.

She was desperate, then, if she would offer her service in that state. She knew what consequences awaited a discovered spy, yet she readily placed her life in Lorrin Raffe's unwilling hands.

The iman chewed on her lip. There were not a lot of options —and Char was giving her a very black-and-white ultimatum. She considered upon what she could compromise, because dismissing the Syren now would be her apprehension.

"...I am prepared to offer you a deal," Lorrin said candidly. "It is in my best interest to ensure no one uncovers the events of last night. And it is in yours to secure a position in a ring. But you need to understand the risk you're taking by joining me. I never have and never will plan on being responsible for anyone other than myself. That being said, I will protect you within the sphere of the rings. Should the Ivory Blade choose you, you will have a place at my side. But you cannot expect me to run to your aid when on a mission. Do you understand?"

The wind was picking up, and sweeping through the empty grey streets. The Harbour almost looked alive when the suns began to set —the nightfall brought a wicked spark from which most daylight citizens stayed well away. The girl lived within the veil that flittered between; an Iman District occupant by day, and a shadow against the walls by night.

Char Gilligan would have to learn of physical survival, as well as intellectual. But Lorrin admired her instincts.

The Syren blinked. "...You will be my mentor and ally, but your back will be turned to my activities?"

"Precisely."

Lorrin thought her deal quite fair. She had no plans of being a babysitter, but she would show favour where necessary. Should Char be prepared for capture or to die for her cause out of her own compulsion, then so be it.

No matter how pitiful or sympathetic the scars of her past, it did not fall on Lorrin's shoulders to prevent more. She refused to consider it.

Now the iman anticipated an argument. Instead, she received a determined, outstretched hand. She smiled and shook it firmly. "Welcome to the rise."

Char's eyes blazed with lifetimes of anger. "Long live the queen."

✝

Both females agreed that they had to go shopping. The Syren's current attire was ill suited for an assassin, regardless of her surprising skill. That majik of hers was her greatest asset. What she wore on an assignment then had little consequence, but she did need to get out of her flowy trousers and hole-y blouse.

It wasn't Lorrin's favourite activity —she preferred a good party and plenty of booze —but Char's wardrobe was in dire need.

"I've never had choices before," the sea creature confessed as they walked the lengths of the mall. "Everything has just been issued."

"Then we'll start with the basics," Lorrin decided, pausing outside of a large department store. "Jeans, t-shirts, leggings, yoga pants and jumpers —and you can never go wrong with a formal dress or two."

Char followed close behind, shrinking from the stares. "Formal?" she echoed.

"For galas," the iman elaborated as she picked a pair of black pants and held them in front of the Syren's frame. "Unless you'd prefer a suit?"

"A dress is fine," she murmured. "I'm just worried…it won't look good."

Lorrin slowly straightened and then folded the clothing over her arm. "Why would you think that?"

There was no amusement or light-heartedness in her expression now. Her pale eyes were shadowed with fear —a fear which the iman had never faced.

31

"…I was simply recommending clothes which are easier to move in," said the blonde tightly. "Nothing unflattering. And certainly not a ballgown."

Char gave a small nod. She glanced around at the rails and shelves and browsing customers; creatures ranging from Seelie to Drakon. Her gaze landed on a new casual sportswear range —a collaboration between the company and the city's rather average diveball team.

"Don't tell me…you're a Phoenixes fan?" Lorrin sighed.

"Absolutely!" the Syren exclaimed, her eyes lighting up. "Aren't you?"

She was referring to the worn cap atop the iman's head. Lorrin shuffled on her feet. There was a bittersweet memory attached to it, like most things from her youth. Now all which flickered in the way of recognition was warm mulberry pie and cool milk amidst the smell of red spider lilies. And vague, repressed renditions of a female with trimmed straw-coloured hair that framed her face.

The assassin's lips tugged upwards half-heartedly at the corners. "…My mother played for them a long time ago."

The Syren's face was wrinkled with unknowing innocence. "Did she retire?"

There wasn't quite enough spit in Lorrin's mouth. "She died."

"Oh."

The consequent silence was deafening —even with the bustle about them. But she didn't want Char's sympathy, nor her condolences. The past grief was dull and the present guilt was numb. When Lorrin's mother had died, the whimsy of the world beyond them died with her.

"Don't be deterred on my account," offered the girl.

"Okay. If you insist," the Syren murmured. Lorrin then had little choice as she grabbed her arm and dragged her over, before fawning over the sweater vests, leggings, skirts and shorts. It was all right. Char could afford the luxury of having basic interests and collecting memorabilia. Of *enjoying* things.

Before long, she had accumulated a large pile of denim and knitwear.

Lorrin's bank account was about to suffer. Then she gasped and pointed at the other side of the store. "Dear Goddess —that dress right there. I need it."

A rack of satin slip-on minidresses was calling her name.

The Syren's eyes widened with vaguely wistful awe.

"Would you like one too?" the assassin offered.

Char started. "Where would I wear it?"

"Out," Lorrin quipped. "Tonight."

In truth, she was still reeling from yesterday's events. The prophecy was persistent static in the back of her mind, and now Kon's proposition felt too convoluted to evaluate immediately. The prospect of working with the Guard —or at least pretending to —was leaving a bad taste in her mouth.

Her solution? More alcohol.

"I thought you didn't want to look out for me," Char frowned after putting two and two together.

"*Professionally*," the iman clarified. "I have no issues with grabbing a few drinks. Besides. It's an excuse to celebrate the formation of this alliance."

Char glanced between her and the rack, delicately chewing on her lip. "I don't know. It's been a long time since I went out."

"I'm not forcing you," Lorrin assured. "Just thought it would be fun."

"…My idea of fun is sitting at an all you can eat buffet with an array of males on the menu," she deadpanned.

The blonde shuddered but grabbed a pastel pink garment for herself. "Scrap the night out for now, then. What you need is dinner."

"You're going to catch one for me?"

"Want another body on the pile?" Lorrin scoffed.

"I'm *kidding*," Char assured as she laughed, genuinely amused. "We won't need to catch anything. I know a little place where they serve it."

"Like a restaurant?"

"Yeah…" The Syren's hand then took hold of a neon green variation of the dress. "And, maybe one drink afterwards wouldn't hurt."

CHAPTER 5

zemir

THERE WERE VERY few things that frustrated Detective Zemir Kal.

A murder case consisting of a handful of witnesses all with impaired memory; no salvageable camera footage from abysmal systems; and an abundance of vengeful suspects, was a new contender.

Jon De Polis wasn't even a stranger to the Guard of Madir —he had been in and out of the Loegon precinct on a few flimsy charges and warnings. Ordinarily, The Court would then have wanted nothing to do with him, but given his fortune and lack of concrete convictions they had overlooked his past hiccups.

Zemir hated politics.

It was messy and grey —a contrast to her black and white view of justice. The inhabitants of the tangible world were twisted and cheating, and the officer found solace in her belief in what could no longer be seen. There were sacred recorded writings of the time when the Daughter had walked among the Seelie and imannity. It had not been prefect —no time ever had been —but it had been better. Less corrupt. What kept Zemir going now was the hope of seeing her Goddess and ancestors when she would pass.

The Kal line had been rigid in their preservation of the fayth and a culture which she suspected to have been lost long ago. The traditional clothing; the music; and the cuisine echoed an era of imannity when it had been untouched by majik. There was something equally mystifying and captivating in its richness.

She was a devout however, and did not question the importance of having something to tether her existence to reality.

"Detective Kal, it's six-thirty," an officer snapped her out of her thoughts.

She glanced up at the Seelie and her closest friend, Fran Denaris. Zemir's second-half weekday shift had drawn to a close, and she was not coming any closer to solving Jon De Polis' case. She began to wonder why she had ever offered to take the case, given the lack of interest when it was brought up.

No one was willing to touch the Iris District, because it likely meant one thing: assassins. Not guaranteed, but that's where they were based. And while it would be difficult to pin the killer, the guard at least wanted to uncover the motive.

The only good news was that one of the Guard's trusted civilian consultants had recommended someone to help earlier, and a temporary partner might arrive on the precinct doorstep in the coming week.

"Thanks, Fran," Zemir sighed, before beginning to pack up.

She was just about grateful for a break.

"Busy tonight?" asked the Faery, inclining her head. Her straight lavender hair swung over her shoulder as her thin flittering wings gave her fragile anticipation away. But the iman didn't socialise, either. She found it unnecessary to forge relationships deeper than a surface level —more meaningful than general canteen chatter and a sparring partner. She couldn't imagine sitting down for a meal or drink with any of her colleagues, least of all kind-hearted Fran.

Zemir swallowed, frowning. "I have to babysit."

"Oh." Fran withdrew, nodding sharply. "See you tomorrow, then."

"See you."

Fran hardly pried, and the iman was grateful for it. But even she could read the disappointment all over her warm pastel visage. One of the most personal details she knew about the Seelie was what type of Faery she was.

This week meant that as soon it was time to clock out, Zemir would drive the thirty minutes home to catch her Drakon neighbour, Lei Baiwen, as she left for her evening shift. With her husband momentarily at The Court, it was then the officer's voluntary responsibility to look after her daughter until nine.

Little Lei Mingxiao was a monster close to bedtime —especially since her little golden horns had begun protruding out of her dark grey hair. Baby Drakon were difficult enough, but toddlers and small children were worse.

Because they could *fly*.

And Mingxiao came slamming into Zemir a few seconds after she dismounted her motorcycle in the parking lot which faced the front of the block apartments. The guard staggered backwards as the Drakon giggled and wrapped her arms and legs around her torso, her little leathery wings fluttering.

"Zee-Zee!" she squealed.

"Lei Mingxiao!" her mother cried, hopping out of their front door with one arm in her jacket. She offered the iman a sympathetic smile while wriggling her foot into her shoe. "...I'm so sorry, Zemir —I've been telling her to wait inside since she can't remember to run anymore."

"It's fine, Baiwen," the officer chuckled, prying Mingxiao's reluctant grip from her. "They're all like this at this age."

The Drakon smiled and tucked her silvery hair behind her ears after she had righted herself. "...Thank you again for agreeing to look after Ming. Goddess knows Tianyu is also thankful for one less expense." She then extended a hand with her keys. "Oh —I wasn't sure if you would be too tired from work to cook, so there are some wraps in the fridge."

"That's perfect. And it's always a pleasure."

Baiwen unfurled her wings —enormous, veiny things with a breadth close to her towering height —and teetered ahead to push off of the tar into the cool sky. She hovered for a moment to offer a wave. "Call if you need anything."

"Say bye," Zemir encouraged Mingxiao, who had buried her head in her shirt.

"Bye mummy!" she called as they then watched her soar.

The guard swung the child to her hip and made for the stairs on the East side of the block, towards the second floor. The coincidence that her apartment was directly above theirs was precisely how they had become acquainted: Mingxiao had attempted to climb up from her balcony to the roof to explore; then her hands had slipped and she swung, slamming into the glass window like a moth.

"Are you hungry now or do you want to eat later?" Zemir asked as she settled on the rug before the television. A colourful cartoon played onscreen.

The little Drakon pouted in thought; her little cheeks puffing. When she attempted to draw a breath, she accidentally spat up sparks and ash. They died and diminished on the breeze, but the iman still inspected the rug for flames.

"It's all right, calm down, Ming," the officer chuckled hollowly. "You haven't done anything wrong. You've always been careful."

This initial stage in her development was temperamental, and what she needed was constructive affirmation. Fire had begun to kindle within her secondary stomach, and the ashes from the embers were expelled at the most unpredictable times. Before the flames would ever roar to a full jet, she had to conquer and control the reflex. The last thing she needed to do was to fear it.

At least she hadn't exhibited her characteristic lightning wielding just yet.

Mingxiao's dusted blue complexion flushed a soft purple with embarrassment as then she tumbled backwards onto the floor; her tutu skirt ruffling up.

Her blue eyes brimmed with an unvoiced apology while she dithered on her back, staring up at the looming iman. "…Hungry now," she mumbled.

"Wait here."

Zemir went back downstairs as quickly as she could after closing the front door. Inside of the steel refrigerator was a lunchbox of six little tortilla wraps which still felt a bit warm, and smelled of crusted chicken and spring onions.

The iman *loved* Baiwen's cooking —it was light yet filling, and had all of the time and love in an echo of her own father. A true lifesaver on her night shifts.

Mingxiao was giggling hysterically along with the cartoon when the guard returned and headed for the kitchenette to heat up their portions and grab some pomegranate juice. The two sat cross-legged on the sofa and rug, and Zemir reached for a discarded paperback on the side table.

A crime thriller titled *Full Deck*.

A sudden shiver crawled up along her spine, and she tentatively set it back as though it oozed some strange majik. Her fingers tugged the edge of her sleeves over her hands. She hadn't been thinking about the De Polis' case until then.

Apparently, she couldn't take her eyes off of the book either.

"Zee-Zee, you can't read now. Watch with me," Mingxiao whined, turned around and tugging on Zemir's leg.

The iman took a moment to draw a breath and compose herself.

What was that on the television —*Whitey and the Whiz*? Some nonsensical serialisation of two little lab rats working to escape their captivity or simply the Whiz carrying out its own experiments. It always ended with an inevitable failure and the bizarre sense of perseverance. The kind of cartoon she had watched on weekends whilst growing up.

She sat straight and flicked her blue hair aside. "Is it a new episode?"

"No, they stopped making new ones ages ago," Mingxiao sighed, though her expression was irked as opposed to forlorn. "But this one *is* my favourite."

"Don't they just keep doing the same thing?" Zemir frowned. It had been funny, for some reason, to see the two characters perpetually fail over and over.

"Nuh-uh," the Drakon countered. "It's different. It's always something new."

Zemir managed a smile. "So you like it because they keep trying anyway, even after so many failed attempts?"

"No. I like it because it's silly," she stated plainly. Then she took a bite out of one of her wraps. "…And the Whiz is super silly."

"Isn't that one supposed to be the mastermind and genius?"

Her face was stony. "I don't think it is."

The iman laughed, wholeheartedly and more relaxed than before, and then started to eat. Maybe not everything needed to have a point; to serve a purpose.

After a mild tantrum concerning the demand to watch more television at seven-thirty and throwing away another chewed-up spare toothbrush, Zemir sighed with utter relief at the sight of a sleeping Mingxiao in her own bed downstairs. She was sprawled across the mattress with her head facing the wrong end, so the officer had simply draped her duvet in that position and stuck several pillows underneath. It made Baiwen's life that much easier if she didn't have to cart her daughter back after coming home. Until nine, Zemir would sit back on the sofa and curl up with the tattered novel again.

Violence is the currency with which the world operates. In the gambling halls, men dealt threats and spoke with silver knives for tongues. Everyone knew that winning your first match was to place your mouth around a frigid barrel —so why would I do it? Why would I dare disrupt the madness…?

Zemir Kal wasn't a pessimist. Neither did she ever raise her hopes too high or insist that there was opportunity in a place in which there shouldn't. She aligned with realists —people who saw things plainly for what they were without siding with much of a stance. The air was stale; the room was dim; her knees were drawn up; her cellphone lit up to display one message and show that it was quarter-to-nine —these were all observations which could be perceived to be plainly true.

Anything beyond that was beckoning trouble.

Yet she continued reading. The book hadn't always belonged to her. Those torn edges to the paper and the evidence of a thorough thumbing through were credited to her father. It had been handed down one birthday in the way of an heirloom; as a remembrance and strange bible to live by. In Idun, she needed it.

…A hunched and spindly male sat at the far table; the one reserved for frequenters and shareholders. Nothing about him seemed intimidating —he simply had the frame of a tower and thin, yellow teeth. Yet I knew that not one patron would dare to speak out of turn; to draw their pistol against him.

Zemir's grandfather, Huhmar Kal, had been a guard as well. He had possessed muscles that Zemir as a grown female could not wrap her hand around, and countless scars to show for his bravery in the Sekon Idun War. It was an honour to fight for one's land —that's what he had always told her. She wondered if he had still felt that way, years later, abandoned with one eye and one leg.

As she grew older, her parents insisted that she leave the story of the brutal conflict between those with majik and those without, alone altogether —that those days were a reflection of a deeply flawed past. Of a time when a city craved war.

…I was fluent in the language of fists. Eloquent in the kick of the foot.

Zemir reached for her cellphone on the table, and checked the time again. Five minutes had passed. The message she had chosen to ignore taunted her vision. It was her brother, Petre, asking when she would come to visit. The iman shifted atop the sofa. She didn't want to visit. She didn't want to go to The Court.

It was one of the very reasons that she had applied for the Guard.

She then sunk back and flicked through the book.

…The ungrateful rich male fattens up on the tears shed by the ones on which he treads. The poor male bleeds and works, and his earnings are divided between his whip and his city. Pity anyone caught between these; without moral, stance and right. He'll be the first to die.

The officer shuddered as though the words were a personal warning. It was no wonder Zemir's father had compared it to a bible.

Her cellphone lit up again. It was Baiwen thanking her, and saying goodnight.

The iman sighed and cast the book aside; slightly irked. She hadn't heard the mighty flap of the Drakon landing. It was unlike her to arrow her attention so finely —to block out her surroundings and miss details she had cultivated to be common. How unbecoming of a guard.

Zemir had been too caught in that book; in the memory of Huhmar.

She drew a sharp breath and turned her hands over, stiffening at the building tremble. They refused to form fists. She told herself to get a grip —to not let the long perfected skill of supressing her fear fail her now. Her hearing wasn't quietening. Her vision wasn't blurring. She wasn't succumbing to what had been drummed into her for years, as inadequacies.

"I am the lord of destiny," Zemir breathed what was in essence, an old mantra; taught by her grandparents —which she didn't like using, because it was only applicable to these episodes. "…I hold the keys of fate."

And as if some other God from another place had heard and listened to her threat, the trembling and rigidity subsided. Was it majik? She wouldn't know. No Kal had ever offered an explanation.

But Zemir still felt like a stranger to her skin. She tentatively ran a few nails along her arm. The sensation barely registered.

A tall glass of cider should do the trick.

But the officer had run out of alcohol yesterday. The iman groaned a little at the thought of leaving the apartment for a bar. Yet she could not fall asleep like this. A little —she would drink just enough to turn the grating static in her head into a dull, comfortable heaviness, as the fayth forbade full-fledged intoxication.

She pushed off of the sofa and went to grab a jacket and her wallet.

Then she paused with a hand on the front door.

'...By the Daughter, Kal, the first time you go out since graduation, you'd better wear something appropriate,' Fran's voice buzzed in the back of her mind. The iman had been rotating the same outfits for years now —at least for as long as Fran had known her. Pantsuit, suspenders —the odd official uniform of the Guard for ceremonies. The Seelie was certain Zemir even slept in fitted trousers.

She didn't.

The officer grumbled to herself as she then trudged back to her closet. There was nothing inspiring on the hangers, and she wasn't about to go to a bar in her traditional *sehrah* either. Her fingers lingered on an eggshell blouse and black flared cotton trousers. A dark blazer would tie it together, even though it had an embroidered coat of arms of the city.

Zemir stiffened. Habit was a fearsome thing.

Fran would never know, anyway.

CHAPTER 6

lorrin

THERE WAS LITTLE stench of iman flesh, thank fuck.
Lorrin had in fact anticipated being hit with that foul smell after turning through several back alleys to what Char Gilligan had described as a street food market.

The blonde wrapped her denim jacket tighter around her midsection and tugged the bill of her diveball cap downwards. It wasn't to evade the law —she simply didn't want the wrong person seeing her there and fabricating their own reasons as to why she would be browsing illegal butchers. There was a variety of meats and delicacies —not only catering to Syrens' tastes.

If not for its secrecy and *extremely* clear signage, the assassin would have guessed that it was a normal, albeit well secluded, fresh produce market.

Patrons —mostly Sea Folk, Seelie and creeps —sat on makeshift stools and wandered the space between the stalls; the smoke billowing from cigarettes creating a line of fog. Vendors shouted out dishes, cuts and prices from each end of the paved road; all manner of voices blending and clashing in harsh chorus.

"Tender iman leg!" a screech made Lorrin veer to the left.

"Lucky Seelie and Elf ear —three for two!"

"Troll's foot," bellowed a one-eyed stooping Mer, "Get your Troll's foot!"
The assassin stiffened and made a face, picturing Kon's giant grey toes on a silver platter or keychain. Then that one slit crimson eye unmistakably caught her gaze, and she tried not to flinch; to look so out of place.

For half an hour, Lorrin Raffe was a black market meat consumer.

Char then tugged on her arm.

"Fajitas are my favourite," the Syren quipped, skipping towards a vendor who appeared marginally friendlier. Another Syren, well-seasoned in the way of life on the shore and riddled with small fishhooks fashioned into deliberate piercings, beckoned the pair nearer. But Lorrin didn't like the shimmer in her lidded sunsset eyes. As if she could openly read her.

"Anything I can offer you ladies?" she purred, flicking her ruby ponytail back.

The iman glanced at the menu, which specified that all meat was male. Fingers, toes, breast, legs and hearts. She was familiar with all of those cuts, yet thinking about them in the way she might think of pizza made her stomach turn.

"Two fajitas please, Valerie," Char smiled.

So Char Gilligan was a regular here.

The seller eyed Lorrin for a brief second, as though in judgement. Or perhaps she could clearly tell that she didn't belong here, and that the second wrap was not for her. "…Sure, Char. Any veg?"

"A bit of everything."

The assassin glanced aside as Valerie prepared the order right before them — down to the slicing and spicing. Of course, she had to acknowledge that no grocery store simply sold packs of these things —at least not on land. Freshly caught produce would need to be cut then and there, and deboned.

"You're pretty unfazed," Valerie murmured; her eyes briefly glancing back from the corner being the only indication of who she was addressing. Char's eyes then widened as she turned in alarm. Her neon green hoop earrings flicked with the movement. So the creature could tell beyond mere appearance.

Lorrin shuffled on her feet despite her earlier resolve to be the picture of calm. "…It wouldn't be my first time seeing a butchered iman carcass. And I'm familiar with how Syrens survive."

Valerie smirked; the action curiously threatening for the amusement in her eyes. "Hm. You brought a decent one, Char. At least she won't rat us out."

"It's not like I'm a fucking officer," Lorrin bit.

"Could've been," said the Syren without missing a beat, setting down her knife. "Land Folk don't usually tag along to…see the sights. Of course, if you *had* been a guard, there are other stalls who dish out female iman, too."

"I'm sure," Lorrin hissed, increasingly queasy.

"Oh, don't pay much attention to that," Char chuckled uneasily, waving a flippant hand. "And my friend can hold her own, Val."

"Hm." The Syren then assembled, folded and wrapped up the bloody fajitas with precision, before presenting them on a few napkins. "…Bon appetit."

Char grabbed them eagerly, and promptly turned away. Valerie raised a brow.

The assassin sighed and dug into her pocket for cash.

Valerie counted each note and coin with meticulous slowness, before nodding in satisfaction and flirtatiously waving off the pair. "Come back soon," she smirked as Lorrin glanced back. A chill straightened the blonde's spine.

The two females leaned against a wall as the smaller one ate ravenously.

Lorrin had to wonder how long it had been since the Syren had eaten meat. The way she licked her fingers and tore through the fajitas with those sharpened teeth made the assassin sure that she hadn't had the means to come to the market in quite some time, nor to hunt in the harbour.

The sort of people who frequented this place saw it as staple —Lorrin had to understand that. This was the reality of a government who wanted to pretend that their society was more harmonious than it was; that some of its citizens did not naturally prey on others. That addressing the issue directly and its implications would open up a large can of worms. No one wanted to think about from where legal meat would come. No one wanted to start another war over that.

So they would turn that eye —they would permit Franq and the Iris District and even the outskirts of Loegon to wither and corrupt, despite the greater country and continent knowing better. Not that they were under obligation to cater to Syrens and other carnivorous creatures. After the sea, Idun was the safest home. And those hunters had been doing it naturally long before law ruled.

"Want a bite?" Char suddenly grinned, holding up the other wrap.

The iman made a face. "You must be joking."

44

"Just being polite," the Syren quipped, the smile falling. And her eyes did not reflect the sentiment. There were layers of distrust there.

"I know what sort of person I am," Lorrin murmured, stuffing her hands into her pockets. "I know of the things I do. How I *choose* to do them. I've washed the world in grey; even where black grates along white. But I have not fallen *that* far."

The creature tilted her head to the side and blinked as she continued to take numerous bites. Then she paused, with the wrap an inch from her mouth. Lorrin could see the steaming vegetables and strips of lightly browned iman.

"...I'm not sure if people would call your occupation grey, Raffe. And I know a thing or two about trying to see the world that way," she murmured, her ears and shoulders drooping. "It would be wonderful, wouldn't it —to pretend that there exists no good and evil. That neutrality is the zenith state of being. But look at me —you know what I am. *I* know what I am. Fishermen know what I am. Each year, they kill hundreds of us despite the decrease in hunts. I can't change that. But I can fight back."

Char had seen the brutality of being little better than an Unfavoured; of the mercilessness of the harbour. The people who lived here were hard, bitter, and accepting of the fact that the city had abandoned them. The extravagant casinos and entertainment plazas were just a slap in the face. Such blatant classism and discrimination had been enough to drive the Syren to wield her own weapon.

To defend herself.

Lorrin glanced at her feet. "Is that why you joined the Central Blades?"

"Mostly."

"What was the other reason?"

Char took another bite. "...I'm so tired of seeing entitled, abusive males at the top of it all. They don't stand a chance in the water, but up on land, they're stronger. Still my tormentors. Why do they get to do that? Nadune Madir is not enough."

The iman blinked. "We truly do have a similar vision."

"Why else do you want that seat?" the creature turned sly before resuming her spirited chewing through the wraps. "I saw the way you covet your boss's chair. You sit in it like it's already yours."

45

Lorrin didn't hesitate. "That's classified."

"Aw, come on," whined the Syren. "I told you *my* reasons."

"No," the assassin insisted. "My reasons are more problematic than yours. Dangerous, in fact. It's…better if you don't know."

"What? Do you want someone dead?" Char scoffed, polishing off the last of the fajitas and wiping her mouth and hands.

Oh, she had no idea. The list was long. The two then pushed off and headed back for the main roads along the flashy nightclubs and bars.

"Death is an occupational hazard," the iman stated plainly, her breath visible in the air. "Mine, or anyone else's. But a lot of people are going to die if I don't sit on that chair. If I don't claw for that power."

Char Gilligan did not grin. Amusement felt wrong, here.

It was better that the Syren see her as a malevolent female who would step on anyone in her way. If any admiration formed as a result, that would only further Lorrin's cause. Because she was not so foolish as to reveal all of her cards.

After the fifth shot, the iman felt her worries bubble away like acid.
What could possibly be so important when the music was loud enough to drown out the patrons' voices and the lights bright enough to blind them if they kept staring at one place for too long?

She barely kept a rein on Char either, who had shimmied her way to the other side of the dance floor and cosied up with a burly, golden haired Mer.

Lorrin considered finding a bed-warmer herself, but it was more trouble than it was worth. She needed a clearer head in the morning.

The dawn would come, but right now it was the moons which kept her company; kept the horrors which awaited beyond the Wall a distant thought.

Granted, it filled her with a shallow sense of being pathetic to sit at the bar counter, leisurely sipping cocktails. But she wasn't drunk enough to dance.

"Night not going the way you planned?"

She turned her head to watch a Seelie sink down onto the stool beside her. A Faery with intricate, mossy stag antlers smirked at her —his slit pupils gleaming.

Lorrin snorted.

Like all Seelie, he had that inexplicable charm and unnatural allure. Still she couldn't help laughing softly, because it was such a tried and trusted pick-up line.

The male took her reaction as a challenge, and continued to smile at her as he ordered a short glass of rum and coke.

Lorrin tucked back her hair and took a sip of her margarita. "…How do you know that I didn't plan my night to be just like this?"

"You looked…defeated," he mused, idly tapping his dark and furred cheek. "Someone who wanted to drink and be alone wouldn't be here, sweetheart."

"Hm," the iman frowned. "Don't call me that, buck."

The Faery noticeably flinched, noting her distancing, but not quite backing off. "…If you came here for the atmosphere, why are you dressed up?"

"*You're* not dressed up for someone who came to party," she cut back.

He chuckled lowly. "Fair enough. So…does this pretty face have a name?"

She smiled a perfected smile. "Maybe."

"Well mine's Sedar."

The assassin finished off her drink, and drew a deep sigh. She wouldn't take him to her bed, but he could be amusing company. She pushed back on the stool, and flicked her hair. "Well how did you plan out *your* night, Sedar?"

This was an invitation.

Lorrin indulged the Seelie; let him lead her to the lit up dance floor and gyrate against her. She didn't mind the touch of his hands on her hips, nor the brazen ventures of them down to the hem of her dress. And she didn't pull away when he presumptuously leaned in. Honestly, he tasted like dirt. Rain-washed, pine-wood sort of dirt, as though she were laying face first on a forest floor.

He grinned as though it had been the best kiss of his life.

Then the world dimmed, and the music softened, as though they were moving further away. Her body numbed, and would no longer listen to her commands. Lorrin knew what these symptoms were. She was familiar with the touch of majik.

47

Sedar brushed his mouth by her round ear. "…Don't be afraid," he murmured. She wasn't. But her body went a bit rigid as a reflex.

"What…what did you…" she rasped, feigning that fright.

The firm arm around her waist tightened. "It's just a little enchantment. You'll be able to hear me now, unlike anyone else, and to focus." The patrons around them moved with a slowness that felt very wrong. The Faery observed her minimal struggle for a moment. "…What do you think of the Unseelie?"

Lorrin paused. "What?"

"Outside of that damned Wall, iman." His tone was flat and low enough to instil a trickle of unease. He wasn't asking her if she hated the Unfavoured. He was asking whether she was a friend or foe. "…There is a strain that I'm sure even airheaded partygoers such as yourself have noticed," he continued. "This city isn't bloody perfect. No matter how much your ruler wants it to seem. Can you say that you're happy here, in the dregs of society? If you knew what was good for you, sweetheart," Sedar whispered, running one hand down the middle of her back, "you would leave Idun while you have the chance."

An Unseelie sympathiser. Lorrin made the mistake of drawing a breath, before her fingers fought to graze the handle of the tiny hunting knife she kept strapped to the topmost of her outer thigh. She didn't have the strength to unsheathe it, but the action was enough to keep her one step from helpless.

Char Gilligan then grabbed that arm.

The enchantment evaporated, and the world and its noise came back at full force. "I've been looking all over for you," the Syren yelled, tugging the assassin from the Faery's grip. He paused, raising an eyebrow.

"…Sorry," Lorrin forced a smile as she stiffly withdrew from Sedar. "I've been otherwise preoccupied."

The Favoured stubbornly lingered, that playful gleam which was in his gaze now dark and sharp. Char seemed to notice. She was all too familiar with the majik of the Seelie. "…Come on, I want to go home."

"What happened to the Mer you were working?"

"He was too…nice," she grinned, in a clear effort to display all of her teeth.

"I think he dodged several bullets," the iman said shakily, also in effort, and hugged her denim jacket closed before stepping to follow the Syren.

The Faery caught her elbow.

His previously cheek was now cold and pissed off, which meant that the females' subtle message had been received. Yet, he could not resist having the last word. "…Stay safe, little iman. Maybe I'll find you after the take-back."

She couldn't decide whether it was a threat or a generous and deluded offer. And she definitely was not about to let him have that word, either.

Lorrin squared her shoulders, staring at him in disbelief. The assassin no longer trembled; no longer hid her experience with Seelie trickery.

She reached out to right the collar of his thin outer shirt, studying those antlers. It was a deceptively sensual gesture —her own mortal form of enchantment. And he drank it up so predictably. That hand then tentatively retreated, and flipped him off. He blinked rapidly; the change in attitude jarring. Her sneakered feet slowly walked backwards into the roaring crowd, sweeping her within it. And she made a promise that even she was surprised to hear herself make before she disappeared entirely. "…I'm not running away from the city, little buck. I'm going to raze it."

CHAPTER 7

zemir

THE OFFICER WAS here again —at *Slow Poison*.

She went whenever she was reminded of how cold and empty her apartment was; how she was the only one in it. That, and the deeply buried comfort which came with being in a quiet gay bar.

The solitude was deafening in these valleys of pity and boredom. She had never sought out a permanent fix for it though, against her parents' wishes. Why couldn't she find a nice person and have a nice relationship, which would end up as a nice marriage? Like her brother. Why couldn't she have a nice *life*?

She swirled her glass and downed another quarter.

People were such fickle things. Zemir Kal liked control. Predictability. In the long term, at least. No one who came to *Slow Poison* during the week wanted that.

She had already swatted away two tall, swaggering Elves away —creatures who promised to be a very gratifying fuck —which had been a shock to the iman's system as she realised that they could quite easily pin her as a guard. It wasn't as though it was illegal to sleep with an officer. It was simply the audacity which they possessed to approach her all the same.

The front door's bell pinged lightly.

Zemir was usually unconcerned with other patrons, but something compelled her to turn at least a little and see who had wandered inside. A tall blonde female staggered towards the counter, earning a fair amount of stares. She dejectedly slid onto the stool beside the guard, and tucked back loose strands of her diamond blonde hair behind a rounded ear. A flush from red blood. An iman, like her.

Someone then tried their luck.

"Hey, beautiful. Need a ride?"

A Wyche who was in way over their head leaned forward against the counter on the iman's other side; curled bronze hair shimmering as they flicked it backwards. Zemir took a long sip. She wouldn't trust the darkness in those crimson eyes.

Apparently the girl had a decent head on her shoulders, because she slowly turned to stare, and raised a vulgar finger. "Sit on this," she spat.

The Wyche irritably retreated; hands raised in surrender.

As the iman then ordered a stiff drink, Zemir's gaze unconsciously wandered from her powdery make-up downwards to her hugging pink dress and sculpted legs. The kind of sculpture achieved from training and rigid exercise.

The detective concluded that she was no more than twenty or so, given her worn sneakers patterned with silly little doodles.

"...Well. I do like a female in uniform."

Zemir started, realising that she was being addressed, and glanced over to meet the iman's green-grey gaze. She tilted her head and pulled up her denim jacket from where it hung off of her slim shoulder. The officer's surprise then turned to dry amusement, and she raised a brow along with her glass.

She had been flirted with before, but had never attempted to put out any smooth moves herself. People simply flocked to her of their own accord. And consequently left, too. Many of them didn't like studded leashes.

"...Does that line normally work?" Zemir asked the pretty stranger, already contemplating what she might look like on her hands and knees.

The blonde smiled with her mouth only, and held her chin in her palm. "Not sure. I've never flirted with an officer."

"Then from where did you muster the courage to try?"

That confidence wavered, and a bit of colour lightly dusted her cheeks as she chewed on her lip. "Because...we're in a gay bar?"

"So everyone in it must surely be available to you, then?" the guard mused, leaning back coolly. "What if I have no interest in relations at all?"

The iman blushed a little more, and turned her head. The bartender then slid her order across the wooden top towards her, but she only stared into the iced liquid as her fingers clasped around the glass.

"I'm sorry," she sighed, tucking her hair again. "I didn't mean to assume. It's just a default and…I've had a…day."

"I'm not angry," Zemir assured, cracking a small smile. "And I do have an interest in people. Chin up. Wouldn't want you looking any more dishevelled."

"Gee, thanks." Her mouth twisted into a shape. "I blame an overeager Seelie." Then her gaze fell to the guard's depleting cider. "…You seem to have had a day, too. Are things slow in the precinct?"

All traces of Zemir's brief amusement vanished. This was still her first glass. She frowned at the dark amber. "I don't talk about work outside of it, girl."

The stranger paused and straightened; her expression unreadable as she cast the guard a sidelong glance. "How young do you think I am?"

"Younger than me."

The officer expected outrage, or perhaps more colour in those cheeks. But the iman's eyes lidded as she proceeded to cross one long leg over the other. From that angle, the guard could spot a small tattoo on the side of her shin, just above her ankle. The outline of a double-edged blade, the tip pointed upwards.

Her denim jacket fell off of her shoulder again.

Zemir tore her gaze away as she hastily finished her drink, before immediately motioning for another. *The Daughter have mercy.* There was something about this willowy female —something dangerously tempting. And the dark mystery only made the fantastical image of her obedient and begging all the more potent.

"What's a guard doing out during the week, anyway?"

"Couldn't sleep," Zemir found herself being somewhat truthful.

"Damn."

"Why are *you* out?" she questioned the blonde. "Nothing to do at UI?"
She laughed, and it was so abruptly genuine. "I'm not a student. Nor did I go to the university. Life hasn't been easy for everyone, you know. But I have a decent

paying job. I work in…Citizen Resources."

"Uh-huh," Zemir quipped, though it came out disbelieving. "I know someone in that field." She then took a swig without breaking eye contact. And the pretty stranger tended to her drink in turn, as though on cue.

"I have to be honest with you," she murmured. "Existence seems to be kicking my ass right now. Maybe it's divine retribution for all the bad things I've done…but something else suggests that it's not a consequence, but a quest. That I have to do things I'd rather not for someone's sake other than my own."

She was still staring directly at the guard, tapping her short, chipping nails against her half-finished glass. And the guard swallowed uneasily, not finding enough saliva in her mouth; quite unsure of how to respond.

The blonde did not have to be honest with her. She especially didn't have to *be* here —unbeknownst to her, unwittingly becoming the subject of a shameless detective's fantasies. Had she no better grasp of self-control?

You're a terrible person, Kal.

With her heartbeat echoing violent drums, she abruptly averted her line of sight. "…Do you tell your life story to everyone you meet in a bar?"

The stranger's light eyes glittered in the overhead light. "No." And she said it with such conviction and rigidity that Zemir believed her.

As though it were only a secret between the two of them.

The guard hid the rising heat of her face with cider. Her head was beginning to fog. "I've never spoken this much with someone I didn't know."

The iman leaned in; however seductive she had appeared before heightened tenfold. "So…maybe now that makes me someone you know."

Zemir's hand acutely twitched. This female was a complete stranger. Even worse —a stranger from *Slow Poison*. The officer really didn't have the time for whatever this might lead to, nor the repercussions of her own tipsy decisions. She knew precisely what would happen if she were to get the blonde to her little apartment, where all of her secrets hid. The thick fence of barbed wire she kept as a barrier came prickling back. "Don't get ahead of yourself, girl," she bit.

"Why? Are you in the habit of doing…other things…with people you don't know?" Her lips were only things worth concentrating upon. Her bleached hair fell forward, obscuring what appeared to be a bitten lip.

The officer didn't blink. "You're not my type."

"That's a shame. But, I can actually say the same."

"Then why are we having this conversation?"

The blonde glanced aside, thinking carefully. "...Don't you get bored of the same thing, especially if it perpetually leaves you unsatisfied?"

There was no way it was that obvious. Zemir began to wonder if the stranger was in fact, iman. Or was the guard simply a clear, open window?

"I like routine," she insisted. "I like feeling like I'm the one steering."

"You can still have that," quipped the pretty stranger, pointing importantly. "There are simply different ways to get it."

The detective frowned. "I am also a fan of consistency."

Now the iman pouted like a spoiled child. "You're no fun. I've never had to work this hard at a conversation. I'll respect your will and wishes. Though it only adds to my intrigue. But...no one likes a pushy busybody."

She was wrong about the first point. The officer had felt her every tug at taut strings which had suddenly tied themselves to her thoughts and leather as soon as she had wandered inside; the picture of a down-on-her-luck young female.

Zemir managed a chuckle. "Fun is certainly not what I'm known for, girl."

The iman laughed again; the sound salving the detective's senses. "Why is that word less annoying coming from anyone but Markus?"

The detective couldn't stop herself. "Who's Markus?"

"Just an ass I work with," she said breezily. Then her features darkened, and she stared at nothing. "...Really wish I could kill him." There was a long pause thereafter, filled with ominous sincerity. She promptly gulped down the remainder of her drink, barely wincing at the burn, and pulled her denim jacket back over her shoulder. She then hesitated, as if searching for words of farewell.

"Uh, you don't have to stay on my account," Zemir murmured, picking up her glass. "I plan to finish this slowly."

"Oh," said the pretty stranger. "I was just going to step out for a smoke. But in that case, I should probably be getting back anyway. Dawn is in a few short hours, and it's a big day ahead."

"Doing what, filing employee records?"

The guard didn't like that she snorted the question, as if the job was easy. But the iman found her rudeness funny, and smiled that smile again that didn't reach her eyes as she turned to leave. "No. I'm being temporarily transferred."

†

Zemir found her outside by an alleyway after that glass. The neon High Street was deserted, barely bathed in the glow of the lampposts above.

She watched her for a brief moment, finding her every movement distracting; her every smoky breath on the night breeze captivating. Her sneaker kicked a stone aside, which rolled over to the officer's boots. Consistency indeed.

"You're still here," Zemir murmured, sauntering closer. Her feet had their own will. The stranger shivered and leaned back against the brick wall as she drew in a lungful of fresh air and flicked ash off of the diminished butt.

"So I am."

The detective was sure that there was something wrong with her, or that she had drunk more than she thought. Why else would she close the distance and enjoy seeing the blonde tense; her breath halting in apprehension? Yet all which Zemir did was coolly lean in towards her ear, spy the pack of cigarettes in the female's hand, and slide one out.

The stranger let her do it. And even though she had a lighter, she let the guard press the end of the roll to hers; their foreheads grazing as she took a drag.

The officer lingered a moment too long after it had caught; her amber eyes drinking in every detail of light jade, and the brown eyelashes which framed it. There was not a trace of timidity —those pale eyelids lidded with a sureness that she was about to get precisely what she wanted. Her stance was cold power.

And the stranger uncurled towards Zemir even as she withdrew; tentative and not breathing. But her free and traitorous hand obliged, gripping the younger female's hip in a way that made her stiffen, before tugging her body into hers.

Zemir revelled a bit in her invitation —in the reciprocation. It was fascinating, the thing pulling between the two of them. Even if she didn't dare to embrace it.

Her hand travelled a little though, sliding up to her satin pink waist and back down to the beginning of her thigh. She quivered slightly at the touch, as though discovering that she was moulded to the guard's hand. So the stranger still wanted this —and perhaps she wanted Zemir to go further, too. But she had no idea just how far the limit to that would be.

"…I thought I wasn't your type," lowly bit the guard, her expression stony as she tilted her head and exhaled smoke.

"And I thought I wasn't yours," she returned, idly stubbing out her cigarette on the wall beside them and letting it fall.

Zemir drew a deep, poisonous breath, and then blew out at the sky. She didn't ordinarily smoke —but she had tried it twice and perfected it at university. She'd pray for forgiveness tomorrow, in the pure light of the suns. Here, now, upon the shadows of the night the Daughter's eye did not fall.

The blonde leaned closer and tentatively ran her hands up along the leather arms of her jacket, her lips parting with a conflicted hope. The detective raised a dark eyebrow, stilling where she was. The temptation to near and taste the smoke on the pretty stranger's tongue was ridiculously high.

But she brought her finger to those pink lips, lazily closing them.

"Uh-uh. I don't do that," Zemir whispered.

Fragile frustration flickered in her eyes. "…Like, ever?"

"Yes, not anymore."

Another instruction of the fayth: avoid intimacy in meaningless relationships, when searching for lifemates. That encompassed hook-ups and one night stands. Sex for her, was not intimate. But to breathe each other's air and have the things which formed both truth and lies touch —that was trust. That was love.

And she hadn't kissed anyone in a very long time.

"…However," the officer continued, taking another drag. Her other hand slid the left side hem of the dress upwards by an inch. "If you'd like?"

"Oh," breathed the iman, shifting against her, before nodding. Nothing other than a soft moan followed her consent as Zemir's hand wandered beneath the garment between her taut legs, and sought out the covered centre of her.

Their locked gazes did not wander —despite the danger in doing it out there in the open; the coldness of the night; the very sin of it, in essence —there was nothing but that moment. Nothing but a stranger's hands clinging to a guard so desperately as she fulfilled a kernel of that shameful wish of having her at her mercy. Nothing but the heightening of that intensity in every varying and stingy stroke; coupled with the unforgiving light in her dark golden eyes.

The iman's breath shortened; her spine arched and her balance began to falter the nearer she came to a pinnacle. All the while, Zemir indulged in two things which would have her repentant with a clear head and straight coffee. She still held a burning cigarette between her fingers; still drew it to her lips occasionally, and she knew that every sound of the stranger's pleasure would echo in her ears for days and days. Her light eyes finally fluttered closed; the sensations too consuming to concentrate on anything else. Her brows furrowed, her bottom lip snagged between her teeth, and her hair blew all over.

What an image for the officer's next few dreams. Though around the time a telling shiver ran through the blonde, Zemir pulled back.

She blinked back to reality, startled. "Wh —"

"If I don't stop now, we'll end up at my apartment," the guard said roughly.

"And…you don't want that?" the iman panted. "We could go…to my —"

"I can't afford that tonight. And I thought that you couldn't, either," hissed Zemir. She stomped out the cigarette and irritably tugged a hand through her layered blue hair. She had lost her nerve and control far more easily than expected. What bewyching spell had the iman cast for her to give in? To follow instinct?

"…Look," she sighed, frowning, "I hadn't even planned to touch you that much before, so perhaps we both need to exercise some restraint."

The stranger gritted her teeth. Then she stiffly withdrew, hugging her denim jacket closed and tugging down the hem of her dress —especially on the right. Her cheeks were lightly flushed but no embarrassment hindered that air of lust and confidence, nor made her avert her eyes. They continued to pierce Zemir's, unflinching. "…I guess we met on the wrong night, huh?"

The detective gave a curt nod.

Then the blonde smiled, and it almost reached her eyes. "No one has ever kept me on my toes like that. You said you didn't want to do anything with me, then you willingly entertain me. Such a game of hot and cold is different with a total stranger. You don't have to worry about what might happen next. I too like that freedom. Yet, I have never met anyone quite like you."

No one who was so closed off, cold and cutting. No one who would abruptly do something forbidden for the purpose of gauging a reaction. And no one who wanted to do certain dark things with which the receiver would be unfamiliar. The guard did not regard that part of herself with any sort of favour —it was fulfilling in the moment, but mostly she viewed it as a blight. A problem.

This young female was in no way unseasoned in the ways of casual flings, but the officer wanted to shield it; protect any innocence she might have left.

Harbouring no care for appearing rude, Zemir then turned to walk away — though a dangerous thought suggested that she stay.

"…And I hope that you never will."

The guard stumbled through her door, her head a little more numb than usual, but not enough for her to forget to lock the door. Her socked feet dragged along the wooden slats like they were unfamiliar, though they knew the path to the bedroom. So did her hands. They reached out ahead, searching for familiarity.

There was no bother with the usual things Zemir did before bed —with her objective met, she could theoretically fall asleep right there on the bathroom tiles. She did manage to fumble her way out of her jacket, shirt and trousers though, before crawling underneath her duvet and curling inwards.

She could feel it now. She could feel everything.

The only sound was her breath. Slow and even. Lazy.

She didn't permit herself to be so otherwise, except on —rather forced —annual leave. She had never even left the city. Those walls were the furthest thing she had seen since birth. All she knew was what was tangible.

It was slightly cold; a little colder than usual for this time of the seasons, but the iman's body was warm with a heat that didn't feel like it was solely natural. It was the kind of heat which kept one alert. Awake.

And when she blocked out the darkness of the room, she saw blonde threads and vesuvianite eyes. Eyes which lowered in respect, while the strands of hair were caught up in the officer's brown fingers. She'd tug at them, guiding the iman's head this way and that, and watch as she put up no resistance.

More, she'd beg —and Zemir would remind herself that it was merely her deprived imagination ruining what could have been a distant memory in a week's time. But she could not get the touch of her skin out of her mind. That look in her eyes, and that voice out of her head. She had expected it to be light and soft — very feminine. But the stranger spoke in a way which held depth; an alto with a heaviness and devastation which could be lethal if she used it wisely.

Which was why it had been so satisfying to hear it strained and breathless, instead. She wondered how it would sound screaming. The guard was sure that the girl had known pain, but *that* sort was the last thing she wished to inflict upon her. She had been eager enough earlier that night. But little would prepare her for Zemir Kal and her urge to dominate.

Those jade eyes would widen, and maybe she would run. Call her strange and twisted; perhaps unbearable or impossible. Like those few before her.

The guard didn't even know her name.

"*Ugh*," Zemir groaned, turning over and bundling up tighter. She tried her best to ignore the bubbling heat in her lower stomach. "…Not again."

CHAPTER 8

lorrin

THE IMAN DIDN'T want to go. She was no longer so sure.

But she knew that she had to drag herself out; to get to the Academy precinct while Verdia Kon's offer still stood. Even if she did it on four hours of sleep, and with a hangover from the torture of the cracked deserts.

Though the feeling of death could be subdued.

The only things which she gladly used that were imbued with majik, were her contraceptive pills and tablets of *Majik Kure*. Tiny capsules of healing crafted by scientists and Maji to make that kind of Seelie majik in any way ingestible to relieve ailments which would not resolve on their own.

Lorrin gulped down half a glass of water with the blue and purple thing, before trudging to the shower. She felt better afterwards; as the majik already got to work on her poor nerves and brain; and stepped into some plain yoga pants to go with a large, partially tucked-in button up shirt. Kon hadn't told her about any sort of dress code, but she didn't think that the situation called for anything smarter.

After lacing up her trainers and shrugging on her denim jacket, the assassin grabbed her keys and carryon bags she used between residences. The Guard of Madir was a little closer to Hemmingway Estate —the former home of Court member and Ember Faery, Lord Dunstun. Now that he had left for the other side of the river, Lorrin had bought the place after fierce negotiations with the estate agent and Kon's reluctant reference.

Opulence beckons trouble, he'd warned her.

But the blonde was fond of the property's large walls and lofty ceilings; of its gilded accents and how the light hit the garden fountains. She would go mad if she had to live in the Iris District apartment on a permanent basis. It was not as though the luxury was something she was used to —she certainly hadn't grown up that way. But she would take full advantage of her dirty money now.

She wouldn't hear the word '*no*' from a single soul.

The drive to the Iman District was leisurely, since she had set out so early. If there was one thing for which Lorrin somewhat cared, it was punctuality. It wasn't that she favoured being on time. Her fixation was on who *deserved* that time. Certain people required more of her, and others had to be grateful for what she offered. Hers was expensive, and few could afford it.

The suns seemed to shine a little brighter on this side of the city —where Her Excellency specifically controlled the iman populous and the Seelie, Drakon, Elves and Trolls who dared to live there. One could not be fooled by the giant billboards advertising coming housing and amenities. Buildings took months upon months to complete without majik, and in the end, they hardly looked as promised. The only places of artistry and value were those commissioned by The Court and citizens rich enough to evade the law.

Lorrin liked being one of those —especially with the evasion perk.

When the roofs of Hemmingway Estate peaked over the horizon, she fantasied about the bubble bath in which she was going to soak in the afternoon. As the fictious rose scent filled her imagination, an intrusive thought speared through the relaxation. That blue-haired stranger from last night was there, despite the two females' hasty parting as unlikely friends. And she was not in any particular way being seductive or sensual. Not like last night outside of the bar. No —the look in her amber eyes was cold and careful; as though she would never deviate from routine. Her presence and air were like gravity: a crushing hold; a lack of needing to be acknowledged; and yet so easily perilous if one misstepped.

If anything, the officer struck her with a chilling apprehension.

About what, the young iman was unsure.

She had been frustrated upon returning to the apartment —no one had ever denied her before, and worse, it had never further aroused her. It was like some sort of punishment, yet little complaint had arisen. The officer had held herself back —Lorrin had felt it in their every touch.

Even after she had breathlessly ridden her own fingers, imagining that they were the guard's, it hadn't been enough. There would never be eyes like those; never be an attraction as strong as that. About that, her mind was made.

The icy recollection thawed a little after Lorrin had driven up the gravel driveway; greeted by the familiar line of teardrop manicured conifer trees and a spotless stone pathway. The gardener must have come around while she was away for the week. She employed no other staff, since it would be unnecessary what with her frequent jumping from dwelling to dwelling. Although '*home*' was here, Lorrin had placed almost as much sentiment into her apartment. It was cosy and compact, while the airy estate echoed with her footsteps and every breath.

There was an upset potted fake cactus which had remained untouched, laying on the key-littered foyer console table. The assassin grumbled as she moved to right it, before visually sifting through the bronze keys. None of them opened a single door to the property. These were vintage collector's items for show.

They had belonged to her mother —and they were the only reminders of her apart from her diveball cap. Janiss Raffe had had the delusional belief that any old key found in the recesses of civilisation would open up a portal to another world; another life. She simply had to find the correct door.

And in the end, she had not found even one.

The disappointment which had buckled the assassin's knees as a young child —that had closed her throat with a lump so large that it left her more terrified of dying than developing a headache —was now a far-off memory, and as severed and old as her delicate milk teeth. If she squeezed her eyes shut tight enough, she could pretend that she didn't even recall it happening.

The keys stayed exactly where they were.

Lorrin recoiled, sure that her skin would bubble and blister like a Wyche's to blessed water if she held them long enough.

She powered for the ground floor bathroom instead, to change her sanitary wear before work, though the bleeding had only started that morning. At least the pain was manageable. What a twisted sense of humour the universe seemed to have, to make such a dastardly thing coincide with her other problems.

On a tangent, she remembered the stash of bloodied clothes she was still yet to destroy. She hauled the bag to the main living room, and threw it onto the dry wood of the rarely used fireplace. She'd need another new bag, but it wasn't worth leaving that DNA. The assassin dug through her pocket for her phoenix engraved gold lighter, the action repetitive and nonchalant, and lit it up.

She blankly watched the fire flare, licking their way over the cotton and plastic and blood —producing that pungent smell. But her nose knew it well. And she'd leave it to burn for all hours of the day.

The iman fought her way back out of the front door as both her bag and denim jacket caught the golden handle, before stomping to the car.

The drive was too fast and angry, but by the time she had parked that irritation had dissipated a little. This was where the central precinct was, after all. She had to rein herself in and make an innocent first impression.

"Hello," Lorrin quipped at reception, displaying the card from Verdia Kon. "I was referred as a civilian consultant until further notice."

"Name and ID," the Seelie guard clipped. "And you'll need one of these." They slid a visitor's lanyard pass across the counter.

She pulled it on and flashed her driver's licence. "Lorrin Raffe."

The Faery's Autumn wings and maple leaves lining their limbs flittered like real ones on the wind. "Do you know the detective you're meant to be assisting?"

"Zemir Kal," answered the iman.

"Hm? What about Detective Kal?" someone said from behind her.

Lorrin turned to another Faery holding a tray of *Sundeers* coffee —a pastel type with lilac waves and a little tattoo of a fire on the bridge of her nose. The blonde's gaze flickered from it to her piercings; to one light amber to the other peridot eye; and to the thin scar which split her right eyebrow towards the end.

The girl noted both the pistol and sword at her side.

63

"Officer Denaris," the Seelie behind the desk sighed with notable relief. "Thank the Daughter. Would you escort this iman consultant in to Detective Kal? Her name is Lorrin Raffe. A CR admin by profession."

The Faery's thin dragonfly wings beat with unhidden annoyance. "Sure, Sol." She nodded to the assassin. "Follow me, girl."

The iman snarled slightly at the word, but immediately straightened it into a grimace when the guard frowned in confusion.

"I wasn't informed of any consultant coming to assist our department," the Faery stated as a harsh matter of fact. "Detective Kal didn't mention anything."

"I think my reference forgot to pass the message on," Lorrin muttered. "He only gave me a little slither of card."

Officer Denaris huffed, and then turned her back to her.

The assassin thought about the dagger sheathed on the inside of her shirt against her midsection, and wondered what the quickest and most brutal way to kill the guard would be. The mess was a worry for afterwards.

"Welcome to Faecide & Homicide," the Faery guard then announced, pushing against the glass doors. "Detective Kal isn't in yet, but that's her desk in the back."

Lorrin looked over the maze of desks. Three people were present and seated: two imans and a Troll. There was a coffee station to the west wall, and the usual cumbersome printers and fax machines. There were even mobile wheeled cork boards with tangles of red string like in the movies.

"What case are you here to work on, Miss Raffe?" Officer Denaris asked as she distributed the coffees.

"The De Polis one," answered the blonde as she dumped her bag on the floor and jumped up to sit directly atop Detective Kal's work station.

"I wouldn't do that if I were you," warned the Seelie.

"Oh, best of luck," one iman guard winced from beneath large, round glasses and a frame of plum braids. Her warm nightly skin was inimanly unblemished. Everything —even her burgundy Harward University sweater over a shirt —was neat and pristine. She sipped away at her pumpkin spiced latte, but that highly scrutinising glint in her stark blue eyes was unmissable.

"Rohna's right," the other iman agreed. "That case is the toughest we've had." The only notable thing about him was his lack of remarkableness. His face was round and forgettable; his body was soft and untrained for apprehending suspects; his entire person a headache-inducing shade of beige. And that flat voice —Lorrin could have sworn that there were babies' lullabies livelier than that drawl. "Even Zemir hasn't found anything," he continued.

"That's why I'm here," Lorrin smiled, swinging her legs.

"*Detective Burns*," Officer Denaris articulated brusquely, slamming his coffee cup onto his desk. "Precinct etiquette. A visitor is here, and this is a professional setting. Refer to anyone by their first name only again and I'll report you to CR."

Lorrin glanced aside, biting back a laugh. It was different to what she had expected. Perhaps her dagger would remain tucked away.

"That's a bit extreme, Denaris," Detective Burns complained, eyeing his cup suspiciously. "What's got you in a mood today?"

The Faery wasn't subtle. She pointed at the blonde, snarling. "Her."

Lorrin blinked rapidly. "Me? Why?"

She only received the click of a tongue in response. The Faery settled down at her desk, and proceeded no longer to have anything to do with the iman. Lorrin nodded importantly. Being disliked was an intimate, constant companion. Having true friends was an obscene venture as an assassin. Her family had left those emotions hollow. And the only person who would protect her and care —who would catch her when she fell, was herself.

"Don't take her too seriously," the female iman whispered as she walked past. "I'm Rohna Nyll —Forensics. Denaris was like this when I joined last year. It just takes some time for her to warm up to you. When she does, you'll almost wish that she had left you alone. However, do take the warning seriously. Kal will kill you if she finds you sitting on her desk."

"Ah."

Lorrin was largely unconcerned with the internal politics of the precinct. The Troll seemed to share in the sentiment, as he had not introduced himself and kept a pair of black headphones glued to his ears. His great horns of fading emerald shadowed everything else —from his lean frame and short umber hair to his small tusks. Even Detective Denaris had not bought him coffee.

But Lorrin wasn't going to work here for very long, anyway. Getting along with the other guards on the team was not a necessity. All that mattered was throwing the detective off of the trail. And avoiding bullets and blades.

"Kal is here," announced Detective Burns.

Lorrin uncertainly jumped down and turned towards the doors to the figure pushing against them. There was an eerily familiar flutter of electric blue hair. The assassin froze, and her astonishment must have been evident because the officer paused in a mirrored stance. All of those sensations came flooding back —though it was difficult to smile or blush when Officer Kal stared back as though she had seen a terrible ghost; her eyes shadowed and her skin blanching. Regret settled hard on her features as she made an effort to mask the unwelcome reunion.

Rohna and Officer Burns watched on with annoying intrigue.

Detective Kal then threw a quizzical look at a calm Officer Denaris. The Faery shrugged; eyes glued to her computer screen. "Sol said Civilian Consultant."

"What?" the guard said through her teeth, powering towards her. She stopped a foot in front of Lorrin, careful not to recreate the scene from a few hours before. The assassin's muscles locked as though they remembered it, too. The rough brick wall, and the skin on the inside of the officer's hand. The sound of her steady breaths being drowned out by Lorrin's quick, harsh ones.

No heat surged between them now. At least not outwardly.

"Well, well, well," the iman cut back. She gave up no ground. There was that look of cold fury in her honey gaze —the one the blonde had daydreamt about. She'd be lying if she said that it had no effect on her to see it in reality.

"What exactly is your purpose here, girl?" Officer Kal sighed without an ounce of interest, but the last word tugged horribly at the iman's gut. It wasn't at all affectionate —she called her that as a little reminder of her place here in the precinct; perhaps even in the whole world. That she had none.

Last night was filed away. This was now, and that was crystal clear. The guard's arms were folded and she was looking down slightly at the assassin in a way that had her legs going a little unsteady.

"Verdia Kon recommended me," Lorrin said, and she mustered all of the bravado she dared. Fluster no longer dusted her cheeks. She didn't need to feel any sort of bad for last night, or any other night. She had just as much of a right to bury the incident and be a bitch about it as the officer. She'd hold up her chin, and dismiss last night as utterly typical. No one remembered in the morning. No one *wanted* to remember.

The detective hesitated, attempting to recall the Troll. "...I really need to have a talk with that male," she grumbled, running a hand through her hurriedly brushed waves. "He can't keep handing out my card as and when he pleases."

Lorrin scoffed. "Well he mentioned that you could certainly use the help."

Their audience audibly gasped —before scampering and making themselves productive when Officer Kal turned to glare.

"Come with me," she ordered, curling her finger to beckon the assassin as she turned to the doors. "Away from those damn busybodies."

The blonde leisurely sauntered after her, with her hands in her pockets. She was all smiles until the guard backed her against the wall in a secluded alcove; her breath uncertain and heavy, her gaze narrowed wildly, with a strained hand beside the assassin's head. "...You and I are going to come to an understanding," she rasped. "Yesterday..." Her voice struggled to put the incident into words. "We are strangers —always have been. And we will *keep* being strangers. We can't act like something happened between us."

"Specifically here?"

"*Anywhere.*"

"What, are you ashamed?" She meant it as a jest.

"Yes," the detective answered bluntly, as though it were a given. But there was no malice in her expression. Her eyebrows knitted in a desperate frown; a glimmer of pain in that amber. Pain that Lorrin couldn't understand.

She had been raised with the impression that the world was more progressive at large —that any sort of prejudice based on race, species, gender and orientation had diminished. Internalised judgement, was something that she had not thought to acknowledge. Unless…the officer had an issue with the assassin, specifically. Even then she refrained from feeling offended. It wasn't as if she was a model citizen, or even a good person. She could understand any shame someone would feel about being associated with her.

Lorrin tentatively tugged at the end of her sleeve. "Don't worry. I can be that professional. And, listen…you know that thing where you overshare because you think you'll never see that stranger again —"

"*This* is our first time meeting," the guard quipped.

A distinct warning and a line drawn. And she'd keep her secrets. Lorrin banished any lingering interest she harboured. Or at least she'd need to. She gave a curt nod and swallowed her pride. "…Agreed."

The officer retreated and stuck her hand out. "Detective Zemir Kal."

She plastered a small smile and forced her hand to slip into Zemir's. Though she let go almost as abruptly as she had offered it. "Lorrin Raffe."

The guard sniffed; little better than indifferent. But that deep gaze stripped the assassin bare. "I hope that you will be of use to me, Miss Raffe."

Lorrin had never spied before, but she had an inkling that she would enjoy it. It was going to be a *joy* to fuck over this female; and the case. To completely pull the wool over her eyes. Zemir was unprepared for the havoc she'd wreak. Now her smile grew genuine. "Just Raffe is fine."

CHAPTER 9

lorrin

THE ASSASSIN HAD done her haphazard job too well.

Zemir was having a terrible time trying to tie loose threads which led nowhere. Thank the Daughter or whatever governed them, for terror. Lorrin was sure that the residents of the Iris District would have plucked the stupid courage to report the incident in detail if they had no fear of being next.

After the findings of the case had been briefed —things that she already knew —the assassin thought about the evidence she would need to manipulate. Officer Kal wasn't working with a lot, so that left ample room. It also presented no guidance. Where would she begin? From what angle would she work?

There were too many people who had wanted Jon De Polis dead. And for petty, stupid reasons. How she had left the crime scene might insinuate an impulsive attack, but she had left it so barren that this case was going to stretch further than for what she had prepared.

Lorrin sneered. She wouldn't be doing this if Verdia Kon hadn't enlisted her to do his dirty work. What a pain.

"What have you actually gathered so far?" the blonde asked, swivelling in a chair across from Officer Kal's desk.

"Please stop that," the guard clipped, her hard gaze slitting.

Lorrin grinned, irrationally pleased with herself. "I'm going to assume that you haven't found any leads. But you've been to the scene, yes?"

"Of course," the detective deadpanned.

"Interviewed any witnesses?"

"All who can recall a slither of that night. Which is next to nothing." The increasing hopelessness was a shot of serotonin. "What about the people who simply live in the area?" the assassin murmured. "I know they weren't there, but maybe life predicts this sort of occurrence."

That's it, she mused. Lorrin would insinuate that it was commonplace; less significant than it seemed.

The detective did not see her vision. "A life is a life, Lorrin Raffe," she said through her teeth. "Whether this happens often is not a dismissing excuse."

The assassin levelled her a withering look, pissed by her full name. "That's not what I meant, Detective *Zemir Kal*. I meant, look for a pattern."

Equally irritated, Zemir paused and folded her arms. She was actually mulling it over. "…That might be the smartest thing you've said all day."

Lorrin didn't miss a beat. "Agreeing with me makes it your smartest move."

Rohna and Detective Burns snickered from the coffee station, where the two were heating up their lunch. The Troll and Seelie remained stiff and absorbed — the only indication of overhearing being additional lines to their furrowed brows.

Officer Kal sprung to her feet; the scrape of her chair echoing through the office. "To the harbour," she barked, straightening her leather jacket.

The iman skipped at her heels. "Yes, Detective."

Lorrin froze and stared at the sleek motorcycle parked a few spaces from her car. It was so polished that she could clearly mark out her reflection on the obsidian body. It even appeared to be dusted in flecks of silver in imitation of stars. She wouldn't have guessed off of the top of her head that it belonged to the guard, but given her true straightforward and prickly disposition, it definitely suited her.

Zemir held her helmet in her hands, glancing at the lack of another.

"I can ride without protection —" the assassin deadpanned.

"—Please watch your phrasing," the detective cringed. Then she chewed on her lower lip in thought; a hard sigh escaping her when she realised the most practical solution. "…I can't allow you to do that in good conscience."

"A car then?"

"Unfortunately."

They veered for the line of black and gold squad cars, plastered with the Idun coat of arms. Lorrin had always been fascinated by that shield —the sheer laughable irony of it, as though anyone below Iman District residency was protected, and why the old kings of the Seelie and Unseelie Courts had decided on it. Aside from the proud twin phoenixes and a crimson sun emblem, it had a harsh depiction of the favoured Faery kind and the not; a floating island city divided by one mountain along the top and one below, upside down. Like a hehlish underworld.

And that brutal motto along the ribboned banner...*from blood, by blood, in blood*. Created even before the Firs Idun War. Having originally been in a Seelie tongue, the assassin could only imagine how much more sinister it sounded in one of those ancient grating languages. It was one consequence of the building of an integrated society that she felt anything for —chilling relief at the dying out of that particular part of their heritage.

Her mother had loved them; those soft, lilting vowels like birdsong and sharp, harsh consonants. The way words sounded like spells and curses.

"Well. Get in, then."

The officer had spoken to her out of nowhere —the engine already started while Lorrin stood staring at the side of the squad car and at nothing.

The blonde climbed inside and stared out of the window.

If she so much as glanced in the driver's direction, she would feel the slip in control. For the second time in her life, Lorrin had to concentrate in order to forget someone. The first was permanent, but this one was to adhere to certain wishes. She'd remember the guard, but it would take a long time to become a stranger to her touch. Especially that seasoned skill she was so clearly hiding.

Detective Zemir Kal was a logical and methodical person. She drove on the speed limit, remained in the middle of their side of the road, and always indicated.

71

The picture of a perfect learner. It bothered the assassin more than it ought to, which left her stiff and scowling.

"Look, I don't want you here either," Detective Kal smirked. "I didn't even know about this arrangement until getting an email back from Kon earlier."

Lorrin started. "If it makes you feel any better, I didn't exactly volunteer," she grumbled. "He thinks this will be...a good change of pace for me."

"Are you always stuck in an office? I'm afraid you can't escape that here."

"No," the iman sighed. "I used to be everyone's errand girl, but I've decided that an office-focused role is actually what I want. I'm sick of my boss, and I want my own schedule and space —my own established position. I've been at it for too long not to be in charge of *something*."

Zemir frowned with misplaced concern. "Patience is a virtue. But if you do a decent job, maybe Verdia will see your ambition."

The Troll already knows of it, she wanted to snap. He just wouldn't give it to her without gaining something himself.

"I'll try," Lorrin drawled.

The guard cast her a sidelong glance, which was not returned. "I thought that you were capable of professionalism."

The assassin huffed a breath, finding her bitterness subsiding slightly. "I never specified to what extent."

She had never heard Detective Kal laugh outright. By the little reluctant smile which momentarily stretched her dark lips, she knew that she likely never would.

The assassin had been taught to run, and fast, at the sight of striped Guard tape. That conditioned instinct kicked in as they approached the familiar secluded street; a patch of old sunning blood squared off by bands of black and gold.

"Do you come to crime scenes often?" the officer quipped.

"No," Lorrin said. She created them.

"Then stay beside me."

The blonde raised an eyebrow, her gaze briefly straying in a flash of weakness. Her personality also escaped. "Is this flirting?"

Zemir Kal had little sense of humour whether drunk or sober.

She bared her teeth, and the warm dark brown of her face saturated with a bit of red. "Absolutely not."

The street was deserted, so no one witnessed their exchange. No one would see how the older iman clenched her fists in either restraint or anger. No one would notice how the assassin tried to put as much distance between them as possible, in order to glance over the guard's back and legs.

"Here," Detective Kal pointed out the splatters of maroon on the tar. "This is where the body was found. Head severed and placed a hand's length away."

"Pretty brutal way to kill someone."

"And sloppy," Zemir remarked.

The girl subconsciously categorised it as strange. Though it stemmed from her job, Lorrin couldn't fathom the strange pique in intrigue which budded from the detective's expression at the fact the murder appeared to be imanslaughter.

In a way, it hadn't been fully premeditated. But in a court, the assassin knew that it would be sentenced as otherwise. She had had motive, opportunity and a plan —however hasty. That was enough for a degree of murder.

An elderly Elf wobbled along the redirected sidewalk.

"Excuse me ma'am," the guard spoke up. The Favoured jumped slightly, and hugged her large handbag closer against her ample chest. Her wrinkled face and ears sagged with millennia of age, and her once copper curls were an unravelling and thinning bob. Lorrin hadn't thought that Elves could live long enough to begin aging as noticeably as imans did. Despite that weathering and frailty, her beady cyan eyes were alert. They'd seen the birth and death of worlds.

They regarded the two imans with an air of odd superiority and caution as she shifted in her lengthy floral dress, lingering on the indication of authority.

"Guard of Madir. Do you live in this side of the Iris District?"

The Elf pressed her thin lips into a line that almost disappeared entirely.

Zemir was undeterred, despite the obvious reluctance. "We only want to ask a few questions —loosely related to this crime. Would you be willing to answer?"

The voice which came out from that thin line of mouth was low and unused. "…What happened here wasn't right," the Favoured spoke, her face contorting into one of thought-out pain.

"Yes," the officer agreed. "It never is."

Lorrin averted her gaze. That comment felt arrowed at her.

"No —I mean it was unnatural," the old female corrected. "Strange things happen in this Daughter-forsaken district all the time. But this," she murmured, glancing at the stain, "this was different. I heard he was terrified before death."

"You weren't…a witness, were you?" Detective Kal questioned, narrowing her eyes as she tried to remember her from previous interviews.

"No, no," hissed the Elf. "I don't even dare to come outside. I live right along the harbour —the sea air's been prescribed for my health. But I hear stories. And I remember the atrocities of long ago."

"About the founding of Idun?" Lorrin frowned.

"Before," the Favoured clipped; the lines in her forehead becoming far more pronounced. "Look, there've always been those who oppose imannity —or even harmony. A lot of them aren't violent. But the ones who crave blood," her voice lowered, and she pointed towards the top of the Gehman bordered Wall in the distance, "are never too far away. Can you hear the rumble of marching feet?"

A shiver jolted up the blonde's spine.

"No one is getting through that cinder block," Zemir said firmly, but her voice lacked conviction, like she was trying to convince herself.

"I've seen this before, over and over," the wizened Elf then sighed, turning sympathetic. "This world will not be spared. Every time you erect a wall between peoples —every time you build a cage around the Unseelie…war follows."

"Are the old kings that ruthless?" Lorrin asked.

The Favoured's gaze narrowed at the iman, in a way to scrutinise. "How do you know of the old kings, girl?"

The assassin paused, contemplating her apparent mistake. "…It's written in the history books," she justified. "Tales of merciless chaos."

74

"Hm. I'm surprised your books say a word about them at all," the old female huffed, hefting her bag. "History gets retold and rewritten with each generation. That is the only constant —because who is able to write those words and what is omitted and left in, is as decided as the flow of water down a rocky mountain." She then paused, realising the conversation had gone off tangent. "...I cannot help you to catch that iman's killer, but I can warn you. It is dangerous here. If you find anything out of the ordinary, or if the Faery kind and majik were involved, abandon the investigation."

"Why?" Zemir demanded.

The Favoured's forehead uncrumpled, smoothing into defeat; her eyes warm with concern. "You may not like the answers," she rasped, moving to carry on her way. "And it may be your head next."

CHAPTER 10

lorrin

THE PAIR HADN'T managed to get a name or statement out of the old Elf, but her story had been effective in setting a chill in the air and their bones —even if neither wanted to admit it. Whether it was fact or fiction, there were truths which were universally acknowledged. That all Faery kind were cunning and fickle, and that egregious Wall was not indestructible. It was only a matter of time before it would crash down, and the Unseelie Court and its allies would remind imannity of their insignificant place once more.

"We can't use anything she said as evidence of any kind without her written consent," Detective Kal grumbled, running her hands over her face.

"Stupid rules," Lorrin quipped.

"And I doubt we'll find any other willing participants," the guard continued, stepping into a pace. "Everyone is scared stiff."

Lorrin's attention had turned elsewhere. Murder was indeed frequent, enough for residents to turn the other cheek, but that presented a problem. If she was going to shift responsibility onto something else…maybe she'd have to *create* a pattern. She'd need to kill again.

"Last night," the assassin murmured. Zemir's expression was already sour when she turned to meet her eye. It worsened with every word out of her pink mouth. "I was at a nightclub called *Moondust*. I met a Seelie —a stag. We flirted, danced…and then he enchanted me with a kiss. So he could ask what I thought about the Unseelie. About the monsters over the Wall, and the inevitability of what that Elf told us —of war. And he advised me to leave Idun."

"An Unseelie sympathiser?" grumbled the detective. "And a Faery kind at that. It doesn't bode well." She then hesitated, straightening her jacket as her expression darkened into something regretful. "…Also, what he did to you isn't legal. Would you like to file a formal complaint?"

Lorrin blinked. Though it didn't stem from a place of emotional concern, she still enjoyed the idea of Zemir eager to charge that Faery. Majik related offences were treated more harshly compared to their mundane counterparts. And if she was entirely delusional, she could relish in the thought of the guard being petty and jealous about how the blonde spent her time. As if it was exclusive to her, based on barely a couple of hours in a shadowed bar and alleyway.

That's right, Detective, Lorrin internally mused. *You're not special.*

"I'm used to the effects of majik," the assassin said as a matter of fact. "I work with a few Seelie. And he didn't do anything else. He just wanted to talk."

"At the time," bit the guard. "You were paralysed, right? Who knows what he could have done if you hadn't broken free."

"I wasn't alone before going to *Slow Poison*," the iman scoffed. "I went with a colleague who is also familiar with majik. I wouldn't be so foolish as to entertain the Faery kind without appropriate company."

Zemir didn't seem convinced, though the evidence stood before her. Lorrin was fine, and displayed none of the deliriousness that lingered after prolonged enchantment. The spells varied in severity depending on the administration — from a simple brush of skin to a full ceremonial blood exchange. Those were rare, and only came up with carnivorous Faery kind; those with canines and talons.

Majik was strongest in Favoured born; with it genetically interwoven. When one learned and acquired such power, it was a diluted concentration of weak incantations, tarot readings and crystals. Even among Wyches.

"If you had been any more intoxicated, foolishness would have had little to do with it," the detective frowned. "He could have done something worse, and you wouldn't have had the awareness and control to stop it."

Lorrin dared to meet her gaze, seeing the sense in her words. Those sharp gemstone eyes almost seemed to have an enchantment of their own.

Then she snapped out of it, and matched the guard's bitterness. "I'm not sure how you see me —as a weak little civilian or just as a clueless iman—but I'm more capable of defending myself than you might think."

"You're speaking to a Guard of Madir here," Zemir sneered, folding her arms and leaning onto one hip. Lorrin's line of sight fought to drift, but she maintained her anger as she processed the insinuation. If she had been pretending to dislike the detective before, the feeling was more genuine now.

No one belittled her experience; made light of her past. And no one would come to doubt her as a thing of death.

She turned on her heel and stalked towards the car as she coldly cut back with, "…And you're speaking to a long-faythless female."

Instant noodle soup was a staple when working into the late hours. Detective Zemir had encouraged the assassin to go home with everyone else at late evening, but the blonde had insisted that she had nothing better to do and that she needed to sift through the witness statements the guard had already compiled.

She needed to know if anyone had seen her.

So she had pulled up Rohna Nyll's chair to the other side of Detective Kal's desk, kicked off her shoes, and was slurping the contents of the cup with desperate concentration. She'd notice Zemir steal a hard, puzzled glance upwards every now and then. It still made her press her thighs together, but she no longer returned the action. If it was professionalism she wanted, then the guard would get it.

That translated to silence and frowns. While the quiet wasn't constant, neither complained about the sound of eating.

Lorrin found the statements were largely identical: The Court members either had a fuzzy recollection of Jon De Polis wandering off on his own, or a vague and unreliable thought of a ghost luring the iman away. The assassin frowned deeply at that, but refrained from panicking. No one had been able to describe the ghost, let alone discern what colours had been its skin and hair. They all simply agreed that Jon De Polis had recognised something in the distance, and it had made him fearful. Like he had known death was coming.

She was fond of that bit.

"Did you find anything I hadn't?" Detective Kal eventually spoke up, setting down her cup and fork.

Lorrin glanced aside and gathered the files, before slowly shaking her head. "It sounds silly, but a majority saw something similar. I'd dismiss the odd sighting of a phantom, but this…do you know any necromancers we can consult?"

"I've already booked one," Zemir sighed. "For ten tomorrow, so get here on time. If you can't stop by the precinct, I can text you the address."

The assassin stuck up her chin. "I don't give out my number."

"This is for work."

"I don't exactly *have* a phone number."

"You…don't have a cellphone?" The guard was taken aback.

"I have several emergency burners."

The officer's gaze narrowed. "Why?"

Lorrin continued to ride on the coattails of haughtiness; giving no thought to the consequences of her words. "So that I'm not constantly monitored by Her Excellency and the Guard. Unlike some people, I value my privacy and freedom."

Zemir's mouth twisted into a shape. Of course the assassin's reasoning was suspicious. Anyone would guess that she wanted to remain off of the grid for an illegal reason. It would be a fair and slightly merited assumption. However, it was not mandatory to possess a smartphone. It was not enforced to be technologically traceable. The only information anyone might find on Lorrin Raffe, would be things related to her citizenship, house address and fake occupation.

"I'll just have to give you my number," the officer relented.

The blonde reluctantly pulled out a small notebook from her bag. She didn't even have the energy to joke about receiving the digits. She was reserving it for midnight; for sliding her dagger along a neck. It was already a stressful venture as it was too late to contact Madam G for a costume. The assassin hadn't even picked a victim yet. Which presented its own issue —without a plan, who now would she fell? There was no one to name as obvious and corrupt as De Polis off of the top of her head. No one else that indulgent. It was wise to go with another predicted Court member, but she had no time to look into it.

Perhaps…Rye could find out for her. He wouldn't *want* to, but he owed her a few favours and she was about to make him an accomplice in murder for the first time to cash in one of them. He would still need to give her an answer immediately —she couldn't wait until the meeting with the necromancer.

Lorrin let out a heavy sigh. In any case, she would have to wear her standard and issued shroud from the Central Blades; the hooded cloak lined with a fur of deep red that resembled a cultish robe more than a cover in the dark.

"Are you finally tired?" asked Zemir, tucking back into her noodles as she lazily scrolled through the system onscreen. "Can you leave now?"

"I can leave. But why should I?" the assassin shot back.

"Because I find you annoying."

The blonde flinched slightly. There was not a second of hesitation. It stabbed her in a way with which she was unfamiliar —a way in which no one had expressed their hatred before. Not even the prickly Markus Arrium was so direct. It wasn't clear, however, why the detective's perception of her should matter —at all. The two young imans knew each other as well as tentative, passing passengers did. Or perhaps that was exactly it: Zemir therefore had little basis to dislike her. Which implied that she was clinging to any reason to keep the assassin at arm's length. A smile tugged at her mouth. She could enjoy and play with this.

Lorrin scoffed, tucked back her hair, and shrugged off the comment. "If you find me annoying, then why am I working here?"

"Who knows," sighed the guard, glancing aside to meet the assassin's gaze. That look held her there in her chair, and caressed her skin.

The iman visibly swallowed, her fingers curling into the upholstery beneath her. Then her smile stretched slightly and she leaned in, tilting her head to the side. "You're the one who approached me after I left last night. You're the one who touched me. Was I irritating then?"

Zemir went still.

An entire battle was waged within that mind before she settled on a few words. "That was a short lapse in judgement," was the attempt to amend. "I said as much before it could go any further, didn't I?"

"That's not what you implied, Officer Kal," Lorrin murmured. "You said that we should stop because you didn't want to take me home. I can respect that. But I feel as though I deserve a decent explanation as to why it felt…"

Now she had Zemir's attention. Her amber gaze narrowed and the hair at the back of her neck rose. "*Felt…?*" she prompted.

Lorrin slid one foot up along the officer's calf; her expression cool calm. It travelled the length of her leg, inching closer and closer to the widening space between her thighs as she, for some reason, spread them. Lorrin's foot dared to hit its destination, and press down. She felt the detective shiver and contract at the contact, though her face was a poised mirror of hers.

Zemir then did something unforeseen. She took hold of that foot, gritted her teeth, and threw it down. Anger crackled in that snarl.

"Like that," the assassin whispered, withdrawing. "Like something denied."

The guard blinked. She was unreadable for a moment; the brutal internal war rekindled; before her gaze lowered to her lap. "I think I should make something clear, Lorrin Raffe." She regathered the courage to look at her again, but there was no trepidation there. It was icy authority. "I *was* blinded by a selfish desire to have a taste of you, even when I knew I shouldn't. I believe that this professional predicament is a sign that we should remain at a distance. It's not that I didn't enjoy our exchange…I simply cannot afford for it to grow. We can't know each other any more deeply. You will not like what you find beneath this."

The blonde couldn't care less about what she was saying, but she got the gist of it. "So you'll write this off based on an assumption?"

Zemir offered a tired smile. "Based on history."

Lorrin didn't return the sentiment; the relief and easing of tension at the end of a serious conversation. She'd leave it sour.

"You'll crash if you keep glancing behind you," she stated.

The detective sighed in defeat. Evidently, she didn't want to hear it. Some people were content with their trauma. "I really think that you should call it a day. *I* can stay as long as I want," Zemir murmured. "Besides...why would I be in a hurry to go home if I know I'll have a hard time falling asleep?"

It was more of a passing comment to herself, but Lorrin lingered on it. She felt no sympathy nor was she about to offer useful advice, but where the assassin harboured little feeling, or had clung to something she shouldn't —like that heated attraction —it was easy to fill it with malice.

"Just go out drinking again," she clipped.

The detective's brows rose in a way that indicated her offence, but with a clear lack of agency to defend herself. That was somehow worse than denying it —an unapologetic and indirect confirmation that drowning herself in cider might be a regular occurrence. The assassin had dealt with and killed people with similar problem solving skills, but she hadn't imagined someone as wound up tight as the guard to suffer through it. Zemir seemed too righteous; too sure of herself to fall into that habit. And from the name she had overheard her praying to at lunch, Detective Kal was in some capacity, a follower of the fayth. Lorrin knew that copious alcohol consumption was prohibited.

"...Maybe I will," muttered the officer.

And maybe she'd meet another pretty blonde, and cave to her whims, too. Lorrin violently pushed back out of the chair and gathered her things. She was filled with an inexplicable mixture of shame and nastiness —something for which she was too proud to apologise or even *imply* remorse.

The assassin left without a further word or glance behind her.

Lorrin Raffe stood on the second floor balcony which faced East towards the Lois Sea, staring at the swelling moons. She had already changed into leather pants, an off-shoulder green blouse, and had strapped down multiple short blades to her legs and midsection; her right hip's gilded leather sheath reserved only for her ivory dagger. That dark robe billowed in the frigid breeze, blocking the cold and giving anyone below on the suburban streets a vision of Death or its harbinger.

Her previous disposable clothes had finally been reduced to crumbling ashes, and Hemmingway Estate was airing with the coolness of the night as well as an automated air freshener dispenser that smelled of tropical fruit juice.

She called Char Gilligan first; on the phone number she had given her. The Syren picked up on the third ring.

"*Hello?*"

"It's the queen," Lorrin deadpanned.

Char belted a laugh, then audibly moved around before letting out a sigh. "*What can I do for you, your Majesty?*"

The assassin adjusted her cuffs. "I won't be able to go to the Central Blades regularly for a while, so in the meantime I have a mission for you."

There was a pause to be noted, as if the dark creature was weighing out her options and feeling out her limits. "*...I am at your command, Raffe,*" she assured.

"Good," hedged Lorrin. "Gather as much information as you can on the inner workings of each of the rings. I need operations; deals; strengths; and weaknesses. I need to know in every which way I can break them."

Char sucked on her teeth. "*Can do.*"

"Don't spare a single detail."

"*Understood.*"

The blonde frowned slightly. "And delete this call from recent."

"*That's a given.*"

A bit of the tension in Lorrin's muscles eased. "...Never spare."

The Syren had evidently been adequately taught, as she returned the end of the Ivory Blade's creed before ending the call. "*Never yield.*"

Lorrin was then left with the silence of the night, as she dialled Rye's number next. But the Elf wasn't picking up. She tapped her booted foot impatiently and forced herself to keep calling until he did. He couldn't be doing anything of importance. After five more attempts, the Favoured answered on the fourth ring.

"*Ahem. I'm afraid to ask why you're calling this late.*"

She raised the pitch of her voice to something soft and almost unrecognisable. "You should be. Get me the name of a predicted Court member. Any will do. The more corrupt and hated, the better. And I need a brand new, untouched deck of playing cards."

"*What? Why would —don't tell me…another one?*" Rye groaned. "*Wasn't that reckless iman enough?*"

"No," she sighed. "And watch what you say. The detective on the case is looking into something that might steer the investigation in the wrong direction. I need to create a pattern. A villain."

"*Why do you need* my *help?*" the Favoured whined.

"Because you know The Court, and you know its people."

"*That's not enough,*" he reasoned, his voice hissed and breath quickening. "*I've never helped you carry out a plan like this before. I don't need my hands dirty.*"

"They already are," Lorrin deadpanned, having anticipated the excuse. She couldn't feel a shred of pity for him or his position. It was all meaningless and bore no consequences for her, personally. "You seem to forget that you owe me, Rye. I know of the bodies you have buried," she threatened. "I know whose blood you've shed. The blood you've…consumed. And I know exactly who to give that information in order for you to wake to a set of iron bars."

The assassin didn't prefer resorting to blackmail —she and the Arch Favoured were meant to be '*friends*' —but she would exploit every single angle without hesitation if needed. Rye knew that. Which is why he relented.

The Elf was not quite as squeaky clean as he presented. Not so far as claiming a life himself, but not innocent. Certainly not before his holy change of career.

"*…Meet me on the Iris District river bank in fifteen. Butterscotch.*"

"Butterscotch," she returned. One of their operation passwords. Then she took hold of the two halves of the burner, and snapped them apart.

CHAPTER 11

lorrin

SYTHE RIVER WAS the constant lapping of waves in a tiny ocean. As though The Court and academy had successfully harnessed nature itself to act as a blockade between the districts. Crossing the mile-wide body undetected was physically impossible. The only methods were a clumsy or Courtly stable boat — easily apprehended —and by majik. Majik was easier to spot. But no one would question the distinguished Rye going back and forth without reason.

Lorrin had no majik; no special ability beyond toned strength, efficiency and speed. It was a mission to get anything done that required none of those skills. She had had to park her car back at the apartment before walking to the three-way border. The need to get away after the murder still persisted, and there was little chance that the Elf would oblige her in more teleporting than necessary.

Disassembling organic and living matter and reconstructing it elsewhere was one of the most difficult spells a majik user could master. They had to understand DNA, the layout of atoms and the conservation of them. And it had to happen in the blink of an eye. It drained so much energy, life and concentration, that even the Unseelie had refrained from using it to get over the Wall.

Favoured and Maji alike had lost their lives for it.

The assassin peeked up from the roof upon which she had perched a few feet from the river bank, in search for Rye's dirty blond hair.

It was the dead of night and visibility was low, but he would be the only one out there. He *should* be the only one out there.

Sure enough, there stood a figure in deep green by the surf. Golden rings studded his pointed ears, and glinted in the moonlight. She was close enough to mark out his features. But her confirmation came when a flash of blue sparked in the shadows and the creature was on the Iris District bank, misting cerulean.

Lorrin jumped down; guarded in her approach.

"Butterscotch," said the Elf, wiping his nose with a sleeve. A streak of stark red blood stained his shirt and smeared just above his upper lip.

The assassin grinned and skipped to his side, swirling the cape of her cloak as she pulled the hood up a little. "Butterscotch. You're pleasantly punctual."

Rye's face pinched inwards. "As if you would give me any other choice. This had better go off without a hitch, Raffe. I think I ruptured three blood vessels just for this. That'll be six more until you're done and back on this side." Then he turned sarcastic. "…Or maybe twelve, since I'll have a passenger."

Lorrin shrugged, then shook off the amusement. Her brows knitted and she straightened up. "Did you bring the deck of cards?"

"Yes," he sighed, digging into his pocket. "Why did you need them anyway?"

"You'll see," she assured, tempted to smile at her own cleverness. "It's a little on the nose, but it'll be our killer's calling card. A right riddle of one. Let's hope that our detective is smarter than I expect."

The Elf grunted in compliance, before offering his arm.

Lorrin carefully linked with him and drew a breath.

It was instantaneous —the pulling apart of muscle and skin and the restitching of it. She blinked, a flicker of blue danced across her eyelids, and then they were on The Court side of the bank as if they had only taken a step.

Her insides screamed for a brief moment, before a short quiver travelled up the assassin's spine. "I'm never going to get used to that."

"And I won't let you," promised the Elf. "Or I'll die before five hundred."

"Fair. So who's my target?"

The Favoured idly scratched the back of his head and gestured for the pair to start walking. "Right. There is a period during a year where predicted members attend an open house event of sorts, hosted by other court members and Her Excellency. There will be a gala to conclude it next week. Its purpose is for those coming members to familiarise themselves with The Court and pick a possible residence. Your target can be any one of these candidates, but there's a rumour circulating about how the Drakon Rudd Leifsdotter has had a shaded rise."

Lorrin rolled her eyes. "Any excuse to spend money, huh? But I doubt that gala will still go ahead in light of murder."

"Indeed." Rye chuckled lowly. Then his pointed ears twitched, and he glanced to the street opposite them. "Careful now," he hissed, tugging the assassin to the nearest conifer tree. "We may be walking along the unsightly back end of the river, but we might find a night guard or the rare jogger."

The iman was marginally surprised by the state of the gardens around them. Though the trimming and care resembled Hemmingway Estate at least, it lacked the expensive touch shown in the brochures of the rest of The Court. The cut grass seemed duller; the trees a little more ruffled —even the winding cobbled pathways sprouted the odd weed or two, and sported a few protruding bricks.

"*This* is the unsightly area?" Lorrin whispered. "Seriously?"

She had never set a foot on Court land prior to this. The glass fences, towering golden spires and slated roofs were the only glimpse she had ever had of this inaccessible playground of the disgustingly rich and powerful. Janiss Raffe would have completely lost her shit if she knew that her daughter now came this close to being able to afford living on the coveted side of society.

"Rudd Leifsdotter, you said?" the assassin mused. She recalled a fiery, beady eyed hunched male with silvery blue skin; scaled and cold; drowning in a curtain of midnight hair. "I think he's popped up in another ring's discussions before. They dismissed him because his allegations were dropped."

The Drakon didn't have the same gambling habits, but rather loansharking. He used to have carefully constructed schemes where he depleted his inheritance in the process of loaning pense to citizens who could barely afford a waterlogged apartment by the harbour. Of course, there had been very few of those who had somehow managed to stay afloat and repay his absurd investments, which was why he was sitting in the lap of luxury.

"He is staying in the Diamond guest house, on Shard Avenue. Suite number twenty-one, second floor, and first window from the entrance," Rye informed her. "I suggest you don't kill him there, though."

"Oh Rye, what do you take me for?" Lorrin scoffed, patting her sheath. "I'm going to lure him out to the back end of the river."

"You're going to wait until morning?"

"I can't wait that long. I have somewhere to be tomorrow, and need to get back in plenty of time to clean my knives. I'll have to get him out forcefully."

The Elf gulped.

"No, I'm not going to drag him from his bed," the assassin clipped, frowning. "He'll be far too heavy. I'm going to send a reaper after him." She pulled her hood up over her tied golden hair, shadowing her face. "I kind of look like it, right?"

"What about a sickle?" the Favoured pointed out.

Lorrin sucked in a sharp breath. "Shit, I hadn't thought of that."
Rye sighed and pulled a steel-bladed sickle from the air, blue majik wafting off of it. "Here. Use this," he offered. "It's just for show, right?"

"Thanks," she quipped, gripping the handle. "Be here when I get back."

Rye promptly dropped cross-legged to the pavement, ready to give the excuse of meditation if caught. "I'll be waiting."

Lorrin then darted off in the direction of a street sign at the intersection. Shard Avenue was a turn to the left and on for two minutes. The blonde sifted through the trees and hedges until the diamond topped towers of the guest house came into view. She spied the second floor window; the one adjacent to the giant marble filigree doors, and sized up the grown pine a foot from it.

It wouldn't be an easy climb, but she would get to that window.

Her feet skimmed the freshly shaven grass in a few seconds before thudding the branches as she jumped up; her gloved hands firmly gripping the ones above. She had achieved a fair height from the initial launch, and the ground seemed much harder to fall upon from up there than it was. But the assassin kept her gaze skyward; to the target, and rapidly scaled the leafy conifer.

Her breath misted the crystal glass when she leaned in to peer. There laid the snoring Drakon, buried beneath furs and pump pillows. The pile rose and fell in such monstrous proportions that Lorrin tensed; convinced that this Favoured was at least twice her size.

It'll be fine, the assassin insisted. *My blade will slice through.*

It wasn't as though she was about to disembowel the beast —just to lop off his great head. And her dagger was sharp. If not, that sickle would have to do it. Rye would simply have to cope.

Lorrin gently tapped the curved blade on the window. She repeated it with a little more vigour when the wind howled about her and Rudd Leifsdotter didn't stir. A bone chilling scrape echoed, and a scratch marred the crystal in its wake. Now the rise and fall of the blanket mountain abruptly ceased, before growing even taller as the Drakon rose. He was only about one and half times her size.

The assassin took the opportunity to pull her hood down further, and tap the sickle again. Leifsdotter jerked about, before gleaming crimson eyes narrowed on the shadowed figure outside. They could only discern her outline; illuminated by the light which hit from behind. The sickle shone in the light of the moons, and the Drakon's dusty, clipped silver wings flared. He was already pale, but he turned as white as the sheets at the shine of the reaping tool.

Lorrin couldn't hold back a grin.

The Drakon stumbled out of the sea of comforters; those egregious wings knocking over ornate vases and miniature marble statues. And he ran for the door in a hastily pulled on silken dressing gown.

The assassin quickly descended to meet him, her face still hidden and sickle withdrawn. She stood outright in front of the filigree doors; a fearsome, indifferent collector of souls. His wings poked out first, then his curled horns. One wide eye assessed her in the weak lighting, before he produced a flashlight.

Lorrin slipped away towards the gardens.

The harsh light skimmed around her shadow as she wafted between trees and shrubbery, barely catching the hem of her cloak. The Drakon followed cautiously;

with understandable terror mixed with the dangerous desire to solve a mystery.

Was it Death who called to him now —led him from the safety of his own foolishness to steal him away? Had he bargained too much; coveted too much? A deep, aching pull in his gut told him that this was consequence finally snagging at his coat. Perhaps that was why his feet trod forward, and kept pace. They knew where they were going, even if he did not. They knew that he deserved this end.

Rudd Leifsdotter couldn't recall how far he had followed Death even as Sythe River stretched to his left. And then the shrouded figure halted; the sickle glinting as they held it out like the crescent of a moon.

"Have you come for me, milord?" asked the Drakon in all earnest. He clutched the flashlight to his heaving chest, and his useless wings jittered nervously.

The assassin slowly turned to the side, exposing a flutter of blonde. "So you are aware of your sins," she said, in that slightly deeper lilt. "Good."

"Forgive me, *milady*," the Favoured gasped, hurriedly falling to his knees. "I was unaware I was in the presence of the Lady Death."

Lorrin couldn't hold back a soft chuckle. "You may call me as you like. I will accept anything, as long as you acknowledge the fact I have indeed come to put an end to your pitiful existence."

Leifsdotter trembled and tightly bit his lower lip.

The iman turned to face him fully, before twirling the sickle. "You followed me, knowing my purpose? Do you *wish* to die?"

"I…I do not wish for it. I have simply been postponing it for a long time," the Drakon admitted. "Something compelled me to seek you, milady. As though a subconscious part of me had already accepted the premise. That I have seen grace for longer than I deserve, and have taken it for granted." The large creature then lifted his head and revealed tears welling within his now sorrowful eyes. "I do not welcome death, but I will not fight. Not anymore."

Lorrin's gaze narrowed. She hadn't expected this —sickening remorse. It was easy to kill someone who was vile and unworthy of breath. Repentance was difficult to swallow; to live with. But she would get over it. She always did.

Never spare.

Even though this rogue mission was her own, she would adhere to the creed.

"No Daughter awaits you," the assassin dared to drive him down further. "No life beyond here, and no paradise."

"How can you not believe, milady?" Leifsdotter cried in disbelief. "I may not deserve to return to Her embrace, but it provides comfort to know there is a slight chance that I might be permitted to wash the ground beneath Her feet."

The futility of that action was the most irritating part.

The blonde's frown deepened. Without realising it, she had drawn her pale dagger and sheathed the sickle. His words were pissing her off that much.

"The realm of death exists outside of the Daughter's reach and sight," Lorrin lied. "She gives life, and we take it away. The only thing which awaits you, Rudd Leifsdotter, is cold emptiness. You will carry your pain into the void, and your Goddess will not remember your name. She will not offer you a glance."

The Drakon's falling face was almost satisfying. Almost.

Lorrin felt no guilt for denouncing his fayth —the things she had said, she wholeheartedly believed. Her unjustifiable job; her loose life; had no room for the Daughter, Her Parents or Siblings. She couldn't paint herself a saint or pretend that what mattered after death was tangible. *Nothing* waited for anyone. That *had* to be the case. Because then she could sleep at night knowing she wasn't sending every creature she culled to some sort of Hehl. Or worse —a paradise.

"…I will still pray," Leifsdotter rasped, though his body was not so resolute. "Even as you strike me down. I will still have hope."

She had finally had enough. What was the point of arguing with a walking, talking corpse? "Do as you like," the assassin sighed frankly, striding closer to loom above him.

His lips quivered as he continued to cry silently, and struggled to get in the final prayer. "…I was born as the delicate Hand dictated, and now I shall return as It pleases. Forgive my wayward wander from the gentle path, and spare me of Her wrath. I pray the Daughter my soul to pity, when my last breath I ta —"

He choked on his own blue blood, staring at Lorrin's sneer.

Never yield.

The assassin huffed as she carved his great head like a cut on a butcher's table, dark blood spraying and pooling, before it thudded to the grass. It tinged a shade of cyan. Lorrin darted aside before it could touch her boots. If there was any benefit to that Assassin's robe, it was shielding her own clothes.

With the deed done, the blonde reached for the deck of cards and ripped the plastic packaging enough to slide out the contents. She sifted through them, before finding the one for which she had been searching and sticking it partly into the Drakon's severed neck from the underside.

And as unseen as she had been upon her arrival, the iman slipped away to find her partner in crime.

CHAPTER 12

lorrin

IT HADN'T BEEN easy to get the blood out of that cloak. It had turned the assassin's predicted six hours of sleep into three and a half.

Detective Kal was not going to be pleased when she arrived, groggy and still suffering from sharp, intermittent abdominal cramps. Everything was a chore — dragging herself from the bed, showering, dressing and eating. The constricting numbed after a quick pill and blueberry muffin, long enough for her to choose her outfit with care and check on her partially soaking robe. It had been many years since safer options to bleach had been developed, but Lorrin was grateful that Kon had understood the need for the cloaks to be made of something which didn't contain cotton or velvet.

She had spotted dots of cleaner to the splatters of blue, so as not to harm the fur lining. That would be harder to clean and dry. Her dagger had also been vigorously scrubbed and polished. Not a trace of Rudd Leifsdotter lingered on her. Only those red eyes plagued her thoughts. And that expression on his face when she had crushed his hope. Maybe for his sake, a part of her was content to imagine him eagerly grovelling and washing holy ground.

She drove into Loegon with a smile on her face; a great grin from ear to ear.

There was no reason for it when she then arrived at the precinct, though. The building was in disarray as even Sol scrambled to gather their things from the front desk. They didn't bother to give Lorrin her visitor's pass —Officer Denaris had to retrieve one for her.

"What's the rush?" asked the assassin, swivelling in Zemir's chair. Detective Burns moved to sheath his sword, compile some documents, and shut off his computer with a slice of toast wedged in his mouth.

The Troll was the only other calm person in the room, but even he was hasty about threading his arms through his jacket.

"Apparently it's something urgent regarding the Wall on the Gehman border," Rohna quipped, grabbing her keys. "Her Excellency is there. Come with me — Kal won't arrive on time if she comes here first."

"The Wall?" Lorrin echoed, bolting to her feet.

That could only mean one thing: a breach.

Rohna Nyll was an impatient driver. It had been stressed as an emergency, but it didn't mean that Faecide & Homicide needed to be involved. Not yet. She was still far more careful than Lorrin, but the assassin was pleased to encounter another person who preferred to go fast.

The Wall loomed on the horizon —far too tall to define the top, and partially eclipsing one of the suns. There was something about the enchanted, bricked impenetrable stone; something that set a chill in the girl's veins and made her feel small. Insignificant. And most importantly: trapped.

Detective Kal's entrance was loud and observed —because of that sleek motorcycle. She parked and dismounted as though she knew as much; shaking her hair loose as she tossed her head after unclipping her helmet. Lorrin had to tear her gaze away from the engrossing sight; her skin crawling at the hushed whistles which followed. Zemir then stalked along the sudden pathway between parted guards, towards the assassin. All eyes felt glued to the pair, yet the detective only arrowed for her; only saw her. The blonde swallowed, lifting her chin. Zemir was the epitome of cool; an unreal image of confidence given form. Lorrin shifted her weight to one hip, folding her arms. The females regarded each other as though in assessment. One which Lorrin decided that the guard passed. And the light danced in her dark golden eyes as if the iman passed, too.

"Hello, girl," the officer greeted.

"Hello, ma'am," the assassin said tightly. *Fucking bitch.*

She watched the corners of Zemir's mouth twitch like she wanted to laugh. And she wondered into what her trained expression would morph if she'd seen her decapitate Rudd Leifsdotter last night. Or if Lorrin knelt down at her feet and buried her head between her naked legs —

"You look terrible," the detective stated. "Rough night?"

The assassin drew a sharp breath as her unbridled imagination dared to heat. "Probably rougher than yours and twice as gratifying."

Zemir chuckled coldly, shaking her head.

Rohna glanced from iman to iman, blinking rapidly.

Lorrin then watched Officer Kal as she turned to wander closer to the front. But she threw an ambiguous glance back over her shoulder as she was swallowed into the entire Guard of Madir gathered along the base of the Wall. A white limousine belonging to Her Excellency halted a few feet ahead. Lorrin peered for even a glimpse of the iman, never having seen her in person, but to no avail. She was hidden and protected well. But her voice certainly carried; boomed over the crowd of officers and officials as she began to address them.

"My treasured Guard," Nadune Madir began, "Something has happened to threaten our harmonious society. As you know, beyond this Wall, the Unseelie have been compliant for generations. Yet now, with the recent hit on The Court and its members, a few rebellious citizens see opportunity to turn unease into complete unrest. Everyone's way of life —not only those in Gehman —is being tested. Threatened. Last night, an Unseelie harnessing ancient armour was seen flying over Iman District territory. No abductions or deaths have been uncovered, thank the Daughter," the esteemed iman breathed. "The public must continue to be in a state of ignorance until we gather significant evidence to disrupt normalcy. Scholars and Maji will inspect the shield which domes our part of the city, as we are uncertain that it was breached, but we must treat this as an intent to commit domestic terrorism. Before it truly becomes such."

The breeze whistled with murmurs.

Then someone shouted, "How do we know it was that sort of Faery kind?"

Lorrin stood on her toes, and finally spied the famed governor whose ancestors had first erected that Wall. She was shorter than the assassin thought, even in heels, but that sharp elegance was not lost on the lack of a television screen. Her tailored suit was as pale as Lorrin's blade, with her skin a cool tan and hair an opposing peppered black. Her dark irises were stark in her almond eyes like a spot of ink on paper. She was as rigid as that Wall, Lorrin was sure of it.

"The gangly limbs and skeletal wings were a giveaway, as well as the illegal height of the flight," Her Excellency answered. "That is what I have been told."

The murmurs grew louder.

A small Seelie scurried to Nadune Madir's side, before whispering something into her ear. The assassin watched the governor pale slightly and press her lips into a thread of red. "…Guards, I am called to urgent business," she addressed the crowd again. "Faecide & Homicide, come with us to The Court."

"Oh my Goddess, that's us," Rohna gasped, hitting out at the blonde's arm.

Lorrin feigned fear and concern as they hurried back to the car, spying the other officers from their department moving to follow the order. It appeared that Rudd Leifsdotter's body had been discovered.

There was more of that striped tape around the perimeter of the crime scene. Rohna was snapping shots of the body and wide pool of blood. There were no footprints aside from his, was the conclusion, which made the phantom theory more believable by the minute —until Detective Burns pointed out that the killer could have simply worn shoes which left no prints and had picked up no dirt.

The assassin shivered; and though it wasn't out of place, the discomfort was genuine. She didn't want to be here and see that peaceful look etched in the final moments of the Drakon's death. It made bile rise.

How could he have been so content; his soul so unweighted?

"You can wait in the car now, Raffe," Detective Kal then told her —a hand poised in mid-air as if she'd thought better about placing it onto the blonde's trembling shoulder. "You don't have to see this."

The assassin could appreciate Zemir's lack of criticism. That she deducted the issue in a tactful manner which didn't require her direct explanation. But a bigger feeling was obstructing that rational reaction: offence.

"I'm fine," she hedged, offering her a sidelong glance.

"You don't look fine."

Lorrin violently bit down her own lips in an effort to control her shaking, at the least. "I'm not *weak*."

"I…never said that."

A flush then kissed her pale skin as she wrapped her arms tighter around her midsection. "…I'm fine. I'm meant to be working with you, and it looks like this might be connected to Jon De Polis. So I'm staying right here."

The officer raised a disbelieving black eyebrow, but appeared to see the futility in arguing. So she stayed there, beside the iman. The shoulder of her jacket grazed against hers. And the heaviness in Lorrin's chest dulled to a light ache.

The embarrassment lingered. *Hormones*, accused the assassin.

"Someone wishes to wage war in Idun," Her Excellency then said gravely, staring down at the body of the Drakon laying on the grass. Her gaze did not waver even as the great creature was enclosed in a bag. The head was an arm's length to its side; the playing card being zipped up in an evidence bag.

Lorrin Raffe stood a few feet inclined towards the river, out of the way. She wondered if this was one of the disasters she was supposed to cause. Not only the murder itself, but the snowballing of the case. The complexity that Her Excellency was convinced now laced it. The assassin had to remind herself that this had been the best course of action. The investigation might accelerate; answers would be fabricated; and Verdia Kon could be satiated.

"Who was he?" asked the blonde, careful to look sombre.

Detective Kal stuck her hands into her trouser pockets as she sighed. "Another predicted Court member. A skipped legacy, in fact. The other guests and residents are shocked that this had happened during the week of *Ortus*."

"*Ortus?*"

"The rise," Zemir elaborated, "from one side of the river to the other." Lorrin grumbled, turning to glance at the Loegon and Iris District divide. "I don't understand why The Court is treated like the crowning glory of Idun. Sure, I can understand its existence. But must we all aspire to live in giant carved diamonds?"

The officer smirked. "No government is perfect. The Court is a tradition long engrained in our history, along with certain families. It may be horribly elitist, but many members are not as cruel as you might think. Rudd Leifsdotter had a rocky start, but he was turning himself around. Maybe someone didn't like that."

"You don't think…that another member of The Court could have done this?" gasped the blonde. She asked it in such a way that was half bemused surprise, and half accusation. She decided to plant that seed.

"I don't know," the guard admitted. "I believed it was an assassin at first. It still could be, but now it feels like they were hired. Everything is too neat, and a Court member would certainly want to keep their hands clean."

Lorrin glanced down at her trainers. "Hm."

"And that playing card…" Zemir mused. "A queen of hearts? It's biting me." So she hadn't yet proved herself as smart enough. Surely the riddle wasn't that difficult. The assassin's brow furrowed as she sucked on her teeth.

"Was anything else left?" she asked.

"No."

"What happened to the meeting with the necromancer?"
"I've postponed it for now," wearily sighed the guard. "It was all we had at the time, but we may find new evidence here."

The wind flittered through the girl's unbound hair, sticking to her glossed lips, and she didn't miss the detective frowning in her direction.

"You're staring," Lorrin stated bluntly.

Zemir started, and whipped her head. "…Still annoying."
Lorrin moved to run her fingers through the pale strands. "I didn't mind it."

The officer let out a gruff sound that tingled along her spine. "Just when I think we can have a normal conversation, you go and…be yourself."

The assassin then laughed; the burst of sound heavy and unhinged. It was genuinely hilarious —the notion of Zemir having the balls to complain about her personality. As though it were something with which she was intimately familiar. The younger iman huffed and straightened her denim jacket, before meeting the guard's flabbergasted gaze. "You don't know me."

Perhaps she realised it then —from the misplaced darkness in her jade eyes which acted as a deterrent. Lorrin Raffe was as much of an enigma as the case, and solving her might be just as frightening; the consequences of unravelling her just as deadly and wicked.

Zemir turned to face her completely, undeterred by that warning. Her body was far too close for Lorrin to ignore, and her breath shallowed as the officer took another step between them. "Mm," the detective hummed. "I don't."

CHAPTER 13

zemir

COLLEAGUES WENT OUT for drinks together all the time. That was how she chose to justify it. It was late, the pub was cool and dark; classically modelled like a tavern, and thankfully without music.

Granted, this was the very first time that she was doing this. Zemir had never before plucked up the courage to spend a night with other people; to engage in conversation and pay attention to someone other than herself. She could hold her liquor —she had trained herself to do so. But now she would have to observe and look out for those who couldn't —those who were irresponsible with drinking, or who simply were predisposed not to cope.

Lorrin Raffe was irresponsible. And Zemir suspected that it was the only time that she ever actually allowed herself to be. She wondered though, upon who she was relying to catch her when she fell.

The officer stared down into her beer, trying to recall how on Earth Fran had twisted her arm to be here. Maybe she had finally declined one too many times.

"Do you have anyone you don't get along with in CR?" Rohna Nyll quipped, also chucking back the drinks. She was infinitely fascinated with the blonde — likely because she was a new face, and not that she was particularly interesting.

"I do," Lorrin gasped, eagerly smacking the iman's shoulder. "This Seelie manager, Markus. He picks on me simply because I'm young."

Zemir's grip tightened on her glass. There was that name again.

"Ooh, maybe he likes you," Rohna giggled, nudging her side. "Some males don't know how to express themselves, or are too embarrassed to pursue a female who's out of their league."

"You're damn right I'm out of his league," Lorrin grinned, polishing off her rum and coke. "But I hope he doesn't fancy me. I'd rather swallow acid."

"Yeah, what is he, five?" Detective Kal then snapped, and harder than she had intended. Everyone at the table blinked. Had she been wrong? Had she spoken out of turn? Though everyone stared as if surprised that she'd spoken at all.

"…Kal is right," Fran, who was sitting to her left, then came to her rescue. "Anyone who tries to show affection like that is immature."

"It's nice when they're direct," Detective Henrik Burns chipped in.

Lorrin nodded importantly. "Markus is an entitled asshole, rest assured. The only thing I'd want to do with his dick, is cut it off."

The other guards laughed and were highly amused by her unfiltered nature, but Zemir found her use of language crass and unnecessary. She sipped her beer and thought of the ways she would clean such a mouth —of the mercy for which the iman would beg as the officer slid her fingers down towards her throat.

Fran also refrained from laughing; her gaze slitted and on her own glass; but she looked like she'd sooner cut out Lorrin's tongue than anything else.

"Body count," Rohna dared.

Detective Kal involuntarily paused, paying attention.

"I don't keep count," the blonde scoffed, stirring the bright cocktail which was then placed before her. "Who would?"

"Those of us whose numbers are below ten, obviously," Henrik muttered.

"Below five, more like," Rohna corrected. "And you are a married male."

"Woah, that many, Raffe?" Fran commented in a rather snarky tone.

The hostility wasn't lost on the young iman. Zemir watched her stiffen and shift as she smiled that half smile. "…Love is hard. Some of us live our lives in such a way, that relationships never go beyond a brief exchange."

"That's so wise," Rohna agreed, downing her drink.

"Don't encourage it," Fran bit.

"Well, luckily it has no bearing on you," Lorrin smiled wider, though it was still prickly and cold. A subtle indication to back off.

Henrik then cleared his throat. "Come on, guys. We're not here to discuss our most personal habits. Let's just keep enjoying the night out until the amount of work Her Excellency has given us inevitably steals that away."

The guards agreed, before Fran motioned for another round.

Zemir pushed back in her chair. "I'm going to get some fresh air."

This wasn't as easy as she thought. Were these always the topics chosen for the flow of conversation? Were people not ashamed? It wasn't as if her dating history was something to hide, but there was a level of privacy that she believed everyone should maintain. No one needed to know how many people she had had before; how many had run from her; how many she'd likely scarred.

She breathed deeply as she leaned back against the plastered wall exterior of the pub, the colder air cutting her cheeks. Perhaps she deserved no better.

"You don't like this sort of thing, do you?"

Lorrin was standing adjacent to her, hands buried in her pockets. There were little badges pinned to her denim jacket —a vibrant rainbow, two round ones with harsh words, and a little sword. No. That was a dagger.

Zemir snorted. "What gave it away?"

"Everything."

She met her light gaze. "Were you watching me, Raffe?"

Lorrin was straightforward. "Yes."

"Why?"

The iman neared, her upper arm pressing on the guard's as she halted at her side. Zemir drew a very loud, very obvious breath. "You are the most interesting and honest person there," Lorrin said as a matter of fact.

"You say that as though you know all about me."

"Your face can't hide your thoughts," the blonde reiterated, glancing at her from the corner of her vision. "Perhaps that is simply a part of you. The part I know; the part you're letting me see —it's real and unflinching."

Zemir's brows knitted as her body turned towards her. She had a sensational way with words when she wanted to. "You seem to have a lot of good fayth," she murmured. "That I don't in fact, dislike you."

"You don't have to like me," sighed Lorrin, sticking her chin up.

"That sounds like half a sentence."

"No, no," she insisted. "You really don't have to like me. I don't go around with that aim. You can have any opinion of me you wish."

"Hm."

They stood in silence for a moment, watching a few cars speed by. Zemir had always loved quiet, but this one felt weighted with things which were too big and awkward to voice. Too altering. The night sky was expansive; consuming and wide enough to hide beneath. Then Lorrin's long fingers wandered, and brushed along the officer's.

Zemir's steadfast resolve evaporated, and all that existed was that touch. No words accompanied it. They'd ruin it instantaneously. All that was necessary for the destruction of guarding walls was the soft intrusion of understanding. Every involuntary twitch sparked a jolt of lightning.

She still thought the younger iman was annoying. But it was this simple thing of secret that made her adamance waver. That tore apart her inhibitions.

Their fingers were threading. They tentatively clasped hands; like little girls; and their hearts raced as though it was the most exhilarating action in all the world. The detective could barely breathe. Was this how it felt —that deeper connection for which she had yearned desperately these past few years, that was forbidden? It was so fragile and sweet. So addictive. *So…*

Wrong.

This was wrong.

Zemir turned the grip into something harsh as she twisted around and brought their hands up beside Lorrin's head, and her other by her waist. She leaned in close enough to feel her ragged breath on her lips. The blonde started, her spine straightening against the wall, and her eyes wide. They slowly lidded, like she could see right through the guard. Like the sabotaging behaviour was excusable.

The officer's face heated at the realisation.

"You shouldn't want this from me, Lorrin Raffe," she said softly. "Ever since that night —you shouldn't want a thing. I won't be good for you."

Run from me, she wanted to plead. *Make this easier.*

"But I…I…" the young iman was at a loss for words.

The desire was clearly not so easily quenched. Especially without fulfilment. The issue was that there could *be* none. Even once…even one summit to the heights of pleasure would reveal it. If the girl uncovered what waited in regards to Zemir —the unapologetically rough command she could wield —it would cause a fissure of irrevocable disharmony.

Detective Kal willed herself to withdraw; to pull her fingers from hers and not miss the warmth. A frown solidified her intent. "I am not another notch for your bedpost, and I would prefer it if we could remain civil to each other after the case."

"Do you…do you think that whatever it is that burns between us will ruin our acquaintanceship?" Lorrin asked in all seriousness. "And…it wasn't my intention to make you feel unimportant or like a box to tick. On the contrary, I think that you'll be the one I remember the most. But at the end of day, we *would* still part as strangers. We don't have to give this that much meaning."

The guard ground her teeth. "Do you honestly think that giving in just this once will not make us hungry for more?"

Lorrin tilted her head, that mischief glinting in her irises. "I'm flattered that you'd even consider asking that. And, I guess the answer is no."

"Hm."

"We…don't have to restrict ourselves, you know," she then turned a little sly. Her voice dropped in volume. "No one has to know what we do after dark."

Indeed. How tempting it was to have their encounters reoccur, for the entire length of their partnership. That both females had known from the beginning, one night would be inadequate in dowsing the fire they had ignited.

No one has to know. Zemir relished that.

She then ran a finger beneath Lorrin's chin, and tilted it upwards. Her thin lips parted, even in light of what the detective had told her. Instead of her mouth,

Zemir gently brushed her thumb along that pink, and noted the same shade appear in her cheeks. Her body pressed to Lorrin's without her knowledge, and the blonde placed her hands underneath her leather jacket. Zemir permitted them to travel and settle on her hips. Then her thumb abruptly slipped inside.

The iman went a little rigid, but dared to run her tongue along the rough pad of it and moan softly. The fluttering sensation set Detective Kal noticeably aflame. She raised her other hand to tug slowly through the strands of bleached hair. Lorrin's expression morphed into one of desperate longing; her minimal breath short and another moan vibrating through to the officer's skin.

Oh the Parents, the Daughter and all the Gods.

Zemir frowned deeply. She needed to stop. Now. Otherwise they were going to fuck right there and then on the far less secluded High Street.

She carefully untangled herself from the iman, popping out her thumb last. Lorrin trembled slightly as she obediently leaned back to the wall and then pulled on her jacket. She was too surprised to say the first word.

Detective Kal hesitated with internal reproach, but forced something into the silence. "…Perhaps, I might allow a slip in my judgement," whispered the guard, curious and briefly placing her thumb along her own tongue. Overly sweet alcohol hit her senses. "But tonight is not that night."

The blonde stared down at the pavement.

Zemir turned back towards the bar, and motioned for her to follow.

The detective noticed it when they were seated with everyone else and the harsh whip of the wind lingered on their faces. Lorrin Raffe did indeed watch her — carefully, inconsistently but intently. Because she knew that she shouldn't.

It felt like a precious thing between the two of them, even though their hints of animosity were visible to those around them. Spectators didn't know of the true thing which pulled the females together; that made those studying gazes hold for a moment too long. Though it appeared that Officer Denaris caught a whiff of something. As usual.

"You're staring, Kal," she whispered, inclining her head towards Zemir.

The iman choked —reached for a napkin to disguise it, before finally forcing her gaze on the grave Seelie. "…Staring at what?" she rasped.

On the other side of the table, Rohna and Lorrin were too absorbed in fawning over Henrik's cute baby daughters.

Fran had known the detective for three years. Although it wasn't long, there were certain things to which she had grown accustomed. Such as the face Zemir made when she sizing someone up for how they would perform in bed.

"Not her," the Faery warned, swirling her mango scented drink. "Anybody but her. I thought you were smarter than that."

The officer swallowed guiltily. "You think I haven't thought of the risk?"

"*Risks*," Fran corrected, her purple brows knitting. "Plural. Because we both know there's more than the obvious."

There was an air of mystery shrouding the blonde, but Zemir had concluded that was simply a factor that made her more attractive: the unfamiliar. What could someone who had had a mixture of a background and worked in Citizen Resources possibly be hiding that was so seriously detrimental?

"We had words," the guard then admitted. "Outside."

The Seelie glanced down into the glass of yellow. "Did she come onto you?"

"No," said Zemir, and she wasn't sure if it was more the truth or a lie. "We just stood there. We simply acknowledged that behaving in any way which was contrary to good colleagues would make life difficult for everyone."

"So you're exercising self-control for *our* sakes?" Fran scoffed, turning back to glare. "*Zemir*," she hissed, "think of your own consequences for once."

She levelled at the Favoured a withering look. "I've done that my entire life, Denaris. Of course I have to consider others in the repercussions of what I do. I'm a creature of instinct and instant gratification —you know that. So when I refrain from satisfying my own selfish whims, you had better believe it's because I can't bear the impact it will have on the people in my life. They matter, too."

The Faery blinked, and her wings flittering the way they did when she was

106

angry. "...Fine," she ground out, lifting her glass to her tightly clamped lips. It clinked against her bronze snake bites. Then she heaved a relenting sigh. "I only hope you know what you're doing, Kal."

Zemir took hold of Fran's hand, making an unnecessary show of it, and felt nothing. "When I finally admit that I don't, *then* you should be frightened."

The Seelie guard gave her a reluctant smile.

Lorrin's eyes bore so deeply into the space between the two friends that even the blue-haired detective could feel it. She glanced back, matching the intensity in that marbled grey. Rohna had just taken a selfie with her and their colourful drinks, and was trying to post it to her Instantgram story.

"What do you mean you don't have an account?" Rohna exclaimed. "How am I supposed to tag you? Then...I'll make you one right now!"

"Oh, you really don't have to do that —" the iman hurriedly quipped, grabbing for her cellphone. Despite the distraction, her eyes snagged back to the officer. The only thing written on her face was cold confusion.

Zemir's hand casually withdrew as Fran's thin wings beat with satisfaction, and she let Lorrin think what she wanted to think.

Perhaps this was simply another play.

CHAPTER 14

lorrin

LORRIN WAS THE type of female who was confident enough in her own ability that making a rival look bad was either the last resort in an emergency, or not at all necessary. What was not in any way beneath her, however, was finding and presenting incriminating evidence which brought about a quicker downfall. She couldn't be blamed for such…happenstance.

Char Gilligan was proving herself to be quite useful —she had a satisfactorily thick pile of information to hand over when the females met the next morning. The weekend was looking to be another scorcher, and the assassin had prepared for the next two days off in a pair of high-waisted linen shorts and loose white shirt. She'd folded the sleaves up to her elbows and slung a small leather backpack over her shoulders. In one hand, she clutched a coned strawberries and vanilla ice cream bubble waffle from a café called *Hansel & Gretel*.

The Syren boasted a new cotton dress that floated to her ankles; the summery pattern of irises popping against her red hair. It was good to see the creature with more colour in her cheeks; with a glow about her. As though life had seeped back with purpose again, as ironic as it was in their cause.

Lorrin lowered her sunglasses before sliding them over her head to tuck back her curtain of hair. "You look good. And have been busy," she quipped.

"Thanks. I'm very fast," Char smiled, removing her own tinted shades.

The assassin flicked through the sheets of paper in the folder with one hand, picking out the names the sea creature had already collected. Markus' name didn't show up. Not yet. The blonde still couldn't help gritting her teeth in irritation, but at the least, Ron Duncan and Sumah Hossef were there. She had had inklings of backstage shenanigans —ever since she had finally stood before them all at the age of fourteen. Even then her skills in observation were sharper than most.

That was necessary for a girl kicked by life.

The Favoured male who had trained her was also not among the others on the list. Though Lorrin was sure that Hordor Fore had many secrets. Perhaps nothing to buckle the Iron Handle, but enough to make him submit when she demanded the throne. He was simply far more skilled at hiding such ammunition.

"By the way," Char frowned. "I know it wasn't part of the assignment, but I noticed something that could be considered '*off*'."

"Yeah?"

"Verdia Kon frequents Her Excellency's city office."

"He what," Lorrin blurted, her eyes widening. She had just caught up the Troll on the case so far. The Syren looked serious; there was not a trace of mischief. But it couldn't be. Why would a higher-up assassin ring leader associate with the government —the very part of society from which their targets often came? The iman had to wonder if Nadune Madir was blackmailing him. Because it was impossible for the Favoured to hold anything above the governor's head. No one toyed with that female and lived.

"I have no reason to lie," Char added, disappointment etching her face.

Of course she didn't. There was nothing for her to gain directly by fabricating such a report. All and any benefits were to be achieved through the iman.

"I...I'm surprised," Lorrin assured. "And in disbelief. The Central Blades respect Kon as an unofficial kingpin. He was there at the beginning. He has proven himself to be the most loyal. This intel...it changes everything."

The Syren's eyes lidded. "It paints him a traitor."

A chill set in the iman's bones. So the Troll's attire was indeed a disguise — but for the wrong party. Kon was a spy in both factions.

"Watch him next week," ordered Lorrin. "Only him."

"Yes ma'am."

"Note down every single thing he does in the capital," the blonde continued in a low murmur; the Summer suns abruptly frosting. "I must know all business he conducts with any official or Nadune Madir herself. Because if I can make a fool and puppet out of him…" She slowly grinned at the prospect —of dethroning the Troll, gaining Her Excellency as an unlikely ally, and perching herself at an untouchable height. "I can climb up faster than I planned."

Char nodded wisely. "I will shadow him all week."

"Good. Now, enjoy your weekend."

"You're off already? Though that works, since I was heading for the harbour."

"I have anonymous phone calls to schedule," Lorrin explained as she wriggled, loosening one shoulder strap, and stuffed the folder into her backpack.

"Right," said the Syren. "See you at the Hall."

"See you," Lorrin called as she turned away.

She preferred to use her car as least as possible, so it was a long walk back to Hemmingway Estate. She had stepped outside for a quick lunch, and the rest of the weekend was reserved for sunbathing and a few episodes of *Killing Evie*. Or a chilled glass of berry vodka in one hand, and one of the books she'd been neglecting in the other. Her mood lightened at just the thought.

Her feet rounded the corner as she was taking a bite out of the waffle, before she paused at the sound of a hushed argument. Two imans stood on the High Street, one in a cropped shirt and wide-legged loose cotton pants, and the other in a far more formal *shervani*. Lorrin's gaze narrowed on deep blue hair.

She had never imagined Zemir Kal in anything other than black and leather up to that point, but the light outfit suited her. She had stuck to her brand in those trousers; tied above her waist with a large belt.

The male with whom the detective was fighting was tall and stiff —did he wear those garments constantly? The embroidery on the coat was exquisite, but surely he stuck out like a sore thumb when he set foot in public. Though his face could pose the same issue. The blonde had encountered many handsome males in her lifetime but this one seemed carved by God. That lightly bearded jawline was so defined, even at a distance, and his black hair was styled and parted as though he had a team of staff simply for that job. And as beautiful as Zemir's eyes were, they paled in light of the male's. Quite literally —his golden eyes were closer to a burning yellow. He was a prince among the casual citizens.

The assassin's mind whirred as she searched for a category under which to file him. Were the two related? Or was he harassing her?

She listened in for clues.

The guard was irked, and demanded to know why he was there. So she knew him, at least. The male's patience was waning, and he bit out his short words. He wanted Zemir to come with him, and to stop ignoring his calls. Lorrin gasped at the revelation —he was a Court member. She had to know why he was asking after the guard, though. A part of her hoped that he was not some sort of suitor.

"...I'm not going unless it's official business," Zemir insisted. "And you can pass the message along."

"I wouldn't be here if our parents didn't insist," the male gritted.

The assassin leaned against the nearest railing. She convinced herself that the outcome of her eavesdropping would have been inconsequential, but her heart bore the weight of relief. The two bickering imans were a pair of siblings. But that secret consolation was short-lived, because it then dawned on her that if he was a member of The Court, then Zemir was too.

It wasn't any of Lorrin's business to theorise about the guard's situation, but she could draw certain conclusions from this not very private exchange. The Kals were from the other side; wealthy and powerful. Yet their daughter slummed it in the capital, risking her life for Idun by joining the Guard of Madir. Perhaps it was an act of rebellion, or her parents hadn't supported the career. The blonde didn't blame them. Why would anyone voluntarily give their life for the city?

There was another story that Lorrin's imagination spun: maybe Zemir had become a guard to escape The Court; to escape that life. Had her mother and father pushed for the idea of marriage? Imans only lived so long. But the prickly detective didn't seem like the type of person to desire a family of her own, let alone children. A piece of her from long ago could sympathise with that.

For ordinary citizens, the concept of carrying on the bloodline was a historical artifact. It was an age of fast and easy; with entertainment, food, and connections. Hard work was spotty and not many people wanted to keep fucking into the next week. The world had so much to offer —why waste it on settling down?

The argument was over.

Lorrin then flinched in the silence and buried her face in the ice cream and strawberries, caught unaware of her bearings. She dared not look around for Zemir and her brother, and hoped that she could blend into the general city scenery.

Evidently, there were no Gods.

"Lorrin Raffe," sighed the voice of Detective Kal. She stood a few feet away; arms folded and face unreadable. The anger did not linger, but there was clear ice in her narrowed gaze. "What a surprise."

The assassin tried her best to play it off as one, while wiping her mouth. "Oh! Fancy bumping into you. I was just having lunch with a friend."

The guard huffed, unconvinced it was a coincidence but finding it difficult to disprove it. "Where's your friend now?"

"She needs water," explained the girl. "Or she'll die."

The tension in the guard's stance relaxed, but her frigidity did not thaw. "I see. Are you waiting for her, here, miles from the harbour?"

"No, I'm finishing off my bubble waffle before I head home."

"Aw, is the lunch date over already?" Zemir cooed, pouting as the pitch of her voice rose with sarcasm.

Lorrin raised an eyebrow. "Hers and mine might be, but *we* can go on one."

After a beat, the detective's entire front crumbled, and she almost smiled — she might have even laughed if the blonde was someone else. She huffed a sigh and pocketed her hands, smirking down at the assassin almost in invitation.

"I don't go on dates, girl."

Oh. Not an invitation.

Yet a shiver curled up along Lorrin's spine. There was still something so enticing about it —to remove the sweetness made everything else so sinfully blissful. "I have no romantic intentions, Kal," she clarified merrily. "I don't date either."

"Well, I wouldn't call us friends," the officer rightfully pointed out, lowering to perch beside her on the railing. "So we still have no reason to associate with each other outside of work."

The iman took another bite; halving a strawberry slice and getting ice cream on the tip of her nose. It wasn't as if she was trying to get to know Zemir —in any emotional capacity. Whatever she happened to find out was purely circumstantial. Physically, what lay beneath those linen clothes most certainly piqued her interest. She wanted to chart every part of her body, and engrain it in memory.

Detective Kal's fingers then brushed her cheek, and the corner of her mouth. Lorrin stiffened at the touch but permitted her to wipe away smears of ice cream. Slowly. The guard dared to turn adventurous, rubbing the assassin's lips in a way that made her gasp a sharp breath. Where else would she rub that parsimoniously? Lorrin might've blushed in such a situation if she wasn't sober.

Zemir hesitated, withdrew, and then brought those fingers to her own lips in an echo of the night before. In broad daylight. The blonde leisurely crossed one leg over the other. She refused to relinquish any form of composure.

"…What does it actually taste like?" the officer asked.

Lorrin tentatively held the waffle out. Her gaze held hers, unwavering and with intent, as she lowered and took a bite. Years flashed by as she stared into that clear amber; stretching between the seconds they likely sat staring.

"You don't kiss your lovers," Lorrin murmured, as Zemir lingered. "Is that why you're making a hobby out of tasting everything I've had in my mouth?"

Detective Kal leaned back coolly and cleared her throat after chewing and swallowing. "We're not lovers," she answered. "And it's cute that you're calling it a hobby. I will admit, though, that the temptation is higher than it has ever been. Usually I can get through a night without that contact, but you make me want to break all of my rules." She smiled, and it was warm.

The assassin tipped her chin back, intrigued. "Break them."

"Is that a dare?"

"It's an invitation."

Zemir forced a chuckle, but Lorrin was serious. "I'll call you later," she offered, "and tell you my address."

The officer pressed her lips into a line, then pushed to her feet. As she turned to walk off, she glanced back over her shoulder and assured, "I'll pick up."

✝

Lorrin could barely contain herself as she rushed to Hemmingway Estate. She had hardly been this giddy —or invited someone over. No one had been to the house, either. It was usually in a drunk stupor that strangers even made it inside the apartment. Now she was alert, vulnerable and entirely at the mercy of that guard: would she really accept her call? It hadn't appeared as though she were lying. It was an aching, sharp hope which leadened her chest as she sat on a living room sofa in the late hours of the evening.

She had forgone the tempting glass of wine. She wanted to remember this, especially since she was in the dregs of her cycle. Zemir would be the only one receiving attention. The wine wouldn't have calmed her nerves, anyway.

She wasn't apprehensive. The two females had planned this out. The frigid officer simply needed to keep her word.

Lorrin settled, satisfied with the resolution of her inner turmoil, and dialled Detective Kal's number. She answered after the first ring.

"That was quite the fast response," quipped the blonde. "It's almost as though you were waiting for me to call."

"…*I was.*"

Something wasn't right. It wasn't romantic. Zemir's voice was quiet, thin and raspy, as though her airways had been obstructed. Or she had been crying.

"Kal? What's the matter?"

Lorrin didn't like the silence that preceded, "*Can you…give me the address?*"

"Of course. And hurry if you must."

There was then no answer when the assassin frowned deeply after ending the call. Where was the guard? She hoped that Zemir was safe. She kicked herself for not

114

asking if she was at home, but realised that she couldn't afford to sit agonising over it. She had to wait, and prepare to be as hospitable as possible. Her hands then paused in what had become habit —in breaking the burner.

She had grown used to casting things away so finitely. Cutting people out was as easy as destroying the evidence of any exchange ever taking place. Business was smooth and predictable. But the detective wasn't predictable. She frequently changed her mind; entertained people as she saw fit; and found it intriguing when she was sought after. She enjoyed the chase. And for the first time in a long time, Lorrin had encountered someone like herself. It enticed her. She couldn't get a reading on Zemir —her face was a trained and impenetrable wall. When she did let people see, it was brief and enticing.

The blonde was getting greedy. She knew that she had no right.

If she stuck to the plan, she needed to crush the burner.

Yet she couldn't. The phone was the only link between her and the officer in this emergency. She couldn't guarantee that there would be others, but a part of her wanted to be there —at least for now. As no one had been there for her.

The assassin saved Zemir's phone number.

Before she could lose that nerve, she snapped the device closed and laid it aside. Conflict swirled like storm clouds within her stomach. Her fingers curled into her palms. She would break some of her rules, too.

And when the doorbell rang, Lorrin ran to it.

CHAPTER 15

lorrin

IT HAD RAINED. Zemir was soaked from head to toe.

The iman ushered her inside, fussing over her bloodshot eyes and lack of luggage. A subtle indication that she hadn't planned on staying until morning.

"I…didn't get a chance to get anything," the detective admitted. She was still wearing the thin outfit from that afternoon. "There's been…a situation. I can't get into my apartment. But I…I figured it would be okay to come here, since you said I could, and—and my neighbours weren't in —"

"It's fine, it's fine," Lorrin assured, guiding her shivering form up the stairs. "Let's get you into a bathroom."

The assassin had an inkling that Zemir hadn't told her the full truth, but it was not her business and she didn't want to pull it from her. She'd listen if the guard wished to speak. And she'd pat her back if words were too painful.

It was much of the latter initially —after getting her to shower and bath, Lorrin silently laid out a set of sweatpants and a sweater. The quiet hung thickly over them, and fresh tears continued to streak along the detective's cheeks as her shoulders trembled with every sob. The blonde didn't know how to console her. There was the vague memory of her mother singing to and holding her after she had tripped over once in a playground, but that felt extreme here.

And she couldn't sing.

Zemir sat on the sofa as though it would swallow her whole; her spine straight and body poised to bolt. The environment was strange and foreign. She was likely trying to figure out how the girl could afford such a dwelling. And though she had stopped crying, her eyes were slightly puffy.

"I'm sorry you got caught in the rain," Lorrin offered limply, unsure of where to start. She fidgeted on the other end, leaning against the armrest and careful not to get too close. "Maybe I should've called a little earlier."

The officer shook her head. "It's not your fault," she whispered. "But thanks for letting me in. And for the clothes." She plucked at the louis blue sweater.

It was then that the assassin allowed herself to process the fact that Zemir was there, in her clothes, and the length of two rulers away. The officer was slightly taller than her, so the sweatpants pinched her lower calves. The top hung oversized and loose on Lorrin, but it almost hugged Zemir's ample chest.

She averted her gaze. "You're welcome."

It wasn't a segue into asking for an explanation. From the way that Detective Kal fiddled with her thumbs and shifted every few seconds, she wasn't sure about what to share. Lorrin sighed. It was fine if she wouldn't share a thing.

She then gingerly pushed off of the sofa and adjusted her surfer shorts. "Have you eaten dinner?"

The guard shook her head.

"You don't mind crumbed chicken and cream cheese pasta?"

"That's fine."

There was an awkward pause as Zemir simply stared at the wall. The iman bit her lip uncertainly. "...Would you like me to switch on the TV?"

Another weak shake 'no'.

"Okay. Sit tight."

The blonde headed for the kitchen. As she dished out the leftovers and reheated them, her nosy and observant side couldn't resist guessing what had gotten the officer into that state. It was somewhat...interesting, to witness her the way others likely never did: delicately iman. Susceptible to the world and its cruelty. No one was invincible, evidently, but Lorrin wanted to come as close as possible. She wanted to touch the stars.

"Bon appetit," she said, placing the steaming plates and a pair of forks down onto the glass coffee table before the sofa. For a moment, Detective Kal didn't move. There were no tears, but Lorrin could tell by the expression on her face that she was indeed weeping —on the inside.

"…Why are you being so accommodating and generous? So kind?" the guard barely murmured. "You have no reason to be. This…this isn't what we agreed."

"Not explicitly," the blonde admitted after taking a bite of crumbled cheese covered penne and chicken. "Being civil should be an extension of basic decency. Besides —you're not here uninvited."

"You didn't have to do all of this, though."

Lorrin folded her arms and leaned back. "No, I don't. And in Idun, nothing is given for nothing. You don't owe me reasoning —I'm not going to interrogate you. But I saw a bit of past self in you, Kal; in the brokenness. The long faded part that craved comfort; that needed someone to lean on. I've learned to survive without it. I have no use for a shoulder now, but you needed one. And I found that I didn't mind offering mine."

Zemir blinked. There was that familiar guarded mask again. If anything, Lorrin should be glad that something returned to normalcy. She wasn't expecting the officer to show gratitude, or even respond. But she leaned forward, took hold of the other silver fork, and began to eat.

The assassin knew how difficult it was to do innate tasks when one's head was pounding and throat was scratched and dry. It was satisfying to see her enjoy the meal, and some life breathe itself back into her clearing eyes.

"This is actually pretty good," Zemir even remarked. "The crispy coating on the fowl is almost perfect."

"*Actually*?" Lorrin echoed, scoffing. She nearly threw one of her cushions at her. "Why are you so surprised? I'm a decent cook, thank you very much. Also, who made you an authority on the culinary arts?"

"It's in my blood," she gloated, sticking up her nose.

"Who says it's not in mine?" the assassin shot back.

Janiss Raffe had made cooking and baking her entire other life. Before she had played for the Idun Phoenixes, she had been selling cakes and bakes out of their garage. As a child, Lorrin recalled looking forward to helping her mother in the kitchen after school. She'd learned all of the foundations —how to make various batters; brownies; how to make pasta; rice; stews; how to debone a fish; the correct way to cut grained meat. She owed it all to strict instruction and a curiosity that had never quite left.

"Fine, fine," Detective Kal relented. "Perhaps I underestimated you."

The blonde lidded her eyes. "You always have."

Zemir sighed and ate another forkful. "You've given me no reason to believe you competent in certain areas."

Lorrin pouted, but found that she couldn't argue. Such was her role. Instead, she tucked back into her food, making the guard barely smile. The two then ate in a silence that was now bearable; occasionally broken up by trivial, amusing stories about the other officers and staff. Once dinner was finished, the assassin gathered the plates and headed back for the kitchen.

"Wait, let me help," the guard called after her.

"You're a guest," Lorrin protested, holding the dishes from her reach.

"Yes, but I've been a pretty terrible one," was the excuse as she twisted around and grabbed at her outstretched arms. "Let me earn my keep."

Lorrin then didn't refuse her aid with drying things and putting them away. The detective was persuasive and stubborn —and the iman was easily distracted by the sight of her bare midsection when she lifted her arms.

"Alexis, play the washing up playlist," the assassin called out to her wireless smart speaker. Upbeat music filled the space. And Zemir stared at the small white round thing on the counter as if she'd never seen one before.

"How do you afford this place, Raffe?" came the inevitable question. "If you don't mind me asking. It's just…I have an idea of the salary for a CR employee, and this is no ordinary house."

Lorrin had been well prepared. "It's fine. It all sort of just happened, actually. One of the senior managers helped out, and put in a good word for me. I just had a lot of pense saved up from my mother."

"Legacy money, huh," Zemir sighed, polishing the last fork. "Would've been me if I bowed to my family's whims." She immediately flinched, and that wall went right back up. Her body stiffened and her lips disappeared into a hard line.

From that, Lorrin could conclude that she indeed wasn't on good terms with them, and that they disapproved of her life as it was.

"I'm on my own now," the assassin quipped, hoping to drag her back up from the inky depths of anxiety. "Independence hit me hard and suddenly, at a young age. We can't…always account for everything. Devastation does not discriminate, and the Daughter cannot save you from it. And family can only take you so far. You have to live for yourself at some point."

She dithered at the end, wondering if she had overstepped her bounds, but the detective shivered, and slowly uncoiled. "Right," she said tightly.

The words were still stuck; the trust between the imans flimsy and new.
A strange song abruptly began to play. It was less about the lyrics, and more so the young female artist's voice. It was low, deep and husked. It was such a sudden shift in mood that the iman was tempted to laugh it off awkwardly. But she reined in that urge and dared to be bold. The night could still be salvaged yet.

"…Want a drink?" Lorrin whispered, turning towards the guard.

"What sort?" Zemir asked in a voice just as low and caressing.

"Any you need."

"Wine would be good."

Lorrin nodded and wandered to the cupboard where it stayed, and felt the officer's gaze follow. While a part of her wanted to play oblivious, the bigger part won out and she made a bit of a show out of the swing of her hips in the effort needed to reach the wine bottle.

One of Detective Kal's hands casually pressed to the marble countertop beside her, before she leaned forward. The assassin's breath caught at the ghostly contact of her chest against her back.

"This one?" she asked in that tone which still echoed the song, pulling down the bottle that the girl's fingers had been skimming.

"Mm."

She couldn't manage any other words; finding herself frozen to the spot as if she couldn't manage basic motor functions, either. Zemir slipped effortlessly from behind her and asked where the glasses were.

Lorrin pointed.

She then followed the guard back to the living room who sauntered as if *she* owned the place, embarrassingly entranced. She wondered what caused her to get so stupid in the officer's presence. At the mere touch of skin.

Zemir even poured out a portion for her, and offered it with a small smirk. Her hand tentatively closed around the thin neck, before she brought it to her lips. "…At least you won't be asking to taste anything tonight."

Detective Kal choked on the sip she'd taken.

The assassin returned to reality, and moved to clap her back. "Sorry —that sort of just slipped out," she apologised sheepishly and remained at her new seat beside her. "I tend to make jokes when I'm uncomfortable."

"You're a sly one, girl," Zemir stated as a matter of fact; leaning in to close the distance between them. Whatever she was trying to do succeeded, and colour rose to the surface of Lorrin's skin. That damned word again —it rendered her dumbstruck. She didn't know where to look; where to put her hands; or even how much air to breathe. Would she kiss her anyway, in spite of her rigid rules?

No, she wouldn't. She hadn't yet won that fight.

The guard jerked aside, clearing her throat. That sensuous song rang through the first floor, unhelpful to the awkward pause. "…You know, wine isn't actually my go-to alcoholic beverage," she then blurted out.

"Let me guess," Lorrin breathed. "Cider?"

"As it happens, yes."

The blonde didn't like the idea that it might always be like this when they were alone. A mutual attraction which was constantly blocked by none other than their own inhibitions. She wouldn't dare to comment on it, and occupied her mouth by drinking. The wine was dry but there was still the sharp hit of bitter sourness. It was a comforting taste. Familiar and welcoming like an old lover.

After the third glass that feeling strengthened. The pleasant calmness washed over her and all that filled her senses was sweetness. This —this was why she drank. She chased this ease. It wasn't an escape. It was an active quest.

Zemir was surprisingly unswayed by the increase of alcohol content from her usual preference. She was still rather sober. Not that Lorrin was stumbling over her own feet —she had just breached the threshold of tipsy.

The playlist had ended, and the only sound to accompany quiet sipping was the returned pitter of rain.

There was little that Lorrin liked better than to be curled up inside and watch the rainfall. It was slightly different with someone else beside her —it was like an intrusion to her down time. But Detective Kal wasn't noisy, and she seemed to enjoy the sight and sound just as much.

Lorrin was about to pour another glass when Zemir's hand caught hers. She looked at her, shaking her head.

"I don't think that's a good idea. You don't want to wake up with a hangover."

"It's the start of the weekend," Lorrin frowned. "And I have majik pills."
The officer glanced aside, and let go. The iman's gaze fell to her wrist, the warmth of her hand lingering on her skin. She couldn't stop her. But the assassin found herself questioning another glass, nevertheless.

"Sorry," Zemir murmured. "I tried to advise you based on my own views."
"What, the fayth?"
"Mm."
The guard knew that Lorrin didn't believe. If anything, her behaviour should have given it away. From the moment they had first met, Zemir had watched her drink herself past the point of light intoxication. She knew that she smoked from time to time. And she'd said that she wasn't a follower outright, in the heat of anger.

Yet the officer was here, in the non-believer's house, drinking her wine and wrestling with the desire to do unholy things to her.

The blonde shifted slightly. "Let's…let's go to bed."

It was a suggestion to reassure the detective mostly, but there was a little guilt irrationally pricking her for wanting to drink more even if Zemir wouldn't.

"I have three guest rooms," she informed her when they had gotten upstairs. "Take your pick."

The officer simply stared. "I'll be honest. I thought you'd try to lie by saying you only had one bed to share."

Lorrin laughed. "Is that what you would have preferred?"

She looked at her feet. "I...I don't know."

It was such an innocently honest answer that the assassin almost reconsidered asking. Then she gathered the liquid courage to ask, "Would you...would you like to share one with me?"

Zemir met her gaze again. The door was a few paces away. Would they start tonight? Very little was stopping them. They could finally get the carnal need out of their systems. But...the image of her crying flashed in Lorrin's mind. And then suddenly she couldn't —not like this. And the detective looked like no amount of alcohol could provide her with the adequate nerve.

"...Yeah," she still whispered. "I don't want to sleep alone. Not today."

"Okay."

Lorrin attempted to hide her surprise, and led her to the master suite. It was a spacious king-sized room —complete with a four poster bed, silk sheets and a walk-in wardrobe. All the furniture was finished with paint such a deep black that it was like staring at many tiny black holes. A small crystal chandelier hung from the main ceiling —a detail that Lorrin had not changed from the original design.

Detective Kal looked about the room in awe and thought, not bothering to hide her assumptions.

"I know —it doesn't match me, does it?" the blonde said as she pulled her t-shirt off. She had her back to the guard, but she wouldn't be able to miss the arch of her spine, and the fading scars which ran horizontal along it.

"...Who did that to you?"

Zemir's voice was cold; angry. She no longer harboured any trepidation. And she didn't appear to care that it wasn't her business, either. All that mattered was that she was law enforcement, and someone had the markings of abuse. Lorrin hesitated as she reached for her pyjamas. "...They're very old."

Her tone softened. "That's not what I asked, Raffe."

The assassin's muscles locked. "I know."

She didn't want to talk about the Central Blades' training methods. It wasn't that they had whipped everyone and anyone at any time they wanted —it had been the consequence for bad behaviour and mistakes. She'd once counted herself lucky to have graduated with the few whippings that she had gotten. Perhaps that had been why she never had the intention of training new recruits. She didn't want to inflict that pain with her own hands.

People had asked about the scars before, and they had all been met the same answer. They did not cause discomfort, and she did not want to explain.

Once dressed, she turned back around to see Zemir clenching her jaw; prepared to snap someone's neck. Was that agency for her sake? She clung to that deluded sweetness, like the wine. She turned off the main light, and the small lamps on the bedside tables automatically illuminated the shadows.

She didn't like sleeping in pitch darkness —in the thick of it. To voluntarily surrender her sense of sight as well as her awareness had her skin crawling.

"…You'd report it if it happened again, wouldn't you?" the officer murmured, walking towards the bed.

"Yes," she answered truthfully, joining her atop the mattress. And once she was queen-pin, she'd eradicate the method altogether.

The frustration refused to leave Zemir's brow, though, as the two lay side by side facing one another. Lorrin studied her for a moment, her gaze flickering from her jaw to her exposed shoulder, then back to her mouth.

"I think my brother stole the keys to my apartment," that mouth then moved, forcing Lorrin to look at her stark eyes.

"Is that why you were crying?"

Zemir sneered. "I don't cry."

"Sure, sure."

She became serious again, forcefully biting her lips. "…It became too much. He stopped by out of nowhere, ruining my mood, and then when I got home…I didn't have my keys. None of them. I know I didn't drop them. I keep them in a secure compartment in my pocket, unbeknownst to anyone else. Or so I thought. He must have found out and snatched them when he hugged me."

"Why don't you get them back? Will he be angry if you accuse him?"

"That, and he's too far from the capital," she put delicately. "But…that wasn't the only thing that set me off. Many things have been occurring in my family for generations; it's not just me. But they're hehlbent on getting me back to them. By any means. I can't believe they've resorted to this. I'll need to call the landlord."

"Do you need a place to stay in the meantime?"

"I'm not going to impose," she dismissed. "I'll figure something out."
Lorrin attempted to look sympathetic. "…You don't have to force yourself to tell me this," she said, shuffling a little closer. "You're a welcome guest, remember?"

Her forehead creased as she frowned. "I know."

But breathing seemed to become easier.
In the dim lighting, this moment was infinite. What could come against them here, in a space outside of the harshness beyond the windows? There were no angry brothers; no ruthless superiors. There wasn't even the end of the world.

"Zemir," the assassin then rasped. The detective blinked at the use of her first name only. "Can I…" She slowly lifted her hand towards her chest, struggling to say it outright. *Touch you. Comfort you.*

The guard took hold of her pale hand, and lightly stroked her thumb over the palm. She didn't provide an answer for a long moment. But maybe the safety got to her too, because she brought the assassin's hand to her breast —over her heart. Lorrin swallowed uneasily, though she didn't withdraw as Zemir guided her hand to her shoulders, down the centre of her chest, before stopping at her stomach. The blonde didn't dare to lower it herself. But she used her other hand to lift the hem of the sweater upwards. It was a careful and meticulous task —and ultimately rewarding as the garment made it over the officer's head.

Lorrin stared, very unapologetically.
And then she was holding one of them. Surprise at its firmness was brief, though it did compel her to verify if it applied to both breasts. Zemir drew a sharp breath. Colour pooled in the guard's cheeks as the iman wondered if her hands were cold.

"This isn't how I normally do things, by the way," whispered the detective. "My...pride wouldn't allow it."

"So why now?"

Her narrowed honey-coloured eyes stared right through to her speck of soul. "I'm mainly curious," she admitted, her voice mimicking that song again. "Of what it would be like if someone else was in control."

The assassin's gaze flicked down as she chewed on her lips. So she was the one usually holding the reins? What would it feel like if Zemir's hands were on her breasts instead? All over her body, in fact. A shiver echoed through her as her imagination kicked into high gear.

Lorrin's hand skidded down along the officer's skin, to her navel. The region reacted rather potently, going taut with awareness. But the destination was further, beneath those grey sweatpants. She felt her arch into the movement involuntarily, making her warm with anticipation. And then breathing became difficult again. Zemir gasped into the little space between them, weak to the methodical fingers within her. She didn't permit any proper incriminating moans to escape, as though the very thought of enjoying someone's touch would come back to haunt her. But she'd pant for air and quiver at every gentle thrust.

The assassin grew greedy; yearning for as much of an indication that it felt good as possible. Be it her intoxicating breathlessness or the clutch of her hand on Lorrin's waist. But it was all over too soon; Zemir bit her lip and noiselessly shuddered in satisfaction, before looking back up into the girl's lidded eyes. The flood of pleasure had at least, made her grip on Lorrin useless.

That open mouth was dangerously enticing.

But Lorrin forced herself to withdraw her hands; to ignore the throb in her lower abdomen; and to turn over onto her other side. The officer didn't say a word. It was cool and silent again, aside from her own racing heartbeat. Then she said into the whispering night, "...Top me next time."

CHAPTER 16

lorrin

SHE WAS AWAKE before Zemir; in a thick jersey and black jazz pants as she stared out towards the rising suns with a cigarette between her lips. Reality was akin to those crashing waves at the sea; constant and persistent. Lorrin Raffe wasn't the sort of saint to deserve nice things, and fate knew as much. That was why her life was being stifled; restricted as her ambition heightened beyond her share. The universe wanted to put the iman from nowhere back in her place.

But nothing would compare to that power; that influence. Did all monarchs feel as giddy and delirious as she did, knowing they would one day ascend? She'd get drunk on it. So wonderfully and stupidly drunk.

What stood in her way would come crumbling down very soon. Once she'd made those phone calls and put some of the ring leaders in jail or close enough, the fragile balance of the Central Blades would cave. She wouldn't find a puppet to rebuild it —the time for hiding was over. She'd demand things, and everyone would know that it was her who did it. They'd remember her name.

Her gaze drifted as the bedsheets rustled.

Detective Kal rose like the dead, pulled the t-shirt back on and sauntered over, before raking her hair back and stepping onto the balcony. "Hey. Did you sleep?"

"A little," Lorrin admitted, turning back to the view. "You hungry?"

Zemir quirked an eyebrow. "Are you offering me breakfast?"

"Shouldn't I?" the assassin frowned at the skyline. "I'm trying to be nice. No one's ever stayed over this long."

"I *am* hungry," smirked the guard, moving to lean against the glass barrier which prevented her from plummeting three stories to gravel. "But we can just go out and grab something if you're tired."

"I'm never tired," Lorrin deadpanned, blowing out smoke. "You can shower first. I'll get cooking in a minute."

She was answered with a snort.

Zemir Kal wandered into the dining room wearing yesterday's freshly washed and ironed clothing. The savoury scent hit her first, and when she sat down, she stared at the salmon eggs benedict as if it had come from a five star restaurant. It inflated the assassin's ego just a little, and eased the lingering frown on her brow. And the praise became audible once they had started eating. The guard had above average table manners; very upright and proper, more so than dinner the night before — and the iman knew it was due to Court training.

"In another life, you should be a chef."

Lorrin shrugged. She had told her mother a very similar thing. "What do you normally do on the weekend?" she then asked.

"Nothing too interesting," the detective sighed, dabbing at her mouth with a napkin. "I'd either work on a case, maybe go to the gym, or read a novel. Boring shit. I don't *do* fun, remember?"

"Yeah. Boring."

"Although," Zemir quipped; a sudden and unnerving glint in her eye, "I've come up with a theory based on that playing card found at Leifsdotter's scene. It was a red queen of hearts. What if…it's in reference to the Queen of Hearts from that fairytale where a little girl falls down a rabbit hole? '*Off with their heads*' — remember that? Both victims were beheaded."

Lorrin paused in taking a sip of orange juice. The detective had finally solved the riddle. A part of her pleased —perhaps even proud —that the small effort had not been vain. But she pushed the feeling aside and set the glass down.

"Oh, now we're talking about work outside of it?" she taunted.

The officer huffed. "Smartass. We were complete strangers then."

"I do commend your findings, though," the assassin promptly assured. "That's a clever angle. But…what would it mean? That the killer has a sense of humour?"

"I haven't had the chance to think further," Zemir admitted dejectedly. "But I *do* believe that it holds meaning. It could even be political."

Lorrin's attention was firmly gripped now. A political murderer? Something along the lines of '*eat the rich*', and such? That would result in her not needing to frame some poor soul. She leaned forward and propped her elbows on the dining table, hands clasped beneath her chin. "With the theory of a ghost being the culprit on the table, terrorists seems plausible."

"But let's save that for tomorrow," suggested the guard. "We've still got one day to laze around, and I plan to take full advantage of it. Her Excellency will no doubt be on our asses for a while."

"Fair enough."

After clearing the plates and glasses, the two females decided to go down to the beach along the Iman District. That damned cycle had finally ended, and it was a change in scenery from a living room or the decorated lawn. They thought about swimming later, too, since it was hot enough. Zemir didn't have a swimsuit, and Lorrin didn't feel comfortable lending out any underwear, so they would pass through the Lotus shopping mall first. Fortunately, the detective had had her wallet and cellphone on her. That left less opportunities for further indebtedness.

The assassin took her time to shower and pick an outfit. In the end she settled for a pair of dark leggings and cropped t-shirt that had the words '*little monster*' embroidered in red across the middle.

Lorrin couldn't stop thinking about the burner she had left intact. Though she couldn't stand the sight of it —she'd shut it away in one of the numerous drawers beneath a pile of clothes —it certainly burned within her memory, and had almost seemed to heat her very skin. *Zemir's phone number is saved there. And it's the only one*. As if she needed to remind herself.

The drive would distract her.

As surprised as the blonde had been at the detective's immaculate driving skills, The officer was silently horrified with Lorrin's. It wasn't only the speed — the assassin barely signalled, and the lines on the tar were treated as a suggestion. The car rattled from side to side and lurched at every bend. But Zemir kept her mouth shut; she didn't dare to point it out. The only indication of her terror was a fast grip of the seat and the colour draining from her straight face.

No one liked backseat driving.

When they arrived at the mall in one piece, the detective appeared tempted to kiss the ground. The assassin felt no sympathy for it, and nearly told her to get over it. But last night replayed in her head, of Zemir telling her about her family, and she couldn't bring herself to say a single bad word.

"I'm not looking for anything fancy," Detective Kal told her as they entered a department store. "It's not like it'll be permanent anyway."

"You actually *own* a swimsuit already?" gasped the girl.

"I swim," the guard defended herself. "…Occasionally."

All Lorrin could do was laugh —and stifle the sound as she remembered that they were in public. She pictured the older iman either flailing in the water or standing and shivering in it, her expression that familiar sour.

Zemir started walking away.

"Wait, no I believe you," the assassin called as she darted after her.

After trying on several pairs, the officer chose a black and white thinly striped tankini. She was satisfied with the short amount of time they had spent looking. She didn't like shopping, but this experience had not been bad. Lorrin begged to differ: the guard had been irritatingly picky, and then she had sat outside of the changing rooms bored out of her mind. Even the shoe display had failed to catch her attention. She couldn't wait to sit on the sand with a romance in her hands.

Kover Beach —which rhymed with '*over*' —was understandably busy that afternoon. Towels lined the sands all the way to the rocky start towards the houses; parents sprawled and tanning while children ran around and jumped them.

Zemir didn't hesitate to show her displeasure at the sight. It was meant to be a quiet, tranquil visit with the only sounds being the water. Snotty brats and burnt red bellies and backs were not supposed to be a part of it.

Lorrin motioned for her to follow towards a bend, which at a glance had more rock and flora than golden sand. But the detective's feet went in that direction in an echo of hers, deciding that rock climbing would be better than taking the chance that no little kid feet would miscalculate the horizontal length of her stomach, and violently step on it instead.

It wasn't an extreme sport which awaited them around the cliffside. There were boulders and bushes of drying wildflowers, but the focal point was a cave pool. Lorrin had found the spot a few months ago when the beach had been teaming with life. The sunslight trickled through the opening high above them at the top of the cliff, and illuminated the interior. The light filtering in was a bright, vibrant blue. The shape of the skylight stained spots of the scarce sand and large coloured rocks patterns that resembled stars.

The still water itself was clearer than it was on the main shore; in a tropical malachite. Its surface glinted like a diamond refracting light, and to the assassin's pleasant surprise, the temperature wasn't freezing. Small shards of violet, ruby and clear cyan crystal studded the walls and ground, turning the cave into a place of majik. It was the closest tangible thing to something out of a fairytale that she had ever encountered.

Zemir whistled as they placed down their bags and towels. "How did you find this place?" she whispered —anything above that volume feeling wrong.

"I stumbled on it once," Lorrin explained. "The beach had been so full, like it is now, so I just started walking instead of going home. I'm so glad that I did."

"I would be, too."

The imans kicked off their shoes and settled down on the mesh of towels. They'd brought a picnic along; apple juice, hoisin duck and salad sandwiches, grapefruit, strawberries and cheese flavoured potato crisps. Detective Kal's eyes went wide when Lorrin produced a tall bottle of sparkling wine that she'd snuck in her bag.

"You can't have that here," hissed the officer.

"We'll only have one serving each *after* swimming," the assassin quipped haughtily, daring to dig up two glasses. "We're only eating afterwards, after all."

"I could fine you for this," Zemir murmured.

"But you won't."

"Why not?"

The blonde threw a simpering smile over her bare shoulder. "Because it's me."

She had simply jested, but the guard frowned and glanced away, towards the pool, as if she was right.

Her gaze continued to avoid the iman as they later dipped into the water — though that could have been because of the now fully on display hot pink bikini Lorrin had worn beneath her clothes. All of her scars were visible, and while no one else had asked her about them in length, Lorrin remembered the officer's raged concern. As though the marring had been fresh. They stretched completely over her back; a cruelly meticulous lattice of brown, with two reddened and less defined lines on the back of her right thigh.

She jolted at the touch of Zemir's hand on her upper back as she swam up behind her, before her fingers traced a mark on her shoulder blade. The graze was light and unsure as if in study. The assassin drew a shuddering breath and pulled away, unable to bear the sensation.

"I apologise," said the detective quietly. The sound of dripping water boomed. "I should've asked. It just…startled me again. But I didn't mean to unsettle you."

"I know." Lorrin tightly wrapped her arms around her shoulders.

Those words were a reflex response. Because it didn't invite further conversation, and it removed the obligation for her to continue. It held one of the only powers that was universally acknowledged.

"…Raffe."

Her head turned at the softness of the whisper. It was unbelievably tender — gentle in the way that she had not imagined anyone would ever utter her name. The way her mother might've called her '*Lorri*' as she fell asleep. It picked at a very small and raw part of her heart in fact; made it ache.

She wanted to hear it again.

132

"Raffe," Detective Kal answered her thought. To say that she said it with the same reverence as a prayer would be a discredit to her fayth. Instead, her name on her tongue was a sweet sin. Something which they could both intrinsically feel was forbidden, yet it didn't seem to deter them. Instead it was temptation into which one surrendered, head-first. Zemir couldn't even muster the nerve to say her first name. Was it even more damning? Would she fall from the Daughter's favour for it? Lorrin wondered if she could be considered worth that.

She then turned around. This was the longest she had gone without any sort of weapon directly on her person —eighteen and a half hours. She felt more exposed than nakedness, weaker than a recruit soldier. Had the guard always been that tall? She loomed over her even as the females treaded closer.

Zemir didn't know what else to say. The only word that would form on her tongue was Lorrin's surname, even if no sound accompanied it. So she neared, and pulled the blonde against her in the most crushing hug she could administer.

The assassin's gaze widened comically at the embrace, her body immediately going rigid. She struggled to remember the last time someone had locked her in their arms in a way that wasn't to restrain her, forcibly move her, or just the way people clung in the heat of sex.

The realisation of it should have been maddening. But she didn't feel a thing. Thankfully, it seemed Detective Kal wouldn't blame her for a lack of a reaction. It was perfectly reasonable. She withdrew of her own accord and held Lorrin at arm's length, her expression one of cold control.

The girl then froze. Suddenly she wanted to obey her every instruction.

"I am never going to do that again," Zemir said slowly.

The assassin managed the smallest smile before lying through her teeth. "I will forever treasure the moment."

The officer certainly wouldn't either. Her face flickered between a multitude of expressions, before settling on pained. She was waging another war in there — fighting to react normally or reveal how much this would plague her. Given what Lorrin had seen of her personality, the guard was unsure of how to process certain scenarios and their consequences. She could be bizarrely impulsive, and disregard

133

what came after. Because in the moment, it didn't really matter. A selfish thread of Lorrin's thoughts wanted her to do that with her abstinence of kissing.

The blonde then leaned in closer. For a second that lasted a thousand years, the detective let her. Their faces neared enough for them to feel the faintest wafts of shallow breath. Zemir didn't grip her waist beneath the water, and the assassin refrained from clutching her shoulders. Any other touch may ruin the quiet majik of the moment. Their noses tapped. Lorrin watched the officer blink, conflicted, through hooded eyes. Would instinct finally triumph?

The graze of skin was so much like the slight brush of wind that she wondered if their lips had even met at all. The distance jerked to several centimetres.

Zemir inhaled shakily as she swam backwards. "Let's eat."

She still would not cave. There was something admirable in that resolve.

"Okay."

The imans dried off and sat on the towels again, before tucking into the picnic. Grapefruit was another insignificant thing she carried from childhood. She had never liked the stark boring orange of fresh citrus. When her mother had brought home a fruit with a similar orange peel but was red on the inside, it had captivated her. Why was it that colour? Why did it remind her of blood? And why was it so much more delicious than other citrus?

The assassin also reached for the paperback she had packed —*I'm Afraid of Heights*. What a great height it might be from which to fall into love, indeed. The plot itself was a melodramatic thing of nonsense, but highly entertaining.

She didn't miss Zemir's hard look her way, enviously eyeing the bright cover. Utterly amused, she glanced at the detective. "Want me to read it aloud?"

"No. I don't like romance."

Lorrin shook her head. "Me neither. I read it for the comedy."

"Still no."

"Well, what kind of book you were going to read?"

The guard took a bite out of her sandwich. "…A historical crime thriller."

CHAPTER 17

lorrin

ROHNA NYLL WASN'T the only one who noticed the decrease in petty bickering in the precinct the next weekday morning. Detective Burns was also staring curiously over at Lorrin and Zemir, as the guards conspicuously huddled by the coffee station. The consultant and the officer were diligently seated at the desk, completely focused on work. There were no glares, no tomfoolery, and no threats. They had to be watching a new and different pair of people.

Rohna asked as much when she cornered the younger iman during lunch.

"Nothing special happened," Lorrin sighed, heating up a portion of Spaghetti Bolognese. The guard hadn't even needed to ask. The blonde had felt her stare from the other side of the room.

"But you're getting along so well," Rohna hissed. "So suddenly."

"We ran into each other on the weekend," the assassin relented an inch. "We just sat down for lunch in silence. I guess Detective Kal found that tolerable."

The iman wasn't so convinced, but she took the information gratefully, as it was all that she would receive. "It's a sight to see."

"I can imagine," Lorrin chuckled, though no warmth seeped into her eyes. The truth of the matter was that the females had reached a sombre understanding. To Zemir, she was less of the dismissible naïve young iman she had seemed. And to herself, the detective was more approachable. She worried, cried and got angry just like the rest of them. She probably bled the same, too.

The assassin had broken many rules in those two days. Fraternising was one thing, but sheltering the enemy? Sharing meals? Keeping each other company? Her transgressions seemed innocent until she realised that she had mixed feelings about the guard. But one steamy night was inadequate for any clouds to judgement to form. The touch of her skin was not enough to change her fate —disposable.

Never spare.

Lorrin had been taught that a good assassin had many masks. And a great one could wield many at once. Had that truly been her these past few days? Had she dipped too deeply into her role, or…had she donned a mask at all? It had to be impossible to consider that what she'd done had meant and been more than acting the friendly character. That idea set a chill in her bones. And in that cave; in the warmth of the water —had that been someone else? She hoped so.

It better have been.

Her fork clattered to the floor.

"You okay?" Rohna frowned, meeting her slightly pained expression.

She shakily bent down. "…I —"

Officer Denaris shot her a glare as she stalked over, her wings pressed and stiff. It made the weak answer instantly die in Lorrin's throat. The Pastel Faery wordlessly prepared two cups of coffee in mugs printed with '*Zemir*' and '*Fran*', and offered a soft scoff and upturn of her nose as she left.

Lorrin blinked in bewilderment, shaking off her previous panic. She was fine. Her mask had only cracked, due to Zemir Kal's persistent torture. It was torture when she touched her; torture when she spoke gently; torture to see her in tears; and torture to desire breathing the same air.

The assassin was smart enough to evade such pain.

Never yield.

"Raffe," came a bark. Detective Kal was beckoning her over. Officer Denaris stood leaned over at her side, pissy and suspicious. "Finish your lunch," ordered the iman. "We need to go to The Court. Witnesses need interviewing, and…we may have found something."

Her muscles locked all over again, and a sick feeling settled in the pit of her stomach. This was not going to be a good day.

✝

The breeze sweeping through The Court was brisk. Lorrin pulled her denim jacket tighter around herself, wishing that she was wearing dark jeans instead of grey and white jogging pants. Her black t-shirt was soaking up the suns' light, but it wasn't enough. The river understood —it was choppier than usual; very inviting if one wished to cease existing.

Zemir and her Seelie friend were conducting questionnaires, but the assassin was glad to be alone and uninvolved. She wanted nothing further to do with Rudd Leifsdotter or *Ortus*. The grass was still discoloured where his body had fell. What required her energy and attention was concluding the investigation in a way that disregarded her entirely. If she headed for the political route, it could coincide with the Unseelie sighting.

Though why would Gehman hate The Court as much as the other Idun citizens when they had a court of their own? No —the killer had to be a desperate, monarch and elitist hating monster. Lorrin couldn't imagine one, however, no matter how much she disliked The Court. If she wasn't an unfeeling assassin, she wouldn't resort to murder. Detective Kal didn't like The Court. Her reasons aligned with a rebellious teenager, but the blonde could think along the same vein.

She would need to do a little stalking.

A witness yelled, falling into hysterics.

The iman glanced over, amused by the sight of Officer Denaris attempting to restrain the wailing Elf. The creature dripped gold, silk and peacock feathers, and clutched a fan decorated with them in one hand; flapping it incessantly. The commotion died down after a moment with the Elf slumped in the Faery's arms, muttering about Death.

Lorrin raised an eyebrow. It appeared that her makeshift disguise had worked its charm on the other residents.

The guards started walking back towards the river.

"That was dramatic," quipped the blonde.

"The murder really spooked them," muttered the Seelie.

"Besides that," Zemir sighed and lowered her voice. "Her Excellency announced that the closing gala is going ahead as planned."

The assassin started.

"What?" Officer Denaris hissed as though it was news to her as well. "Even with this threat on The Court and its members?"

"They all still want it to happen," Detective Kal grumbled in frustration. "It's the complexity of these elitists. Maybe they think it will lift their spirits. Any one of them could be next, but they don't want all of that investment to go to waste."

"They fund it themselves?" Lorrin asked.

"Apparently."

The Faery was still stuck on one detail; her wings flittering rapidly. "Wait, why did Her Excellency inform you about this but I haven't heard a thing?"

"I can't answer that," Zemir deadpanned. "However, I can conclude that she will want many guards for security."

"I hope it's voluntary," Officer Denaris seethed.

Zemir did not agree. She didn't say anything; she simply looked down at the ground and pressed her lips together —and while it left the Seelie confused, the assassin had an inkling that she knew why. The detective's family could try to use the gala as an excuse to get her over here.

Lorrin struggled to understand why The Court members would want the event to still be on from a safety point of view. It had no bearing on her, but she had to question their sanity. A few hundred thousand pense surely did not equate to their lives. Then again, it was possible that the fools planned to gamble that life simply for the thrill of it. Who could outlive the rest —they could turn it into a game. The assassin's mouth twitched slightly as she fought off a grin.

Perhaps nothing stopped her from playing along.

"What was the clue you found?" she then asked the guards.

Officer Denaris' wings beat with annoyance as Detective Kal pointed to a conifer near the scene.

"We found a fragment of cloth snagged on a tree," Zemir answered.

Lorrin's blood froze in her veins.

She willed her body to still; not to give away her loss of nerve at the revelation. It didn't mean that it was hers. Many people likely came into contact with the trees. With these gardens. And now that she'd been on Court grounds with permission before a number of witnesses, it wouldn't be strange to find a few threads of denim dangling from a pine. She forced a breath.

Although...if the piece they found happened to be a hopeless black, suspicion would rise. They may not find traces of her on it, but they could eventually link it to the Central Blades. Danger still beckoned; still whispered her name on the wind. Depending on how Rohna handled the situation, Lorrin would need to vanish and return to normalcy.

Yet a part of her hesitated. Attachment was a death wish when undercover, even her first, and it wasn't that she particularly cared for any of the guards —at least not superficially. An odd hollowness seeped in at the thought of them all going back to strangers. But that such was existence. Few relationships lasted until one's expiration, and she had no need for any of them.

The only thing which mattered was weaving herself in the great tapestry.

Which meant that while she had not yet been caught, those phone calls would need to be placed today. The turning of wheels had to resume. And by the end of the week, if law enforcement was still on her side, she'd be the acting queen-pin. The horizon still shone with possibility. But she had no Gods to Whom to pray.

A powerful, far-off thud made the ground tremble.

Like something had rammed into a metal door.

The three females tensed, glancing westward. A cloud of grey dust began to rise from the top of the Wall.

"Holy shit," hissed the Faery.

The radio on Zemir's thigh switched on. "*Code 2, I repeat code 2! Hairline fracture along central panel of the Wall. We have a 11-83 and 10-29h. All available units to Gehman border. Code 2, I repeat Code 2!*"

"We're too far," Lorrin cried. "Is it a breach?"

"Thankfully, no," Officer Denaris clipped, adjusting her sheath. "Otherwise we'd be fucking running to the squad cars."

"We can't just do nothing," Detective Kal bit, unstrapping the radio. "Come in. This is Officer Zemir Kal and Fran Denaris. Code 6 from The Court."

"*Copy, Officer Kal. 10-23. You're too far.*"

"Copy that." She then groaned deeply, tugging her hair out of her face. "…We can't just standby from here. Let's head back. Leave Rohna here with forensics."

"Copy," the Seelie quipped, turning to where they had parked.

"Raffe," Zemir said, shaking her free from her state of paralysing fright. Her eyes of amber blazed. "Let's go and witness history."

CHAPTER 18

zemir

THE UNSEELIE HAD shattered the dome shield in order to leave a fracture in the Wall. There was no way of knowing what exactly they had knocked into the fortified structure —helicopters dared not to fly that close over Gehman. But it had to be enormous, and brutal. After years of trying to pierce through the majik, direct and blunt force was the tactic to which they had resorted.

The closest they had come to breaking it was a century before, when they had tunnelled beneath the ground. Since then, Her Excellency and her predecessor had spent a fortune reinforcing the Wall's foundations, and building on to run further thousands of kilometres down. The Unseelie Court's only option was to come from above, after breaking the shield. And they were not privy to the complex spells which fabricated it.

Until now.

Zemir was determined to be a beacon of collectedness —and to her surprise, Lorrin Raffe was pale and shaking. It was indeed terrifying; not knowing if this was just the first step to the end, or the next step in subduing the threat. She wasn't feigning strength. And Gehman would forever haunt, forever loom over the rest of the city like the shadows of a beast.

Fran was just as outwardly calm as her —they had gone through the very same training to mask certain emotions for the sake and reassurance of others. The

Seelie was ordinarily stoic and aloof, but her heart was in the right place. Time and effort warmed her, and that frown flipped at familiarity. When Zemir had first met her, the Faery was someone from whom she wanted to stay away. She was unapproachable and entirely focused on her position. She wasn't chief or anything so high and mighty, but there was a respect she had carried from the Academy. Rohna, Henrick and Harris —even people who saw her once a day like Sol —they all had a reverence for Fran as though she had singlehandedly saved Idun once.

Like she was a thing of legend.

Zemir was the first person in a long time to make her earn that sort of worship. She hadn't let the Faery look down upon her; but dead in the eye, as if they stood on equal footing. Fran certainly thought the iman arrogant and haughty at first, but she soon proved that she was a match for the Seelie.

The respect had grown to be mutual.

Hordes of civilians were lining the streets, before an extensive black and gold blockade behind which the Guard had stationed themselves. News stations were parked and clambering for any sort of information beyond speculation and the visible evidence. There thankfully appeared to be no casualties or injuries.

Getting through was a nightmare, but a few officers were guiding squad cars towards the blockade. The imans threw open the doors and stared up at the Wall. From here, the fizzling majik shield flickered in and out of view, but was clearly damaged. No scholars or Maji were present —they too, were too far.

Her Excellency was positioned at the heart of the chaos among the Guard of Madir, briefing the arriving officers. An unidentified object had rammed into the Gehman side of the Wall, but the shield had not been tampered with prior —it had cracked upon impact. The battering object had been imbued with majik itself.

"I think we should go into a state of emergency!" shouted an officer.
The reporters were going to have a field day with that.

"The wall was only fractured!" another reasoned. "It's not like it's hollow!"

The barrier shield needed to be repaired, and that fracture needed filling — but otherwise sitting at home seemed inconsequential. The Unseelie were going to get in regardless of what the citizens were doing.

"I will go and speak with His Holiness!" Nadune Madir then announced.

The entire Guard went quiet for a good while.

The governor saw it as the opportunity to continue. "We have three options. The first: we can bury our heads and pretend that nothing is happening. Two, we can retaliate with bullets and bombs and further ruin this strained peace we've known for many centuries. And third...I can go to the Unseelie Court with diplomacy and intentions of reconciliation."

Personally, Zemir thought it was a rather stupid idea. It wasn't as though Her Excellency was unfamiliar with Gehman. It was an untamed and lush wilderness —a region preserved in time when laws did not reign and instinct did. Those Faery kind there were monstrous cousins of the Seelie; and gripped by ages of bitter resentment. They believed that their land had been stolen from them, along with their people and power. And their King...he had a reputation for culling anything that didn't roll over for his amusement, or resemble the festering dark.

Her Excellency may be walking to her early death for the sheer audacity.

"The King will slit her throat," Lorrin whispered beside her. She knew of the recounts of terror. "You have to be explicitly invited to survive an audience."

Perhaps the governor knew that. At least, her Seelie advisors should. Zemir wasn't going to jump to inform her, anyway. The less involved in the dispute she was, the better. Or else she would find herself by Her Excellency's side, at the foot of that throne. And Nadune Madir would definitely remember two little imans warning her to request an invitation.

Detective Kal pressed a finger to her lips.

So it was decided that a request to see the Unseelie King would be sent. The disbanding of the crowd and News stations were their priority. The Majik District would be contacted promptly to begin repairs.

The officer could vividly picture the mad creature lazing in the shadowed, debauched throne room; cloaked in black or nothing at all; and laughing heartily when the letter arrived. How he'd rip it up and make one of his subjects eat the pieces. And then he might accept the request after all, simply to size the iman governor up and watch her squirm.

"May I…may I have the rest of the day off?" Lorrin asked in a quiet voice which sounded thick with ash.

Zemir frowned, tempted to say '*no*' until she noticed how close to the brink of death the blonde had become. There was no colour in her cheek; no glimmer in her eyes; and her lips had faded to a ghostly pink. It was almost alarming —the detective had grown used to a fierce and cunning young female. Someone who *refused* to give a shit; not that she couldn't read a room. She was so confident in who she was, yet she didn't wield it like a weapon.

She seemed almost invincible.

It turned out that she too, had a soul. That she could feel fear.

"Okay," Zemir sighed. "I'll see you back at your house."

"Mm."

The detective had to wonder, as she watched her walk away. How had she ended up saying '*yes*' to her offer of a temporary spare room? She had planned to ask Fran instead, since Lei Baiwen didn't have spare rooms. But she had thought better of it when she realised that she'd need to explain a lot of painful things. Maybe she would tell her one day, but a rushed and desperate account wasn't necessary. The Faery would make it a much bigger deal than it was. That counted as another reason why she had said '*yes*' to Lorrin Raffe. She had made no fuss. Just been there, offering no pity and demanding no explanation.

Now she would spend the next few days in her home. It certainly made their arrangement easier. The two hadn't done anything since the first night —since that *accident* in the cave. It had been too secret in there; too beautiful. It had bewyched her into reacting too slowly. But it had also given Zemir an increased drive to bed her. The electricity of their every touch lingered as on the wind in a storm, and she couldn't wait to get another taste of it. She'd thoroughly daydreamt about how she wanted to do it, and the anticipation had finally reached its peak.

Thank the Daughter their entanglement wouldn't be at her apartment after all. She would delay using her collection of toys and leashes on the blonde, until she was comfortable with her alone.

Fran caught up with the pondering guard as soon as Lorrin had disappeared.

She was tasked with ushering the crowd away and reassuring the public that the matter was being resolved. Her wings hummed and blurred in flight, giving her easier access to the sea of heads. Zemir followed the Faery's lead on the ground; her stare enough to send a few citizens shuffling off without a word.

"I didn't get a chance to ask you earlier," Fran began, hovering half a metre above her, "but I couldn't help noticing in the office how well you're getting on with that iman girl, now. You heeded my advice, right? You didn't fuck her over the weekend, did you?"

"No, I didn't. Not everything is resolved that way, Fran. We simply decided to behave like rational adults," Detective Kal huffed, signalling the direction of evacuation. "There will be no more hostility, lingering stares or petty taunting." She was embellishing it slightly, but that was the essence of their unofficial truce.

Fran glanced down and gave her a withering look of evaluation, but seemed to conclude favourably. "...If you say so."

Zemir realised that she should be feeling some level of guilt, somewhere. Yet she couldn't muster a slither of reproach for keeping Officer Denaris out of things. Lying was forbidden, and often left a sludgy feeling in the pit of her stomach. That was why she preferred to say nothing at all.

It was growing more and more difficult to wrap up the truth.

Her landlord, being the frugal old Seelie he was, didn't keep any spare keys at hand. It would take time to have one cut. And she would have to pay a fine, despite her reasoning. Unfortunately the grumpy dwarf of a Faery hadn't seen the issue with going all the way to The Court for a key that was not even confirmed to be in her brother's possession.

But she *knew* that it was. Petre Kal appeared genteel and proper enough, but beneath all of that polished training lay a snake just as vicious as the rest of them. Not including her, of course. Zemir had escaped by the skin of her teeth —with bundles of nicked jewellery and gold. There had been little she could do at the age of sixteen, but Baiwen and Tianyu had been more than generous in guiding her.

Years of gruelling school and the Academy had shaped her into the far wiser female she now was —one who understood that money could not buy one's way out of everything. There were consequences for what the Kals did in the shadows, and they were inevitable. Petre's future children were going to feel them.

If she chose to have any of her own, at least they would be spared. In fact, she would never let the hand of karma seize them —they'd deserve a life where no one sought them out for their ancestors' sins.

But it wasn't that the guard wanted revenge on her family now. That wasn't what the burn that lingered in her chest meant. She was sure that the sharp heat was only pain. Fully suppressible and trivial. Because what she wanted more than anything, was freedom.

She wanted to crawl out of the clutch of legacy.

CHAPTER 19

lorrin

SHE COULDN'T FIGURE out from where the vomit had come. Surely she couldn't be that weak; that merely seeing the first threads of the prophecy stitch themselves into Idun caused a physical reaction. Perhaps the very prospect of the foretold events actually coming to fruition made it sink in so deep, that her natural instinct was to reject it. She couldn't believe that the disasters were occurring now, when she hadn't gotten a grasp on the power she yearned to steal.

The other disasters were her own doing, but for something so out of her hands; for the Unseelie to pluck up the nerve to bash the Wall…it felt so far removed from her. Her ambition felt small and insignificant.

Was she truly going to be forced to play a hand she didn't have?

Saving the city had been a fun side quest she had thought of in the heat of the moment. She couldn't imagine actually facing the force of His Holiness. He had ancient majik, and an army. She had a little knife, and a Syren.

Her anonymous calls had sounded a lot more like distress signals; her voice and limbs unsteady and shaking as the words on the pages swam in mockery. She could only hope that the emotional side of the officers with whom she'd spoken had been touched and moved. Would it hurry the process along? That would be a welcome benefit to reap.

Now that was out of the way, she was calling in on Char Gilligan.

"*Hello?*" answered the Syren.

"Raffe," Lorrin rasped as she feverishly paced the kitchen. She had changed into cotton shorts and a spacey *NESA* jersey. "Did you hear about the Wall?"

"*Yes.*" There was a quiet pause in which the blonde was certain that Char was grinning manically. "*...Are you worried about me?*"

"Not particularly," the assassin huffed, halting. "I just can't afford to lose my right-hand female. That, and I wanted to catch up with you while I had the chance. So, what do you think? Will the dark Faery kind finally take it all back?"

"*I think His Holiness is stronger than Nadune Madir gives him credit for,*" the Syren mused carefully. "*I think he's being underestimated. Gravely so.*"

Lorrin began to pace the tiled floor again, chewing on her lips hard enough to draw blood. "...Can the Unseelie Court be stopped?"

The Syren's voice tightened. "*Do you want me to lie?*"

That was an answer in itself.

"*Well,*" she spoke up, pitying the painful silence, "*I think you and I both know that there's only one way to stop an Unseelie with a goal.*"

The iman sucked on her teeth. "Bargaining."

"*That's right. It's the only weakness the Faery kind have —truth and vows. The only way to catch them out.*"

Lorrin went quiet, unable to respond. She wasn't good with the truth, but she could keep her word. An assassin was a dead creature if they didn't make good on their promises. They'd find themselves on the business end of a blade. Though how was she going to trick His Holiness with the truth when she herself barely had a grasp on it?

How ridiculous would she look, sashaying into the Unseelie Court to tell the King that his plans were going to unravel, and that she would be the one to stop him? He'd laugh at her face, and tear her into ribbons.

"*By the way,*" Char pierced her thoughts, "*Jerrek Burr's head was delivered today in a golden box. Bloody gruesome —his brain had been partly eaten, lips ripped off, horns broken, and his eyes were missing. I think they used an axe, 'cause the edges of his spinal column seemed hacked off. Oh, it also came with a note. You'll want to hear it.*"

"Yeah?" Lorrin muttered, half there and half not. She couldn't care less that Burr had finally met his end. It wasn't a surprise, and even the Syren was treating it as a trivial development. The only thing of concern was that if the Drakon really had gone to plead for his life, His Holiness had not indulged him. He had tortured the Favoured anyway, and sent the Central Blades a souvenir to show for it. The Unseelie King didn't like traitors, and he usually saw chosen death as honourable, but if he had refused even the Ivory Blade ring leader, he wasn't easily going to spare Favoured citizens.

"*It said* 'I'm coming for the subordinate's heart next'."

The assassin felt her heart skip a few beats, and then abruptly race. A harsh chill swept the room, prickling her skin with gooseflesh and raising the hair on the back of her neck. Her heavy, unsteady breathing was likely audible on the phone, but she wasn't bothered to conceal her fright. Who would, in light of that note? The word '*heart*' stabbed her gut. Lorrin had no doubt the King meant it quite literally —he'd carve out her heart and mail it over. Rye had said that His Holiness' vengeance took the form of a beating heart. Was it hers, then? Was that part of her what he needed to wage war?

"...That could be a number of people," the iman whispered feebly.

"*Mm.*" If the Syren hadn't known the risk before, she could guess it now. Even Char was doubtful, though tactful. Because every assassin knew that Lorrin Raffe was Jerrek Burr's subordinate. His glorious, brutal, right-hand female.

The sea creature was still not finished with her report. "*By the way, Kon is calling you in. Congratulations, your Majesty.*"

Fucking shit.

Lorrin should be happy. This was the realisation of her own goal. It would be easier to take over as a ring leader. This was what she wanted. Yet all she managed was a grimace and strained, "I'll be there tomorrow. Never spare."

"*Never yield.*"

The assassin drew a hard breath and leaned forward onto the marble island. It was damn suffocating in the house now. She needed a smoke.

The setting of the suns was calming. She could look out at the dusty fuchsias, golds and vermilions and forget about the world for an eternal second. The tufts of cloud blurred with her every exhale; a fantastical reminder that she was dust and nothing more. A flicker in forever. Once upon a time, that had bothered her. She supposed that it still did, but for a different reason. Then, she had yearned to live longer for the sake of having breath. Now she wanted to live long enough to etch her name into history. It didn't matter that she would die soon —what mattered was afterwards. Would people say the name Lorrin Raffe and know who they were talking about?

The sweeping views from Hemmingway Estate had always been unparalleled. Incomparable. It was one of the reasons the place had been so perfect. The city loomed yonder, and the sea crashed a little further. Deep blue stretched to the horizon, and the assassin often thought about what lay beyond that.

Zemir found her there, elbows crossed and leaning forward on the railing in falling socks, staring out wistfully.

The officer walked over and leaned back in the opposite direction, her elbows behind her. She glanced down. "Hello, girl."

Lorrin turned her head, meeting that steely gaze. "Hello, Kal."

"Feeling any better?"

"Not really. My boss died."

"Oh. My condolences."

"No, I hated him," the blonde said firmly, before taking a long drag. "I'm uneasy because now I'm going to get his position."

"Verdia Kon said so?"

"Mm." She looked towards the sea again.

"Is this not what you wanted?"

"Yes. But…I'm overwhelmed with everything else that's happening around us," she admitted truthfully. "My promotion feels trivial. Almost…foreboding."

Lorrin expected her to agree and enforce her feelings as appropriate —at a stretch. Perhaps question why her greatest concern was succession rights. Instead, Zemir's eyes stayed trained on her in thought.

"It's not your fault. I know it feels like the world is ending, but sometimes we deserve that for which we yearn."

The assassin scoffed as she flicked ash off of the butt. "I don't deserve it."

The guard frowned. "What makes you say that?"

But if she truly thought about it; if she let Lorrin's comment sink in, she would find the answer in every moment her mask had slipped. In every moment she had been herself before Zemir; undecorated and thorny.

"Self-destruction," Lorrin said instead. "And sabotage. The outcome of something may be precisely as I envisioned, but I'm never satisfied. And then that culminates into anger, and ruin. I run from the things I yearn."

The expression on Zemir's face didn't change. She didn't provide some sort of motivational speech or wise advice. Maybe there was nothing that she could offer. Then the detective turned and looked out at the glinting water as though it had the answers. "...Maybe you and I are a lot more alike than we seem."

Lorrin wasn't sure how it had begun —had they even finished dinner? She'd put a little effort into it: macaroni and cheese with chorizo and bacon. The vague feeling of something having been forgotten lingered through the rough caress of Detective Kal's hands on her bare skin. They'd been talking, and then the next thing she knew, she was on her back on her bed as Zemir spread her out, pinning her hands above her head. A soft rasp betrayed her; gave her excitement away.

The detective had neared, almost enough to taste the smell of ash, and stopped just short of the ghost of a graze. The air felt static with electricity. And the dim light from the lamps didn't catch Zemir's eyes from that angle, making them dark enough to mirror the vastness of space. They flicked back and forth, searching for something in hers. "...Raffe."

Oh, the sweet whisper of her name.

Lorrin's eyelids had shuttered. "Yes."

The guard had mentioned that she had indeed being roped into security detail for

151

the *Ortus* gala that was somehow, still scheduled as planned. And the blonde had expressed her wish to go too —simply for the sake of investigating for her own cause —but the officer had shut her down immediately. No good would come of her accompanying her; as security or consultant. Then Lorrin had sighed and wondered how else she might get in…and that was when Zemir had nudged her leg with her foot. Ran it up to her thigh.

A teasing echo of what the assassin had done the week before. Only now the room was illuminated; the sky not yet indigo, and the cold harboured.

It was warm —hot, maybe, and the detective's casual action only warmed her further. She had bitten her lip in response, understanding the hint. That foot had turned into hands; calloused and determined.

They slid her *NESA* jersey upwards against her ribs, skimming over her bra which became unclipped just as fast and skilfully. Her chest was smaller than Zemir's, but the assassin didn't mind. The guard familiarised herself with her breasts in seasoned worship; proving it to be far more enjoyable than the previous partners who had ever tried their hand.

And as if in reminder that she'd never meet her mouth, the officer latched onto each pebbled peak instead. Lorrin arched with the sensation, her breath escaping in near silent gasps. Zemir wouldn't let her run her fingers through that vibrant dark blue —she continued to hold the younger iman on the mattress.

Lorrin felt her body shiver. She had never given up control in such a manner before. Whether while fighting, training or fucking.

So this is what Zemir had meant when complaining about not leading. The younger iman had been at the bottom before, but always at the expense of a male or someone's spark of curiosity. The person on top had never looked at her like this —as though she had misbehaved or didn't deserve any pleasure. Yet the girl somehow still felt it, despite that expression and act of withholding. Her mouth dragged lower, towards Lorrin's navel in hot, easy leisure. Her hands carefully stripped her of her shorts and underwear, before bending each of her legs back towards the headboard. The assassin watched in tantalising anticipation as Zemir knelt before her, looming and naked.

"I don't want to hear any crying, girl —do you understand?" she murmured. Now her eyes swallowed the light, refracting it like jewels. "I'll go easy, since this will be the first time. But you know what to say when you want to stop. In the meantime, I'm going to push you to the point where pleasure turns into pain."

They had discussed it briefly at the beach. It had fascinated Lorrin. It was different from how she topped —all she did was take lead. This would involve power play. She had heard of the concept of what Zemir had explained; about her dominant and rough preferences. The analysing part of her brain reasoned that it might have stemmed from being meticulously controlled for all of her childhood. Or, she loved seeing people on their knees. Which would be another thing that they had in common. Most importantly, Lorrin wanted to understand that part of her. From where did all of the bravado and effortless superiority come?

The officer had been very stiff and uncertain when she'd told her. It had made the blonde smile. And imagine her crawling above; luminous amber piercing to her very core as she undressed. The assassin envisioned her stingy with touch and fulfilment. How she'd make her feel rewarded from time to time. How far she might push her limits to see her beg.

Lorrin had chosen a nonsense safe word for that —something so absurd that it might instantly kill the mood, too.

"Okay."

"No," the officer reprimanded.

"…Yes, Kal."

The guard slid one initial finger within her; the laziest motion of sawing back and forth to ease Lorrin into it. Her spine curved here too, and her own fingers gripped the sheets. It tingled through every nerve; seeped through each bone.

"Just from one?" Zemir hissed.

"I…it's been a while since I…since someone competent —"

"I don't recall asking for an explanation," the guard bit. "Or comparison."

Lorrin gasped and flushed pink, her lips struggling to clamp shut as she drew shuddering breaths. Where had this cutting side of the detective come from, and why on Earth was she enjoying it so much? It wasn't out of fear. It was more like amusement. She was doing her a favour.

Zemir added another digit, and reached forward for a breast. Lorrin's toes curled and a sound louder and more prominent than a mere rasp escaped her throat. And the guard smiled in satisfaction in light of it. Now her movements shifted to a more flexible wave; the assassin could feel the knuckles hinging at each descent. The withdrawal was never all the way out —those fingers lingered as if indecisive of leaving a home. Her muscles took a few seconds to remember the feeling, quivering in their efforts. Then they loosened, relishing the bliss.

By the time she was full with three, her body could no longer cope. Her back lifted off of the bed and she came apart —but the pleasure was intense and quick. When she had processed it, her breath was already evening out and the numbness was fading. It was horribly unfair.

Zemir's smirk stretched. She'd rebuild that upward climb.

"Onto your stomach," she instructed.

Lorrin obediently turned over, wrapping her arms around the pillow beneath her. She felt it so sharply, that her entire body shuddered. The guard ran her hands over her skin; her sides, legs and back, as she pressed her mouth to her spine. So she didn't mind kissing her there. Lorrin closed her eyes and relished the sensation. Was that how Zemir would kiss her mouth if it came to it —slowly, hotly, and with her tongue? Her heartbeat echoed all over at the thought.

She travelled up to her shoulders, lazily biting the pale skin. The assassin moaned softly as she shifted on the sheets, grinding her ass into Zemir's front. The temperature of her skin was rising. The detective tensed, momentarily surprised by the eagerness, before burying her head in the crook of Lorrin's neck and reaching for her right between her parting legs from the underside.

The blonde drowned out the consistent sounds which then erupted from her with the pillow, filled with those glorious fingers again. The position was far more potent; far more lethal. Her nerves pulsed with ecstasy, getting closer to their limits —all while the guard dragged her lips against her neck and sucked.

"Deeper —*deeper*…" Lorrin groaned.

Zemir heard, though it was muffled.

Her free hand tangled within the assassin's hair, and tugged lightly. "Tell me, girl," she whispered into her ear. "Tell me how it feels."

Lorrin lifted her head from the pillow and drew a sharp breath, unable to hide the pleasure shooting through her. Her legs stiffly slid along the silk. "So good. Please...pull my hair...harder."

Zemir noticeably paused, before chuckling softly and roughly tilting her head back as she kissed her temple. "Perfect."

She moaned at that word; at how pleased the officer seemed. It stopped being an accommodating experiment. She was immersed in it now. Her body on fire, breath short and pleasure searing. Rationality dispersed, and the officer bit down on her neck a little harder. She could feel her blue hair over her arched back and down her arm, like an extension of hers.

Lorrin swore towards the ceiling, shaking feverishly before waves and waves of rapture washed over her and she came close to screaming —but never quite reached that loud. Zemir was disappointed, but understanding. She kissed her shoulder, parting her blonde hair so that her lips reached her ear. And amidst Lorrin's panting recouperation she promised, "...I'll taste you next time."

✝

Fatigue had won out before pain. The younger iman could have gone on if the events of the day hadn't utterly twisted and rung her out. The guard didn't mind. She lay beside her still form and traced the bites she'd left and the lines of her scars. Lorrin wondered if she might press her mouth to them too, but that was too far for the moment designated for catching their breath and resting. Intimate in a way with which neither of the two females were familiar.

The assassin had minded her touching the fading marks before, but now the action was rather soothing. She hummed in satisfaction, the corners of her mouth curling in a lazy smile. Sleep hovered out of reach despite her consciousness feeling like it was already slipping. Her head then turned towards Zemir. Her eyes were filled with light again. Their gazes held so seriously; so sincerely.

"…Can I have tomorrow off too?" she murmured.

"What for?"

"The promotion," Lorrin clarified, before breaking the contact. "They…they need a replacement effective immediately."

"Verdia didn't ask me for that," the officer muttered, frowning.

"He expected me to ask you, I think."

Zemir sighed, and rolled over onto her back. She stared at the ceiling; unblinking and with her hands clasped behind her head on her pillow. Lorrin looked at her imploringly. Truthfully, she was still clearly rather pale now that the flush of heat had cooled. She didn't care if Detective Kal thought of her as weak based on her reaction to the impact on the Wall and her boss's death.

She simply couldn't miss the ceremony.

And thankfully the bites which had been left were easily concealable without the need for a polo neck or excessive makeup.

"…Fine," the guard finally breathed, her eyes closing. "And congratulations."

Lorrin settled down under the duvet. "It'll be far more sombre than that."

CHAPTER 20

lorrin

THE ENTIRE CENTRAL Blades Hall held its breath.

While death was an occupational hazard, ring leaders usually lasted more than a few decades. Jerrek Burr's leadership had risen with the suns, and set with them. The ceremony to transfer power was formal and carefully observed by all of the organised assassins. In order to ensure obedience, leaders and vassals had to be unanimously accepted. No expectations, aside from Verdia Kon's influence. And though the Troll promised full endorsement in light of her intel into the case involving The Court thus far, Lorrin Raffe could not assure that the Ivory Blade wanted her in charge. She was their crowning glory, but that didn't completely stifle sparks of jealousy. That admiration and pride could easily turn into sour resentment. Who would want their biggest competition giving orders?

If only they knew of what she had planned. A lot of blood was going to be shed in the coming week.

Lorrin walked into the gilded Blood Corridor draped —or even perhaps drowning —in the customary ruby cloak. Underneath that was a plain white piece of cloth tied and wrapped around her midsection in semblance of a floor-length dress. An embroidered stark white flamberge dagger ran down from the shoulder blades towards the bottom hem; a speck of snow in, very fittingly, a pool of blood.

There had been one female ring leader, a century before her. Selena Whittaker

157

—Elf and master of the haladie blade. Her fist had been iron and her smile, poison. Lorrin vowed to be worse. She'd carve her hand into tungsten, and she'd grin a grin that dripped blood and madness.

Kon was standing stiff and upright at the dais ahead of her, also donned in red. His expression was hard and indecipherable, but there was an understanding in his forest eyes; a secret they shared from moments prior. Getting dressed in the makeshift gown —which was a simple draping around the waist for males —from jeans and trainers and a t-shirt had been a mission in itself, but having to come around through the back entrance had been in her opinion, an unnecessary pain. All of the preparations felt excessive: hair, eye makeup and lipstick. The only useful one was the cleaning of her right upper arm, onto which they would ink a white and gold bejewelled ivory tusk.

It'd hurt like a bitch, unlike her existing tattoos for which she had gone to a Maji artist. But still the least of her worries. Kon had asked if she was nervous. Had the tremble in her shoulders been that noticeable? But he had reassured her that no one else would see, so long as she breathed.

Breathe, breathe, breathe.

The assassin forced the air rhythmically in and out of her lungs in intervals long enough to calm her; to lessen the thudding of her racing heart. Because what was to stop anyone from whipping out their dagger and plunging it into her back?

Shoulders back, spine straight.

She ascended the short stairs before the great apse with stained glass in the ceiling, which bathed anyone standing beneath it in shards of garnet and spinel. She made it there without a single slip or an ironic and premature assassination attempt; to her silent, unseen relief. The window of death was narrowing.

The Troll held out a mighty hand, and she forced herself to take it. Her small, pale fingers resembled a child's. If she dared to show him any contempt here she would be branded unworthy on the spot. As someone who didn't know their place. He led her to stand at the top, just in front of the spot where a throne might sit. She placed her hands together at her middle, one over the other. They then turned to face the rings, heads high above the solemn crowd.

She spotted Char Gilligan immediately; her form shimmering as though she were prepared to disappear if the need arose.

"Gathered creatures," Verdia began, like some kind of priest. "Jerrek Burr of the Ivory Blade has passed away. Like those before him, he will be honoured on the first working day of the next month. And his second in command will take over absolutely. Namely, Lorrin Raffe; purebred iman."

It shouldn't be the case at all, because the Drakon had been tortured and killed. In that event, the succession would be postponed and decided amongst the other leaders alone. But no one would admit he'd been killed by the Unseelie. That would be a detail forever lost in their history.

"Should anyone in the Ivory Blade not accept this succession, speak now." Lorrin's lungs burned and her muscles pulled taut as she waited for the cries of protest to begin. She had no known enemies among her colleagues. Any outrage would be to her utter surprise.

Yet the Corridor remained quiet.

Eerily and crushingly so. Every assassin waited for a fool to break the silence, but none revealed themselves. Her composed jade eyes met with several pairs in the audience, and they conveyed surrender or validation —or reserved, blunt nonchalance. She'd take it. No opinion at all was more favourable than opposition.

The blonde almost caved to the pricking in her eyes. But she wouldn't be the fool herself and expose such emotion.

"Since there is no protest to the ascension of Lorrin Raffe to the head of the Ivory Blade and gaining a seat on the council, I hereby invite the iman to recite the Central Blades Assassin's Creed."

The words had taken root within the fibres of her very being long before she had graduated as a fully-fledged contracted killer. They had carried her through sleepless nights and her mother's funeral. They weren't good or just, but neither were they evil and cold. The creed was perfectly grey.

Interestingly, it was in an ancient iman and Elf tongue —she had become accustomed to everything old being in a language of the Seelie.

Lorrin raised her chin, gazing towards the depiction of the Unseelie being expelled from the city along the ceiling of the crossing and transept. "*Officium nostrum est; electi et acuta instrumenta, ad emundandam terram madentem sol rubicundus, proditorum, mendaces, avari, et impii. Sacrificio sanguinis tantum subbelle civitatis justificatur. Non parcas propter poenitentiae fraudem. Semper radicem extrahe. Macula peccati semper manet. Cultelli nostri e panno temporis peccatum secabunt. Ego autem, Lorrin Raffe, pharus esse vovi.*"

Her voice rang clear through the chamber structure as she'd been born to say just this and this alone. There had been one similar ceremony in her lifetime, but standing at the dais was different from cowering with her hands clutched on someone's jacket. Her eyes had sparkled then, as though full of wonder.

How had she envied the leaders and vassals who had stood here?

Verdia's heavy hands then rested on her shoulders. "It is done."

It wasn't over yet —she still had to get the tattoo.

But the formalities concerning her, had concluded. The other assassins would now feast. Lorrin still needed to present herself to the other ring leaders. There'd be more friction there. Especially since she had made those phone calls. Even the great Troll may find himself regretting his endorsement. Because if Char found anything to suggest traitorous behaviour in favour of the state, the blonde was going to dethrone him faster than he could flick his embroidered coat.

The crowd filed out of the Blood Corridor, leaving only the council. Though something told her that the Syren was still present.

Six males in identical robes but with their usual garb beneath, gathered before the dais. They were grave and stiff —apart from Hordor Fore, who looked something along the lines of proud. Had he hoped for this when he plucked a tiny, violent teenager from the Care Home? Had he seen the makings of a leader? He had been the closest and furthest thing she had had to another father. He didn't nurture like one; there was not an ounce of warmth in the Elf. But he had offered her protection and guidance. She'd received plenty of love before that, he kept telling her. There was no use for it now. The time for childish desires was ending. Now it was the age of war and justice.

Markus Arrium glared, unsubtle, with his jaw clenched so tightly that Lorrin wouldn't be surprised if a trickle of blood slid down the Faery's chin. If anyone would be displeased with the development, it was him.

The girl permitted herself to smile now that the audience was absent. All of the ring leaders would grow used to the sight soon enough.

"Welcome to the seats of the Central Blades," Hordor spoke first. "While it is a surprise to see you up there, it is a pleasant and welcome one."

Lorrin bowed slightly in thanks.

He wasn't going to be smiling when she slit his throat.

Each leader offered something in the way of congratulations, until Markus was the only one who had remained quiet. She had to admire his self-control. It must have been a strain to bite his tongue. He was no longer permitted to treat her with blatant disrespect. And that no doubt boiled his blood.

"Look Arrium," Lorrin quipped, knowing which buttons to push. "We're finally on equal footing."

The Seelie flinched; his ears and tail twitching. "Equal?" he finally unhinged that jaw. "You've *just* been appointed to office, Raffe."

"Yes, but our law does state that my duty begins immediately. I get to be in all of the meetings; I get to veto —why, I even get to command my ring. Think of all the terrible people of which we'll rid the city. Of course, this means we'll be seeing a lot more of each other. Doesn't that excite you?"

"I'd rather throw myself off of Sythe Bridge," the Faery said brightly.

The iman smiled, thinking, '*be careful what you wish for, little dog*'.

"Do you now have an objection, Arrium?" Verdia Kon came to Lorrin's unwanted rescue. "Because I asked that question in regards to her complete acceptance during the ceremony and you didn't say a word."

"Do not misunderstand me, Kon," Markus softly snarled. "I may despise this little girl, but it has little to do with a lack of competence. Quite the opposite. But she may do as she pleases as the new leader of the Ivory Blade. It doesn't mean that my personal dislike for her consequently vanishes."

Markus believed that an iman shouldn't be as skilled as she was; much less a female. And she had culminated that skill in a far shorter time than he.

The Troll snorted. "…You are grown adults. I trust that you will show more decorum. I don't want to see an increase in bickering and spiteful arguments. The two of you were irksome enough before."

"Aye," Sumah Hossef quipped, nodding. The Mer flicked his robe to rid it of dust, before raising his goblet of water to his lips. It was likely becoming too dry for him. "…It was like watching a pair of children."

Lorrin felt her cheeks warm, but kept her expression flat. "That ends here," she declared, levelling a stare at the Seelie. Or he'd die trying.

Markus raised his chin. "Indeed it does."

The pain was bearable. It had to be, if the middle-aged and thin-skinned Fore had been subjected to it. The design overall was not as intricate as she'd imagined, but it still needed to be filled in. The curved outline was one thing. The back and forth of that mechanical needle, row by row, was quite another.

At least she had changed out of that dreadful gown and cloak. She could now lounge in her jeans and bra; put her feet up.

"You must have other tattoos," the artist commented. A short wingless Faery that resembled something of a mix between a goblin and Troll. "You're so calm."

Lorrin held her head high, knowing that Verdia was watching a short distance away like a guardian. "The ones I already have were majik," she bit out. "This is my first real one."

"Oh?" chuckled the Seelie. "Maybe you possess a high pain tolerance."

She would like to think so. As a child, the prick of a needle had been trivial. The sight of blood had never disgusted her, and she'd never shied from violence. Bullies were inevitable in almost everyone's life, but Lorrin had been a bigger bully. She hadn't actively sought out weaker victims —there were simply things she didn't tolerate and her fists were handy resolutions.

"All done," the Faery quipped once the machine had stopped buzzing. The assassin watched the creature treat her reddened and risen skin. She would have to deal with the aftercare for as long as a month. Majik tattoos removed that inconvenience, and provided no risk for complications.

That was the cruelty of it: a truly permanent tattoo where the pain was lasting signified the eternal obligation of being in the Central Blades. This was where her allegiance lay. The only way out was death.

"Make sure to follow the aftercare properly, yeah?" the Seelie warned as it hopped down from its chair. "I'd hate for you to have to come back."

"Will do," Lorrin muttered, gingerly threading her arms through the sleeves of her thankfully loose fitting t-shirt.

Verdia saw her out; having to duck his head under the doorframe. The Troll looked strange in casual clothes; dark jeans and a button-up shirt —eerily like someone's father. But he had never been and never would be that kind of person to her. The Favoured was an obstacle —something to get rid of to attain her goal. To her knowledge, he didn't have a family. Not of his own. But it was better that way. Assassins didn't have time to mourn.

"I'm going to need you to come by more often," the Troll said gravely. "Finish solving that case, and lead your ring."

"I'm working on it, Kon," she drawled, resisting the urge to roll her eyes. Rohna had worked ardently that day to find out that the piece of black cloth was a rare composition which prevented absorption. Useful for a fussy Court member, but more so for a careful murderer.

She'd tell him as much, but he could draw his own conclusions.

The girl cleared her throat. "...Forensics reported that they found a fragment of an assassin's robe snagged on a nearby tree. They haven't figured out that it's one of ours, but I could tell. Now it's been confirmed. It does make the terrorist organisation narrative take a backseat, yet I wouldn't rule it out."

"So it *was* a violation of orders," muttered Verdia. "And you are right —all options must be explored. It may very well be a converted double agent in our midst. Let me know immediately if they can identify anything else, but this is sufficient enough for the Central Blades to go on. Somebody is responsible for two possible unauthorised killings. And the punishment will not be light."

Lorrin nodded. "Oh —there was something else. The Court still wishes to hold the *Ortus* gala at the end of the week. Detective Kal is on security detail, but she refuses to allow me to do the same. I have no other way of getting in, if not with the Guard of Madir."

In all honesty, she would have asked the ever single Rye to be his plus one. Unfortunately, his reputation would be in jeopardy should he associate with her.

"Is that all?" the Troll snorted. "Kal has a good heart, I'm sure you've noticed. She'd sooner sacrifice her life for this city and its people. That incident with the Wall likely drove that point home. I believe she doesn't want to tangle you up in high society politics —and danger."

"I *need* to be there," bit the iman, throwing him a glare. "I have to assess the scene, too, should the suspect be one of us. No one knows an assassin better than another assassin. And Kal doesn't know that I don't need babysitting."

The Favoured paused and stroked his chin as they continued down the street. "Hm. I see the merit in your argument. Well, it happens that I have an invitation, given my various connections. Would you like my guest ticket?"

That was suspiciously convenient. Had Nadune Madir given it to him?

Lorrin pressed her lips into a line. The person she wished to observe was the same one onto whose arm she'd be holding. It certainly kept him close, but it may also make him extremely careful when speaking with the other guests. Especially Her Excellency and the officials.

She had no other options. This was her guaranteed way inside, as prosecution had an unknown timeline. The other ring leaders could remain in power for longer than anticipated —and she didn't need more blood on her hands just yet. That, and Zemir wouldn't let her ask other attending colleagues.

"I accept," Lorrin answered, turning to him. She'd need to call Madam G.

"Then I will see you at The Court. The theme is Red Carpet."

CHAPTER 21

lorrin

MOST WYCHES WERE nothing but trouble.

It wasn't because of the majik they practised —there were Wyche attendees at the Hall of Excellence Academy. Dark majik was forbidden in all of Idun apart from Gehman, but it didn't mean that every citizen followed every law. It wasn't just Wyches either —plenty of Favoured citizens dipped into prohibited territory often enough to be suspiciously nefarious, but not enough to be thrown at His Holiness' feet. And a majority of offenders only used dark majik for small quotidian matters to accomplish insignificant tasks.

Madam G was not one of those. She was unapologetic, sensuous and sly. She wielded the sort of power that ensnared your life within her clutches at even the slightest interest. Loyalty wasn't important to her —she bowed to pense and who had the most of it. Even so, she had developed a soft spot for the blonde assassin.

As a seamstress, she made most of her profit off of illegal dark majik practice. Her regular clothing and costumes were merely made with the aid of it, so as to eliminate staff. But special orders were actually laced with it —in a mist of nightly poison and deception catering to the customer's requirements.

Lorrin only needed an ordinary evening gown, this time.

"*My little Raffe, right?*" the zealous Wyche cried over the phone. The jingle of her jewellery could be heard from a mile. "*It's wonderful to hear from you at last. Have you got a new order for me?"*

"Keep it down," the iman warned, glancing around one of the many stairwells of the precinct. It was white and clean and deserted; one florescent light flickering constantly; but she could never be too sure. "I'm at…a different sort of work right now. But has business been that slow without me?" she then chuckled.

"You have no idea, girl," Madam G said darkly. *"The last thing I made was a little Seelie's ballet leotard —the basic one, mind you; not even a show costume —because they were all out in her size in regular boutiques."*

"Aw, you've been slumming it, Madam."

"Oh, stop that nonsense," the Wyche huffed and clicked her tongue. *"You are my favourite customer. I told you to call me Gerti."*

"I'm not used to that," the assassin admitted.

"Hm. Very well," the immortal relented. *"So what do you need? A new cloak. A flapper dress? Perhaps a frilly tutu —"*

"—Just a plain evening gown," Lorrin hissed. "A simple, glamourous gown."

Madam G paused. *"…What for?"*

Information was a commodity, and the Wyche wanted to know everything about everyone she could. Like a second currency, if you will. Should the need arise, the immortal would sell on information to the highest bid. Had a customer refused to pay? She would ensure their secrets were known citywide.

In this case, while it was unlikely for Madam G to betray her without a second thought, it didn't rule out that she might tell the wrong person that an assassin was attending the *Ortus* gala intended only for prospective Court members and capital officials. Even not all existing members had been invited —though only on the basis that there would not enough tables otherwise.

"…I have found myself as someone's expensive plus one on a night out," Lorrin elaborated vaguely.

"Oh?" said the Wyche. *"Don't tell me you've found a partner out of this too."*

Everything in the iman cringed as she audibly winced. She couldn't imagine herself settled with someone. But her mind drifted to a certain blue haired officer, and the disgust didn't wrench her stomach. She swallowed. "Don't joke, Gerti."

"*Fine, fine. So is there a theme or did you have a colour in mind?*"

"It's Red Carpet, but I want something understated. I need to blend in."

Madam G sucked on her teeth. "*Are you sure, girl? Depending on where you are going, simplicity will make you stand out even more. I thought you said you were meant to be arm candy?*"

"But what about spying?"

"*Ever heard of hiding in plain sight?*" the Wyche laughed. "*Besides, darling, I don't think I can pull off making you blend in. You have the sort of face which is unforgettable; can't be ignored. Your temperament is worse. Why dampen that? Of course, I can create something that'll compliment that bright, beautiful shine. Something which will not clash with it.*"

Lorrin smiled softly. Flattery always got the immortal everywhere. "…You are the best, my Wychey godmother."

"*Of course, love. Now I must insist that you come down to the store.*"

"What?" the blonde gasped. "But, Madam G —"

"*I'll see you in a few days, then!*"

The call was over before the iman could even protest. She only scoffed and sulked at the behaviour to which she should be accustomed. She hardly went to *Madam Modiste* in person, for the fear of being associated in the future. The Wyche knew her secrets, and she knew hers. Their relationship was a constant battle of wits in the form of subtle reminders. If one ever outed the other, their agreement would be null and all Hehl would break loose. It was a great charade at some level, to trust someone with information which could be your end.

The slink back to the office felt long.

She slid back into the opposite chair at Zemir's desk, before laying her head on the table. She might have started banging it against the surface repeatedly if the detective didn't tap her on the shoulder as she returned from lunch.

"Bad phone call?" she murmured.

Lorrin raised her head slightly, and then groaned as she lowered it again.

Fran Denaris brisked past and clipped, "Marshmallow."

"Officer Denaris," Zemir frowned. "Cut her a little slack."

167

"For what?" the Faery huffed, turning and placing a hand on her hip. Her thin wings were stiff and straight up. That predicted warming up which Rohna had mentioned had not even begun to come to fruition.

"She took the recent events rather hard," the guard sighed.

"I think it's an unnatural reaction," declared Fran. "A little bump to the Wall is nothing to take a sick day for. There's barely a crack."

"It was a build-up of stress," Lorrin then rasped. "It wasn't because the shield was compromised. Everything that's been bombarding life took its toll."

Officer Denaris eyed her blankly, before turning on her heel. "…Then you need better stress management."

Zemir half moved to chase after her. "*Denaris.*"

"Cope," she quipped.

"…I'm sorry about that," the detective then sighed, raking her hair back from her forehead. "She truly isn't usually like this. I can't think of what specific animosity she still holds for you."

Lorrin managed an action that resembled shaking her head. "I'm the one who should be apologising. I didn't come into work, after all."

"You were sick," the guard reminded her. She sternly stacked a pile of folders. "It might have partially been as a result of overwork, but people crash differently. Never apologise for the consequences we cannot avoid."

The assassin wondered if that could apply to the prophecy, too. Would it truly be her fault if the Unseelie King triumphed? Because fate had decreed long before her birth that Idun would fall. Could outcomes be changed; could lives be saved? Most importantly, did she even possess the strength to do it?

The weight upon her shoulders was immense and crippling by the day —even by the hour. She hadn't lied this time. The way that she dealt with stress was to expel it. Since it was impossible to get rid of an abstract culprit, her body flushed out the next best thing. It had been like that even as a child who knew little of such turmoil. Stress had been a foreign problem until she had found herself entirely alone in the world. With her mother, she had wanted for nothing. Her childhood had been happy —at least the earlier years had. Distress had been introduced as soon as that majik was gone.

Rohna Nyll was the friendliest face in Faecide & Homicide. She was also the biggest threat to Lorrin's cover as she concerned herself with evidence, but the blonde decided to take all complications as they arose. She could appreciate someone who smiled and roped her into nonsense.

"Have you found anything else about that snag of cloth?" the assassin asked, hovering over Rohna's desk after forcing herself up.

"Oh right —you weren't here yesterday when the team briefed," she realised. "I guess Detective Kal didn't tell you everything. Well…after finding out it was made of rare materials, I did a little digging," the iman admitted, taking off her glasses and tucking them into her braids. "There is no registered fabric store or tailor who offers it as is. Either it's bought in a manner that's a little shady via underground markets, or outsourced entirely."

"From out of the country?" Lorrin muttered, already feeling the sweat beading her brow. She didn't actually know from where the Central Blades got the cloaks, but maybe she'd find out now with a council seat.

"From out of the continent," the guard corrected, blue eyes shining with the excitement of a new challenge. "I'll have a much harder time finding it in such a widespread database, but it's doable. Eventually. In the meantime, this does suggest that the murderer could be associated with unsavoury causes."

"So we're going with terrorism?" whispered Lorrin.

Rohna's mouth twisted thoughtfully. "I doubt it, because to afford such an expensive looking material for something like a coat, it would have to be a well-established group or insanely rich rogue."

She was right on both counts.

Lorrin drew a shaky breath and turned to saunter back to Zemir. "Well, I wish you the best of luck finding the source," she offered —and a little genuinely. She was curious, regardless of who or what it pinned. Because it was unlikely to come back to her anytime soon.

"I have a task for you," Detective Kal informed her as soon as she returned. "It's not too difficult. We're just trying to narrow down our list of suspects."

"Sure."

Zemir handed her a short pile of documents. She flicked through them to see names of radical groups in the entire country of Euradon; active, disbanded and eradicated. "Research these. Write summaries and a final list. We need to know which ones would likely target The Court and stand with Gehman."

"Can do," the assassin sang.

It was easy work she'd done at the Central Blades before. But as she filtered her way through the pile, a few things began to sink in. When she thought about it, framing a terrorist group could have unsavoury repercussions. Idun might find itself with a real threat in retaliation, or the framed organisation would only drag the investigation out further and consequently pin the blame on a sacrificial no-name to escape conviction. A benefit would be little chance of actual arrests — though it wouldn't matter in the end considering the Unseelie Court's pending advancement. All which mattered was her evading the law long enough to actually meet with His Holiness. The only non-variable.

She glanced upwards over the screen of the company laptop at Zemir. Her focus was on her own computer. Soon, the detective wouldn't matter, either. From the moment she'd known who she was, Lorrin had known how she wanted to run her dagger through her. But a startling thought pushed that bloodlust aside. She no longer wanted to see the guard's betrayed gaze of hatred and scorn.

She wanted to see it warm, and full of life.

CHAPTER 22

lorrin

SHE HAD NEVER had this problem before.

Granted, there had never been the opportunity to grow a bond between herself and another person. Either had always slipped away before first light. And they would never see each other again. Ever.

Perhaps that was the root —the fact that she'd spent more than a night with the same person. They'd gotten used to one another. No longer aimless dots in an expanse of pitch darkness. A thin, delicate line had been drawn in the distance. Now they were linked. Tethered. Forever.

If one dot was erased, the memory of it would remain with the other. There was no ridding themselves of the line which labelled them familiar. Nor of the danger of familiarity. Because when things became familiar, attachment ensued.

Lorrin Raffe didn't like feeling attached to anything. There were few things she allowed herself to frequent, but she maintained distance. One so careful that it resembled a puddle when the plunge inside would be to drown in a sea. The illusion of closeness which people seemed to appreciate, though for which they rarely asked. She assured that friendliness was not friendship; that flirting was not love. That kindness was but an unassuming weed.

That was why she was grappling with the idea of a hero.

Who on Earth would place others; good people, bad people and everyone else along the spectrum; above themselves? Why did their lives matter any more than the one saving them?

Lorrin wanted to ask Zemir, knowing that she was that sort of fool, but she couldn't think of a way to make it sound polite. Apparently, something vile and considerate couldn't stomach the thought of seeing the officer cry again.

The assassin used to laugh at tears, if anything.

Usually she'd feel nothing at all.

This new manner of experiencing emotion wasn't sitting well with her. She could barely even concentrate later than night when Zemir had her sprawled out on the bed; her head between her pale thighs with one leg up over her shoulder.

Lorrin's gaze was to the ceiling. She registered the feel of a tongue, and while she could appreciate the technique, no pleasure accompanied it. Not much of anything came from it. Her body didn't react either. She was numb and vacant, entertaining the detective's wishes.

When they had started she'd been more into it. She had sucked on Zemir's neck and touched her roughly; greedily. She had been satisfied with the sound of her breathless gasps and bitten moans. Yet now, upon her turn, Lorrin did not pant for air and her back stayed flat against the mattress.

The guard tentatively stopped, licking her lips and frowning. The assassin was still staring upwards blankly, her breath quiet and even. Barely audible. Zemir sighed and withdrew; needing the blonde's full attention. Then she moved to sit cross-legged beside her.

"What's the matter?" she said into the dark.

The dark...Lorrin herself had suggested that. But she could not recall having meant it literally. They didn't have to do every little thing in the shadows, despite it being the best place to keep a secret. No one else was in this damned estate. Why could they not do anything in the light of the suns?

"I'm afraid," the younger iman then admitted for the first time since she was thirteen. "Of what comes next." Her broken voice reflected that little girl; though fierce and irrational, the world was far bigger than what a child's eyes could see. More brutal than they could comprehend.

"In terms of what?" asked the officer.

Lorrin inhaled sharply. "Everything."

She wondered if Detective Kal ever felt fear. If she ever faced something which shook up every part of her. There had had to be a time when the iman had cared only for her own survival. The iman hoped that she had not come to despise it.

"Well, you don't have to worry about this," Zemir quipped, gesturing between them. "At least that's something which we can control."

Lorrin slowly sat up before bringing her knees to her chest. She shifted back to sit against the headboard, feeling like she would blow over without it. There were things that she wanted to say. Terrible, vulnerable things made to ruin. And she didn't want to ruin it; the thing that they had now. At least they *had* it.

"...Yeah," she agreed. "One less thing to worry about."

Lorrin was well versed in being a bottle.

"Do you...want to sleep, then?"

"No," the assassin answered instantly, turning to look her in the eye. They were closer than she thought. The tips of their noses grazed. It took her back to that cave. It was less clear here, even with the haze of the bedside lamps. If Zemir gave in now, the world would not whisper of it.

"...Hey. Do you have a dildo?"

Lorrin paused. The question was so blunt, unapologetic and out of left field that her lips twitched in the forerunner of laughter.

"Yes," she answered, sliding her fingers between the older iman's. "Several."

"Pick a colour and size."

The assassin bit her lip. "...Red. Seven inches."

"Is that your comfort zone?"

Zemir's fingers curled in against hers. And Lorrin smiled a little wider, liking the challenge. But now was not the time to push her limits. "Yes, it is."

"Where can I find it?"

"Bathroom cupboard. Top shelf."

The detective slipped away. Lorrin sat there, the flush to her skin returning as she thought of every way the guard would want to use the phallic piece of silicone.

She heard her return, before feeling the bed dip with her weight. It felt unwise to turn around, so she curled into Zemir's body as she knelt at her back.

"Open your mouth," she instructed.

The assassin parted her lips. It slipped along her tongue; thick and slightly cold. Her mouth sucked gently from memory, but the officer didn't permit it for long. The dildo was withdrawn —to skid along her chin, neck and the valley of her breasts. She shivered at the trail of dampness it left all the way to her thighs.

But Zemir denied any further adventure.

Then her dark fingers were slowly parting her sunslight hair aside, back over her bare shoulder. That hanging hint of a kiss did not fall; her mouth refused to stray from the rest of her body. So she'd sigh at the lazy biting up the curve of her neck, and throw back her head as the guard's hands mercifully wandered up along her leg to the still unsatisfied centre of her. The older iman lazily kissed her way towards her ear. The blonde flinched and tensed, before quivering as Zemir tilted her head forward to meet her jade gaze. That expression was liquid lust. And Lorrin was glued there beneath it.

Her spine curved as the leisurely thrusts between her legs hardened. Zemir picked up her pace; the toy reaching new depths as her other fingers rubbed just above. The assassin could feel it then; searing gratification pumping through her veins. One hand bunched the sheets, and the other cupped the guard's cheek. Then her eyes shuttered and her muscles trembled as she grew overwhelmed —but she knew that Zemir's stare lingered.

Watching how she unravelled before her.

"Moan for me, Raffe," she murmured.

Lorrin obeyed.

It was utterly foreign to her —the fluster of nervousness or reverence. The only person she had ever considered to be a role model was her mother. After that, there had been no one else to trust. No one else to whom to give her time.

When had she started waking up expecting the detective to be there?

It was frustrating —in the same stupid way that it felt to be unable to open a jar or unpeel a stickered label. Why could certain functions within the body not come with a complete off switch?

"You're staring," Zemir said at breakfast. It was simply bright, sugary cereal — because Lorrin had been in too much of a daze since she had woken up.

The assassin blinked, shaking her head as she realised that her eyes had been trained to the officer's face. She offered no apology for her blunder; nor for her alarming embarrassment. Instead she levelled a far more obvious stare in taunt; and ate at the pace of a spiteful teenager —her eyes lidded and lifeless.

Her gaze flittered from the officer's to her mouth, neck and shoulders. Though no longer visible, Lorrin knew of the bites she had left in her wake. Possessive. That was what she felt. And illogical.

She was tempted to scream.

A childish development deserved a childish response.

She reasoned as much in the bathroom.

"This is not what it looks like," she hissed to the mirror, pointing. Dark circles were forming beneath her eyes. Her hair was somehow dishevelled despite being brushed half an hour before. "You're better than this."

Was this internal negligence being reflected outwardly?

If there was one thing she hadn't experienced, it was a schoolgirl crush. She'd been taught how to kill and not feel before those hormones had kicked in. Now it had caught up with her, regarding the one person it really shouldn't. How would she force herself to stab the guard —if worst came to worst —when she wrestled with rising urges to have her; to keep her close?

"...Never spare," Lorrin said through gritted teeth. She painfully curled her fingers against the frigid sink. "Never, never, *never* spare."

She was yet to fail. Her perfect execution record was yet to be broken. She couldn't permit one measly iman to take that achievement away. Just because the sex was more enjoyable than it had been with anyone previous, or that her striking golden eyes were endless unexplored pools.

"Raffe," Zemir's voice called from the other side of the door. "Hurry up. We're going to be late."

"Okay, okay," she snapped back, shaking her hair loose. When she looked back up into her reflection, the flush had receded. She tried a frown. A smile. Her brows knitted together, and her eyes shimmered with something blunt-edged and dangerous. She rummaged through her makeup bag for eyeshadow.

The assassin quickly smudged it over her eyelids and underneath the curve, surrounding her eyes in a smoky outline. She defined it with a whip of eyeliner, before parting her lips for a bold red tint.

What an ambitious mask.

Thank goodness she'd gone for black jeggings and a maroon satin shirt. After adjusting the tuck of it, she gave the steamed mirror one last glance —before reminding the female there to never yield.

She felt different as soon as she walked through the glass doors.
Her entrance demanded every eye. Zemir had already thoroughly gawked earlier, and had promised an evening of Lorrin atoning for the sin of looking anything like her. But no one else could pull of her beige pants suit. And the vow hadn't sounded like a joke. The detective truly felt entitled to the crown of looks which killed. The blonde didn't even really work there, yet she walked in as though she'd started the Guard of Madir from the ground up.

The guard walked abreast, clearly a master of the art. Riding on that delusion, Lorrin pulled her aviator sunglasses off and tucked them into her hair.

"Is there a memo I missed?" Rohna questioned, eyeing the pair of imans.

"No. They naturally outshine us," Detective Burns dismissed.
The ever quiet Troll had stared for an entire four seconds. Officer Denaris's eyes grew so wide that the assassin was sure she'd bolt from her chair and fly at her; hands outstretched in a chokehold. Though the Seelie had never disclosed specific reasons for her hatred, the iman was sure it was because of her good instincts.

Perhaps Lorrin simply radiated manipulative, cold murder.

She was certainly feeling it after the phone call at five in the morning from Char Gilligan. The Syren had delivered her findings on her spying on Verdia, and Lorrin's mood had plummeted from the heights of euphoria to the abyss of unease. Her suspicions had been confirmed: the Troll was dealing in political matters alongside Her Excellency. It hadn't been an issue at face value —there could be a number of reasons why he felt the need to know all of the inner workings of parliament. But that wasn't the case.

Verdia Kon had been deceiving both the Central Blades and the capital in becoming a spineless double-sided coin. He didn't seem to care deeply for Nadune Madir, but he appeared to be drifting from the underworld and yearning for a more normal existence in an honest profession. And the governor was his key. She would sweep his dirty history under the gilded rug, and provide an unshakable reference to allow him to walk right into her circle.

It had made Lorrin grind her teeth together. She'd sooner put Kon six feet under than have him as an enemy —or some sort of strange ally. But she couldn't take that chance. In order to bring about his downfall, she would have to offer Her Excellency something more than the Troll had.

She realised that she had a trump card that she could play many times over: the prophecy had crowned Lorrin the only means to save the city. And there was nothing for which Nadune Madir cared more.

She'd do it at the gala. The Court Seeyer would have to verify.

The cleverness of it replayed in her head all throughout the day. It kept her unfocused and giddy. She couldn't wait to get out of the precinct forever; leave these insufferable people, and crush the entire Guard beneath her heel.

Rohna Nyll couldn't resist an interrogation when they both went to get a cup of coffee. Her face must have given her elatedness away.

"Are you going through a midlife crisis?" the iman guard asked her bluntly. "You look like a rich, scorned widow."

Lorrin smiled and slowly stirred the spoon through pitch black liquid. "Feels that way," she admitted cryptically. "Everything but a widow."

"What brought it on? You were dressing like a college student all this time. Are you suddenly feeling like an adult?"

The assassin sighed and leaned back against the short counter. "Let's just say that one of my stressors…is about to be permanently eradicated. I'm celebrating early. And I wanted to feel powerful today. Capable."

The way she said such a basic word —her tone turned it into a sword, dripping with acid. A weapon she'd wield against anyone who believed her to be otherwise. It was sort of pitiful; as though she'd gone through life so far encountering people who deemed her weak or good-for-nothing.

Rohna eagerly patted her deep red shoulder. "I already thought so."

Lorrin wanted to hold off a smile, but she couldn't.

CHAPTER 23

his holiness

DARK FAERY KIND were not meant to be beautiful.

Unlike their whimsical Favoured counterparts, the Unseelie represented all which was unholy, malignant and covetous. They possessed no charm; no love and no compassion. Not as other creatures understood it. What coursed through their veins was black ink and bad poetry; narratives which dictated pain, suffering, loneliness and insatiability. One constant: they were never satisfied. Like a spoiled child who knew nothing but gratification and cared for nothing but the self, the Unseelie existed in a perpetual state of tantrum and thievery.

They took what they wanted. Ate what they wanted.

There were stray pocketfuls of traitor Elves, Syrens, Trolls and Wyches who had sought enlightenment in Gehman. They too, had been encouraged in the art of pride. But still, they were creatures of higher function.

There was little room for branches of thought in an Unseelie; for a gathering of complex conference and analysis —not that many Seelie could think better. The dark Faery brain ran at full capacity at every moment. Either hungry, bored, or enraged. Hunger could be fed, boredom could be entertained at court festivities, but anger lingered. Festered. An Unseelie child learned of rage before the first proper grumble of its stomach.

Nothing is given —everything must be worked for.

There was no Unseelie who understood this better than Ixor Horjen —the last living old king.

He wasn't an old king in life himself, but his father had sat on the throne as such. With purple blood like his, Ixor had ascended as the rightful heir. The small faction of Gehman had not been enough. Freedom from the Idun law had not been enough. He wanted his blight to spread into all corners of the city; every inch of the territory which had been sliced from him and given to the imans.

Dark Faery kind had entertained primitive imannity; toying with them as a house cat did with an insignificant, curious mouse. It was amusing with a few. But when a handful became a populous, easy prey morphed into vermin. The once rolling hills; fresh springs and proud mountains vanished beneath the touch of majik and machine —of a species just as greedy with an unquenchable desire for…something which Ixor had hardly been able to understand.

They too yearned to conquer; to rule.

All of a sudden the timid creatures were monstrous rats —giant and destructive. All of a sudden, they were just like the Faery kind.

The Unseelie King only wished to return the favour. To uproot a weed.

His Holiness had laughed; aloud and heartily at the presentation of a letter from Nadune Madir requesting an audience.

He wasn't sure what was more amusing: the iman governor asking, or the audacity of it given the consequences for an unwarranted visit. What impression did she have, to think that he might accept the request? He almost wanted to allow her to come, simply to see the horror in her eyes as he killed her anyway.

But he wouldn't do that.

Unlike common Unseelie, he'd been bred to be far more clever. His word was law, because his subjects believed him to know better than them. He had plans in place for his reclaiming of Idun. Careful plans which unfortunately needed every iman alive, because his Seeyer had delivered a prophecy the week before.

He'd need the heart of one, and although he knew precisely who she was, he wanted as many as possible to witness their end. What an honour it would be.

The Favoured mattered not; that Drakon was a warning for that. What had pissed him off the most, though helpful, had been Jerrek Burr's flimsy sense of self-respect. Had he no pride for his ring? No loyalty to his people? All it had taken was a swift flog and he had spilled all the information Ixor wanted to know.

Pity that his efforts had not been rewarded. The King was no one's saviour, and he would spare no other species at the take-back.

The prophecy itself indicated that a female rivalling his influence —though obviously on a smaller scale —with a heart of pure blazing death would be the key in a lock. A speck of an iman named Lorrin Raffe from backwater Idun. He'd need to carve her heart and gift it to the Daughter. He was planning to send a summons to the girl for the end of the week, when his preparations would be complete. The assassin's fresh, wicked blood was what he needed to bring the Daughter back to dwell among them.

The old kings had written and told stories —of Her duality, malevolence and righteousness. There were stacks and stacks of books filled with hymns and praises in the old Oak Library. Many had fall apart and withered away, no doubt to Her disappointment. Ixor's favourites had been the stories. Of creation and the destruction to come. Imannity would be long extinct by that time.

She had been given a handful of dirt by Her Parents, to build a world from it; to breathe a piece of Her into it. She had weaved majik and wonder and darkness in a perfect symphony. Then formed imans as an afterthought, in resemblance to Herself but different enough to cast them aside should She grow bored.

When Ixor met Her face to face, he'd lament about the regret they must share. Court was not as entertaining as it had been three hundred years ago. Nothing else bubbled his blood anymore quite like the screams of torture.

"Your Holiness," a drone spoke, pulling him from the governor's letter. The fuzzy fellow bowed politely; wings hung and trailing the filthy floor in respect. "All is prepared for the rite."

Ixor smiled. "Lead the mothers out."

Dark Farey kind had always observed the day of *Rehpro*; referring to '*plenty*' and '*multiply*'. Aside from the royal nest, greater Unseelie could not have children of their own. It was on that day this day that the Unfavoured burrowed through a hole that Nadune Madir and her foolish scholars had no knowledge of; right in the shield they believed protected them. They wouldn't attack the Favoured —they never did. The purpose of *Rehpro* was to steal.

A huddle of female Unseelie shivered together in the high moons; their shapes defined and tall, mimicking the Elven and iman form. All were draped in silvery spider web and crowns of wildflowers. Few had wings, and even fewer sported furry ears and tails. These Faery kind were closer to Seelie blood, but it ran dark and their wings were bits of hollow ribbon veined together.

They had been waiting five months for the reason they wasted away in their homes; bound to tidying and cooking.

The mothers —wanting, hungry females who yearned to pass on instruction —only because of deals passed down from generation to generation with the few orphanages and Homes in Idun regarding little abandoned healthy babes of Elf and iman descent. Greater Unseelie needed the structure of those genetics for the beautification of their nests. Children not yet tainted by the world outside; by what lay beyond that Wall. They would be imbued with dark majik, to grow a little twisted and absurd; to resemble their new mothers.

No one would miss the children. No one would know that they were gone.

No one asked questions.

It was an unexplained phenomenon that no new-born orphans existed in Idun.

"Come, come," the drone beckoned the horde towards a thicket on their side of the Gehman border. Under the brambles and overgrown fungus, a crumbling gap no bigger than a toddler's width and height led from the Unseelie Court to the Iman District. The mothers were ushered through; each contorting and bending to fit, and whispering words of thanks and praise to the Daughter.

"Blessed be the moons!"

"Blessed is the Mother of mothers!"

"Holy is the *Rehpro* night!"

Then they ran —with reckless abandon into the shadows between the street lights. Hushed giggling echoed as the mothers danced towards the buildings. They did not know where the correct cradles were, but they would find them. The cries of desperate infants were distinct.

This was their night to be free, and to dream. Children always brought dreams with them. When the suns rose, the looseness would cease and the mothers would be but females again, to be trampled beneath their fathers' and husbands' feet.

Dark Faery kind stole away unloved babies and left lilies in their place.

It mourned a loss and signified a new path.

Like angels of death, or perhaps mercy —for giving the unwanted children a place and a life to live. And the little ones would be grateful, for they would live forever.

CHAPTER 24

zemir

"TELL ME A story, girl."

Lorrin sighed, rolling over onto her stomach as her panting breath returned to normal. Zemir's gaze slid along the curve of her body; where her back sloped into her ass and legs beneath the lazily lifted sheet. She preferred this state above all else. When the younger iman was still warm with strain, her hair raked and unflattering. It was as though only the guard could see the beauty in it.

The officer had been in a real mood. In public, she could feign manners. But within the closed doors of the lavish house, she had given Lorrin a taste of a side she wouldn't want to see. She'd bound her slim wrists with a pair of fluffy pink handcuffs found in the same cabinet of toys before holding a fistful of that blonde hair and hissing into her ear a demand to know what she had been thinking that morning. What had driven her to shift away from the image she had created and to mirror Zemir. Did she not have her own character?

The younger iman had trembled at the strong implication of compliance being a wise choice, but refused to answer. As though she'd done it simply for kicks.

The guard had consequently kept her on the edge without ever reaching a pinnacle; her whimpers for mercy satisfying for a good while. Zemir had given into the pleas after she'd screamed at the first full unravel.

After that punishment, the detective had proposed a round of roleplay —a cop interrogating a daring and giggly suspect. At least, that's how it had begun. In all fairness it must be difficult to laugh while cuffed to the bed post, back on the mattress, with a relentless vibrator between mercilessly spread legs. It was the first time the detective had heard Lorrin beg. It was music to her ears. Nothing of note had come up in the brief '*interrogation*' portion, but Zemir couldn't think of why she had wanted something to. Though she couldn't deny that it had satiated a thrilling craving for witnessing the blonde shedding tears from the intensity, or watch her flounder beneath authority.

"A real story?" Lorrin now asked. Her voice was quiet and rasped.

"A fairytale."

The guard didn't want to hear something true.

Those jade eyes held her in place with force. Zemir laid on her back, the sheets only reaching her bellybutton.

"...There once was a little girl and a little boy," Lorrin began, frowning at her fingers as she fiddled with them. "Neighbours...the two neighbours would go down to a park at the end of the road to play silly games of pretend. They were the best of friends, even though she was tough and manipulative, and he could hardly bear the very thought of conflict."

Zemir stared, unblinking. She had come to be a little fonder than she ought to of the CR employee. Observed her a little too closely. Feeling her skin beneath her fingers or directly against her own body wasn't enough. Mere touch was not sufficient. When her desire had been satiated, she had been sure that her general association would die with it. Instead it had bloomed. There was something about her by which the officer could never be fulfilled. Was it the way in which Lorrin looked at her; as if also searching for answers to a dilemma so foreign and daunting? She *hoped* it was the intoxicating way she'd call for the older iman's name, and that look in her eyes which begged, '*take me well and hard*'.

Whatever it was, Zemir no longer wished to leave the estate.

"They married when they were wiser about the world," the blonde continued the story. "She still solved her grievances with a tussle, and he would hold her back."

It felt real.

Fairytales had morals and clear distinctions between good and evil. Reality did not display such ideals; such clarity. This story felt like a recount. And the detective was tempted to think that she was, at present, peeking through a window into Lorrin's life. A subject about which she was only privy to bits and pieces. She wasn't sure why she wanted to know more.

"Does this have a happy ending?" the guard asked.

The iman turned back to her and tilted her head. "Do you want it to?"

Zemir did. She wanted to believe that some things did work out. There had to be a stupid hope that strife could be overcome in the real world, otherwise people wouldn't treasure fairytales. That fondness could only be rooted in experience; in a reflection over the past and seeing it riddled with favour.

"I believe that some of us *do* get to be happy," the officer remarked, staring intently up at the filigree pattern above. "It would be discourteous to deny those few of it. Your story may be a fairytale, but a narrator's pessimism takes away from the reward of little worry; little fear; and an abundance in love."

She couldn't see it clearly, but Lorrin's gaze was following her movements —small, subtle signs of life. As though she could watch them for eternity.

Then she spoke again.

"…They had a child. A girl. As headstrong and undiplomatic as her mother, but with the tenderness of her father's heart." As she glanced back down at her hands, the light-heartedness died. "…Life was harsh. The fact of it was that death knocked upon every door, and some opposites lose their magnetism. The male left his wife and child for the embrace of whatever God had commanded him to do so. The family didn't stay together. They fell apart, and amidst that break, the girl's mother did anything she could. But it wasn't enough. Her daughter's heart had already hardened; her fists had become bloody; and her belief in happily-ever-afters was buried with the idea of love itself. Eventually it would all be drummed out of her entirely."

The word '*entirely*' was so cruel and final.

And Lorrin told this part of the story as if there was an incentive to rid herself of it —to expel some kind of unpalatable idea about which she had long debated.

"That sounds like a sad ending," Zemir murmured.

"It's a *realistic* ending."

The guard's brow furrowed as Lorrin refused to glance her way. She had no doubt about it now —the younger iman was telling the story of her childhood. It was painful and unwarranted, but the most vulnerable that she had ever allowed herself to be before her. Zemir could appreciate that. She understood how much courage Lorrin had gathered and held together with trembling hands, just to get the words out. And at its conclusion, she still had not managed to own it; to call it hers.

Detective Kal didn't say anything. She simply curled a finger in a beckoning motion, enticing the blonde to shimmy closer beneath the sheets. And she did the thing which she had insisted she would never do again: her arms wrapped around Lorrin's slim waist after they had both turned inwards. Her head rested on her shoulder; blonde strands falling over and into blue. She didn't miss the tattoo of a tusk which had not been there a day or two before, healing on her upper arm.

The younger iman was uncertain in reciprocating initially —not that the officer had expected it —but tentatively hugged Zemir against her with one hand on her shoulder and the other pausing just short of her lower back.

✝

There was quiet majik in waking to find someone tangled up with you.

The guard hadn't slept for very long, but had spent that time watching the stress ease from Lorrin's furrowed forehead as her body shifted and curled against her in unfamiliar comfort. When was the last time someone had embraced her with wordless promise that even she deserved the chance not to suffer?

The suns' light was softly streaming through the curtains when Lorrin finally stirred, staring into the detective's eyes in a mixture of confusion and shame.

Zemir shook her head and parted her pale hair away from her face. There was no shame in needing such a basic courtesy. There was no shame in healing.

Words felt like tainting ink the entire morning.

Neither female uttered a single one; only communicating in unsteady touch and small gestures. They had taken a shower together, standing stiffly and very aware of one another. It was a first for them both to be in such an intimate space without being an all too well known, physically intimate. But Lorrin's body remembered the feeling of Zemir's fingers; she breathed a shallow sigh at every drag of them. The officer had clenched her jaw in restraint.

She'd thought about kissing her.

Aside from the pleasure of it, how cathartic it might feel to place enough trust in her to believe that every slow hook of their lips and each shudder was at her most honest. But Lorrin's gaze was too hollow and her face too vacant to accept that sort of affection and find meaning in it.

It had taken so much from the girl to say as much as she had, without crying or breaking completely. The fact that she was still up, still moving; still *living*, was a testament to a strength that the officer had not considered before. Lorrin Raffe was strong —and needing a semblance of love didn't change that.

She didn't eat breakfast. Perhaps she thought that nothing would stay down. But she stood at the balcony again in flowing pants and a woollen cardigan draped around her shoulders —her favourite place on the whole estate —and gave up on a cigarette a quarter of the way through.

Zemir stood in the master suite, hands in her pockets and dressed for work. She could have offered to stay with her; to smooth the ruffle of last night; but they were on the precipice of solving the case, and she was needed at the precinct.

She did, however, leave a note with the words that Lorrin needed.

Please eat something.
And never deny yourself happiness.

Fran Denaris was the picture of reserved concern as Zemir breezed into the office; her confidence projected too high. The Seelie didn't say anything in regards to it, but Detective Kal knew that she was trying to decipher the situation through every pitiful glance.

Each seemed to silently ask if the detective was still sure of what she was doing. And to her frustration, she wasn't confident in being able to answer.

Her spare keys had been cut, but she wanted to dwell with Lorrin a little longer. Her cooking was delicious and her estate was glamorous, yet what made the officer linger was the host. She wanted to stay for the sake of draining a little loneliness out from her life. Perhaps out of her own, too.

Rohna seemed to share the same sentiment of walking on eggshells as Fran, but she didn't pry in any way. The guards had all likely concluded that Lorrin had skipped the day because Zemir had been too harsh the day before.

"I was looking through our data bases," Rohna said after calling the detective over. "And I found something a bit strange. Every citizen's biological information is stored from birth and on reserve in conjunction with the Civil Healthcare system. Of course, there are a few cases where infants are born outside of hospitals and therefore not automatically on record. But as far as I'm aware, you have to be a Euradon citizen to work in Citizen Resources."

"Okay," the officer said carefully. "What does that have to do with The Court murders?"

"Well…I was looking through Lorrin's profile for the purpose of identifying that piece of cloth —in the event it wasn't the killer's —but I couldn't find any biological data. No prints, no classifications, no hospital records or CHC number. The only proof that she exists are her passport details, address and name."

"Then she has to have been born in the country at least," Zemir frowned. "She owns property —or at least her family did, so she has the right to live here. But it *is* strange that her birth certificate isn't listed."

Especially since she'd heard the story of the picturesque start to her life. Why wouldn't she have a certificate, or hospital records? Had they been tampered with after her family's fallout?

"Right?" said Rohna. "It's understandable if a child never got injured enough to need serious medical attention, or their parents never consented to getting them vaccinated. But this…it's as if everything's been wiped. If she legally is a citizen,

189

her information was then removed. Completely erased from all systems."

Zemir couldn't understand how any of it could be possible. Even if her mother had wanted to tamper with her daughter's information for whatever purpose, it would've meant that she faced many obstacles in securing a job in CR. Then Zemir's thoughts drifted to the person who had recommended Lorrin in the first place. Verdia Kon had always insisted himself an ally. He operated with such oppressive dignity and quiet deftness that it felt illogical to question him. But when the iman thought of it, there had been instances when their paths crossed in public of the glint in his forest gaze darkening with a sinister warning not to pry. Not to ask more than she was supposed to.

"Detective Kal." Rohna had turned deathly candid. "If it can be proven that she has a connection to the evidence found, it will raise many questions."

"I know."

The investigation may fall apart. The consultant would become the suspect. In the worst case scenario, the officer would have to arrest the girl, and live down her contempt. After moments which were more than surface deep of bonding and very slowly strengthening the threads of reliance and fayth, an arrest would write that off as a delusion. And hate would seep into affection.

Maybe remaining strangers had been the wiser choice. They were entangling themselves within something dangerous; something that would leave them changed. But the law was the law, one thing upon which Zemir had been trained not to compromise.

"I will ask her about this," the detective assured the guard. "Though she might not give straight answers."

"We have to find out the reasons," Rohna pushed, her expression softening in a way that only fondness for someone could permit. "Even if they are unsavoury, or a simple misunderstanding. The city comes first."

Zemir only nodded. If she had been asked the week before, she'd have agreed in a heartbeat. But with the persistence of the Kals and the rekindled desire not to shut herself entirely to the world, it left her compliance in shambles.

"By the way, my research on that piece of black cloth so far is pointing to the

Ajian continent. It's actually similar to the ones used in the desert."

"Oh?"

The iman had stopped listening fully, but she knew a few things off of the top of her head. Ajia was two oceans away. The closest lands were colder; covered in snow many months of the year. And the continent in which Euradon was situated was vast enough to have a wide range of weather from one coast to the other.

Why would anyone outsource that far?

Or, maybe that was the entire point.

The case was becoming more of a constricting rope. More importantly, it left Zemir's conviction about the true nature of the younger iman wavering. Had her intuition been correct in thinking that revealing each layer of the girl would show parts as dark, unlawful and complicated as her own?

Now they seemed even more treacherous.

It wasn't as though she knew Lorrin well enough to be in a position to plead her loyalty. What they had was manageable because of the mystery each had maintained; a constant pull to gather fitting pieces to a puzzle. That benefit now reared its ugly backside, and the detective was now left with the most important question that she would ever ask.

Who *was* Lorrin Raffe?

CHAPTER 25

lorrin

SHE HAD MUSTERED enough energy to pick at a piece of buttered toast and get to *Madam Modiste* on a whim stemming from the fact that she couldn't think of anything better to do. Though she was unsure of what she was seeing in the mirror. The wrap of satin was a deep red; though closer to ruby than blood, and trailed the floor like the train of a wedding gown.

Madam G in black and lavender was at her right, smiling triumphantly as she assessed her pinning. Lorrin could barely move an inch without feeling the prick of one of the numerous pins the Wyche had placed. And she had to remain still as she then circled the pedestal to outline the slippery fabric for sewing.

"Don't you love it, darling?" she asked the iman —though it was a tone which discouraged any refusal. "I knew I had chosen the right colour."

She didn't hate it.

The gown was a shape which flattered her narrow hips and tall frame —and in any other setting, the colour would have been her favourite part. Considering how their pervious one-sided conversation had developed, she wasn't shocked by the ambition. In fact, she was grateful that it seemed fairly simple in its design by comparison of her previous costumes. Yet she couldn't shake the foreboding that arriving at Court in such a bold look would turn all manner of heads.

"Madam G —"

"Gerti," she said curtly, inspecting the slit she had accounted for along the left leg. "...Is this too high? Will your sheath be visible?"

"Does it need a slit?" the assassin deadpanned.

"Easy access," the Wyche explained.

Lorrin had to wonder for whose hand.

She huffed before squeaking out an '*ouch*' in response to a moved pin —for which there was no apology; rather a teasing scold. She straightened and mused over the note that Zemir had left that morning. It had gotten her from the balcony, at least, and thinking about something other than the hand which fate had dealt her. She was growing tired of games, but that didn't seem to matter with the Unfavoured card master knocking at their door.

"Is something on your mind, Raffe?" Madam G asked, far gentler than usual. She had paused in her fussing and patted a nimble hand on the iman's forearm. The Favoured was a female who did everything large: life, business and leisure. She boasted gowns with skirts nearly as wide as she was tall; hats adorned with flowers; silk and gossamer and tulle and lace in dark, inky colours or bright hues. And when that nature receded for concern and sympathy, the atmosphere deflated and only made Lorrin feel worse.

"I couldn't possibly burden you, Gerti," she murmured.

A small smile stretched her dark purple lips. "But customer satisfaction must be at a hundred percent," reasoned the Wyche.

The assassin managed to smoothen her brow into less of a frown. "...I don't deserve to be your favourite."

"Yes you do," Madam G insisted. Her ringlets bounced as she shook her head. "...I won't know what disheartens you unless you decide to tell me. I understand your hesitancy, however. But I hope that you have enough trust in me, despite my tendency to be loose-lipped. Besides. I doubt whatever it is will be juicy enough for the neighbourhood."

Lorrin levelled at her a look of amused disbelief. "You know plenty of my secrets, Gerti. And I know yours. But you have to remember that even though we lock ourselves in such an unstable and unspoken agreement, that we also owe each other nothing. I appreciate your pity, but I don't think I want to offload. Because if I start, I won't stop."

The Wyche blinked, momentarily taken aback by her honesty.

The iman knew that if she got to a point of breaking down, she would eventually speak about the prophecy and her role in it. She didn't need the Wyche spreading rumours when she was uncertain as to what extent she wished to be involved in the defeat of the Unseelie Court.

"It sounds to me as though you have more self-awareness than I," Madam G remarked. Then she grinned. "And I can respect your guardedness."

The blonde heaved a sigh, allowing herself to relax.

Aside from oversharing, she was even uninclined to reveal that Zemir Kal was rearranging her priorities and making her question what she had been taught. A part of her had needed that hug —of that she could minimally admit in the privacy of her own mind. But it hadn't been enough to nullify the apathy, nor launch a crusade to chase a happiness that did not exist.

It had crossed her thoughts for only one second: if it was possible for her to disappear and take the officer with her. Would she want to leave? The assassin couldn't be certain of how much she wanted to escape her family, and if it would outweigh all that was to happen. But it couldn't.

Because people like her didn't get to live happily ever after.

The only warm embrace she would experience was that of death.

"I don't think I am afraid of what comes after, anymore," she muttered aloud.

The Wyche glanced up from where she knelt at the floor. "After what, hon?"

"Dying."

Her voice was soft and sure; knowing and convinced. She had tasted all which she deemed worth having and all of which she was worthy. There was nothing more after the impending invasion that could bring a greater sense of fulfilment.

"You have not found love, little Raffe," the Favoured chuckled softly. "You have only lived half of your years, and you have only lived in Idun."

"I don't need the unpredictability of love," Lorrin declared. "I am satisfied with the flickers of it; the newness of it. Once you know someone deeply enough to prevent their death and obsess over their wellbeing, it is too late."

"How bleak," Madam G gasped, the marker poised in mid-air. "While it is not enforced that most creatures on this world were placed here to find a mate, I can see the emptiness in your eyes. It's been there ever since we met. Since you started killing, I'd bet. I'm not saying that the love of another will bring back that light, because only you can let love in. But don't remain lonely, Raffe."

Not '*alone*'. Because the assassin could find that peace without a mate. Even so, it was possible for someone to unlock that part of her which would give herself the forgiveness she craved. No one could love away her past, but she might find a way to settle with it given someone's effort.

Her mind went to Zemir.

She didn't show compassion frequently nor obviously, yet the blonde felt her hand reaching out. Still felt her arms around her in such a secure embrace that there was no way that she could ever hurt again. The guard was selective with her comfort, but generous in it. Of the vulnerability she'd glimpsed, Lorrin saw that she was just the same. Perhaps they were each other's keys.

And she hated herself for thinking that, knowing that she could never burden her that way, nor would the detective consider loving her.

The gown would be ready to pick up the next day, but Lorrin didn't return to Hemmingway Estate. She didn't leave a note, either. Something like guilt had bloomed and withered in the conclusion of it; that she would dare to run just as the proverbial distance between them had begun to lessen. Because the last thing she needed was to leave a trail of crumbs for the detective to follow.

She went back to the Iris District to clear her head and get a new perspective on things. Maybe a different environment would flush out the wishful thoughts of domestic sweetness. Of futile hope and idle dreaming. That, and she needed to catch up with what was happening at the Central Blades.

Char Gilligan had only reported one arrest so far since Lorrin had arrived at the apartment, but she still wanted to scope it out, just for sake of seeing the sheer panic in the other ring leaders' faces.

The Syren was dressed in far more casual leggings and a hooded jersey over a Phoenixes t-shirt; as though she was beginning to get a grasp on fashion and her own style outside of the Ivory Blade. Her expression was cheery enough, but she was stiff; still shackled to the ideals of her captors. But Lorrin would be her ticket to a better existence. While the past was irrevocable, revenge was the first step to satisfying the burn of resentment.

The assassin couldn't be sure of the Syren's every intention and their sincerity —only a mindreader could verify her testament. She could very well rise to sit on that throne to find Char holding a dagger to her neck, yearning for it herself. While she could keep the young female in check, Lorrin would place a semblance of trust in her in a way that reminded her of her place.

What the blonde needed was obedient soldiers and loyalty, and even if she didn't readily have either, she would enforce the latter. All she needed to do was provide a reason as to why it was worth her being placed at the head.

"Are you ready?" the sea creature called from the kitchenette.

Lorrin emerged from the bedroom, her platform boots thudding along the floor. She had pinned her hair back at the sides, away from her face, and slid on a large pair of gold rimmed sunglasses. Having been limited to the party clothes she owned for something close to formal, her final decision was a simple black drawstring minidress and an oversized pink leather jacket which hung off of her shoulders. Between her lips hung an unlit cigarette, and in one hand she wielded its lighter. She flicked it on and off.

Char sat upright on a stool and stared in awe —in that moment understanding that at least for now, her position was to follow.

The assassin made for the front door. "Let's go fuck shit up."

CHAPTER 26

lorrin

THERE WAS NO dress code for the Central Blades council —especially the females. The only unspoken rule was sophistication and professionalism, which everyone took for grim business attire. A shapely dress, leather combat boots and sunglasses were far from that pristine vision. The consequent eyes the iman and Syren received made Lorrin both curious and amused. She stalked to her new chair and sat down on it primly; one leg crossed over the other as though this was a colossal waste of her time. Then she lit the cigarette flicking up and down in her mouth, and leaned back to exhale towards the ceiling.

Smoking was not prohibited, though the council were at present looking down on it given the circumstances and the culprit. It was unfathomably audacious for Lorrin to have entered the way she had; to have sat down in the manner she had. All of that could be forgiven, but the smoke was a new and deep insult.

Verdia Kon turned his gaze skyward as if in silent prayer.

The other ring leaders' vassals and attendants stood at the end of the room, sneaking glances at Char, who was idly picking at her blue-painted nails and scrolling on her cellphone. A certain leader's vassals were notably absent.

"Right. Sumah Hossef has been arrested on charges of laundering, tax evasion and assault. He has not been granted bail as of yet, either," the great Troll sighed, his brow furrowed in frustration. "And I fear that he will never be."

"What?" Ron Duncan clipped. "How was any solid evidence found? We do not leave paper trails."

"It was an anonymous call," Verdia bit, his hands curling into fists. "And that tip off was sufficient in inciting an investigation. To top it all off, a folder full of paperwork was filed in against him."

Lorrin swallowed a laugh and frowned in a masquerade of disturbance behind her sunglasses. She even withdrew her cigarette and leaned forward. "Who would do such a thing? Hossef is one of the best."

"It has to have been a rat," Markus huffed, his tail twitching with rising anger. "Someone who poked their nose in where it was not supposed to be."

"I agree," Verdia said lowly, glancing at the vassals.

They all hurriedly shook their heads.

"Have their quarters searched," suggested Lorrin. Her chin was raised, her back straight and the cigarette poised to stab if she chose to fling it. Gone was the disrespectful fledgling leader who thought herself too lofty above certain issues. Her eyes were chilling rage —as if Sumah Hossef was a close friend of hers.

She was offering a small taster of the treatment that was to come, should anyone find themselves desperate enough to sell out. It didn't matter who was being betrayed, and it didn't matter that she herself had pulled that rug from under Hossef's feet. She was about to set an example for all the Blades, even if it meant framing one of those poor vassals cowering by the door.

"My, my, Raffe," Markus smirked. "Ruthless suits you."

She clicked her tongue and waved her hand dismissively. "Bring the culprit directly to me, should you find them. But be quick about it, I don't have all day."

"Well aren't you eager to exercise your duties," Verdia murmured, looking down at her proud form. "Even if it may be your own assassins."

"Traitors are not tolerated, Kon," Lorrin warned, looking him dead in the eye. She let the words sink in; let them bite down and leave their pierce. The Troll stiffened enough for the blonde to be confident in his reception of the message. He was the next to fall, after all. "...I will not show mercy to any of them, even if the rat is found to be within my ranks. I'll consider it a good day of weeding."

Verdia huffed, and lowered into his seat, before motioning for his attendants to begin a search of the grounds. There were offices on the property as well as apartments nearby, so that would keep them for an hour at the most.

Char Gilligan obediently followed, prepared to carry out their plan. One of the vassals was about to be in for a shock when copies of Hossef's incriminating paperwork were mysteriously found in their possession.

As the others protested, the members at the long table eyed the new head of the Ivory Blade with wary curiosity. Perhaps they saw it now, that she was not going to be someone with whom to trifle. It was entirely their loss for writing her off based on something as insignificant as her parts.

Her thoughts wandered again.

She frowned at the sight of Zemir Kal in her mind; her gaze judgemental and disappointed. Perhaps hurt. But that was something in which Lorrin prided herself. She'd been born missing people's expectations. The guard wasn't about to make an angel out of her, and she wasn't going to be Lorrin's conscience either. Because when it all went awry, Zemir wouldn't be there at her side.

Nobody would.

"Gentlemales," the iman quipped, billowing smoke. "I look forward to getting acquainted with each of you. We're a tight knit unit —let's not permit a fit of envy to ruin that. I believe that Hossef was careful and prudent. Someone leaked private information. I urge you to be vigilant of your underlings, assassins and seconds-in-command. Kill the blight before it spreads, no?"

Gasps and whispers were hushed by Verdia's soft snarl.

"Lorrin Raffe," Hordor Fore finally spoke up; his face pinched inwards. "You may think that you can come here and enforce your own policies, but you forget yourself. This organisation is based on trust and years of tradition. We do not raise our blades without cause."

"What if you're the next one in jail?" was her argument. "You might wish that you had listened to me then, and sought out your pests. I'll remember to say, '*I told you so*' at your hearing."

The Elf growled. "I do not harbour traitors, Raffe."

"I should hope not," she scoffed. "You recruit more than half of us."

He was silenced with that, and the attention divided between them.

Lorrin was very aware that Verdia would want a word about this incident, but he would have to wait until the *Ortus* gala. She didn't wish to divulge any unnecessary information, and she didn't want him perpetually privy to it either. Her rise was going to be from underneath the pillars of what was for now, greater authority; not from above nor from the front or rear.

The best overthrows were done silently. Cleverly. She'd remember their rage, regret and shame for as long as she would be permitted.

Markus Arrium levelled at her a glare which sent ice down her spine. He couldn't know of her plot, but the irrational worry that he could pick apart her performance like a surgeon, rooted itself in the back of her head. She had always been on edge when it came to the Jackal Seelie —he saw everything too clearly; heard things that he shouldn't; hid within the darkness too well. He was smart and formidable, and it had pushed her to sharpen and mirror those skills. He might take it as her showing some slither of interest, but the twisted game which they played would only end with blood. She simply had to poise herself to be in a position to strike first.

And his death would be savoured, she decided as she took a drag and averted her shadowed eyes. Like a last meal.

Fore's demise was going to be quick and messy. He was going to leave the world painfully and uncared for, knowing that his protégé couldn't care less about him and that he was someone to whom she attributed none of her success.

The careful balance of the Central Blades was about to be toppled. All which the iman had done was sow the seeds of accusation and doubt. Tenuous bonds were easily broken. And the trust which Hordor had mentioned? That was bullshit. The house demanded to be divided against itself.

One of Verdia's attendants burst through the doors. "We found the rat, Kon."

The Troll shot to his feet, shaking the table. "Already? Who is it?"

"One of the Iron Handle trainees. Having them searched immediately ensured a quick discovery. There was no time to hide the evidence. I also have witnesses to verify the culprit appearing paranoid and afraid during the search."

All eyes were on the old Elven Favoured —the one who had insisted upon an innocence. It was no longer possible with recounts. He blanched and cleared his throat, attempting to gather up the tatters of his dignity. Lorrin continued to smoke down her cigarette, as the action hid her egregiously smug grin. Char lingered in the back, controlling her amusement with far more skill. It had been her, the clever Syren, who had frightened the trainee into believing her a ghost.

Hordor beckoned the party back inside. A trembling iman was dragged at the rear, begging for mercy. They couldn't be older than seventeen. There was the raw emotion of desperation in their eyes, which meant that the Elf had not yet broken them. The crying rang through the room, making everyone uncomfortable. When one pleaded for their life, self-respect and pride vanished. The iman fell to their knees, scrambling for their master's feet. Insisting that they had had no part in it. Of course they hadn't, but their wails were not going to deter the Ivory Blade leader. This was a necessary sacrifice.

"Let me speak with them," Fore said gravely. "I was unaware of this." He couldn't be certain of what Lorrin wanted to do. Though he could guess.

Lorrin didn't bother to retaliate. She reclined and leisurely finished off her cigarette, wanting to see how it would all unfold. It was so rare for the Elf to lose his nerve in public. But this was only the first stitch she would unpick.

"You would give your ear to a traitor, Fore?" Markus, of all people, remarked. His voice was steady but there was warning in his posture and slight glower. "I say we proceed with Raffe's suggestion and make an example of what happens to those who do not embody the community we hold dear. It is not every creature for themself —we are a network. And this unofficial assassin broke that synergy."

"How can we even fathom letting them back in?" Lorrin murmured.

Hordor's eyes went wide. "You know very well what that entails."

"Mm," she hummed, snubbing out the butt on the windowsill behind her. "Am I suddenly at fault for following procedure? I always thought that the way the Central Blades dealt with traitors was lenient. Do you think that others will learn when they realise that they could get away with it in the past? I know that we only draw a knife to those deserving of it, but why is this the exception?" She then sighed and pushed out of the chair, growing impatient. Her every breath and move were watched. Her hand parted her jacket, revealing her dagger strapped to her midsection. "…Look, Fore. You may value an individual over the other assassins in our rings, but it cannot cloud your judgement. Punishment must be dealt to those who break the rules. And I don't think that flogging and banishment truly reflect the image we wish to perpetuate. It will not teach something to those who wish to follow in those misguided footsteps."

She looked to the iman, reining in a waft of pity at the sight of bloodshot eyes and streaming tears. She wondered if they followed the fayth. Because only prayer would save them. Only the Daughter could keep them from Hehl.

The leader of the Iron Handle ground his teeth and flushed in frustration and rage. No other member seated at the table spoke in his favour; no one saw any issue in Lorrin disposing of the trainee. Not even the strangely quiet Verdia, upon whom Hordor had perhaps counted. The Troll was frowning at his clasped hands, deep within concerns of his own. Mulling over her words, was Lorrin's hope.

She marched to the accused, towering over them in a manner which sent bold pulses of power through her system. Still the other vassals threw the iman down at her feet, like an offering. From there the blonde noted the fresh lashings which had already been administered, and bruising of rope tied to their wrists. That could not be blamed on her; it had not been in her instructions. But it would not be worth bringing up, since the last thing the trainee was going to see was a flash of ivory.

"P-please, Raffe," they rasped with a voice already broken, shakily reaching for her boots. "…Please, I'm —I'm innocent, I swear!"

She sidestepped the gesture. Their face was obscured with their fallen hair; a thankful hinderance to an icky feeling resembling sympathy. It would do no good, and she didn't know them. That made it easier to stomach. She wouldn't have to look into those eyes and see betrayal. The assassin turned back to the council.

"Let it be known from now until our fracture that all traitors and double agents as so instructed by their own will, of someone in or unaffiliated with the Central Blades, will be executed for their wrongdoing by any of the ring leaders."

They all nodded in grim agreement.

Colour drained from the traitor's face. "No, *please*! Please!"

The protest between the guilty and the guiltless differed in at least three ways. The first, was that those who had things to confess knew of their sin, and so accepted death as the natural consequence. Those who were innocent fought for pardoning, or if unattainable, a quick and merciful end. Secondly, a guilty creature stood tall. The faultless cowered and thrashed. And the most important difference: one knew where they were going afterwards. The other did not.

Lorrin had run out of pity. Her face was reserved and cold indifference. She was no longer acting. There truly was no feeling within her mind at that moment. There was no space for grace. The assassin stared down at the iman from behind her sunglasses, blocked out the cries, and wondered at what age they had been ripped from their family. If they had had a good childhood and once known happiness. Because if they had, she wanted them to cling to that memory.

She raised her blade.

The teenager was mid-scream when she swiped their neck.

The room fell into a frigid silence at the harsh splatter of blood. Something very fundamental in the assassin rings had been altered by the day's events. By the first female leader of the Ivory Blade. And no one would forget it.

A towel was presented to her. Lorrin tilted her head and beckoned hers and Verdia's attendants before turning on her heel. "Clean this up."

The Ash Blade ring leader met the assassin and Syren on their way out. Char Gilligan was not so polite about it, and regarded him as a feral child would a tall, shadowed stranger.

"Arrium," Lorrin greeted briskly.

"I'll cut to the chase, Raffe," assured the Faery, adjusting his cufflinks. "I am not entirely sure what the purpose of your little…charade, today, but I was intrigued."

Lorrin paused and removed the sunglasses, before sweeping her hair with the movement of placing them on her head. "I'm afraid that I do not understand what you mean. I wasn't pretending. There's a very real dead body in the Hall."

"Not with the purging," he smirked. His hands slid into his pockets as his tail did the most annoying thing —wag with excitement. "It's obvious when a child parades around in their parents' clothing."

The iman frowned in alarm. The Syren's hand flew to her own sheath, but her master motioned for her to stand down. "Prove it," she dared the Jackal.

Markus took an unwarranted step closer. Near enough to be the forerunner to a threat, but not so much that it immediately rattled her. "Listen, little girl. Never forget your place among us. What you did today, though I backed you to avoid a proper investigation being launched by Fore, was a disgrace to our legacy."

A male so set in the ways of the past when the future dared to meet his eye.

Lorrin lifted her chin. "A disgrace?" Her vicious certainty unnerved him. Not a muscle in her body twitched in fear. She refused to falter before him. And she treated his assessment as a poor attempt at a taunt. "I'm just getting started."

"Oh I'm sure," said the Seelie, his eyes squinting as he then almost smiled. "I didn't approach you to catch you out. I believe that if you'd let me, I can help you to remodel the Central Blades the way you want to, with the right methods. This might be my initial speculation, but I smell a take-over on the horizon. I want in."

Char was about to pounce.

Lorrin shook her head, considering it. Or at least appearing to —because there was no way in Hehl that she would take Markus as an ally. He always held a knife behind his back, and never threw his trust into one entity. If he was asking her, he had already spoken to the others. More importantly, she had dreamt of the day she would kill him for a long time. He couldn't aid with her rise.

The assassin turned, motioning for the Syren. The attention she then granted the Seelie was left at a glance over her shoulder. "I want you to recall the feeling you got when I suggested killing that morsel. Of wariness," she stated, redonning her sunglasses. "It will be your only companion."

CHAPTER 27

lorrin

THE ASSASSIN REALISED that if she wanted her reach to gain traction outside of the Central Blades, she would need allies in other parts of the criminal underbelly. And the first place which came to mind was the meat market.

It wasn't as busy this evening, but the scent of smoke and blood lingered all the same; curling between the stalls and high into the lung lights above which stretched from one apartment building to the other.

Char was sure that she could convince Valerie to join their cause, and in doing so they may acquire the backing of most of the culinary black market. Lorrin wasn't so certain that the Syren would welcome them back after her first impolite impression, but she believed that there was no better approach than a conversation between one sea creature and another.

The Syren was surprised to see the iman back at her stall, but she smiled at the punk look she was going for. The creature wore her bright red hair down on this occasion; pinned back so she wouldn't contaminate the food. What had gone unnoticed before, was a ripped fishnet t-shirt over a bra and cargo pants.

"How can I help you?"

"We're not here for food this time, Val," Char quipped. "Today we've come for business."

The vendor paused, eyeing the pair with suspicion as she set down her blue and white chequered tea towel. "What sort?"

"I want to take over the criminal underworld," Lorrin declared, rather bluntly. "Most of it, realistically. And I need the right people in different factions to help me get there. I was originally aiming to achieve it of my own merit, but I realised that allies go a long way. What I need from you, is the meat market."

The Syren blinked, then slowly grinned. Her nails tapped the wooden counter. "...What makes you think that I have that much sway in this place?"

"Nothing, but I'm not going to beg you," the assassin assured. She was not proposing this on the basis that it was her first resort. With no one being wholly trustworthy, she was simply following Markus' example and gathering as much possible support as she could convince.

Char nodded. "She's going to head the assassin rings. If we have her on that throne, then everyone will have to fall in line. If you choose to join us now, then you will have a better seat than those who didn't pick a side."

Valerie tilted her head and sucked on her sharpened teeth. "Which sides?"

Lorrin matched her smile. "Mine and death's."

The Syren glanced down and nodded slowly. "So what you're saying is, there is no choice and what you truly crave is me putting in a good word for you."

"I'm so pleased we're on the same page," said the blonde.

Valerie scoffed and looked at Char, who simply huffed triumphantly.

The assassin didn't think that she was demanding too much. The agreement was straightforward and beneficial to both parties. Should the Syren do nothing, she would be asked again where her allegiance lay when Lorrin had succeeded.

"Can I think about it?" asked the vendor, flicking the tea towel back over her shoulder. Her eyes were icy, despite the blazing colour of them.

"I can't guarantee how much time you'll have to do so, but go ahead," the iman offered. "You don't need to reply with your decision. I will know the results of your efforts or lack thereof, when the time comes."

It was an inadvertent threat, and the Syren seemed to understand that. It was interesting to see an expression on her face which wasn't smug or knowing. Lorrin was sure that the look was angry fear, and she loved every bit of it. She wanted to see more, from those who would dare to stand before her with such confidence.

Valerie nodded slowly, and her gaze followed as the two females left.

†

Lorrin Raffe was riding on the dregs of accomplishment and even less of energy. A good night's sleep was tempting, but that only reminded her of the detective, and how she had held her close. And that was the last thing she wanted plaguing her thoughts. As disgustingly hypocritical as it was, the only way she was going to stop thinking of what was not hers, was a distraction.

The vodka in her hand was an effective one, but the Drakon across the room seemed to be better. The dim lighting blurred everything into blue and pink.

He had been stealing glances at her ever since she had wandered inside, drawn by the vicious music which discouraged conversation. It was the perfect setting: a tall young iman alone at the bar of a nightclub, uninterested in chatter and only for someone she could drag to her bed.

The assassin had changed into a black long-sleeved top; a matching cropped denim jacket; silver platform sneakers; and a lattice of strung silver stars secured over a figure-hugging black skirt. She couldn't possibly have gone out with blood stains and murder fresh on her mind.

A pair of heavy footsteps neared as she downed a shot.

"Hello there," the Drakon leaned down to say into her ear. His muscled body loomed over her; characteristic of such a creature, with his dark midnight wings folded loosely at his back in a subtle indication of their breadth. Because that measurement corresponded to another length. It wasn't impressive, but it would satisfy her. A shiver did run down her spine at the sound of his voice, though, even at this low volume; mangled by the rock music blaring from the speakers. At the very least, that would carry her over the threshold.

Lorrin lifted her chin, meeting his dark green almond eyes. His pink mouth consequently grazed her cheek and jaw, before curling in a smile. Her back straightened. He had a pair of dimples in his lightly scaly porcelain skin.

207

"Hello," she purposefully murmured, just so he would have to remain where he was. A little way past him, she could see a cluster of people who were either his friends or strangers he had joined earlier that night. Regardless, there was an Elven female in a long sleeved white midi dress glaring in their direction.

The assassin glanced back at the Drakon and placed a hand on his shoulder. "I couldn't help noticing your stare," she told him.

"Same here," he returned, brushing his fingers along the side of her face. She trembled again, but it wasn't due to anything pleasant. It was because that touch was so like...Zemir's. The bitter feeling was promptly swallowed.

"What's your name?" she asked.

"Nam-joon," he answered. One of his hands stayed on the counter beside her, and the other went on a short audacious adventure from her knee to the edge of one star on her thigh. It left pebbled skin in its wake. "What about you?"

"Lorrin. Join me for a drink?" the assassin suggested, lowering her hand to his chest. She felt the muscle flex beneath his *Timmy Highfiger* t-shirt.

"Oh, Goddess yes," he hissed, sliding into the seat at her right.

The iman's gaze drifted to the Elf again. She had more of her back to them now; her arms folded as she spoke furiously with another female.

"Do you know her?" Lorrin couldn't resist asking after the Drakon had ordered a cider. She tried to ignore that detail as well, and focus on his face.

He glanced behind them. His expression turned sour, before he turned back and shook his head. "Ignore them. I'm...I'm trying to forget."

"People don't usually go out somewhere with the person they're trying to forget," Lorrin quipped, resting her chin in one hand.

"The consequences of dating within a friendship circle," he sighed.

The assassin nodded, though she couldn't relate. "...To be honest with you, Nam-joon, I'm here to forget someone, too."

Those deep forest eyes then met her jade, and an odd understanding passed between them. He seemed experienced enough with flirting and females, but at the same time, his temperament suggested that he wasn't the sort of person who did this on a regular basis. It wasn't that he was a bad person —she was alone in

208

that label. However, they could still be a benefit to each other. She could get him out of there, and he could override certain memories. At least for that night.

"Do you want to come home with me?" Lorrin dropped her voice again, and slid a hand towards his. "We could help each other forget."

He frowned in deliberation, thinking about it for about three seconds, before nodding determinedly. "Okay. Let's do it."

They finished off their drinks with laughter and shallow conversation. It was an odd comfort. As they then walked out, the assassin made sure that the jilted Elf was watching. She made a show of linking her arm with Nam-joon's; feeling deliciously triumphant as she threw a glance over her shoulder and smiled at the sight of the fury of scorn as her friend attempted to hold her back.

The walk to the iman's apartment was sobering and brisk —the breeze flushed her cheeks and caused her to shiver feverishly. The Drakon unfurled his wings to drape over her shoulders, offering an adorable grin when her head lifted.

"What we're about to do doesn't mean that I shouldn't be a gentlemale about it," he murmured, tugging at her waist. Lorrin averted her gaze and smirked, lazily hitting out at his chest.

But he was serious. He stood patiently at her side when she opened the door and locked it behind them. His hands stayed inside of his pockets as he took in the space, as though he might remember it in the morning, and followed her to the bedroom. She kept the lights dim here, too, for the sake of that gnawing fear. But her gaze focused on Nam-joon as he reached to take off his t-shirt made for wings.

"Oh," she remarked aloud, unapologetically watching him undress.

The Favoured tugged at his wavy dark hair when he was wholly bare, before meeting her lidded gaze. He was almost a different person. His eyes flared with a dangerous glow, and he stretched his wings out almost as far as the four walls about them would allow. Lorrin reconsidered her earlier assessment, and slowly eyed his body up and down with renewed delight.

He closed the distance in a few strides, prompting the assassin to shrug off her jacket and unfasten the skirt of stars. She let him slide up her top, though, and pull it off over her head. His wings flared wider at the sight, and knocked into a bookshelf. Then his gaze narrowed on her knives. She insisted that they were for self-defence. He didn't look entirely convinced, but he unwrapped her further, raking her hair from her back to unclip the lacy bralette. Then she gingerly stepped out of the other skirt, and her underwear.

The Drakon neared, his lips parting in expectation. "May I...?"

The iman didn't move, but when she felt his breath on her lips, she flinched and turned her head so the kiss landed on her cheek. His mouth felt uncertain; even against her skin the action was tentative and careful.

"...I'm sorry," she rasped. "I...I don't do that."

His brows furrowed in thought. "That's all right. I wasn't sure about it either."

She smiled, and it reached her eyes. "But you're welcome to the rest of me," she whispered, reaching out for his chest.

Nam-joon looked her over with feral lust, before picking her up off of the floor and tipping her over onto the bed. Lorrin lay expectantly as he knelt above, her hair tumbling outwards in a pale halo.

"I've never met anyone like you, Lorrin," he told her.

Something pricked the assassin's eyes, but she chalked it up to dust. And the thought melted away when he started touching her; sliding his adequate fingers between her legs and watching her quiver. Her spine arched slightly upwards at the stimulus, and thanks to the alcohol lingering in her system, a small moan escaped her lips. That spurred the creature on, who licked his upper lip and shifted in a way that had his muscles rippling. To her pleasant surprise, her toes curled into the sheets and she clutched the pillow behind her head. Lorrin didn't like being proven wrong in any capacity. But she'd tolerate it here.

The pleasure was comfortable and easy —as though they'd known each other for years and had learned the right places to touch. For the first time, that didn't frighten her. At the times which it had, the sensations had been intermittent and electric —like a storm which startled her senses. This was constant static.

His fingers didn't move with seasoned speed nor skill, but he could be taught. She reached down to guide his movements. If not her own, there was only one hand she begged for, and it stuck in her mind like a stubborn ghost.

But she tensed and unravelled for him noiselessly —at least unconcerned with hiding how much she had enjoyed it. When her eyes opened, he was closer; with a thick arm either side of her. Under any other circumstances she would've kissed him; felt the heat of his mouth as well as his body. Something that shouldn't be, was barricading that engrained instinct. Something annoyingly earnest and tender.

What had that guard done to her?

Nam-joon didn't notice her frown as he gripped her sides and softly kissed her shoulder instead, then the middle of her chest. Lorrin sighed and shifted on the mattress as his mouth trailed downward, lingering at one breast and her taut stomach. She couldn't concentrate on any touch; her thoughts whirled around a rougher pair of hands; a more unforgiving tongue.

But she stiffened when he migrated to her warming centre, before grabbing at his hair and watching his wings spread to their full span. Her gasps and wobbly affirmations were genuine. The Drakon was far more knowledgeable in feasting. His tongue reached places that were so rarely licked, she wondered if they only existed for him. The build was swift and engulfing.

She screamed in ecstasy —writhed with beads of tears forming in the corners of her eyes. Her nerves hadn't been that riled up in a long while. The creature gathered her up in his arms, pulling her into his lap. The iman knelt over him and panted, clinging to his strong shoulders. She stared through tangled hair like spindles of web in the air. All she could see in the swimming room were those glinting eyes. Perhaps in another life she might have come to frequent this Drakon. Maybe they could have been friends. Her hands moved to part his hair, before running upwards along his beautiful emerald horns. She traced the twisting shape of them, while his hands skidded her back.

He strained against her —nudging gently as his cock tried to stand.

"...If you call out someone else's name while we do this, I won't mind," Lorrin rasped. She raised her hips, still holding his horns, and freed him.

Nam-joon bit his lip. "Me neither."

The assassin took him slowly, all at once recalling how it felt to mount a male, her breath heavy and forced. But as soon as she was seated, she raised one leg up

211

over his corresponding one, and gripped his arm. He took hold of that freer limb and rolled her hips into his. She quivered and curled into him, biting back a sharp whimper. The real thing was different. There was heat; a throbbing heat, and a whole other person. She looked up at him again, overwhelmed and unsteady, with a face she had given someone else before.

The Favoured clutched her tighter and curved her spine backwards, making her throw her head. His mouth latched onto her breast; rough and painful. Pleasure shot up her body, consuming every other sense.

"Hold onto my horns again," he then hissed, manoeuvring her hips.

The assassin grinned. She'd use them as handles.

Now both of her legs hooked over his, linking at the small of his back. The iman grunted as she lifted herself high enough. He met her halfway and thrusted into her, drawing out a shaky moan. His dark wings trembled at the sound. She strained to run her fingers along the arch of one, making him growl and harden further. A bubble of laughter erupted from her throat.

Lorrin forced her attention on this; on him. She abandoned every important and urgent issue and rode a stranger as though it was the last she'd get of euphoria. It likely was. It heightened when Nam-joon groaned out her name instead of his ex's. And right when cognitive processing turned into deliriousness, her mouth opened. But the only word within it was '*Zemir*'.

The warmth of the sex was fleeting.

When the iman caught her breath after sleeping with Zemir Kal, she would still be warm well into the night. Even if they didn't hold each other like the world was splintering. There was a terrible reassurance in the detective's embrace; one she knew from which she had to tear herself away.

And she was delusional in thinking that anyone would measure up to that which she had gotten used to. It was disgustingly selfish —for the officer to make Lorrin so immersed and enamoured that she could no longer find that same feeling in another's arms. To whom was she meant to run after Zemir's death?

After detangling herself from Nam-joon, the assassin had taken a long hot shower; worn a pair of sweatpants, fluffy socks and a thick sweater; and yet she could feel the chill of outside. The window was barely open as she inhaled and blew out smoke into the indigo sky, yet a violent shiver shook through her.

The guard was nowhere near a distant memory —everything about her was at the forefront and in bold. That amber was inescapable, and it was refreshing to meet someone whose only goal wasn't to decipher and know her. Dare she say, it was meaningful that Zemir had shown her such respect.

And there Lorrin was, brooding and fresh from bedding someone else on a whim. How dare she dream of the officer in light of her audacious hypocrisy. It wasn't as though the two females had explicitly agreed to be exclusive, but there definitely had to be something wrong with the blonde to stoop so low.

"*Shit,*" she bit into the cold, pissed that her plan had failed.

The Drakon yawned as he padded over, dressed again apart from his t-shirt. He shook out his wet hair and offered her another dimpled smile.

"Well. I take it that it didn't work?" he verified. The expression on his face wasn't hope. It was sympathy. And it was mutual.

She could only offer him a glance as she took a drag. "No."

He chuckled softly. "Sorry. And here I am, starting to think that I wasn't that into my ex to begin with. I guess *your* heart is more stubborn than you thought."

The assassin snorted and wiped her cheeks as streams of something wet slid down along them. "I hate it."

"…That you can't get over them?"

She straightened, then shook her head. "That I never stood a chance."

Fear gripped her again. Lorrin Raffe was infatuated with the detective, and there was nothing that she could do to undo it.

CHAPTER 28

zemir

THINGS HAD GOTTEN worse since they'd last spoke.

Citizens within ten miles of the Gehman border Wall had been evacuated; the officer had been forced to return to her apartment upon finding a locked house; and Nadune Madir had received approval of her request for an audience with the Unseelie King. A thick darkness was seeping into Idun, and the guard was finding it difficult to keep her head above it.

Lorrin hadn't come back to Hemmingway Estate for nearly thirty hours. She hadn't even left a note.

The feeling which welled within Detective Kal's chest was dull, heavy and sickening. She thought it might simply be a strange sense of hurt, as though either had a bearing in each other's lives. But it was more paralysing than that. Far more aggravating. It was as if the girl had stolen a small slither of her away, and would never return it.

She hadn't gotten the chance to question the iman about her records either — and the disappearance was only compounding suspicion.

She couldn't be certain yet that Lorrin was missing or had been abducted. She could be staying with a friend, safe…and far away. The blonde could even be warming someone else's bed. The guard's skin had crawled and she had gritted her teeth at that thought, though she had no right to be angry or judgemental. No matter what she inwardly wanted, she couldn't impose it on the younger iman.

The best possible outcome was for the two of them to part ways and find other people, after all. Yet Zemir struggled to accept it. Not so abruptly.

She couldn't imagine being involved with more than one person at a time in regards to the casual scenario they had had, even though she was aware that people certainly did it. She could try to understand it in the case of love. But she could barely understand love itself.

In the same vein —the absence of Lorrin's presence, laughter and even smoke had revealed precisely how alone amidst it all the officer was. All with which she was left were flashes of sultry glances and the recollection of the feel of her.

Zemir wished that her sheets had been imprinted upon so that she could lay among them and remember their every encounter. So that she could contain that memory and keep it near. Hemmingway was too far.

The detective was quite tempted to do as she usually did: to push matters of the heart back to the recesses of her mind and bury herself in work. Emotion was detrimental to a person like her; honest, volatile and easily obliterating. If she could maintain her composure and pretend as though she still felt nothing, then their parting would not hurt. She'd permit little regret to take root in their allocated reminiscence slot, and she'd refrain from displaying her weakness so plainly.

The city came first.

And that in itself was dying.

"Detective Kal," Fran Denaris spoke up on her way past her desk. She was sullen but resolute —and only for her friend's benefit, as she was still unaware of the occurring inner turmoil. Her long ears twitched, along with her thin wings while going over the empty space opposite. "...Is the little iman still not back?"

"No," she sighed. "Should I file a missing person's report?"

The Seelie gave her a look. "It hasn't been the minimum hours required. Also, what did you fight with her about —clothes? It was shocking initially, but you're both overreacting. Now you've scared her off and she's throwing a tantrum."

"We didn't fight," Zemir clipped truthfully. "I'm pretty sure we resolved it. She's not the type to '*throw a tantrum*', either. I think she's just tied up with her promotion. But…I worry that you're right about her being scared off."

"I can't blame her, just this once," chuckled the Faery. "You are a force."

The officer threw up her hands half-heartedly. "I'm gathering that."

Fran then leaned in and lowered her voice, the sheath of her sword swinging. "Kal, you know that you can be honest with me, right?" she murmured. "I know you well enough to understand you hate confrontation and telling me things straight. But you look plagued with something, and I can't relax if you're agitated."

The guard blinked, before her gaze flickered down to her hands atop the desk. "I don't think you'll like this one."

"Have I ever liked any of them?"

"…Point taken."

As surface level as Zemir would like to think their relationship was, the Favoured had been there for her on more occasions than she could count. It was Fran's good nature which made her a fussy hen, but she never pushed and all she wanted was to ease the burden anyone felt. Her tough love knew no bounds.

"If you think that telling me will make you feel in any way worse," the Seelie continued, turning to return to her desk, "then do not force yourself. Just know that I am here, and I'll try not to judge."

She would very much judge, but to what degree was dependant on the guilt. And the detective felt quite a lot of it considering their first conversation about Lorrin and how she should have been off-limits. It wasn't simply a territorial thing —a common trait of the Faery kind —Fran didn't want to see her closest friend spiral over some iman. As far as she thought, it had just been fun.

Zemir didn't think that she could tell her of the moments when it hadn't just felt like satisfying a desire; when some prickly part of her had begun to smooth over from the strike of affection and comfort. No one had ever treated her like Lorrin had —from the first glance they had shared. The Kals had made it seem as though love was a tool to be used for some sort of gain, but the younger iman had brought back a flicker of light; the budding of something which she didn't want to lose. Even if that revelation couldn't manifest itself with her specifically, the guard at least wanted to experience it with someone else.

The radio on the Seelie's belt switched on.

"*Attention all available precinct guards. We have a 904G at Code 1, Werren Park, Loegon. 955, requesting investigation. I repeat, Code 1 for 904G requesting investigation. No casualties.*"

Fran's lavender brows rose. "A fire?" she mused.

"It's not for us," Detective Kal sighed. "No casualties."

"Then why the broadcast?" wondered the Faery, frowning at the device.

Zemir shrugged. Though she would have liked to get out of the office for a few minutes and investigate something other than classist terrorism. Given the recent events with her brother, nothing about the case was sitting well with her. What if her family were targeted next? She couldn't bring herself to feel bad about thinking that she would not mourn their deaths.

"*…Amendment, we have a 10-54!*" the transmission continued, rather frantic. "*I repeat, 10-54. Code 2 at Werren Park, Loegon. Body appears old, but unclear. Requesting investigation for a 10-54. Code 2!*"

The Seelie huffed in triumph. "That would be us. You wanna take it?"

"Come with me," the guard urged, unstrapping her radio. "And bring Rohna." Fran gave a quick salute of two fingers as she turned away. "We'll take a car."

The iman reached for her jacket off of the back of her chair as she responded. "Come in, this is Officer Zemir Kal from the Academy precinct. 10-8, I accept and am bringing a team. We'll be there in ten minutes."

"*Copy that, Officer Kal.*"

The evening ride to Werren Park was settling to her nerves, but as she rounded the corner, the billow of smoke rising from dead flora tightened her muscles again and caused sweat to spring from her brow. The fire department appeared to be on standby, and a small crowd of people and local residents had gathered. The guards couldn't be certain yet, but it didn't seem like an accident.

"Officer Kal. What happened here?" Zemir asked the guards present after dismounting her motorcycle. Fran flanked her right as she half flew, half ran to the scene. Rohna followed in behind them, her kit slung over her shoulder.

"Officer Grandmire. We received a distress call about a fire two hours ago," a Troll guard briefed; his great arms folded. "After the fire department had been alerted, we all made our way here to see no casualties and no damage further than the park grounds. Once the fire under was control, we realised that it could have two causes: the result of an accident involving a flammable substance, or arson."

The detective sucked on her teeth.

The burning was expansive —it spanned two-thirds of the park and everything within the area was charcoal. The trees were spindles of hardened ash, and the ground parched wasteland. It was more of a safe place for endangered plant life, so there had not been a playground or buildings for the flames to consume. There was only a small office to the edge, near the entrance. It was metal and untouched.

"And…what of the possible body?" Rohna quipped, peering over the much shorter Officer Denaris' shoulder. The Seelie wasn't pleased. If her wings of light were tangible, they would have slapped the iman across the face.

The Troll frowned further, his muscles tensing. "The skeleton was partially unearthed to such an extent that it could have been a hasty burial. However, I doubt that this is the case. If your forensics team could look it over, we might discover that it is significantly older than a recent murder."

"This way," the iman guard beside Grandmire offered.

Zemir snapped her fingers and pointed ahead. "Nyll."

The female nodded and marched to follow the other officers.

"I want to know more about the cause of the fire," she then informed the Troll. "Have you found anything so far? A lighter, or a lamp?"

"No, but we're starting to lean towards arson," a Mer guard spoke up from behind lengthy aquamarine hair. With a new breeze growing unforgiving, she tucked it behind her ears as she continued. "Officer Lamar. The perimeter of damage is clean-cut, ensured by an outlining ring of fire resistant spray. And there was a trace of gasoline in the air before the blaze was dowsed. Enough to line the ground as it appears, but not enough to linger."

The iman detective stroked her chin. "Let's collect some soil and bark samples for evidence," she suggested. Her gaze turned skyward. If this was arson and the scorching was so controlled, then perhaps there was more information to glean.

"…Officer Denaris, fly overhead and try to see if the damaged area creates some sort of a…shape."

"Yes Detective."

The Seelie pushed off of the ground and flew a few meters. She only took a few seconds; flittering this way and that as she attempted to see it from a range of possible angles. Then she halted, very abruptly, and demanded a camera.

The personnel and onlookers immediately backed away from the blackened ground to allow a clear shot. The Faery took several, each with the flash engaged. Her descent was hasty, but even Zemir wanted to study what had been captured. She, Grandmire and Lamar huddled to catch a glimpse.

In aerial, the shape was rather distinct. There were wavy arms from the large circle in the centre, and smaller ones at the edges of those waves. The flash of the camera made it easier to contrast the browning fringes and unscathed flora around it, and even though the burning had gotten a bit wild, it was unmistakable.

"It's the red sun from the Idun coat of arms," the Mer gasped.

The iman tapped her cheek. "Land of the dripping red sun…"

Fran turned grave. "The name given by the Faery kind."

"So it was arson," Officer Grandmire stated gruffly —though his voice was loud enough to boom. "Not only that, but it's likely radical."

"We don't know for sure, yet," Zemir warned, knowing it was unwise to stir fear. Hushed murmurs rippled through the anxious crowd and fire department.

"Detective Kal! Over here. Detective *Kal*!"

Rohna was calling from the clearing a few meters away, frantic. The iman levelled at her a look of disapproval, subtly glancing at their audience. The guard made an effort to be more discreet, but it was evident that the situation was urgent from the expression of desperation which still contorted her face. Zemir sighed, turned on her heel and pointed at the Seelie. "Denaris, try to calm them down."

"On it."

With that, the detective hurried to the forensics team, expectant. "What is it?" There was black and gold tape around four posts, enclosing the square where the body had been discovered. Bones jutted out of turned soil; quite white, dry and misshapen. If her bearings were correct, the patch was somewhere close to the centre of the sun shape; once hidden beneath trees.

Rohna stepped forward with her notepad, smudged with charcoal and dust. "I believe that we have identified the skeleton in part, and roughly the era of death."

"Which would be?"

"We need a palaeontologist to verify," another guard clarified.

"Right," Rohna deadpanned. "…Sorry, my mind is in a million places because *look* at those bones," she urged. "They're too elongated to be iman, Elf or Wyche. They're not big or thick enough to be Troll, and there are no tusks. No horns for a Drakon, and it is clearly not of the sea."

"So tell me what you think it is, rather than what it's not," Zemir prompted.

"Oh, yes —judging by the length, and skull, we believe it to be Faery kind. Specifically Unseelie, due to its frailty and of what we could glean from the few sharp teeth. But an expert on aged bodies must be consulted on that."

Detective Kal rolled her wrist in a continuing motion. "Because…?"

Rohna adjusted her glasses as she pouted. "The state of the body and its site indicate many years of decomposition. This wasn't recent, not in the slightest. In fact, born-majik slows the progression of death. For it to be so dry and brittle…"

"This was buried *years* ago," Zemir gasped, looking back down at the body. A chill set in her own bones. Her mind whirred at a thousand thoughts per second. Werren Park was a national one. But now that part of it had been set alight and precious plants turned to ash, a body had been discovered beneath. Whoever had concealed the dark Faery had known what they were doing. And if it had happened that many years ago —there was only one conclusion. "…Search for more bodies within the burnt area," she suggested.

Where there was one Unseelie, more were sure to follow.

CHAPTER 29

zemir

THEY WERE CALLING the unidentified Unseelie skeleton '*Red Ray*'. Though it seemed pointless after the very first day, because just as the iman had thought, one body multiplied. The mass grave accounted for fifteen Unseelie so far; the haphazard layout suggesting unbothered and rushed burials, in random shallow ditches within a meter or more of each other.

Sol was attempting to smoulder the flames of the media, but it had become public knowledge all too quickly. The News had dubbed it '*The Dripping Red Sun Massacre: a myriad of bodies unearthed in arson stunt at capital national park*' —which was unusual in the sense that it didn't rhyme or implement a semblance of alliteration, yet it would still prove effective in rendering the city frigid with paranoia. While the media reaped the profits of what was sure to be long exposure, Zemir Kal only had two things on her mind.

Lorrin Raffe, and the *Ortus* gala. The latter being, by some fucking miracle, once again scheduled as planned for that evening. Her Excellency had departed in the morning and was due a few hours before the start of the festivities —should she still have her head on her shoulders. The detective wanted to speak with her there about the mass grave.

The blonde iman was a less straightforward case. She had postponed declaring her missing, and didn't even fathom calling. And on what number? She operated with burners, and had probably destroyed the phone on which she had once called her. She couldn't understand it.

In the shamelessness of nightfall, she'd lain in bed and thought of sunlight and cigarettes with a hand between her legs. In turn, the officer wondered if the idea of dark blue and leather had ever crossed Lorrin's mind. If she dreamt of it. Perhaps Zemir was deluding herself with such fancy, but despite her resolve to feel nothing, clearly it was at least surface deep.

The girl was stuck in her head.

The guard wanted to hear her voice. Just once more; a soft whisper in the dim lights against her pierced ear. It was the sort of grey quiet for the dead, otherwise. She couldn't even have little Lei Mingxiao over for company because she had gone for a sleepover at a friend's. It was the start of the weekend.

She had resorted to sitting through Rohna's lengthy update to the Werren Park case earlier, for fear of being consumed by her musings.

All of the remains were around the same stage in decomposition, indicating that they had been killed and buried together. She estimated their age to be one century and a half —from the Sekon Idun War. That fact had sent chills down her spine. Could her grandfather have played a part in it?

Still Rohna needed to consult another professional.

So Zemir had to bury herself in her other cases instead —with little yield from the terrorist group stakeouts and no progress on the black piece of cloth. It was now that she needed the younger iman. Though upon an idle search of group emblems, she stumbled upon a curious note of daggers.

Tattoos, robed ceremonies and conspiracies.

One twisting blade in particular bore a striking resemblance to the one which was Lorrin's newest addition to her canvas. A white and gold tusk, like that of an elephant. The officer hadn't spared it much thought, since it seemed to hold no meaning besides aesthetic pleasure. But hand in hand with the dagger at her ankle and the one pinned to her denim jacket, the guard was left to ponder questions. She would get an answer from her the next time they'd meet.

Assassins —the culprits she had suspected initially —used daggers, pistols and swords. It wasn't solid speculation, since Zemir was sure that Lorrin could wield a knife regardless, but when she thought of her mannerisms and character, she turned into a two sided coin. One was kind and drunkenly friendly. The other was like the expression she'd seen at The Court; cautioning and deadly. The look of someone who had claimed a life before. But the detective knew of her past. That side to her could have stemmed from years of mistreatment. Self-defence did not paint her a serial killer.

Besides —why would Verdia Kon recommend an assassin to the Guard of Madir? The job description hinged on death, and all Lorrin had done was help to seek justice. Despite no information showing of her in their systems, the younger iman just couldn't possibly be a stealthy killer. When on Earth would she find the time to do it —Zemir had been with her for most of their partnership.

She banished the thought.

Yet her fingers itched to dial the last number the younger iman had used. It felt futile, but…there was nothing for her to lose.

Back in her apartment, her most appropriate evening suit on a hanger on the closet doors, she paced the space in her undergarments and called the number in her recents. After a beat of silence, her eyes went wide.

It rang. There was no answer, but it rang. Which meant that the phone was unbroken, and that Lorrin Raffe hadn't meant to disappear. It filled Zemir with adequate relief, though the worry remained. She would file that report.

But it was enough to eye the dark suit of velvet with silvery embroidered swirls akin to the ones decorating the coat of arms before her, and not dread what might come in a few hours.

As someone who had been raised in The Court and its culture, attending as a guest was lacklustre. Of course, she was not actually going to the gala as an invited individual. That made it more palatable. The main event was to be held at Madir Manor and its surrounding towers —further away from Sythe River as possible.

She hadn't ridden there on her motorcycle, to her annoyance, because her suit might have gotten ruined. Like some sort of commoner, she had taken the ferry and then called on a Yuber.

The conifer trees lining the paved driveway to a mammoth of a building were wrapped in small lights. On the path itself, a red carpet had been unrolled. The air smelled of warm Winter Solstice despite it being Summer, and was thin and crisp. And some Maji or Favoured had riddled it with tiny spores of light and glitter, to add to the majik. The suns were yet to set at this hour, which bathed the scene in warm gold.

In all, the setting was flawless. Not a leaf out of place.

As Zemir found her way to the entrance for the Guard of Madir, a few guests were already wandering inside for dinner or dawdling for photographs. Decked in extravagant jewels and fabrics, the only goal was to flaunt their wealth and dine in close proximity to Her Excellency.

The guard slipped inside through the staff doors to find a few of her fellow officers gathered already —some changing only now, and others briefing. They had been given only one guideline on clothing: something adequately decadent, in dark colours. The attendees had been told to stray from black, indigo, midnight and royal blue, so as not to cause confusion.

The detective stood admired: she wore a deep-necked, tucked-in silk blouse and fitted trousers beneath an outer coat of sorts which flared at the waist into an A-line train. Along the collars and hem were those swirls of silver and dusting of glass stones. She had pinned her freshly curled hair into a loose bun; the deviant curls framing her face and brushing her nape.

Fran Denaris hadn't been assigned to security, so Zemir was alone. She would have no excuse to turn Petre and their parents away. Hopefully her brother's wife Jocelyn would be there —to smooth the ruffling. Such was her only talent.

No one knew of her familial ties with The Court, but she knew it inevitable for the Kals to be at the gala. But she didn't possess the nerve to face them. Not tonight. Likely not ever.

She wasn't listening to the Academy Chief as he went over their duties for the gala; her attention was scattered and mostly rooted in the mistake that the event would reveal itself to be.

Her eyes tried not to soak in the interior of the manor after the officers had been dismissed and fitted with earpieces. But it was blinding.

As expensive as it had appeared outside, the ballroom and dining tables were decorated as though for a grand wedding. Giant bouquets of ivy, white lilies and orchids hung from the ceilings, sat on the white and gold tablecloths, and on the pedestals in all corners of the room. More light spores floated overhead, while strings of light were hung from one doorframe to another. Suits of ancient armour were displayed on the draped walls; gleaming and protected by majik shields. And at the dais at the northernmost part of the ballroom, sat something resembling a throne. Thinly veiled by a wide gilded Goldspire Ginkgo dripping with teardrop diamonds on thread, it blended...less than seamlessly into the décor.

Above it, was an arch of two Drakon sculptures in their lost alpha form; long wingless bodied serpents dancing into an embrace with manes of fur and fearsome snouts. Absolutely detailed and commissioned only to honour Nadune Madir's roots and ancestors. There were rumours that the governors had descended from the Favoured creatures so long ago that only drops of that blood remained in their veins, permitting them to live ten to twenty years longer than the average iman.

Zemir was sure that it was the work of her Seelie physicians using restorative majik at the cost of their own lifeforce. The vast difference between the species' life spans was likely what justified it in the governor's mind.

Even now the small string ensemble was weaving a slow melody to act as a soft filler to the otherwise chatter-sprinkled silence. It was sweet and Elven, but it sparked memories of The Court that she'd rather forget. Like a hive, the district shared a taste in that lulling music; in the rich and small portioned food; the bright and glinting attire; and the swept corruption. Every member knew of the sin, and every member turned the other cheek.

It was enough to spurn her appetite.

Instead she observed every guest who arrived through the doors closest to her. Every frill of tangerine, gold, snow and emerald. Their ambitious sense of style had not changed, even with the general simplicity of the theme. The urge to outdo one's neighbour went unstifled.

No member stood out to her at first glance, though —it was all smiles and snorting laughter. The bickering was poison to her ears, but she had to filter and endure it for the sake of Her Excellency and her damned pride. The night needed to go off without a hitch. The Kals were nowhere to be seen. Yet.

It was going to be a long night. She was permitted but one glass of champagne. And she decided to drink it now, despite the early hour. She swiped one from one of the glittering side tables.

A few minutes later, the manor was filled with the majority of invited guests. And Nadune Madir and an attendant emerged from the curtains behind the golden tree. She wore a plain one piece suit in classic ivory, and from the collars of her jacket was a train of her own. On the back, the coat of arms was embroidered. The only overly showy piece to her garb was the large pin at the top of her gathered hair which resembled a bronze flame.

The band played a short fanfare. A Troll was holding up her arm, guiding her movements. Zemir frowned and wondered what the Unseelie King had done to her at court. She was alive, at the least, but evidently she had not left unscathed. Her usually coloured face was pale, grave underneath the small smile she wore. Her spine was as stretched and straight as a pole —in a way which made her walk stiff. To the untrained eye, she was the picture of snobby elegance.

"Dear guests and candidates," the governor began when all attention had been drawn to her, with the aid of a golden microphone. Even that was bedazzled. "It is my great pleasure to welcome you to our closing gala in celebration of *Ortus*. Now that the traditional ceremonies are out of the way, it is time to reward your efforts. And I know that this year is a sombre occasion, so let us keep those who could not be with us in our thoughts and hearts, and know that the Daughter keeps them in paradise greater than our humble court. So go forth in love and dignity, and welcome to The Court."

Respectable clapping rippled through the crowd. Her Excellency then waved her hand in the most subtle movement after the microphone had been taken by her attendant. The consequent dispersing meant the start of food being served.

The boring portion of the evening.

When the guard had reached halfway through the tall flute, there was still no sign of specifically severe *sehrahs* nor of *shervanis*. It was a very good thing, but it continued to fuel a sense of anxiety since she had not yet pinned them.

The atmosphere was stifling.

Zemir tugged on the thin collar of her trailing coat, clicking her tongue. She should have returned it to the store and spoken to the tailor. The trousers and outer garment were a touch too tight, and hugged in on her hips and thighs. Because Daughter forbid she should be mistaken for a male.

The officer drew her crystal flute to her lips again to take a sip of champagne. And as she did so, her line of sight rose and fell on a familiar tall blonde and a gown of an interesting shade of red by the foot of the dais.

She cringed. How oddly becoming.

Lorrin Raffe's jade gaze shifted around the room before catching hers. At first, the officer could do nothing. Her muscles refused to recall their function, and her expression likely resembled dumb awe. *Where had she been.* That was supposed to be the only thought. Yet she found joy invading her anger; relief flooding her worry; and a sudden and disgusting urge to draw the blonde towards her.

Sweat beaded her brow as she forced her face to reflect an expectant look. There was a beat of hesitancy. Then a crafty smile stretched Lorrin's matching garnet lips. She raised her own flute, in a knowing, taunting salute.

Her neckline was low and gave a view of the middle column of her chest. The gold and white tattoo on her upper arm was visible and glittering; bringing back the question that had been forcibly pushed down.

Zemir gritted her teeth. *Fucking bitch.*

Then Lorrin set her glass on a passing silver tray, and turned to begin stalking towards her. The detective's eyes widened and her throat turned dry despite her relentless swallowing. Though she attempted to keep her composure —she stuck one hand in her pocket and leaned into one hip.

Unfortunately, the intimidation was slightly lost on the receiver.

The blonde's smile held as she paused before the guard —even more so when she glanced over her suit. To her irritation, Zemir couldn't stop her own gaze from raking down the length of ruby cloth and the slender leg exposed beneath it.

"You look stunning, Officer Kal," Lorrin purred, inclining her head.

Such brazen shamelessness. The guard shifted slightly in her stance, still feigning disinterest. "...Raffe," she returned, keeping her expression flat.

There was a bit of a harsh pause afterwards, as if waiting to be filled with a compliment in exchange. But the detective could not bring herself to give it.

"That is so like you," laughed the girl, understanding her bite. "Even now, so ready to remind me of your displeasure."

Lorrin had chosen her words carefully. She knew precisely which chords to strike, and how to play Zemir like an instrument. It was *infuriating*.

"Why are you here," the older iman interrogated, lifting her chin as she took a step forward. If she was going to ignore the disappearance issue so blatantly, then the guard would too. "I thought I made it quite clear —"

"I'm here as a plus one," answered the girl. Unbridled sass spread, as did her grin. "I believe you know Verdia Kon."

The officer followed her line of sight. That damned Troll. He stood beside a cluster of officials with a drink in hand. He appeared at ease; so naturally among them that he might have been one himself. It was unclear as to why that bothered her so. Maybe it had more to do with Lorrin being obliged to be with them, on display like some sort of accessory.

"What have you come for, Lorrin Raffe?" Zemir reiterated her question. She was serious —unnervingly so. The younger iman glanced down at her suede heels before daring to return her gaze with matched warning.

"...To rectify."

CHAPTER 30

her excellency

midday, hours prior…

NADUNE MADIR HAD lived her entire life at a court of sorts, but she had never encountered the likes of the Unseelie. As Idun's governor she was familiar with the lawless and the vile, but Gehman was a new wave of depravity.

The journey had been fine —as was every ride in that egregious squadron of cars —and the greater part of the district was in fact mystically beautiful. She had wondered where the citizens were, as she had not seen any among the mushrooms and trees. It was abundantly clear as to why that was when she and her attendants stood at the entrance of the King's throne room.

The castle, or something similar, was far larger on the inside than it appeared; its wide, arched ceilings soared to heights of ancient turreted palaces but was only a stone fortress of three stories. The air was damp and musky with the scent of something the iman would rather not name, and all light of the suns was almost blocked by large drapings of thick black tulle.

It was unbelievably better that way. So that she could attempt to ignore the huddles of erotic displays about the space. It wasn't easy —the laughter, rasps and moans writhed with the music and chorused in the fog of smoke and humidity.

But her eye passed it all and arrowed to Ixor Horjen. He sat sprawled on the chair carved out of a single oak trunk in nothing but low slung leather trousers and surrounded by a swarm of Unseelie. His ropes of coiled dark hair trailed the floor, tangling in itself and between his lovers —smiling, leashed things too thin to have the strength to fly with eyes large enough to survey the Loegon delegation. Ixor's visage bore more of a likeness to imans, but his teeth too were sharp and his longer ears pointed and drooped. He had two pairs of wings shaped like a Drakon's but appearing moth-eaten and twice as large. He carried them due to his great height; taller than Troll's.

And atop his head, secured by the tight curls of raven hair, was a large twisted jewelled crown of iron. His set sapphire eyes were feline, just like his form. They commanded the room in such a way that it felt as though everything might stop merely from a subtle blink.

The Loegon delegation trembled beside her; Seelie, Troll and iman alike. The King struck fear in all.

Slender hands slid across every inch of his light grey skin —slowly, in a show. They even ventured over clothing, especially the barely covered female who sat astride one of his thighs with her back to the guests and hand between his covered legs. She threw a wicked smile over her bare fuchsia shoulder as her translucent sheer dragonfly wings quivered with anticipation.

"Your Holiness," the iman governor bit. She had never once allowed for her officials to speak on her behalf.

The Unseelie King set down his goblet and offered a curl of his lips. "Your Excellency," he returned the sentiment. "What a surprise it is to see you here. If I had known to be expecting guests, I might have cleaned up a bit."

Nadune huffed. It was a test. A very tasteless one.

The disrespect was in fact a warning for her to remember where she was and who held the power right then. Just because a treaty of peace had been signed for their districts, it did not mean that it would remain honoured.

"...Is your court usually in this state?" she inquired dryly.

"Every minute of every day," he purred, tugging on something silver. It was a thin

230

chain connecting to the bust of the sheer gossamer draping and collar of the female who sat in his lap. It shifted her forward, so she might start kissing his temple. "Is it not to your tolerance?" Ixor murmured. "Perhaps it is not what you do in that little city of yours, but you can try to be accommodating, can't you?"

"Each peoples has its traditions," the governor replied, not knowing where to keep her gaze. "And I was taught to respect tradition."

His eyes stayed trained to her. "I'm so glad we could reach a compromise." Then he leaned back a little further, fully lounging. "Now, speak. What is it you requested an audience for, exactly?"

The Unseelie enjoyed games. Imannity existed only to amuse him.

"You already know, Your Holiness."

He didn't move a muscle. "I'm afraid I do not quite understand. I never leave my *prison*, you see." The viciousness was left in the emphasis alone; those eyes were cold and lifeless. "You have to explain yourself, madam governor, in full. Or else I'll lose my patience, and do this."

He leisurely produced a thin longsword from the armrest of the throne, and struck the Faery closest to his other side so swiftly that the only evidence of it being done was the body thudding down the steps from the dais.

Nadune flinched at the sight of the bleeding corpse —as did some of her attendants, but all held their tongue. Her heart ached for such a meaningless and unwarranted slaughter, and she silently offered a word of prayer for the soul. Such was how she had been raised.

"To *you*, if it wasn't clear," the King clarified, handing the sword to another subject who promptly cleaned the blade along a cloth and motioned for the body to be taken away. It was all resolved within a matter of moments.

"You need not demonstrate your famed nature to me," the iman assured. Her stomach turned, more so than she had anticipated.

The King pouted. "Really? Then you should have told me beforehand. Then I would not have slain my most prized saddle."

"They were your beloved prize, milord?" the female on his leg whined.

"Don't fret, pet. You are, now," he whispered, glancing towards her for the first time. He offered her a smile with his mouth only; one which lacked warmth and assurance. Still she simpered and dared to steal a kiss.

They spoke of death and ends so casually, as if it was slumber. To immortals, she imagined that this was indeed the outlook. Lives meant nothing but little to them, and excessive culling was a sport. It was done out of boredom, as opposed to wretched sacrifice or justice.

Her Excellency cleared her throat. "One of your citizens broke the shield and the Wall. Or tried to, in regards to the latter. There's a fracture on the surface."

The King's sharp eyes flicked right back to her. "Oh? Is that so. I don't believe that I have sufficient knowledge of this. Otherwise no such disaster would have occurred. I will speak with my general at once, madam governor."

His horde of Unseelie giggled.

Nadune Madir sighed, understanding how stupid he was attempting to make her look. Ixor was no fool himself, and he wasn't about to confess outright to being a threat. But she would yank the truth from him, because at least he could not lie. He had not lied all of this time. But his words were no trick; he had known to some extent of the scheme.

"I realise that I have taken much of your time, Your Holiness," she said, eyes narrowing. He mirrored the action.

"Indeed, Your Excellency."

"Thus I shall state my point."

"*Finally*," he groaned, then shifting into the movements of his new favourite. She stroked him lightly; her hands purposefully grazing unseemly parts of him, while her attention was both on him and the governor. She didn't possess irises, so her gaze were two voids of gold, yet her stare could not be ignored.

Nadune put her hands on her hips and parted her feet. "...You are frightening my citizens. I need you to stay away from that Wall."

The King showed his teeth. "Fuck your citizens —their wellbeing is not my responsibility, and you cannot confine my realm any further than you already have. I will have my people go wherever they please."

"Then I will have *my* people shoot them down."

Ixor straightened. And with that development, the vast throne room stilled. Quietened. The rough melody of flutes, harps and drums ceased. There was not a drawing of breath or beat of a wing. Nothing moved and all gazes were trained on him and Nadune. Then the King rose from the trunk, tugging his pet along behind him after she had climbed down, and gingerly descended the stairs.

He stopped short of a meter from the delegation, but he seemed to have grown further between that time. He towered so that the iman and her attendants had to lift their heads to peer at his sneer.

The Unseelie in the chained garments lingered obediently, and hung her head in reverence. But she bore his sword in one hand behind her back.

"You dare to threaten my Faeries after I showed you grace in accepting your daft request?" the King asked the governor. His voice was quiet and gravelly. Controlled, for now. "I almost turned it down entirely for the sheer nerve you displayed in requesting. You are aware that that it is not how it's done?"

"I understand that you only give audience to those you invite," Nadune held her ground, furrowing her eyebrows. "I am grateful for your cooperation."

The Unseelie snorted, but it was now with unbridled disgust. "I do not think that you understand at all, Your Excellency. The last creature who showed up here without my invitation was sent back as but a hacked head in a pretty box."

A violent shiver ran up the iman's spine as her anger mounted. "You can't do that to me. The treaty clearly states —"

"Can't..." he interjected, pulling on the chain, "or won't?"

In a rarity, Nadune found no words.

"You have a lot of fayth," murmured the King. He still had not altered his tone. "And I have little interest. I had hoped that this would be far more amusing, but you have exhausted me. You should leave, while I still possess abundant mercy."

The governor winced and clicked her tongue, still not fearful but now growing nervous. It wasn't so much that he might kill her and the delegation, but that her death would not even ensure Idun's safety. She had to make Ixor see a reason to keep her and the city alive.

The slight woodland Faery at her side hurriedly whispered in her ear. There was but one way to subdue the Unfavoured, in a simple capacity.

The Unseelie was moving to turn back to his throne —and in her desperation, Her Excellency made a grave decision.

"Your Holiness," she implored, "I want to make a bargain."

He paused, as did the world with him. His subjects tilted their heads in utter fascination, and the saddle by his side stiffened; her eyes widening with alarm. It took no genius to realise that her hasty offer was most nefarious. If not at her own expense, it was at this court's. But the governor was left with no other choice. She needed security —especially for the weekend. And she would place herself in the path of the King's wrath for her people.

Ixor Horjen stared down at the iman a moment, at an impasse. The tension in his handsome face eased, but the trouble in his eyes didn't dissipate. "...Are you certain?" he asked, but it came off more as an accusation.

His small semblance of consideration was almost laughable, but conversely it reinforced the severity of the circumstance. Because just as it bound him, so would it bind her. Still, Nadune nodded.

"I will give you one chance to retract. State your terms," he huffed.

"You will do no harm to the Wall, and I want no disturbance this night."
The King sucked on his teeth. His gaze was largely unreadable, and no light shone within it. "...Did you experience the disturbance *last* night?" he asked cryptically. "Something about suns and flames. I imagine that it came as quite the shock, but I wish to have the bodies of my fallen returned to me. And should I find a single one of my diligent Faeries returning in the coming days with the slightest mar from gunpowder or arrowheads, you will *beg* for death."

Her Excellency froze. The Werren arson case had been his doing after all. She should have guessed that he wanted the bodies reburied in Gehman, even after all of these years. The governor was not so proud that she absolved herself from due blame and accountability for the massacre, but she would not admit her role. Nor that of her predecessors.

She averted her line of sight, marginally ashamed. But her voice did not falter. "Are those your terms, then?"

"Yes."

The Faery warned her to consider his wish. It would be difficult to explain the law and intent of a bargain to the citizens for such a high profile case. But it was too late for that. The public were aware that she had come here, and they knew that the skeletons were Unseelie. It held enough plausibility, even though The Court would be the ones to bear the impending heat as to the origins of the mass grave. *Graves* —plural.

Nadune thrust out her hand. "Then let us seal it."

A glimmer of mischief passed over his visage.

He neared and bowed slightly, before extending his bony arm. His hand enclosed hers completely; uncomfortably. Then the warmth of majik seared their clasp, and with it engraved a carving into their skin. She felt it on her back —scarlet blood seeped through her pristine white coat. To bear the pain she bit down on her lip and accepted another Seelie's soothing majik spreading from her shoulder.

Violet dripped from Ixor's back as he clenched his jaw as well; to his trousers.

When the light between their palms faded, the King withdrew and tugged his pet along, giving Nadune Madir the view of their contract. It took the form of a curling serpent from the bottom of the nape to the small of his back, surrounded by varied phases of the moons and six-point stars.

The blood beneath her suit was still warm. She gripped onto two attendants as she glared up at the throne. Her knees would falter should she walk on her own.

"It is done," the Unseelie said over his shoulder. "Depart from here. *I* will do no harm to your precious fence. Enjoy your day of *Ortus*, madam governor."

He was grinning then —fully.

CHAPTER 31

lorrin

THE BASTARD HAD left his cellphone number. She'd called it twice.
On a little canary sticky note pressed to the microwave, Nam-joon had added his
Instantgram handle and '*thanks for the help. I may not have been able to return
the favour, so call me if you figure out how I can. P.S. It doesn't need to be sex.
We can just talk.*' She had actually laughed, and pocketed it. He was soothing in
a different, silly way. She might befriend him after all.

It was an odd thing to remember while poised tentatively before the detective.
Perhaps it stemmed from the stab of reproach. She had been wrong. That was a
rarity. But she concluded that it would not matter, for the Unseelie King would
come for her heart and Zemir would be dead.

"…To rectify?" the officer repeated.

She was so beautiful. Since the moment they'd met, Lorrin had thought so. Today
the effort was minimal, yet the result unparalleled. Her lips were rosewood and
unpainted. It was a grand shame that they had never managed that kiss. Now the
guard would need disposing of without her having had a taste.

Lorrin was ready to do it —to end her.

Or so she was sure. The day had been spent in front of a mirror, uttering the
phrase '*Never spare, never yield*' over and over until she'd convinced herself to
draw a blade. It would be quick and without feeling. And she would only hope

that Zemir ended up in paradise.

"I find myself accumulating…a few misdeeds," explained Lorrin. "Being here will help me to atone for them."

"How."

Rage was clearly hindering her ability to say things intended to be questions. Her words were blunt, short and unsurprising. They hurt in a way Lorrin did not wish to give gravity and meaning.

It had been a taxing day. The council had quickly dwindled to her, Kon, Fore and the Jackal Seelie. None had been foolish as to point fingers, but the Troll had promised strong words. He'd get them later, after her meeting with Nadune Madir. If he was lucky. Fore was crumbling, and the assassins were turning to the only person who felt trustworthy in such uncertain times: Verdia.

Char had recreated her scheme, ensuring three more executions. In truth, they had not come at a better time —Lorrin had managed to use the gala as an excuse for her haste. The Troll was keeping a close eye on her, but she wasn't going to do anything to him here. Tonight was for Zemir Kal.

"You'll see," was the assassin's answer.

She then turned to leave, but was stalled by the guard's loud and sudden intake of breath. Her body frosted; her eyes were glued to a small group across the room. They wore striking pale garments of glittering satin and tulle, bore no smiles, and were inimanly well-groomed. The picture of chilling perfection.

The girl opened her mouth. "Who are they —?"

"F-*Fuck*," Zemir choked out, before her adrenaline kicked into high gear and she bolted from her post. That was when Lorrin recognised one of the males there. The officer's cunning thief of a brother.

The blonde wanted to chortle —but not knowing the detective's whereabouts was detrimental to the plan. She picked up her skirts, and turned through the doors. The iman was very fast. It shouldn't have rattled the assassin as much as it did. The ornate hallway was empty and cold, as though the breeze was penetrating some crack in the walls. She paused and listened for footsteps.

There were several, but only one pair which sounded like running.

237

And it was heading outside.

Which was perfectly fine, because that would mean not getting any blood in Madir Manor. Not that she cared for Her Excellency in any way.

The sound was lost upon the soft grass in the side gardens, but at that point Lorrin had regained a visual on her target. Zemir was hunched over the raised flowerbed; her form rising and falling and trembling as she hurled a string of profanities to the small castle-like building next door. She had torn off her outer coat, leaving it strewn on the ground at her feet.

It was an intriguing sight. Not amusing, but rather, it inspired investigation. And that tangent was what led her to approach without malice.

"Kal?" she called, so as not to startle her from a closer distance.

The sound made her jump all the same, before she whipped around and cursed again. Her neatened hair had already begun to unravel, and she looked dragged through Hehl and back. Lorrin halted and pressed her lips together in thought. It wasn't a mere hatred. Zemir had a developed fear of her family —raw and open and real. The sight of them was enough to send her spiralling.

Another similar thing which they shared; even if her trigger was thought.

She sighed and slowly made her way over. The officer continued to hyperventilate, but made the effort to draw breath and distract her thoughts. She looked skyward and muttered something indistinguishable; sweat trickling to the deep neck of her satin shirt.

The assassin couldn't think of a single word say. So she stood there, at a little distance from her, leaning against the smooth tan plastered wall of the flowerbed. And offered her warm silence. Which was received gladly.

There was a large conifer tree which grew beside them, undecorated and plain. It was the most fascinating shade of green, though —almost dusty in its saturation. It demanded more attention than that of the neat rows of zinnias and lilacs in the bed. Their colours were proud and radiant. The bulbous tree stood just as it was; just as it would always be, and commanded Lorrin's gaze. It was such a contrast to the opulence inside, and seemed to loosen her midriff just a touch. There was air and life here, in the quiet garden beneath the two lowering suns. She could not imagine it splattered red.

Then the quiet was broken, by a whisper so soft and unapologetic that Lorrin felt her heart lurch. "…Why did you leave?"

The iman blinked to rid her eyes of some irritant that had abruptly made itself known, but found another blockade within her throat. If her mouth formed words, would it be able to discern which ones were needed to answer? Or would more spill out, with a mind of their own —wicked, brutal morsels about her escapades two nights ago. So these were consequences. She hated it. The feeling of rot, from the inside of her, festering as though she had eaten Faery food.

"…I only know two things, Detective Kal," she finally managed. "To run, and to hurt. I'm covered in these little thorns, and when you get close enough to touch, you'll bleed. They don't choose, so I do. That's why I run."

Zemir turned to meet her gaze. "Do you never tire?"
She didn't seem to care about the cuts. She would willingly sift through an endless garden to find her again, despite the tiny, curled things of iron?

"I…I have been running for a very, very long time."
"You will fall."

She already had. "Oh, I know," the assassin said. She had known it for a very, very long time. "And when that happens, my feet will rest."

"And what about the rest of you?" murmured the guard. Her breath was even now, but her eyes empty and pinkish.

Why was she so skilled in asking the questions about which Lorrin every day refused to think, let alone answer? She effortlessly picked at her very being, as if to get to her shrouded core. The pricks were trivial. But she wouldn't like what she found there. Lorrin herself didn't like what was there. How could she dare to reveal it to another person? To *Zemir*?

"…I have grown used to the ache," she settled for. "So I get up and run."

Their hands were inches apart. The girl didn't know whose fingers moved first, but at some point she could feel the rough skin of the officer's, intertwined with her own. As delicately as the hold had been outside of that bar. Or even more fragile. It almost whispered of things which dwelled in shadow.

"Maybe don't."

Those words hit her in a way that made her…angry. The frustration was with herself alone. *Maybe don't run from this*. She stared into the amber which seemed to have regained some manner of life. What a lovely shade of honey. In her silly dreams she still imagined waking to those every day.

But what choice did she have? The detective was going to put two and two together eventually. She'd find some link, and she would arrest her. It was all for naught. Now that it was no longer simple fun, it was painful.

"I already did," Lorrin found her mouth confessing. "I…I slept with someone else a couple of days ago. It didn't help, I assure you. In the end, I wanted to run again. But it left me glancing over my shoulder at you —at that long night before disappearing. I…I have never done that before. Looked back."

She was taking those thorns and using them as weapons. If the guard refused to pull away and protect herself, then the assassin would *choose* to inflict pain.

Zemir's fingers twitched, but they didn't withdraw. The blonde frowned down at the lack of hostility. And the older iman did not demand an explanation, nor did she condemn the assassin. She didn't say anything at all —and turned to look up at the cloudless sky again. Lorrin couldn't understand what tumbled within her mind then. And she hated that the silence returned —apprehensive and tightly wound. It wasn't as though she expected anything favourable in response. All she wanted was *a* response.

"…No one shackled us to one another," was the eventual answer.

Expectation was the enemy of such free will.

"We —" the girl rasped. "We did it to ourselves."

"How so?"

The feelings which she processed fluctuated between vexation and desperation. "Well, I expected you to want only me for the time that we would mess around. I couldn't fathom you eyeing another, even before we reached an agreement. It's horribly selfish…yet I can't apologise for it. And then I went and did the thing I worried you would…and now I feel like the biggest bitch. There's no number of times I can apologise to make it better. So I…I don't deserve —"

240

Her hand had moved; curled away, and her voice had exercised its last sound. She couldn't bear to turn and witness the disappointment on the guard's face. This was the final emotional wound she would inflict. Then she would draw her dagger and drive that blade into —

"Raffe," Zemir murmured, reaching for her hand again, but now with purpose. She clasped the trembling thing firmly, enough to keep her there. Lorrin was weak to her name on those lips. "I forbid you from dictating what you can and can't deserve. Since you fail to judge accordingly."

"No," Lorrin tried to reason; barely managing to let out a pitiful sob as she shook her head. "You don't understand. I *truly* don't —"

"Don't say it," the officer warned, tugging her closer. "Or have you decided to disregard the note I left you?"

She would never admit that she indeed had. That she had needed to. Searing tears had sprung at the sight and turned her vision blurry. It couldn't matter what the officer told her. By the end of the night, she'd know of the people who had been slain at her hands...and take her last breath.

The assassin jerked free, and stumbled to her feet. She could already see the blood which would drip from her hands; the red which would splatter the skirt of her gown. She needed to put a great distance between them.

Detective Kal's expression was frustration. "Wait, where are you —"

It was Lorrin's turn to flee, and run. Such an intrinsic part of her that her feet never questioned and her lungs forever burned. It was an effort not to glance back as she pushed back into the manor.

Though unlike before, her footsteps were unechoed.

CHAPTER 32

lorrin

THERE WAS ONE thing over which the assassin had any control now: her audience with Her Excellency. Verdia Kon could not be there, which proved more difficult than she had anticipated, but she had finally tracked down Rye.

The Elf was dressed in official silver and cream Hall of Excellence robes — likely a forced endeavour, as he relentlessly attempted to loosen the collar and shake out the sleeves. The rings studding his lobes were platinum to match. The Court Seeyer was stuck at his side in less regulated attire. An impossibly willowy Seelie the general hue of dry wheat with the fragile wings and antennae of a moth, towering at seven feet. She recognised the famed iman upon first glance —and stiffened appropriately. Her phenakite eyes lined with blonde lashes tracked Lorrin's every movement as though *she* were on security detail.

Though overall, the Faery felt estranged from the extravagance around them, even in her chiffon off-shoulder draped gown and moonstone circlet.

"The bloody queen," she whispered flatly, her head inclined towards Rye but her gaze unwavering from the girl. The antennae twitched; perking and drooping.

Lorrin blinked, unnerved but noting the purpose of her presence. Her opinion *should* be impartial, but the apprehensive standoffishness was understandable. As the instigator of the prophecy, the assassin was embracing contempt. If she was someone else; some other iman, she would have shown herself malice, too.

"Is she...*aware* of this plan?" asked the blonde, scrutinising the Favoured's tall form. "It's not all going to turn against us to have her witness, is it?"

"She is utterly neutral," the Elf reassured, then standing straighter beside the Seeyer, likely feeling inadequate. "But...she knows everything. And what's this '*our*'? This is all on you, Raffe."

"I just want some certainty in this," she huffed, manically threading a hand through her flatiron hair. "Madir's alliance will be all I require now. What with my first task of the night already in shambles, and Kon on my scent."

"I will keep him distracted," Rye sighed. "You need only show Tinnia before Her Excellency, and then have her verify your role. She will cooperate with you, provided that you uphold your end of the deal."

"Of course," Lorrin quipped. "My garden is your garden, Tinnia."

The Faery's blank façade soured as her wings ruffled a bit.
"She only permits officials and members of the Hall of Excellence to address her by name," the Elf quickly clarified. "To you, she is the Seeyer."

"...*Right*," the assassin mused, her brows arching. "Got it."

"Best of luck, End-Bringer." Rye gave a parting nod of his head —to which he received a small wave and vulgar gesture from Lorrin —before returning to the gala. The iman hurriedly corrected her posture when she was left alone with the Seelie; pinned beneath her sharp glare.

"I'm sorry; did that offend you?" she whispered.

Tinnia snorted and unfurled her wings in a brief stretch before her antennae lowered —the entire image of ethereal superiority dissolving into something more mundane as she strode towards the entrance which the governor had used at her opening speech. "I see the future, iman. I am no holy maiden."

Lorrin smiled, then barked a laugh.

As the two females returned to the main room, she couldn't help noticing how unsteadily Her Excellency raised a crystal flute to her lips, and how upright her spine sat. There was almost no curve at its shoulder and base. Her knuckles and mouth had blanched with the strain of supressing pain, while a thin sheen of sweat dampened the stray strands of dark hair at her forehead.

It was not her place to ask if she was well. The sneer of the Troll at her side made that abundantly clear.

A stream of adoring and eager citizens queued a short way past the dais, each waiting for the chance to pitch a business venture; gain her favour; or simply to praise her on yet another trivial government achievement that Lorrin couldn't be bothered to recall.

Or maybe it was gratitude for her mere presence —the fact that she had made it back alive, and with all of her limbs and sanity intact. Well. She couldn't vouch for the lattermost. Especially when Tinnia's dark brows furrowed in the direction of the egregious tree by which the governor sat in one of the dining chairs.

All the while they waited, the assassin thought about the dagger sheathed at her upper thigh behind her leg, by the slit. And she thought about Zemir, who had finally returned to her post, but was actively sweeping around the room in an effort to avoid her family. The younger iman would guess it was a party of her father, mother, brother —and his wife, from the way they stood together. And she hadn't understood it before, yet after observing them for but a few minutes she had a sense of the bundle of emotion the guard must be struggling to untangle.

They did not smile; they did not dance; they did not make conversation with anyone beyond their tiny circle. Nothing indicated any enjoyment of the gala in any capacity. The mother was her least favourite —Lorrin had simply been standing and minding her own business when the short greying female had stormed past, wine glass in hand, and rammed into her shoulder.

The Seeyer had, as she always did, seen it happen and done nothing. All she offered was a stare at the entitled iman's back as she went on her way; oblivious to the debris she left in her wake. And give the slightest twitch of amusement as Lorrin muttered to the retreating shadow, "…Bitch."

Nadune Madir was nearing. She was taller this close up, but not beyond the average height. Still she seemed otherworldly, as if she truly was a distant child of the Drakon. She certainly commanded the room that way. That control slipped when she gazed upon Tinnia. Because the Seeyer only ever meant two things: a vision, or another day at the Academy. But there was nothing scholarly about this.

It wasn't very secluded, but there were no gossipy tongues in The Court itself. Everyone's secrets were protected here.

"Your Excellency," Lorrin bit out the words she had rehearsed, and they still left a bitter taste on her tongue. She could manage a small curtesy with one hand crossed over her wildly beating chest, as could the passive Moth Seelie. "We thank you for being so generous with your time."

She purposely omitted anything along the lines of good health.

"What is the meaning of this?" the governor asked, glancing at the Faery.
"I am Lorrin Raffe," quipped the assassin. "I am here with a...proposition for you. I am accompanied by the Seeyer only so that you know I speak the truth."

Nadune pressed her lips into a line which made her entire mouth disappear, before beckoning the pair a little closer. "...Let us hear it, girl."

"Your Excellency, I will not ramble," the assassin promised. "You wouldn't know me, but I am about to hold the fate of Idun within my palm. I wish to take on Gehman, only because the Unseelie King seeks me. I have the power to rid us of tyranny. Unfortunately, the only way to achieve this is by rivalling his madness. I want to head the underworld. What I seek an alliance —with you."

The older iman's eyes flared, before she turned to Tinnia. "What verification of this do you possess, Seeyer?"

The Faery sighed and spread her wings like tired, dusty rugs. She explained, in clear speech, what the prophecy entailed. Of the disaster it outlined, and the only ways to divert it. And of Lorrin, and what fate decreed of her.

Though the iman had been unsure what Nadune's reaction would be, she had not fooled herself into hoping for an end where the circumstances were accepted immediately, let alone eagerly. The governor's band complexion took a queasy turn. Of course the prospect of becoming allies with a different, younger and more reckless criminal should terrify her. Leaving it in her hands should beckon death. But Her Excellency was more poised than that. She gripped the arms of the padded velvet chair beneath her, and thought over her options. And then she asked one question for which Lorrin had been fully prepared, but had not expected.

"Why should I favour you over Verdia Kon?"

She knew the Troll, and she knew that the assassin knew him. And clearly, all which he had gotten up to in the past months. Maybe years. The governor might offer her the benefit of the doubt on the grounds that the blonde knew how to manipulate their alliance to her advantage.

"I want a legacy, Your Excellency," she answered truthfully, clutching at her neckline. "To be immortalised in history and on our walls. I may be realising this by accumulating power, but such is the only way to climb in the underside of our city. After my parents died, I wasn't offered many options. Yes, I chose a darker path. But now I wish to turn it into something better. We the Blades have always existed to serve Idun, ultimately. I don't want to change that. I only want the promise of your aid; that you will stand with me should I need it. And I *will* need it. To overthrow stubborn males stuck centuries in the past, I'll need them to bow to me. I cannot do that without your reinforcement."

It felt lengthy, but she wanted to be clear. Neither The Court nor the governor were required to spill blood. They needed only to clean her hands.

Nadune frowned. "...Your ambition appears to hold little greed, ill will and pride. I can admire that. Though I must admit that I feel backed into a corner, Miss Raffe. I am already a benefactor to your Troll overseer, yet here you stand; subject to the end of our city and in the middle of a coup of sorts."

The assassin fought off a smile. "You are very preceptive, Your Excellency. I can't deny that it is audacious of me to come to you in this manner. But I assure you that I am a better choice than Verdia Kon. He is becoming more reserved and is advancing in age —mentally, that is. I am not an incentive for death, just to be clear. I want to lower the casualties as much as anyone. I simply fear that he is not what the Blades need, nor will he be crucial in this crisis."

Her Excellency showed no reaction. Then her attendant bowed his great head and leaned down to murmur into her ear. Her gaze didn't stray from the girl, but her eyebrows neared further and the emotion most likely to reveal itself in light of the Troll's advice, seemed to be anger.

"You don't want to make an enemy out of me," Lorrin dared to warn. "The prophecy is more of a joker card to me than it is to you. Should you say no, I may have no obligation to your good people."

She might have been arrested then and there, if it were not for the fury swirling within her own eyes. It gripped the governor with an odd…apprehension.

"No, I don't want an enemy of a future…*queen*," the older iman said carefully, narrowing her eyes in inspection. "And I always keep the city in mind. The issues which arise from your proposal, child, is the unforeseen risk of you going on a culling spree in light of my support. Even my influence will not protect you then."

"When I sit atop it all, I will not take a life without your permission," was the hasty lie. Even Tinnia arched a brow as she glanced at her sandaled feet.

"Is that so," Nadune mused, straightening again. She didn't give it away —if she was foolish enough to believe it. "…This is a delicate thing you are asking of me, Lorrin Raffe. I need time to think it over. Tinnia, when do the events of this '*end*' take place?"

The Seelie adjusted her perfected mask. "Your Excellency, if I told you that, it would twist the vision. It must be your choice —uninfluenced, and plain."

"…I see."

That was the end of it. She didn't need to wave her hand in dismissal nor to declare it. The iman and the Faery took their leave after a bow of respect, and retreated to the corridor. Tinnia wandered off along it to find Rye without a word, but Lorrin was not done. There was one thing left that she had to take care of. She patted her leg, sure of the weight of the knife under her skirt.

But when she had glanced there, Zemir had left her post once again.

Instead, she was a few places behind her in the queue.

CHAPTER 33

zemir

ZEMIR WAS UNRAVELLING. And it hadn't been a quick snip from a pair of scissors, either. The deteriorating of her reality had become unstitched like the way a beloved scarf had snagged a hook or nail, and a thread would then be pulled and pulled over a long stretch of time. Since she had learned to walk and speak. When the damage finally went noticed, it was already too late. She had escaped The Court at the harder tug of that thread, but the tangle had only worsened by joining the Guard of Madir. She had thought it a step in the right direction, yet even that decision was revealing itself to be an error.

Was that all she was destined to accumulate? Mistakes?

Corruption, power and greed had been with her since birth —even before that. Generations before her, imannity had sought to establish themselves in the world without a thought to consequence. Without a thought to life. Whether theirs, or that of their enemies. It almost felt like a terrible game.

The iman didn't like people who played games.

Gamblers, scammers, betters —even the elderly citizens who enjoyed a round of bingo. Her books and novels had made the pastimes and jovial hobbies sound damning and nowhere near worth the risk. Of course, it was a spectrum, and the individual needed to regulate themselves. But she'd just rather lump them together somewhat and avoid it all.

She had never considered Nadune Madir to be that type of risk taker.

Politicians and reigning sovereigns were hardly clean —especially the latter. But the governor of the Madir Dynasty was different. She ought to be. There was traces of Drakon blood within her line, and with that came honour and notoriety. Responsibility. Zemir had been taught that the governors of Idun had been noble people —elected leaders deemed trustworthy and patriotic.

The Werren Park case did not reflect that.

Perhaps the label '*massacre*' was apt.

The only thing which the detective could take away from the attack and fallout, was that the government had been desperate to cover it up. As part of its service, was her own hand an inadvertent accomplice? Would anyone believe her if she said that she hadn't known?

Part of her hoped that Lorrin Raffe would, despite her obviously being another mistake. It had no business with her shaded past nor what she might be up to, now. And she definitely was up to something, given that she had just had an audience. From what Zemir had seen, it was unlikely that the young iman would be so brazen to try her luck at targeting Nadune —their exchange had looked civil. But the officer hadn't missed the small and crafty smile on Lorrin's face whenever she glanced aside, and walked away.

Nor could she ignore the troubled expression lingering on the governor's face.

Her Excellency was a proud female. Zemir didn't need to stand before her at the foot of a dais to conclude as much. Despite whatever marring weighed down on her posture from the Unseelie Court, she was here at the gala, fulfilling her duty. Her purpose. All which she seemed good for was being a beacon and symbol of something abstract and incapable. A marble statue to be worshipped, of a God who promised a utopia.

"Officer Kal," Nadune said, her brows rising in slight surprise.

She knew her by name.

"Your Excellency," the guard returned flatly. A subtle jab of disrespect.

The governor's lips thinned. She wouldn't want to cause a scene here. "…Are you enjoying the gala? I ensured that all guards would each take a break in rounds, long enough to participate. Is there an issue?"

"This isn't about the gala," Zemir assured. Her eyes narrowed accusingly. "I don't know when next I'll be able to ask you, so I had to do it here. I…I need to know about the Werren Park incident."

Her Excellency visibly flinched. The Troll at her side lowered in concern, but she raised a dismissive hand. Every strain in her body told the detective that this was the last thing she wanted to discuss. Here, or anywhere. Her regal image took precedence over such personal opinion, however.

That was how she had planned to ensnare her.

"…What about it?" the governor murmured. Her voice dropped low enough to still be heard within the sea of melody and laughing chatter. It was also rough and contained; in warning.

Zemir ignored it.

"Do you know how the bodies came to be there, Your Excellency?" asked the guard. "The public is terrified, knowing that the evidence of war rests beneath their feet. There could be more, in other places. Under people's houses. Under the offices. In the playgrounds. In the harbour…"

"Officer Kal, what are you implying?" Nadune clipped. "Even the Sekon Idun War was before my time. I had no knowledge of the graves."

"Oh, really?" she challenged, straightening. "I beg to differ. Because as far as I am aware, the planting of endangered flora is authorised only by the officials in charge of environmental affairs. And Werren Park was a hive of such plants — ones which are illegal to dig up."

Her Excellency abruptly shifted on her chair. Her back appeared to protest, and her attendant took delicate hold of her forearm accordingly. The iman huffed, growing more and more frustrated, but refused to cave. "You seem to have come here with some sort of agenda, Detective. Why don't you outright accuse me of something rather than going about it so cryptically?"

Zemir found herself buzzing with an unfamiliar yet addictive sense of spite. Her lips stretched into a smile. "…Where's the fun in that?"

"Excuse me?" Nadune snapped, frowning in offence.

"It's just, you're falling short of my expectations," she sighed. There was now a festering desire to no longer give a shit. She didn't care about her job; she didn't care about the governor; and she considered not caring about her life, either. How could she, in good conscience, serve and protect a city built on brutal oppression and possible genocide? "From a young age, I was told to love my home —Idun. My parents told me. The Academy told me. And I never questioned it, until we found bodies under the ground on which I walk. I know that we have a tenuous relationship with Gehman, but the Werren Park case sheds an unsavoury light on the nature of it. I'm not going to defend either district, but power has been abused, Your Excellency. It always has been. Foolishly, I thought we'd be different."

The governor didn't say anything for a long moment. The guard's words were unfiltered and harsh, but necessary. At least Zemir thought so.

Apparently the iman on the chair didn't agree.

She slowly crossed one leg over the other, straightened up as though nothing was wrong with her spine, and glared down in all seriousness.

"All that I do, I do for the sake of this city. All I give, is for our people. I have never planned to be part of a war. The mistakes of the Unseelie King's and my predecessors should be atoned only by them. I cannot speak about His Holiness' present choices. He uses underhanded strategies to forcibly take back what was taken from him long before my birth. *I did know about the graves* —is that what you want to hear? What does it change, is what I want to ask you. I am not the one who killed them. Have you forgotten your pledge, Officer?"

The guard clenched her jaw, but showed no defeat.

So this was what was to become of her beloved home.
Nadune was right about one thing, though. What *would* it change? There was still nothing which could put the citizens at ease. There was no story that could be spun to keep the cause of the deaths a secret. The truth was going to emerge, but Zemir's dilemma now, was deciding whether or not she'd be there for it.

The conversation was over. At least at the gala. That was laughable. As if she would ever get another chance to confront her.

She stared the governor down, and clicked her tongue. "…Have *you*?"

The look of being taken aback was the tiniest consolation.

The anger stayed after she had whirled away. Anger at her uselessness; anger at her station; anger at the system. There was no democracy. And Her Excellency had made the unfortunate mistake of rendering an officer her enemy.

In her blind haste, she slammed into someone dressed in cream and pale gold. "Oh, I'm sorry, I —"

"—No you're not."

Zemir drew a deep breath as she studied the person properly. She knew that voice, and that face. A tall male much like her in appearance, with brighter eyes and less life in his countenance. The blood which ran through his veins was hers. But that was where their similarities ended. The detective was fair and just. She didn't possess that signature Kal sneer. That cold, cutting hatred. He hid it well beneath a plastered, practised smile. "...Petre," she rasped.

"Zemir."

There was no love in his tone. In any part of him, in fact. Jocelyn was a saint.

"Where...where are mother and father?" she demanded, lowering her voice further as she offered him a hostile glower.

"Why should I tell you? So you can avoid them, too?"

"Obviously."

Petre scoffed, and ran his tongue across his too-white teeth in irked disbelief. "I cannot believe it took you being security for an *Ortus* gala for us to see you again."

Zemir glanced about the room, tensing ostentatiously as her fists clenched. "I didn't choose to be here," she hissed. "...It wouldn't surprise me if our parents had something to do with that. And would you keep your voice down —I'm not actually supposed to be talking to you."

"Now *you're* ashamed of *me*?" he drawled, clutching at his chest.

The officer rolled her eyes before her arms folded. "Maybe I have good reason to be. Are you not in possession of something which belongs to me?"

"Why on Earth would I want anything of yours, sister?" Petre deadpanned. "But do tell me, have you been...*chilly*, this past week?"

She huffed, understanding his stance. "No, I've felt the warmth of a hot, naked body," she smirked. "...She and I have been inseparable as of late."

252

Her brother stiffened, clearly thrown off by the failure of his scheme.

"Where's your wife?" Zemir continued to take jabs at him. She phrased it in a way which might imply something disgusting to a passer-by.

He pointed to the dessert table.

Jocelyn Kal poured over the display of cakes, puddings and bowls of gelato; her *sehrah* and silky, pinned head scarf a matching ivory and embellished with goldsand stones and fire opals. After deciding on a thick slice of decadent Death by Chocolate; the same shade as her skin; the iman turned and wandered over. Zemir's brows rose at the sight of her swelling midsection.

"By the Daughter, brother," she murmured, whistling lowly. "Was it breeding season while I was away?"

These were not her views on the matter. She was simply calling into question the appalling and outdated ideals of their family.

"That's the best you've got?" he shot back.

"Oh my —Zemir!" Jocelyn exclaimed, sharply darting over to embrace her from the side with one free arm. "You look lovely, dear. Isn't this fun?"

"Whoo," she deadpanned, rotating a finger in mock excitement. Then her gaze fell to her stomach. "...Oh, and congratulations."

"Thank you," the iman beamed; a grin from ear to ear which only rounded her soft face. Such a contrast to her husband. She was dazzling, truly —and the only kindness amidst a gathering of hostility. "Are you here with someone?"

"Lyn, no —she's on...*duty*, remember?" Petre hissed, leading her aside. He spoke of Zemir's work like it was a disease his wife could contract.

The officer stuck up her chin, and cleared her throat. "What, I can't have a job and be seeing someone at the same time?"

"I —I didn't say that," her brother sighed, before fishing into his pocket for his cellphone. No doubt to message their parents.

Jocelyn offered a tentative smile as she clung to his arm. "He didn't mean it like that, Zemir. It's just...your vocation is very dangerous, and you might not find adequate time to be social —"

"I *am* with someone," the guard lied.

Petre started paying attention. "What —who? Don't tell me you're talking about the hot, naked body. *You* bagged someone capable of getting a ticket to The Court? As if. Would mother and father even approve?"

For a moment, she imagined introducing Lorrin before them. What a disaster it would turn out to be, and how much they would laugh about it for years after. It wasn't that her parents would disapprove on the sole basis she was a female — although they would sniff in disappointment, Petre was already carrying on the family line. They would disapprove because Lorrin was reckless, conniving and a total conundrum. They wanted someone mouldable and compliant.

"You know, I don't think they would," she quipped, tapping her cheek. "So let's keep this between ourselves, shall we?"

"Zemir —"

"Sorry, but I need to go and find her. I haven't yet had a meal." The officer promptly sidestepped the couple. "Enjoy the rest of the gala."

She distinctly heard the sound of Petre clicking his tongue; of Jocelyn sighing; and of a cellphone's dialling tone.

She needed to slip away to a part of the manor where her family couldn't go. It was more than enough to bump into her brother and sister-in-law. She'd feign being fine, and could go to therapy for that. But if she had to stand before her parents…she'd never make it back to Loegon.

A flicker of red snagged her gaze. She needed to catch Lorrin, too. It was no longer about her own suspicions, but hearing the confirmation from that mouth. There was so little tangible truth around her, that she was willing to hear some from anywhere. Certain things no longer had consequence, so she was prepared to throw everything away.

The meaning of her life had disintegrated.

Her stubborn heart still beat a little for Lorrin, but she refused to think of her in that way before knowing with whom she was truly dealing. Before she'd landed a blow to relieve her own frustration. And the sight of glimmering swords and shields lining the walls sparked an idea.

CHAPTER 34

lorrin

THE ELUSIVE GUARD was lost within the stiff forest of people.

A few heads jutted up over the plateau of browns and greys; the spots of dye or majik strange, blossoming wildflowers amidst the wood. It should have been easy to distinguish a suit of black from the bright coloured swirl —the lights bounced off of the diamond and gold, startling her wandering eyes in the dimming of the room. The smoke and laughter and music were a haze to navigate for the senses. Still, she couldn't spot pinned up royal blue waves.

Her jade eyes had stayed on her for her entire audience —through the brisk but polite enough greeting and into the hushed discission afterwards. Whatever it was, only quiet rage had been Nadune Madir's answer. She wanted nothing more to do with it. Zemir had parted bitterly, before slipping into the guests.

Lorrin needed to get out of there.

Her feet darted for the nearest set of doors for the chance to breathe air, but the action drew the attention of the last person she'd want to notice her escape. The solid bulk of Verdia Kon blocked the exit. Lorrin's head lifted slowly to spy a deep frown below one and a half horns.

"I thought that you were here as my invited, Raffe. So far, you have treated me as anything but."

His deep voice grated her ears. And he wasn't annoyed with her, specifically.

What irked him was how masterfully she managed to evade his watch.

"I came here to take care of someone, Kon," she hissed, grinding her teeth to stop anything else from accompanying the words. "Of whom I've lost track due to a previous engagement."

"You mean a little audience with Her Excellency?"

It wasn't a question. It was a test to see if she might confess the truth. Though why would she, when none of it would matter next week?

So she lied.

"...I was just saying a hello, since the first time we had met was during my work with the Guard of Madir. I didn't mind saying my piece with the Seeyer, who had her own things to report."

The Troll's eyes lit up slightly. "The Seeyer? Had she had a vision? You must tell me everything which you heard."

She scoffed and moved to continue on her way. "Unlike you seem to think, I do not listen in to people's conversations when it does not serve me, Kon."

He let her duck and pass, but then caught her arm in order to add on. She stared up at his face with a look that said a million thoughts. Mainly, '*let me go, or I'll stab you*'. But it was here where the Favoured found pity, and his expression softened as he released his grip. "...I do not like this path that you are on."

Instinct dictated that she feel offence. "I've upheld my end of the deal."

His stance stiffened. "I think you know what I mean."

Ah —this was about her new personality. Or rather, the waking of a dormant one. Was this the advice of a parent or superior? She had never digested his wise morsels well —even when she had regarded him with respect. Rather than a figure from whom to seek knowledge, she had pictured a senile Maji in the woods.

The assassin tilted her head, genuinely surprised. "I always take the path less travelled. And if you find me loathsome now, just wait."

She had vanished into the corridor before he could respond.

The long stretches of arches and windows cleared a little more of her head, and air whistled in and out of her lungs. She would prefer to wander there for the rest of the gala, but she had someone to find.

Her search was pulled towards the doors which led out to the side garden with the bare conifer tree. Perhaps the detective had tried to escape her family again. Though after her audience with the governor, she hadn't caught another glimpse of them. Lorrin's hope was that they had left.

So she turned down the other way, towards the back end of the manor. The light was far dimmer here. It didn't bode well, but she would rather be anywhere but in the main hall. If she were to stare the centrepiece chandelier head-on, it would no doubt cause her head to spin.

The iman was sure that she could smell the tang of grass, when her feet halted at a corner. But the iced touch of a long blade's edge made her sharply inhale — right against the front of her neck.

Her eyes flicked to the side. A pair of amber ones stared back.

The black sword was not immediately withdrawn. It lingered, like the wind after rain. Her skin strained; she needed air and preferred not to be cut into. Zemir caught whatever breath had been escaping her, before hardening her grip on the weapon. The sharp edge no longer pressed in, but it didn't leave.

"...You're not supposed to be here, Lorrin Raffe."

The iman swallowed a gasp. This was how it was meant to be.

The two females were at odds, through and through. A blade to each other's necks. She'd known that from the very beginning. The entire proposition of a little fun had been a grave error. Meeting her in *Slow Poison* the night before business had resulted in just that —a bitter and torturous demise. Not that she was known for consistently ingenious ideas. If this, right now, was not their end —it would be soon. Then why did betrayal rip apart her heart, and why did she feel so beaten?

"I came looking for you," rasped the blonde.

That sentiment was welcomed with a growl. "Security personnel only."

"Can you...can you lower the sword?"

The guard frowned, wrestling with the idea. It struck and caused a ripple of unease through the assassin. Had the officer already solved the puzzle?

Her pale fingers soundlessly inched along her thigh.

Then the blade was retracted and swung aside. Zemir blinked rapidly, sifting through her thoughts. "You…you're normally more alert than this," she carefully murmured. "Did you drink the wine? It might have traces of Faery majik."

"A couple of glasses," Lorrin admitted, running a hand along her neck. Would Zemir have slit it open if she had believed the assassin to be someone else? Or perhaps even that might not have stopped her.

"What did you speak to Her Excellency about," the guard then asked —or demanded as her gaze narrowed. "I saw you in the line."

"Tell me about yours first."

She stuck up her nose. "I am not at liberty to discuss it."

"I see."

Detective Kal stared at her blankly. Her quiet was something which the younger iman had become used to. "…You're make this really difficult, you know. When you go around where you shouldn't, and ask questions you're not meant to. And, even the notion of…caring about you is…*ludicrous*! Why do I want to be put at ease? Damn it all, Raffe I don't know what to think anymore."

Lorrin blinked. "Wh…what?"

Zemir looked like she was losing it. There was burning rage in her glare and she had become dishevelled. What devils chased her here in The Court?

"Listen," she bit, glancing down into the darkness beyond. "I've got several questions, and all you've done is avoid me. So now I need the truth. Nothing more and nothing less. Because maybe if we were going to be strangers again after this, it wouldn't matter. But we aren't parting like that anymore, are we? We…can't."

She was right. They couldn't return to such simpler times.

"True. We can't."

The two imans met each other's eyes again, and two things became instantly clear. One, was that this was the end. Finally. Lorrin would not return to the precinct, or aid the investigation. That was over. Incomplete and fruitless. Two, was that it was the end of *them*. Of all of their games and desires, and of the buried feelings they had accumulated. Now they would wither, as all relationships came to pass.

Only one female was going to walk back into the manor.

"…If you are prepared, I will flash my cards," the assassin chose her words

258

with intent and purpose. "Ask away. Though I hope that elderly Elf's words will ring in your ears forever. You may not like the answers."

"No, I don't think that I will like them," agreed the guard. "I don't think I'll like them, or you."

"I thought we had established that you never had to," the girl reasoned.

"Yet here I stand, trying to make sense of it," she scoffed. "Did you know that Rohna told me to investigate you? You have close to no records in this city, Raffe. And I am trying very hard to advocate for your innocence."

The assassin looked at a sconce on the wall. So that had been her downfall. She had always expressed to Verdia that erasing records would draw attention and cause a collapse. It had not done so in the past only because assassins were not spies, and no one had entangled themselves with law enforcement before.

"I won't lie," she assured the guard, reaching for the dagger. She produced it slowly, so that she could see. So she could study it. A beautifully crafted leaf blade with a golden handle, fashioned like the ones from the hot land from which such exotic animals like elephants came. It had petals towards the hilt like two bent teardrops, and little diamonds and aquamarines. She twirled it idly. And as much of a visual masterpiece as it was, it was still a weapon intended for killing.

"Where did your records go," the officer icily hedged, hefting her sword.

"Away."

"I need something fucking better than that."

Lorrin took a daring step towards her, and the black sword rose. "When someone abandons the life they knew before and takes up a blade, their public identity is reinvented. To the city, we exist as we are in the shadows. The most of us you see is where we go outside of work hours. The public places we live when we're not in service. The most you get to see, is what we show you. Always."

Zemir sucked on her teeth and shook her head in rising frustration. Her eyes didn't leave that dagger. "...Did you ask Her Excellency to pardon you?"

The questioned was dripping with disgust.

"Not at all. I asked her for favour."

"A favour? From Nadune Madir?" Her grip tightened further, and the tip of the blade pointed to the girl's chest. "How did you ever —are you implying that you threatened the person I had pledged my life to —"

"Not *a* favour," she corrected. "I asked for something grossly more political than a once-off exchange. And I did not threaten, nor had I never planned to. Her Excellency has a choice. And she has not given me her answer. In the meantime, I assure you that I am rather untouchable."

It must have been truly baffling. Zemir had likely never faced such a moral quandary —though that term was generous. She was confronting the bad guy. Now she had to be the good guy and seek justice. Right?

The fire in her eyes was dying. Exhaustion fogged that lustre.

"...Who are you, Lorrin Raffe?" the guard finally asked, her anger breaking into a mixture of devastation and bewilderment. "Who the fuck are you?"

The assassin pointed her own blade; pressing it against the other.

"I am not entirely who you thought," she put delicately. "And you have every right to swing your sword at me, but know that our matter is trivial in light of the Seeyer's true purpose beside me. That Wall is going to fall, Kal. And the Unseelie King is going to come for it all. *I* am what stands in his way. I am the only one who has something he cannot be successful without."

The long sword grated against the dagger. "And...you'll give it to him?"

"Not if I value my life," sighed Lorrin, swiping away. "I'm quite fond of my heart, and its ability to remain beating."

"So, you want to save us?" Zemir muttered. "...The city."

The odd pause stayed with Lorrin. Against her wishes, it took root and curled around that damned, rapidly quickening bargaining chip. She did —or she had. She'd wanted to save them. But the ever faythful detective wouldn't want to keep sleeping with a murderess, let alone grow to love one.

She made a blow to the officer's blade, throwing her off balance. Which she quickly regained, before swinging it downwards to her pale neck. The assassin gasped —barely parrying it. Barely holding it back as her spine bent to bare the force. A part of her had hoped that Zemir wouldn't really do it; that she wouldn't try to kill her, too. Because in the moment, Lorrin found she...couldn't do it.

Still the guard hacked at the air about her, aiming for her shoulders but not focused enough, so that the girl could push back. She stared into that gold and couldn't recognise the fury she beheld. Though she knew that she deserved it. She would still fight for her life in a battle where she was at the disadvantage.

Over and over they swung and blocked; making the sound of metal on ivory echo through the halls —which was far better than gunshots. Strain worked their muscles to a point where their accuracy wavered.

"You think yourself a hero, with that knife in your hand?" the detective hissed, nodding to the ivory dagger. This question was oddly hopeful. Zemir wanted her to say she could be more righteous. To quell the fear that her views were in fact, not black and white. To reassure herself of a delusion into which she had sunk.

The long blade was on the base of Lorrin's throat, while she pressed hers just below the guard's pierced ear. They were an endless inch apart; separated by the strength with which they gripped their weapons. Which was fierce.

"...What if I don't?" said the girl; her voice even and low, but that expression and her eyes laughing as though in taunt. Then she turned candid —almost cold. And she demanded, "What if there's no such thing?"

Zemir barely flinched. Then she told a lie. "I don't believe that."

She didn't *want* to believe that.

Then she pushed her back with a sharp swipe, towards the wall. Lorrin stumbled, but remained planted. Her eyes slitted, still wielding that blade. "Because I've been nice to you? Because there are those out there who appear so evil?"

The officer was tired now. Every muscle in her body screamed —not just from fatigue and exertion, but the entire war roiling within her too. Her chest heaved, and the sword's tip hit the floor. It scraped the stone, before she leaned forward on it entirely for support. For a moment all the assassin did was stare as she caught her breath. Then Zemir found her footing.

"Because of every time I saw the inner you, Raffe," she breathed, closing the distance between them. Lorrin stiffened and gripped her dagger tightly. But her feet did not falter. The guard commanded her every action. "...You are not a villain. Not entirely. There were times when those carefully built walls trembled and cracked, and I saw the raw imannity. You showed me that much."

Oh, for fuck's sake —her fayth was multiplying. The iman's own mistakes had only fuelled a very stubborn fire. Her jade eyes widened and pricked with a sharp sting as she turned her cheek. "...Maybe I shouldn't have."

"Maybe I'm a little glad that you did," the guard whispered. Her nose brushed the assassin's and she felt her laboured breath. "Maybe I don't...fully hate you."

Lorrin flinched, finding her hands slippery. "So you still hate me a little?"

Why was she faltering. Was this not the time to be awful and angry? In the rapid tumble of her mind, Zemir Kal had come to the conclusion that the blonde had simply been caught up in something about which she had no say as a young child. Of *course* she hadn't had the say at first —but that hadn't been the case in taking the Central Blades. That was all her own ambition.

There was confliction at every corner. But Lorrin's defences lowered, and her own breath shallowed in foolish anticipation. She couldn't help it. This moment could repeat forever and she would never change her reaction. She would always near. "Zemir..." Her lips parted in a selfish wish. *Just once*, she'd beg.

And Zemir would always pull away, reminding herself that it was forbidden. That it was now downright wrong. But she didn't do that this time. Her hand took hold of her red satin waist, and tugged inwards. "...I must be insane."

Lorrin was sure that she felt life at the touch of the officer's mouth on hers.

It was the most incredible feeling. Both of their lips moved with experience, yet it was as uncoordinated and uncertain as a first. Each hook and release echoed in the stale air; each breath was heavy and forced. Suddenly the assassin didn't know how to kiss, and relinquished any inkling that she once had.

This was how it was done: in the cold, darkened, restricted corridors of a grand manor in expensive Red Carpet garb, with swords and daggers in hand.

Lorrin slowly and discreetly sheathed her blade back under her gown and gripped one of the officer's shoulders. The kiss snowballed into a thing of haste as their lips then parted. With that, she was certain that the strongest muscle in Zemir's body was her tongue. The embrace was still slow and heart-fluttering, but the movement of it curved her spine and drew out a soft moan.

That was it —she knew it then. Of every kiss in which she had ever taken part, not one had evoked a pleasure like this. Her body pressed forward, craving more of the guard's. Now she understood how males could grow hard from it alone. And the mirrored desire fanned the flames. There was an eagerness in Zemir's control; one which slipped through every strained sound from her throat and every sure dip of her head as they stumbled backwards and the sword clattered.

It was an art of possession —each declared the other to be theirs, and pulled them close to illustrate the fact. If they stopped, they would no longer have such a claim. And though it did not mean love, the assassin felt terrifyingly numb with it as the touch faded and the detective withdrew to breathe.

She grasped for one of the blonde's hands, and slowly led her away.

Anywhere she'd tread, Lorrin's feet would follow.

She wasn't being guided to her end. The officer's anger had almost dissolved and there was no malice on her face; in her dark honey-coloured eyes. The same spell clutched her too. She simply wished to kiss her again in the light of day.

The suns were dipping to the horizon. The sky was yet to be fully painted with all of the colours of dusk, so it was still gold.

Lorrin wanted to name the tree. If it would be denied the lights and glitter, she wanted it to feel as magnificent as she did right then. Important. There were no longer thoughts of blood and ruin in her mind. She cast them aside. She had failed to rid the world of the self-righteous guard, and she of a loose-moral killer —but perhaps they had both grown to be wrong about themselves.

About each other.

Zemir whirled and twirled her about the patch of manicured grass, as if they were dancing. The girl felt lighter than air with each spin —with that look on the detective's face. Longing. Painful, forbidden longing. But for as long as she would indulge in it, Lorrin would have her. Then the guard backed her into the short wall and ran a hand up the back of the red gown. It hugged inwards midway down her upper arms and left her wide shoulders bare, covering up the scars.

The assassin watched her like she was all that was left to live for. "…I don't know what to say. What made you finally break your rules?" she murmured. "Do you not fear me and what I can do?"

The officer drew a deep breath, her lips smudged with dark red, and buried her head in the crook of Lorrin's neck. "What do you do if you discover —in the worst way possible, from someone you respected —that everything that you had known as what's right and the truth, was anything but?"

The younger iman paused thoughtfully. There was no definitive answer she could provide. There was nothing she could say to soothe the tremor of a breaking reality. So she offered only a practical and realist solution. "…We live on."

Zemir's grip on her tightened as she let out a shuddering sigh.

They'd live.

It was the only thing they could do.

"Kiss me again," Lorrin rasped, because there was nothing worth more than that and nothing else worth doing. "Senselessly."

The guard straightened and raised her chin. Her eyes were frigid but they still gleamed with light. "…Say please."

Lorrin smiled, masking it with a light scoff. She wouldn't say it here, which Zemir quickly realised as she tugged her body closer. The look on her face was flat annoyance. Still, she leaned in and pressed her mouth to the assassin's neck, before working her way upwards.

What a disaster. A miracle.

Neither female walked back into the manor.

CHAPTER 35

lorrin

FOR AS LONG as she might live, she would never admit to Zemir Kal that she had planned to kill her the night of *Ortus*. That was the last thing she thought as they lay in the messy bed of the master suite at Hemmingway Estate.

She did think about the details she had omitted, but at least she hadn't lied. Maybe that habit would stop now that the guard knew that she had been more of a hinderance than a help, and that she had killed the victims of the case.

Why on Earth was she huddled here with her; bare and burning and immersed; knowing all of those crimes? Lorrin couldn't understand how she had still tangled herself with a grey mystery; kissed and kissed and kissed every inch of her tarnished body; wept and clung to her; told her that the only sound from that mouth should be that of pleasure; and brought her to the edges of obliteration while stealing each breath from her lungs. If it hadn't been so beautiful, she would have cried it out for all of Idun to hear and whisper.

"Won't you arrest me?" Lorrin mused against Zemir's dampened forehead, absentmindedly dragging her fingers through her sapphire hair.

It took her a moment to rise. "…I should."

"But?"

The officer shifted on the silk, skidding her hands up along the assassin's sides. She bit her lip at the groan which vibrated through to her fingers. "I wish the world would end tomorrow, so that I wasn't shackled by things like morals and fayth."

"Do not denounce your fayth for me," begged the girl. "You don't have to feel the need to reconcile with it in order to have me."

"I can't have you any other way," Zemir sighed. "We've been dangerous for each other from the very beginning, Raffe. But you are a very beautiful rose."

"I can't disagree with the first part," she said. "But…is that why you stayed? I am eternally grateful, but I need to understand. If you're fighting with yourself about it, then maybe we…maybe we're forcing —"

"Lorrin."

The girl went still. Zemir rose to her knees, placing each either side of her sprawled body. She'd said her first name. Alone, and with pain. It was intimate and unnerving. That face was sincerity and restraint. She wasn't forcing herself. She was willingly caving. Lorrin slowly reached for the sides of her face and pulled her downwards. As her mouth comforted hers, she realised that she was showing too much. When had the detective stripped her of every piece of armour? And when had that stopped being her greatest fear?

Zemir pulled away too soon. "We should get up and eat."

"Must we?"

Her voice lowered, and her eyes glinted with mischief. "Get your ass downstairs and food into our systems so I'll have the energy to fuck you again."

The assassin smiled. "Yes ma'am."

"Shouldn't we at least talk properly about last night?"

The officer only glanced to the side in indication of listening as she continued washing up. "Should we?" she murmured.

Lorrin was not so sure. Which was wrong. She didn't second guess herself. Did Zemir…not share in her blooming feelings? Though it'd make sense.

"Y-yes," she stammered. "Yes we should. I need answers of my own. Because it…it didn't mean nothing. Not to me."

Zemir chuckled softly and dried her hands. Though the way she did it made it seem like the tea towel was more of a device used for punishment and torture. The assassin swallowed, her gaze following the harsh twist of the fabric.

Then she turned to face her fully, hanging the towel on its hook and striding over to where the blonde stood. Lorrin's feet instinctively retreated in time, until her lower back hit the centre island. Her heart rate spiked as she realised how easily she had been cornered and given up the upper hand.

"Well?" Zemir then said. "Let's talk about it."

She drew a deep breath and begged for her simmering blood not to betray her. "Firstly," she whispered. "…What am I to you now? Do you just…want to ignore my job. And what does it all change about what we are?"

The detective's expression didn't falter, though something flickered in that gold. "Does it *have* to change anything? We could simply remain as we are —in this limbo where the world is washed grey and nothing matters anymore."

The blonde frowned. "That's not a healthy outlook."

"Why do you care? Neither of us ever tie ourselves to people. And this…this is all new. I'm not ready to give it weight it so…finally."

Lorrin bit her bottom lip and dropped her line of sight. It wasn't permanent.

"…Just know that we are no longer what we were before, okay?" Zemir then sighed. "We shouldn't voice any more than that."

The assassin couldn't say it, anyway. That she had fallen. She didn't possess the courage to state it so plainly —that she was dangerously in too deep.

"It wasn't supposed to turn out this way at all," she did manage, daring to look back up. "You weren't supposed to turn into the least terrible thing in my life."

Zemir didn't look flattered or surprised. She barely showed a reaction of any sort, aside from the raising of her eyebrows to indicate some base level of interest. "What do you want from me, girl?" she asked. "I barely understand what I feel."

She panicked. It wasn't that she didn't care. It was simply too much for the officer; and she was making that clear. Greed was such a dangerous sin.

"I…I want you to do what you always do. I want you to stay. I want you to crush me beneath your gaze; to make me feel unworthy."

The tenderness had morphed into something less endearing. Last night had been what they had needed it to be: sweet. Now she craved the heat of her again —whether she feigned her disappointment or not.

"Oh?" The officer's dark brows rose further as she fell for it. "To stay...You wish to grovel at my feet in reverence, Raffe?"

She meant it as a deterrent. Lorrin couldn't truly want her with the staggering depth of the first plunge into love. Perhaps if she made their predicament sound as unwelcoming as possible, the assassin would relent. As she should.

"Yes," Lorrin breathed.

The guard blinked. "What?"

"I would kneel before you, Kal."

"It's...more than lust?" Zemir asked, her voice flat and her head inclined to depict boredom. "I didn't realise that you were capable of such."

Lorrin didn't possess the adequate confidence to smirk; to brush it off. Her fingers curled over the countertop and her spine curved with the nearing of the officer's body. And in a breathless rasp, she laid out all of her cards.

"Yes."

She wasn't sure how the older iman could make her so vulnerable and pliable. She had never been so honest before. Zemir then paused, searching for something within her lidded jade eyes. Then she placed one hand by her elbow. The assassin shuddered just at that. And the officer appeared to notice it, though she tried not to let it show on her face.

"You understand that this is a problematic dynamic, don't you? You were at my mercy professionally, and you still crave to be the same...this way?"

Lorrin managed a nod. "It never stopped you before. Is it not too late to mark those boundaries?"

"Then I suppose I cannot lie and say that it does not entice me to see you like this. Cooperative. *Weak*." She accentuated the last word —bit it out.

The girl flushed. She couldn't deny it.

"Oh," the officer then mused, her warm brown fingers then inching upwards along Lorrin's arm. The light hairs raised in their wake. "Is this the only weakness that you'll tolerate?"

The younger iman had hardly struggled for words before. "…Y-yes. Only…if it's for you, Zemir," she whispered.

Her mood shifted to somewhat pleased, and she smirked. Not smiled —there was no warmth in that satisfaction. It was frigid and calculating.

She reached to tilt Lorrin's chin back, before her fingers strayed towards her neck and loosely curled around her throat. Lorrin's eyes lidded as the detective tugged and brought her mouth tantalisingly close. No one had ever held her this way. And it was absolutely salacious. Zemir then guided her head, completely in control of its tilt as she stared into jade.

Her breath was shallow. "You are a horrendous idea."

The assassin's lips parted.

"…And I will enjoy every minute."

She would never get over their every kiss. Her nerves crackled in an overload, and she was hyper aware of every sensation on her skin. There was only one thing which prevented it from being near perfect.

She kissed her now as though the action was a reward which she had not yet earned. And she inhaled sharply in surprise when the officer pulled away, even though the touch lingered. Her cheeks burned pink at the controlled, expectant look on Zemir's face. It wasn't anger. It was testy amusement.

"Did you think that I will permit you to be satisfied before I am?" the detective asked, unbuttoning her black shirt.

The assassin swallowed, unapologetically staring. Then she grinned.

"Answer me, Raffe," she instructed, raising her nose.

The girl found herself licking her lips. "No…no, I did not."

The guard smirked again, the valley of her breasts and the column down her midsection bare. She then took hold of Lorrin by the waist and lifted her up to sit on the island. She gripped her shoulders and stared with wide eyes, surprised at what she had managed. Then Zemir pushed her backwards so her spine kissed the cold marble. Her large t-shirt rode up along her thighs, inviting the officer to bend her legs up and back at her leisure. "…There's a good girl," she said.

Lorrin trembled and bit down a soft and betraying sound. The officer's honey-coloured eyes shimmered as her hands continued their exploration of her lower half. They inched closer and closer between her legs —before they found their destination. Zemir's small smile widened as she watched the willowy iman writhe gently beneath her. Her fingers felt out the shape of her, before lightly running up and down in the laziest motion.

The assassin whimpered, her arousal climbing up to irrevocable heights, and rolled her hips down in a way of begging. A sound like soft laughter filled the room, before the officer's fingers moved away. Still Lorrin dripped; the closeness yet lack of fulfilment nearing painful.

"I want to find something out, Raffe," she mused, licking those fingers. "You are skilled in talking your way around things. Are your words pretty stars in the sky, or do you truly harbour the strange desire to bow to me?"

Lorrin took a moment to clear her thoughts. "…I do want to. You bring out a side of me that's wilful but…good. I want to be good for you. At first, it angered me. No one had ever made me want that. But it feels…natural with you. Perhaps your profession influences it a little. But know that you are magnetic, Zemir Kal. And I am but a helpless shard of metal."

The officer was a little surprised at her words for a moment. Such poetry for a heavy and heated situation. Her gaze averted, before her eyes lidded in thought. Then she nodded, and cleared her throat.

"All right. Follow me."

She turned to saunter into the living room. Lorrin got back to her shaky feet with slight difficulty, despite no reason other than yearning and frustration being the cause. Zemir was seated on one of her sofas, arms out either side and over the back cushions. Her shirt fell further open. She smiled coldly as Lorrin wandered in; who instinctively lowered to her haunches at her spread feet.

"Make me feel something, Raffe," the guard ordered. "Then we'll see about another kiss."

Lorrin tentatively reached out for each of the iman's thighs. She stroked them slowly, looking up at her through her thin lashes, before pulling them apart. "Yes."

She slid the tan lace down over Zemir's hips. She glanced up at her once more, and the officer's jaw tightened. She leaned down to circle and angle the assassin's neck again —then pleased by her gasp. Her fingers slid slowly up and down along her skin, varying their grip. "I am liking this a lot more than I should."

Lorrin smirked. "Wait until you come undone for me."

Those fingers lingered, and then withdrew to slip into the sunslight strands of hair. The assassin's breath caught as her eyelids shuttered, before Zemir's hand grazed her cheek. It had turned into a drug —her touch. Lorrin knew it.

She then dove for her arousal. The guard audibly gasped as she felt a mouth there —where few had ever been before. While the blonde would not boast in her experience, the officer would know by the way her tongue moved, how her lips puckered. How she knew to worship far better than any priestess of fayth.

"*Raffe.*"

Zemir's voice was rough and thick. It made Lorrin's stomach roil with heat. The fingers in her hair tightened their hold, before guiding her head to show her where she should concentrate. The assassin attended her desire, a moan emerging even though it was not her pleasure.

"*Lorrin —*"

Again, she whispered her first name. In such a breathless, husky rasp that the younger iman had to pause to let a shudder run down her spine. Then her hands tightened on the iman's skin, keeping her knees apart. The guard hissed, moving to indicate that her grip was too rough. The assassin immediately corrected her mistake, before moaning deeply at the sight of Zemir throwing her head back.

She called Lorrin's name over and over, assured her of diligence —before a violent quake with which the blonde was intimately familiar began to take over the officer's body. Lorrin withdrew. She then watched, mesmerised, as Zemir then stiffened and groaned, arching over the backrest of the sofa. Pride welled within her at the notion of getting Zemir there. And when the officer panted as she straightened up, the iman knelt back on her legs to await further instruction.

"Well, I'll be damned," Zemir breathed, running a hand through her blue hair. This smirk was laced with amusement. "Come and get your reward."

Lorrin bit her lip at the invitation. She rose, and then climbed up over her lap. The blonde quivered slightly at the sensation of their touching skin. Her bare legs atop hers. The detective circled her sculpted waist with one hand at her back and dipped her chin with the other. She gazed into the pools of gold, tempted to pinch herself to ensure that this was reality.

Her lips then pressing against hers proved that it was. She let the officer lead, let herself be moulded as she saw fit, and hesitantly gripped her shoulders. *This* was a reward earned. Lorrin hummed softly at every pull; every tug closer and every breath. Her fingers moved of their own accord —they clawed at the black shirt, pulling it down toned arms as the girl grew desperate; hasty.

Detective Kal's hands wandered again, and one mercifully settled between an ache threatening to consume her whole. The other at her spine. She gasped at the ceiling and trembled, before holding on tighter. Her unsteady body curled into the repeated beckoning motion, chasing release. All the while, the guard's mouth wandered over her heaving chest and shoulders. That gave her what she wanted. The assassin writhed and cried out her pleasure —and Zemir's name.

Was it better simply because something more than lust tethered them?

The officer kissed her hurriedly, groaning in satisfaction —before firming her grasp on her and twisting them around on the sofa. Lorrin blinked rapidly as she found herself on her back. "No one else," Zemir hissed. "No one else is going to do it like me. Is that clear?"

The iman's expression above her was almost wild —strained and yearning. Sweat beaded her brow and the skin of her chest and abdomen —which were no longer hidden away by her shirt. The assassin stared for a long moment, burning the image within her mind. It was a beautiful sight; to see her control slipping. To know that Lorrin herself was the cause.

"Yes, Kal."

She kissed her again, in a way which clawed; unable to satiate an ache which burned between them. It had never been like this before. Lorrin drowned in Zemir; relinquished herself and pleaded to feel her anywhere. Everywhere.

The guard's hand started to slide downwards against the oversized t-shirt, descending further along the quivering tautness of her midsection, before reaching the hem and drove the garment up all the way to her ribs. Lorrin's underthings had long been discarded, but Zemir still licked her lips and stared. Still brushed her fingers along the wetness and felt again how much the blonde wanted her. It was with an intensity that was irrational. "Fuck," she softly cursed, and Lorrin felt the echoes of the tremble which then travelled through her.

She mustered the nerve to ask as she shifted her hips. "...Me, please."
The detective paused, her eyes twinkling with conflicted amusement. The assassin dared to grin. And in response, Zemir's lips twitched in a crescent as she leisurely slid her fingers back in and ran a hand up the middle of her chest and neck, before lingering on her breasts. Lorrin drew a sharp breath and arched into the movement, her own fingers consequently curling into the upholstery.

Through every desperate moan, her body jerked in time with each stroke; still yearning for more. Nothing was going to suffice. But everything was going to work. Those fingers didn't last long, as the officer lowered to lick her, having missed the way she arched into her mouth. She gripped her unsteady hips and drew her nearer, ensuring that her tongue reached new crevices and claimed them all. Lorrin jolted and shook against the sofa, tears springing from her eyes.

Her nerves throbbed with the warnings of pain as she still cried out words of unbridled encouragement. It felt far too good to put an end to. If she couldn't have Zemir's heart, then she'd take everything else.

"*Faster*," Lorrin sobbed, throwing her head back over the armrest.

The guard did not heed to her wishes. Who did she think herself to be, to command and direct? Instead, she was met with two fingers and an idle tongue. And maybe that disregard was what pushed her; what drove her over the edge and turned her lidded vision spotted white and blurry.

No one else indeed.

"Lorrin," Zemir whispered her name. She pulled her back up to her lap. The assassin quivered and panted, left with little strength and focus. The older iman cupped her cheek, before caressing it lightly. "You know what to say."

She nodded, determined to recover within the next minute.

273

The detective hummed, brushed her thumb across the girl's lips, and then pushed off of the sofa. She glanced back over her shoulder. Her finger curled.

"More?" the iman asked.

"Oh yes. You're under arrest, Raffe."

The twisted irony wasn't lost on her.

When she had followed her back to the master suite, Zemir was perched there on the bed with the pink handcuffs in hand. Lorrin staggered over, still short of breath. But all which mattered was that grin on the officer's face. She shifted, legs open in invitation. "Hello little prisoner. In order to consider you for parole, I need to see that you're obedient and compliant with the law."

She was the law.

"...Yes, Officer."

The cuffs closed around Lorrin's wrists behind her back, and all the while, eye contact was never broken. The assassin shivered at the impatient touch of the guard's hands. She pulled her hips closer, slid the hem of the t-shirt upwards again, before opening her mouth and delving for the centre of her. The younger iman moaned, short and breathily; her spine arcing towards that mouth as she instinctively struggled against the cuffs. That's when she realised —she wouldn't be allowed to rake through that blue hair.

"My, my, little prisoner," whispered the detective. "You seem to have learned a thing or two. Repentance suits you well."

"Thank you, Officer," she rasped, looking down in time to see where her hot tongue speared. All she could do was watch Zemir do as she pleased; in no hurry to devour what had seemed to have become her only means of living.

And her every shudder served as encouragement; a spur to keep licking.

The detective's hands roamed her covered sides as she guided the tilt of her lower half. Her tongue traced the fold, slipped between and circled to the apex, where she lingered with the intent to drive the assassin wild.

Lorrin swore breathlessly; a violent shiver raking through her body. Then she gasped, catching her mistake. "I mean...Wait, I'm sorry, Officer —"

That amber was unfaltering. "I'll remember that."

The response was dismissing, not threatening.

Lorrin whimpered, keeping the sound between her clamped lips, before deciding to concentrate on finding the elusive climax.

Her leg slid up beside her on the mattress, so she half knelt above her. Zemir chuckled softly at the brazenness, but held her steady. The position provided her with more...simply more. She tilted her head and licked with vigour, enticing Lorrin to rock her hips in slow thrusts. It was all that she could do. And the end was within reach. Then it crashed into her abruptly and without warning.

The pleasure which surged through her was enough to buckle her knees. She stumbled, fell to the floor, and quivered against the guard's leg. A hand slipped into her hair, and stroked soothingly. She was permitted a few minutes rest in that position. Then the caress turned into a rough pull, tilting her head upwards so she could look at the older iman. She stood and stared down at her, her expression controlled and eyes set. Wordlessly, Zemir then pushed the fistfuls of blonde downwards below her navel.

And Lorrin, eager to please, began to lick.

At nightfall, it finally dawned on her that they no longer confined themselves to the darkness. They had spent those satisfying hours out in the light of the suns. Exhaustion and ache had found them at last, and all they wanted to do was recharge. She had never experienced it quite like that; an endless onslaught of ecstasy. If their bodies didn't adhere to iman biology, they might have gone on.

"...I'd like to take you somewhere tomorrow," the assassin told the detective. "If you won't go to work."

Zemir had been debating it all afternoon. She saw little point in returning at that point, but she wasn't old enough to retire. Her trust in the Guard of Madir was irrevocably fractured, and the only things for which she cared now was sleep and sex. Lorrin fit somewhere in between.

"It's not a date, is it?" she murmured.

"No," the iman assured. "I just…need some leverage. I want to show you off."

"What," the officer snorted, turning her head to stare at her. "Why —"

"—I'm an assassin," she said outright. "I have been for ten years. There are things that are about to happen which I can't explain right now, but I will when the time comes. Just know that you…you are important to me. Whether I am the same to you or not. And what I also need you to know, is that I want to take the organisation over and make changes, but there is one thing that won't change. Something that I understand you leaving for. I…I kill people, Zemir."

When her name left her lips, she sealed her fate. Her eyes stung, then welled with and leaked an emotion so stupidly delicate that she almost turned onto her other side and dismissed it. How had she thought a person of fayth would respond? At least she hadn't tried to gloss over it by specifying '*bad*' people.

Because that would also be a lie.

But Zemir's dark fingers slowly threaded with her pale; she tugged her a little closer, and refused to let go. She held Lorrin's hands —the very ones which had committed those crimes, and the blonde felt pieces of herself crack.

Then the guard found a few words. "…I know."

Lorrin couldn't breathe or swallow.

She hadn't said that she didn't care, or that it didn't matter. It *did* matter, and the officer's shattered care was written clearly on her face.

"I know."

Those two words were an acknowledgment of a truth —and a revelation which meant that Zemir didn't know what to feel. How to feel. But she was still there with her, and that was all that mattered right then.

CHAPTER 36

zemir

SHE HADN'T EXPLICITLY agreed to go anywhere.

But Lorrin looked like she could use the support, and there was nothing better to do. Being near her hushed the thundering battle within her mind to a degree. She didn't think that anything would remedy the destruction of what she had once decided to give her life for, but she'd try just about anything.

That's why she stood outside of the Central Blades Hall beside Lorrin Raffe. She didn't look so eager either. Her outfit didn't help. It was more of a costume —a tight lilac mini dress, white denim jacket and large, expensive sunglasses.

Zemir had hated that she'd hesitated that morning in deciding whether or not to drape her fanciest embroidered coat over her blouse and suspended trousers.

Lorrin had turned pink and insisted so —as part of her little plan.

It was still madness to waltz into the place where most assassins gathered. Would they let her in? But the most important question she had to ask herself was why she was still with the blonde after finding out all that she had. She knew that she was a killer. She knew that she was an enemy of the law.

But…the world was going to crumble.

The simple answer was that she couldn't devote enough thought to it in light of the recent revelation. So she would do whatever the Hehl she wanted to, and disregard what came next. Fayth and Her Excellency couldn't stop her.

She followed behind Lorrin closely, eyeing the Hall and taking note of each detail out of habit. The few assassins who roamed past them flinched and exchanged perplexed glances —which was reasonable. Zemir strolled with her head high and hands in her pockets. They didn't know what to do, given Lorrin's presence. They would wait for a brief.

The main room where the blonde stopped was filled with a long table that felt too big for it; and seated along its sides were a Seelie, Elf and familiar Troll.

Verdia Kon shot to his feet.

His expression reflected shock and horror. He wouldn't be so stupid as to reveal the relationship between himself and the two females. But even he had to wonder why the guard was there, with the Idun crest on her back no less.

"Raffe, what in the Hehl are you playing at?" snapped the Elf.

"That's an officer!" blurted the Seelie.

"Questioning," Lorrin corrected, frowning. "Please be respectful." She beckoned her over to the prestigious chair at the head, and patted it.

She called the shots in the bedroom, but the assassin was clearly in charge in this professional capacity. Zemir sauntered over, her gaze glued to the Troll, before sinking to the velvet and assessing the audience. The ring leaders and other assassins simply stared, blinking in bewilderment with hands on their sheaths. She'd been told not to fear. They wouldn't dare do anything without orders.

Lorrin leaned in towards her, sliding a hand down her blouse which slowly lowered to her trousers. "Spread your legs a little," she whispered.

She obeyed, gripped her waist, and swung her over one thigh. She perched sideways with her legs between the officer's; an arm at her waist. Lorrin removed the sunglasses as she wrapped her arm around her shoulders for support. "Good cop," she murmured into her ear, and then lowered to kiss her slowly.

And though it was intoxicating, Zemir didn't miss that hardly a single sound interrupted them. She wanted to glance at all of the assassins' stunned faces. What warranted their hesitation? The quiet whispers seemed insufficient.

It was only after half a minute that Lorrin withdrew and turned back to the room. "Please excuse me," she said bashfully. "I can't, um…sit down right now."

The detective chuckled softly, placing her other hand on the hem of the dress.

"Raffe, you've been unhinged all week," the Seelie was the first to speak up. He was a Jackal, with a bushy brown tail and a sneer. "What logical reason could you possibly have now for bringing your *guard* girlfriend to the Hall?"

It was mostly to unnerve Verdia Kon, but Lorrin simply smiled. "Well, well, Markus Arrium," she answered, "Why doesn't it surprise me that you still think that you're miles above me?"

Zemir grazed her lips along her ear. "*That's* Markus?"

The assassin nodded, before idly tugging at one black elastic strap. The officer pulled her nearer and slid that hand which rested on the purple hem; inching it up far enough to reveal the tip of a dagger.

"He's nothing, Kal," Lorrin murmured.

The officer only offered a grunt.

"This is not a matter of status or influence," Arrium hissed, hitting the wooden table. His ears flattened in rage. "It is an issue of security and competence. The Guard of Madir is not an ally of the Central Blades. You *know* that. How can you, in good conscience, reveal our location, and the subject of our meetings?"

Lorrin stiffened; her smile disappeared and her posture shifted from carefree to deadly as she adjusted the sunglasses atop her hair. "They aren't an ally, but they do not have to be an enemy either. Especially one who no longer wishes to have an affiliation with them. And do *you* have a death wish, pup, to imply that I am incapable of doing my job because I get laid more often than you do?"

The Faery let out a growl.

"That's my girl," Zemir whispered as she kissed the spot underneath her ear, slowly stroking the inside of her thigh. Was it her role, or herself who said that? At least that was the excuse she could hide behind. The detective owned nothing, least of all Lorrin Raffe. But the title had a hot, pleasing ring to it.

The assassin drew a sharp breath and raised a taunting brow. "*Your* girl?"

"Raffe," Kon sighed, growing tired of the performance. "What he means is that you don't seem to have thought this through. Even if this officer is breaking from the Guard, it doesn't give her free entrance into *our* affairs."

"Oh, are you saying she's not trustworthy either?" Lorrin snapped, jerking on the detective's lap. The older iman attempted to hide her intrigue at the sight of the blonde so riled up on her behalf. Or in fact, angry at all. It was different from her quiet rage —the subtle signs of her merely being pissed off. This emotion was free and open, while her cheeks flushed with colour. It was the sort of anger that might gain a very opposing reaction from Zemir than shame or reproach.

"Well —" Verdia began.

"—I say that exactly!" Arrium cut in.

"I second it!" the Elf spluttered.

The officer tapped the assassin's leg. She didn't have to carry on the charade. The point had been made, and if it was easier for her not to be there anymore, then she would go outside and wait. Close enough to step in if she needed to, but at a safe distance to appease the Hall.

But Lorrin clicked her tongue and pressed her lips to her forehead. "I have no reason to think over your objections," she told the council. "I think that there is value in colluding with the government. She has my trust. If you have issues with that, perhaps we should hear about your own alliances beyond these walls."

The attendants and vassals began to whisper.

Just as she had hoped they would.

Verdia was the most troubled. Zemir made note to make eye contact with him as often as possible. He would glance away with fearful haste, the little blue draining from his face so he resembled a sickly phantom. '*Haunted*' was an appropriate word to describe him in that moment; in the entire meeting. It would now look bad if he gave the slightest hint that he knew who the officer was. It could very well get him killed. The only reason it was being tolerated for Lorrin Raffe was because her behaviour was no surprise. She had always been like this, while Verdia had kept his dealings concealed.

For him to acknowledge Zemir would open a can of worms in relation to every aspect of his business, and whatever else into which he had gotten himself.

"Are you implying that the rest of us have allies in places we shouldn't?" the Seelie snarled. "You have some damn nerve."

"I don't know, Arrium," Lorrin mused, cosying up close to the guard. Zemir slid her hand higher against the younger iman's side, underneath the denim, and brushed her light hair back over her shoulder —so that she could start kissing her nape. The blonde hummed softly as she caressed her warm, dark cheek. "*Do* you have any allies where you shouldn't?"

The Faery grumbled and hissed something incoherent to the sour Elf. Verdia glanced at the pair briefly, understanding whatever it might be that they had kept a secret, before addressing the females. "Listen Raffe. Your behaviour has been erratic and puzzling. I'd like to say that we're worried about you, but that may be only on my part. This isn't the way of the Central Blades. Your ascension was supposed to be a golden opportunity, yet you seem to be squandering it with wild rages and executions. This isn't the way of the assassin."

"*The way of the assassin?*" Lorrin echoed, rolling her eyes. "You males need to get over yourselves. It isn't my fault that there've been so many traitors. You should be thankful that I found them, before they could rat the three of you out. Besides that…you have led the Blades for *years*. There have been far too few females among you, but as soon as I step in I'm irrational and out of control? That sounds an awful lot like typical misogyny to me."

"I knew she'd deny it," Arrium snapped.

Lorrin didn't retaliate immediately. All that she had wanted was to illustrate to the subordinates the ring leaders' instability. How united they were against her. How utterly predictable they were. And they certainly talked —the assassins at the door whispered and typed away discreetly on their cellphones.

The Troll ran a hand over his face. "This has gone on long enough. Raffe, we have come to a decision. We feel that perhaps this role was too much for you, too soon. You're going to be removed from your post, effective immediately."

The iman tilted her head in thought as Zemir paused, withdrew from her neck and idly tapped the dagger on her thigh. Lorrin didn't respond right away. She wanted the devastation of it to sink in thoroughly. Yet even though this was a part of her plan, the guard could tell by the way her spine lengthened and the press of her coloured lips that the anticipated words hurt, regardless. That the very notion

281

of her orchestrated trap working perfectly still shred at her.

Because they weren't faking it.

The officer squeezed her knee, and offered a peck to her stiff shoulder. So she gathered the strength to regain control of her forlorn stance, before tentatively patting Zemir's arm in gratitude. Her chin was raised high. "…Your effort to silence me is in vain," she eventually informed the creatures.

"We're not '*silencing*' you," the Elf sighed, exasperated. It was clear that his conclusion on the situation was disappointment. "What a victim mentality."

"Now you're gaslighting me, Fore?" Lorrin gasped, clutching at her chest. "I just wanted the best for this organisation —after years upon years of torturous, barbaric training and mistreatment."

The attendants' murmuring was growing louder.

The council finally chose to acknowledge it.

"Please be gracious about this, Raffe," Verdia insisted, his expression morphing into one of pain and embarrassment. "And make it easier on all of us."

"All of you or just the council?" she cut back.

The Favoured frowned in disbelief. "Now, listen here —"

A loud knock interrupted the rising noise. All attention was diverted to the doors, where a short Syren with light coppery waves stood. Her hair was gathered into a ponytail, and she seemed more formally dressed compared to the other assassins. Her louis blue pants were smart and pleated; cream silk blouse tucked and flowy —even the thin colour-matched cardigan with a minimalist Idun Phoenixes logo on the pocket blended. In one hand, she held an ivory dagger. In the other, were two elaborate letters. One golden with filigree, and the other charcoal and mossy.

"Char Gilligan," Lorrin quipped.

"We have mail, your Majesty," the sea creature announced gravely.

"For the council?" Verdia asked.

Char scoffed. "For my queen, only. The black one is for me."

"*Queen*?" Arrium bit.

The blonde ignored the Seelie's outrage and beckoned the redhead over. The gold letter was finely sliced open with the dagger's blade, before being presented to the assassin. Her hands were trembling slightly. This was also planned, but she didn't know what was written in it. That became clearer as she tugged the letter out, and skimmed over its contents. Zemir couldn't resist a few glances over her shoulder, despite being sure that the information was not for her to know.

But Lorrin then shifted slightly to address the Hall aloud anyway.

"Her Excellency Nadune Madir has chosen to give me her support," she began —which set off a ripple of gasps. "Effective immediately, she endorses me as the absolute head of the Central Blades."

"What?" the Troll blurted; his face gaining colour with rage.

"Lies!" Arrium echoed the sentiment, jumping from his own chair.

"This is her official seal," Lorrin stated, narrowing her eyes as she slid the letter over atop the wood. "Do you think I'd forge that?"

"There are witnesses who were with Char outside all day," a member of the Ash Blade spoke up. "It was delivered by NPS properly and orderly."

"I-rre-futable," Lorrin articulated, before sighing deeply.

"You can't just take over the Central Blades," the Seelie hissed, straightening his tie. "There are no procedures in place for this. Her Excellency might have given you the green light —only the *Daughter* knows how —but we are still fairly a democracy. Do you think you can simply do as you please without any prior discussion and consultation?"

Lorrin idly stroked the top of Zemir's head as it was buried in the crook of her neck. "A democracy —you're quite right, Arrium. Perhaps it's time that the Central Blades worked under such fairness." She turned to the onlookers. "What say you, fellow assassins?"

They dithered, at first unsure of whether they could even answer. Then they worried that their choices would irrevocably ruin the function of the organisation. Would the ring leaders forgive them for needing something new and different? For wanting to do away with the practices of old and usher in a new leader with more liberating ideas?

Zemir ran a hand up along the younger iman's back. She quivered against her, before leaning down to whisper into her ear. "What do you think they'll do?"

"Honestly?" she murmured into her light hair.

"Now and always."

The guard glanced about the room, assessing everyone's body language as they all spoke over one another. The ring leaders were prepared for murder, while the attendants and vassals didn't seem so certain. Lorrin had the upper hand after providing them with a choice —which was something of which they had been deprived. Though at the same time, would they ultimately end up trading a set of overbearing lords for one indefinite one who called herself queen?

"…They will be divided," Zemir sighed, turning to meet the assassin's gaze. It was full of apprehension. She hardly succumbed to fear, but she was worried that maybe the blonde's ambition was too far from reach. The detective did think that she had aimed too high —but it was too entertaining to leave alone. She wanted to be a part of this; to help her do something extraordinary.

Her lips captured hers before she could give herself the chance to think. The kiss was soft and dragged; only meant to comfort her and calm her nerves. But Lorrin's eyelids fluttered and lidded when they parted, before she curled one hand on the older iman's thigh —dangerously close to the zip of her trousers. The other gripped a suspender strap.

"Later," the assassin breathed, "I want you to push me up against a wall."

Zemir chuckled, staring at her mouth. Then she lightly gripped her chin, her expression hardening into something taunting. "Say please."

That jade shimmered, and a shiver rippled through her. "…Please."

Suddenly she couldn't swallow. "*Goddess*, Raffe —"

Verdia loudly cleared his throat. His face was bluish —likely from the two imans' antics and the frustration the letter had brought. But the officer smirked with pure triumph at the former possibility. "Evidently," he ground out, "a consensus cannot be reached on the spot. We will organise a formal vote, and the results will be reviewed at a later date."

"Why?" Lorrin questioned. "If you fear losing terribly, just say so."

"It's not a competition," the Troll growled.

"Oh my *Goddess*, yes it is," the Seelie exclaimed. "Don't sugar-coat it, Kon.

There will be a victor, and the vanquished. This isn't only about the council being broken apart. This is about the future of the Central Blades. And there's no point in campaigning, because that's what we've been doing for all of these years. They know what we're like, all too well. And why would they choose that?"

"Are you admitting defeat?" Fore gasped.

"I refuse to call it that," dismissed the Faery. He turned to Lorrin. "If the way forward is with Raffe, then perhaps we should ask ourselves why that is. We shouldn't stand in the way of progression, after all."

Lorrin was seething.

This was not what she wanted.

"*You're* surprisingly quick to change your stance," Verdia muttered, noticing just as swiftly. "How is that meant to reinforce anybody's confidence?"

"I can't help it if I find myself to be opportunistic," the Seelie huffed. "And smart business is smart business."

"This isn't an investment summit," Lorrin countered. "This is about people's lives. Those which serve, as well as those which are targeted for violating rules. As much as we'd like law to be absolute in this world, there will always be those who refuse to abide and we exist to punish them as well as protect this city. Be careful how you speak about the Central Blades."

That should be enough to tip the scales in her favour.

Zemir smiled against her jaw. There was a strange sense of pride in seeing the assassin handle these issues on her own so masterfully —she was magnificent. The other assassins appeared to realise this, too.

"I want Raffe as the head," one boldly declared into the silence.

"I want her there, too," said another.

"She cares about us —and about the organisation's purpose!"

Like the build-up of the wind, an uproar rang through the Hall declaring Lorrin Raffe the head of the Central Blades. She gave her best look of surprise and delight. But this was the easy part. Now she had to finalise the demise of the remaining council members. It wouldn't be straightforward as it had been with the others. These males were clever and dangerous —more so than the blonde.

"What do you intend to do about us?" the Elf asked the inevitable question.

"I'm offended that you feel the need to ask me that, Fore," the iman sighed. "I am not as ruthless as you may think. No one is being deposed. I will merely have final say in matters, and represent us to the public. The Central Blades will not be incorrectly feared with a young female iman at the head."

It was more of a lie than anything, of course.

Zemir leaned back and smiled at what was indeed defeat written all over the ring leaders' faces. But she lingered on Verdia and Markus —one confused and in despair, while the other glared at Lorrin's lily white neck.

Impatience was a fuel to their flickering inferno.

It was the assassin's first time in Zemir's apartment, but it was overshadowed by the two females' fumble for the bedroom. Her dress had been tugged up her hips and her underwear, down —before they made it there, and her back arched against the wallpaper. Pinned, as requested. It was breathless and unceremonious; Lorrin could barely get a sound out while the older iman claimed her mouth and reached up between her thighs. Zemir delighted in the feeling of her quivering legs loose around her waist; the desperate dig of her fingers in her working shoulders.

"*Fuck*. More," Lorrin rasped, throwing her head as she shuddered.

Zemir chuckled and bit her neck, hefting her higher. But she craved more than that. She wanted to put a bejewelled velvet collar around her delicate neck and parade her around in thin red lace. Lace that only she could touch and remove, and lick what was beneath.

"Please," begged the girl, tugging through blue. "I want to have you, too."

"Not yet," the detective breathed, finding her lips again.

She kissed her with far more feeling; as they had in the Central Blades Hall, but not for show. This was for them alone. She poured in a little more of her budding emotion; of undeclared affection that could be implied —yet to be voiced as she didn't have a firm enough grasp on *what* it truly was.

But if Lorrin would have it, she'd give it.

She wanted something more than they had had, but she couldn't call it love. It wasn't mature enough; it was in its early stages of wild lust and the endless need to feel one another closely. All of which she could be certain, was that she wanted no one else. That she craved no one else.

She kept her on the wall a little longer —binding her wrists in one hand above her head, while the other remained buried. The assassin curled towards her and moaned; unrestrained and without consideration for the neighbours either side of the walls. It only worsened when Zemir lowered to suck on her exposed throat and along her collar bone; heaving deep breaths when she surfaced for air. All of it —every shaky sound and the rising heat of her skin —Zemir couldn't get enough of it. She didn't want to compare, but she found herself unable to deny that every time with Lorrin was better than any she had ever experienced. No one had thrilled her this much; pissed her off to such an extent —and made her enjoy it. The two moved with learned sync; as though what they had done before was practice; and gave it new meaning. Delicate, lush and consuming meaning.

"*Please...*" the blonde gasped, her hands turning into fists up on the plaster. The pitch of her unsteady voice rose as Zemir's lips grazed her earlobe, then softly bit down. A highly sensitive part of her body were those ears. Simply blowing into them rendered her weak. But as much as her flushed expression aroused her, the officer straightened to claim her mouth. There was lost time for which to make up. She let go of her fighting wrists —which then immediately found their way around her neck tangled within her dark hair.

When Zemir felt dissatisfied with their position, she took to the bed and fully stripped. It was narrower than the king-sized suite, but Lorrin seemed to like it more. There was nowhere to which to escape, and she could hold her there. It was then that the officer relented and surrendered to the assassin's eagerness.

Lorrin guided her to sit up against the headboard, before seeking to feel every richly bronze plane as she lowered before her. Her hands ran down her bent legs, spreading them so that she might see all which she was doing. All the guard could do was stare back as she licked her slowly. Her light eyes never strayed; they held

Zemir's right there, where she was. She drew a breath and arced towards her in turn, shuddering with each swipe of that tongue. And it was deliciously, sinfully gratifying. Her fingers gripped the crisp sheets and blonde hair as her body fought to remain upright. All on which she could focus was that look, and how that gaze beckoned her to the edge. "*Goddess*, Raffe," she hissed, tugging at silken strands. "You'll be the end of me."

The young iman smiled and hummed; and Zemir felt those lips curl with the sound echoing through her skin. And she let herself moan —allowed her senses to be filled and saturated as she gave Lorrin the satisfaction of knowing that it felt good. Her mouth alternately latched onto her trembling thighs, leaving her mark on her in its wake —and intensifying every ripple of pleasure flooding the guard's system. Instinct was to bite down any cry loud enough to rattle her common sense, but the sight was far too rousing. She had watched Lorrin on her knees before, but there was something different in the glint of her eyes. Something in the way the officer had little control, sitting there with her legs open. It was heady, and it demanded all of her attention. She had never thought of it doing it this way; in surrendering and permitting herself to be desired.

She wished that she had done it sooner.

And the discovery of the younger iman's true self ceased to pester.
Lorrin's pleased groan was muffled during the unravelling of her. When she had crawled back up, she slid one leg upwards along hers, entangling them together. Zemir panted and caressed her cheek, then guided her head to look at her again. What was in those eyes ran deep. Deeper than what she would ever understand.

So she would offer a kiss in consolation, and another climb to ecstasy as they lay on their sides. She watched the girl with a fascination that would never go. She studied her every smile; every gasp between the parting of their lips. And she observed each reaction to a different spot on which her fingers concentrated.

"Please…show me your closet full of kinky secrets," the blonde leaned back to whisper; her eyelids shuttering as she neared her limit.

Zemir frowned slightly. "…There's no way to unknow that part of me."

"I don't want to unknow any part of you."

It wasn't in reference to just heat. The iman wanted every bit of her; that of which she was proud and of which she wasn't. Whatever fell in between. No one had wanted that much of her before. No one had dared.

She smiled; small but genuinely, and then leaned in to swallow up Lorrin's unsteady moan at the start of her undoing.

$$\dagger$$

Char wasn't smiling when the two imans met her on the High Street close to the detective's apartment building. The road was bustling with weekday evening activity, flooding them within a small crowd.

The sea creature was clutching that black overgrown letter. Whatever bravado she had possessed inside of the Hall was gone now. She stood like a shy child, avoiding eye contact despite their opportune location. "…It's for you," the Syren murmured. "It's from Gehman."

Lorrin pressed her lips together tightly as she took the envelope. "I know."

Zemir shuffled on the sidewalk, hands in her pockets. After the meeting they had asked Char to drop by far later in that day —leaving adequate time to satiate the spark of desire. Only it hadn't been enough, and she hoped that the letter did not contain horrendous news. Otherwise she would be awake all night holding the assassin in reassurance.

She tore it open; hands shaking again; before her eyes darted over the curious print. The Syren and the guard held their breath until Lorrin loosed her own. Acceptance —grim and bleak, settled over her features.

"…So the end begins."

CHAPTER 37

lorrin

SHE WAS TO go to the Unseelie Court in three days.

His Holiness had congratulated her on her newly appointed position —one of which she had no idea he was aware. Yet it made devastating sense. It sent chills down her spine that he might know of all that had happened at the Central Blades Hall, and what it entailed. He could only take her heart when she sat on the head chair and commanded as similarly as he did. All she could think was that he was a male who wasted no time.

Zemir didn't know how to ease her anxiety and terror. All she could do was cook, clean and guide Lorrin from one daily activity to the next. Though she was familiar with the fear, she was an acquaintance to death. Lorrin was a good friend. The officer hardly encountered the Unseelie, and she didn't know how to deal with majik. Her life had never been guaranteed to be taken from her because of a singular choice. She would never knowingly walk to her end.

The guard did try to understand, but it was a struggle. When all Lorrin would do was lie on the sofa and stare out the window, Zemir would have egregiously long phone calls with Fran Denaris to keep herself from staring with her.

The blonde was slow to anger. There was a pang of jealousy, but it was dull and ignorable. Her tangle of affection for the officer was one more complication to the web of utter chaos, but she took comfort in the fact that she stayed there at

Hemmingway Estate. When it mattered, Zemir was there at her side.

She'd even lied for her sake.

On the occasion that she had overheard the two guards' conversations —either when she had been so still that it appeared like she was asleep, or when the older iman had just been less discreet —it had dwindled into '*I'm fine*' and '*I'm at a friend's place*'. The Pastel Faery couldn't be so slow witted as to believe any of it; that Zemir in fact had other friends at all; but she didn't ask further questions. That would be her demise one day.

It felt like the guard was putting space between herself and the assassin, but she knew that it was simply that she couldn't help her in the way she needed. Because Lorrin wouldn't tell her how.

What on Earth could she say? How could she explain the prophecy? She had gone through possible scenarios, yielding the same miserable outcomes, and had been thoroughly deterred. The officer might try to stop her, and therefore bring a quicker end to the city of Idun. Though a dark part of her had an inkling that she wouldn't try to stop her at all, because her death wouldn't matter.

"Hey, it's time to eat."

She lifted her head from the cushion to see a bare pair of long legs. Zemir held two steaming bowls of rice and beef stir-fry. It smelled delicious —but Lorrin didn't have the strength to eat. Which was strange. Hunger wasn't a companion, but she loved anything to do with food. She had never found herself in a position where eating was the last thing she wanted to do.

"…I can't," she rasped.

The detective sighed and set the bowls on the coffee table, before kneeling at her side. Her hand tentatively brushed her hair aside, revealing the evidence of another thing that she filled time with: weeping.

"Lorrin," Zemir said softly. "I know it's difficult. I know you feel hopeless. But it will pass. A summons doesn't necessarily mean tragedy."

The assassin pressed her lips into a tight line. A piece of her fell away at the spelling out of what was going to happen. "…I'm not hungry."

On some terrible cue, her stomach protested the lie.

The older iman scoffed. "I will not watch you starve. We all need a nudge, remember? You reminded me of that."

She refused to remember such a thing.

She lazily watched Zemir blink in disbelief. "Where is the girl who fearlessly defied my every order?" she demanded. "Who took what she wanted, and never apologised? Bring back the iman who stood before creatures with majik with nothing but her wit and a knife and wormed her way to the throne of a new era."

"She's dying," Lorrin rasped. The detective frowned. "...Since that damn letter from the Unseelie King," she continued, "her days are numbered. And don't tell me that going to Gehman doesn't mean death. As the new head of the Central Blades, I *know* that it does."

"You mean to imply that you have two and a half days to live?"

"Possibly."

The assassin anticipated rage, or more silence. She was being troublesome and she knew it. Yet in her bracing for the worst, the officer offered warmth.

"...So, there's a chance that you won't die."

She couldn't answer that and give her hope. She couldn't give *herself* hope. It was better to act as though she was already doomed.

"I don't want to see your last days like this, then," the guard whispered.

Lorrin's vision focused, and she studied her face.

Zemir wasn't unfeeling. Her eyes told her so. They glistened with the tell-tale sign of tears, and swallowed great depths uncharted emotion. As crushing as the ocean. Neither one of them wanted to explore it. Neither were brave to leave the shallows —the comfortable waves which they could surf until they crashed down onto the safety of land. The deep trenches of love beyond the attractive reef were far too frightening, and there was nowhere for their feet to tread.

They'd drown if they fell.

She kissed her —clumsily. It was slow and repetitive. A breathless push and pull, and test of the waters. After a few seconds of hesitancy, Zemir cupped her dampened cheek and returned it, perhaps uncaring of what it might mean. Or maybe she knew exactly what it meant and what she was doing; as she rose and climbed onto the sofa alongside her, refusing to stray and break the contact. But her nature won out and she twisted them around to pin Lorrin to the cushions. Her tongue swept into her uncertain mouth, guiding even this, while her hands settled at her waist and the back of her neck. The assassin could only arch upwards and grip her shoulders, before hooking around them with one arm. Was it possible to convey how she felt with a kiss alone? She wished it so. She wished that she didn't have to choose between a fate she didn't want, and a person for whom she longed. Zemir entangled herself with the dying girl, and gave her awful hope. But it was lovely, and Lorrin would take it. Because even if they couldn't reach the ocean floor, at least they could pretend that they had dived deep.

When they had forced themselves apart for the sake of dinner —their t-shirts crumpled and cotton shorts loose at their hips —the blonde still struggled to find the motivation. To her surprise, Zemir sat cross-legged knee-to-knee with her on her left, and held out a sizable forkful from her plate.

"Eat."

It wasn't an order, despite its blunt instruction. It was a plead.
Lorrin slowly opened her mouth. This food was going to waste, should she fail to bargain with the King. But the beef was crisp and the rice was soft; soaked in a thin sauce which had enveloped even the green peppers, asparagus and carrots.

Life blossomed within her chest and she half smiled at the officer.

"It really is in your blood," she muttered.
The consequent look of relief which flooded Zemir's face was priceless. Then her brows narrowed, and her delight plunged to troubled.

"…What's the matter?" Lorrin asked.

"You don't have to answer me," Zemir sighed. "But I would like to know why this has affected you the way it has. Have you always been like this?"

The guard didn't want to see her wither.

"No," she answered, and it was the truth. "I don't usually deal with this sort of thing. I think it's just shock. The biggest one of my existence. But you don't have to worry about me slipping into a state of permanent detachment —I'm not entirely new at this. At ends."

Zemir shook her head. "No one should be *used* to it, Raffe. It's okay to feel grief; new and afresh. It's all right to feel helpless. You just need to reach out your hand, and find someone to help bring you back."

The assassin impulsively reached for her hand. She stared at their fingers for a moment, and burned it into her memory. Then she glanced back up into her softened gaze. "Will you bring me back?"

How dare she plead for her permanence.

Zemir drew a very deep breath. And repaid her honesty. "I don't know." Instinct told her to pull away. But the guard tightened her grip, and brought their hands between them; warmth laced together with ice cold. She squeezed once, and leaned forward to rest her forehead on hers. "…But I can try."

Her voice was barely audible. Yet it was more than enough.

Even though they had removed themselves from the secrecy of night, there was still a beautiful serenity about it. And to have someone there, holding her together, kept the thought of the Unseelie King ripping her heart from her chest at bay.

The detective spooned her beneath the duvet, acting as a living water bottle. She could feel her steady breath at the back of her neck, and her blue hair falling along her shoulder. It was…strange. Sleeping like this with another body against her was not something that she had ever thought she'd do.

And the officer was beyond respectful —her hands stayed loosely clasped at her stomach, unadventurous. But she wanted a distraction. She didn't want to fall back into the endless darkness which had eaten at her earlier.

"Zemir," she whispered into the dimness.

"Mm?"

She slowly pushed back against her, before sliding her legs up and down on the silk. The exact words refused to make it out of her mouth. The exact request. Her confidence had diminished; her resolve limp; and all she wanted was to feel something other than the weight of the sky. "Please."

The guard gripped her hip, halting her movements. Though she couldn't resist skidding her hand down along her thigh, riding up her shorts. "...Are you sure?" she asked. "I don't want to disrupt if what you need is peace and quiet."

"Don't go," Lorrin insisted. "If anything, I don't want to be alone tonight."

The whir of her thoughts was more bearable without silence.

Zemir paused at the echo of her own sentiment all of those nights ago. It had only been a couple of weeks, but they seemed buried long ago in the past. For her, the blonde had comforted her that way when she had needed it. But to that hour, she couldn't pin a particular reason as to why she had agreed to it. She hadn't hated it. Yet she couldn't scrounge for the meaning behind the desire.

"Please," the assassin asked again.

After a moment of deliberation, Zemir sighed and slid her hand up under Lorrin's t-shirt. The girl flinched, before shuddering slightly as the touch skimmed her breasts. She felt the other hand run down her midsection and descend beyond the band of her pyjama shorts. Lorrin let out a shaky, shallow breath at the slow insertion of fingers between her legs.

"*Raffe*," whispered the officer. "I love the way your body moulds to me." Her lips brushed by her ear. "Begs for me."

It certainly did. It had since they had first met.

Lorrin quivered, biting back a curse. Her every breath coincided with the guard's movements. It was absolutely electrifying. One of the simplest methods, yet somehow perfectly effective right then. Her soft panting only became more frequent as she rolled her hips in time. Zemir's fingers were leisurely and deep, while her other hand moved from her heaving chest to her neck —to guide its tilt backwards as she kissed and bit the nape.

Lorrin's moans turned strained and pleading. The cold had been chased away, and all which remained was the rising heat pulsing through her system. It seeped into the room; as did the sound of her breathless pleasure. It was music to Zemir's ears, given her hums of satisfaction.

"Just like that," she hissed, biting harder. "Louder."

There was something in the praise and demand; in the officer's voice. It filled

Lorrin, utterly, and bent her to her will. She'd been all hers longer than reality.

She gasped out '*yes*', three times. Then again. And again. Yes to right now; yes to forever. Yes to her; to them. Whether that was the flicker of a moment or all of eternity. And she came undone with it.

The position provided a far more potent climax. The assassin writhed and trembled, Zemir's name on her tongue —and ensured that the detective felt the ripples of it. She *did* feel it —and groaned against her spine in response; the sound layered with frustration.

Lorrin smiled, and reached backwards to run a hand through her dark hair. "I wouldn't mind returning the favour," she assured.

Zemir's grip on her waist and breast tightened. "No," she ended up grinding out through clenched teeth. She definitely wanted to, but her self-control was well exercised. "We can't. You need to sleep —to rest."

Lingering bliss clouded her regular cognitive functions, and she sighed as her cheeks flushed in embarrassment. There was obviously no shame in wanting to touch her too, but she was making it seem like an offence.

The disappointment was suppressible. "…If you're sure."

Detective Kal still had ways to make her heart useless. She shifted behind her and mumbled, "I'm never sure when it comes to you, girl."

CHAPTER 38

lorrin

"WHAT ARE YOU up to?" Zemir asked as she wandered into the kitchen the next morning, yawning in indication of a hypocritical lack of sleep.

Lorrin patted the pile of books and her smart-tablet on the island in front of her. "Researching some history."

"Whose?"

"Gehman's," she murmured, pouring over the next thick leather-bound. "If I have no choice in going there, I need to go with some knowledge on how the court operates, and adhere to the proper courtesies and customs."

"I thought you wanted to stay off of the grid. Why do you have a tablet?"

"Bought third-hand," was the explanation. "And it's sim-less."

The guard neared, before leaning over to read what she was reading. Her buttoned shirt hung off one of her shoulders, and her socks were falling down her ankles. Despite being a mess, her hair retained its silkiness; glinting in the rising suns. Even the frown which sullied her visage made Lorrin's chest tighten.

"...That's not what happened," she quipped, pointing to the page.

It was a chapter on the Sekon Idun War. The blonde had known it as a conflict which had divided The Court and Majik District from the rest of the city. The Maji and scholars hadn't wanted to mix so freely with the larger population, lest their majik ended up in the wrong hands. The rich had simply wanted an exclusive playground. The book spoke of that Wall and Sythe River, and its purpose. Every citizen learned that the Wall was meant to protect them from Gehman and the hostile Unseelie Court. The King's resentment of it was common knowledge, and his reclamation was more of an inevitability to be avoided and postponed for as long as possible, than an uncertain probability.

No one knew that it would all happen tomorrow.

"Inaccuracies in our history books?" Lorrin scoffed. "*Real* surprising."
"Mm. That battle in Loegon didn't end with the imprisonment of Unseelie before sending them back," Zemir said gravely. "They…those are the bodies the Guard found buried in the park."

The assassin started. "The Dripping Red Sun Massacre from the News?"

The guard nodded. "It wasn't even a fight. It was an elaborate trap to deplete His Holiness' numbers. It was brutal, and it was wrong."

Lorrin glanced at her from the corner of her vision. "I'm not for genocide, nor do I harbour '*hate*' for the Unseelie. I feel that they hate us more. But detective, I must know if you side with them."

Zemir blinked, quite taken aback. "The dark Faery kind do hate us, Raffe. As we fear them. It's not about loyalty. I strove to side with what's right."

Not justice, anymore, because justice had failed her. The younger iman could understand that. And it *was* wrong —no matter who the victor was, or who had started it. That mass grave was wrong, and many would see it. The veil over the truth of Idun would be parted, and the suns would shine down on the ugly reality.

"…Do you know what else Her Excellency covered up?" she asked.

The officer slid onto the stool beside her. "No, but I can guess. The Unseelie aren't one for bending the truth. No Faery can lie. Our history books tell a story of willing division; of one faction breaking from another. I'd like to think that it was forced, and that one grew tired of the other. The Unseelie and Favoured work better without imannity thrown in, so I believe our ancestors poisoned something. We caused the rift, and we've only been making it worse. While I can agree that the dark Faery kind treated other species cruelly and haven't stopped, I don't think that caging them will lessen their thirst for our extinction."

"Maybe Nadune knows that," Lorrin sighed, picking up her tablet and opening a new tab. "She's just biding her time. She should've made a bargain back then."

She typed '*bargaining with the Faery kind*' into the search engine of her web browser, before pressing enter. Numerous links showed up as restricted —the only accessible ones being those concerned with Seelie and Wyches.

"A bargain has to be mutual," said the detective. "If she attempted it after the war, it must have not been beneficial to the King, and thus he rejected it."

"So I have to offer him something he cannot refuse."

"He already has that, according to you," Zemir murmured, meeting her eye. "What you need to think about is what you want; the city; and what's the best damage control. You have somewhat of an upper hand, Raffe."

That fact hit her for the very first time. It gave her a glimmer of fayth.

The doorbell then rang, causing Lorrin to flinch.

The guard stood, and headed for the foyer.

"Did you order something?" she called after her.

"…Uh, sort of."

Lorrin turned to see Char Gilligan saunter in, wearing dark blue jeans, knee-high leather boots and a Phoenixes vest top. Her assassin attire. She had been sent back in the blonde's stead to the Central Blades to inform them of her summoning — and that she would only return once some '*paperwork*' had been completed.

"You called Char over?" the iman spluttered.

"I figured you could use some more support," Zemir reasoned. "And I believe that she's your second-in-command. The best person to have at your side right now is the one you trust the most."

She didn't trust the Syren *that* much, but neither female corrected it.

"All right," Lorrin said tightly. "Do you have any advice, Gilligan?"

The Syren padded over and glanced over the books. "You're certainly not going to learn everything from that horseshit."

Lorrin drew a defeated breath. "I'm gathering that."

"And I wouldn't be publicly searching for bargaining techniques either," Char added, frowning at the screen. "You want to end up on a watchlist?"

"Okay, okay," she snapped, flipping the bubblegum pink cover over. "How about you tell me what I should do, instead of what I shouldn't?"

The Syren sighed and climbed onto the other stool beside her. Zemir returned to her previous chair; sandwiching the younger iman between them.

"Quick question, before we go on," the redhead quipped, smirking. "Are you two *actually* dating? I know about the rumours. Talk about the ultimate irony."

"No," the two imans answered in unison.

Lorrin shot her a look, which the detective returned.

"It was...a performance. And this isn't about us," the assassin sharply dismissed. She then tapped her cast-aside tablet. "Now, how do I bargain?"

"You must understand what the King wants, and what you want," Char said, leaning forward on the island. "A bargain must present a desirable compromise between the two parties. For example: a Seelie asks you out on a date, and if you refuse, your future children will be cursed. Depending on how easy it is to get out of—like if you don't even want children—you can bargain with them to turn the ultimatum into something more like...if you go on a few dates and hate them, then it will be *their* children who will bear the curse."

Lorrin's eyes narrowed in bewilderment.

"That's terrible," Zemir scoffed.

"I second that."

"That's just the way of the Faery kind," the Syren protested. "They make crazy demands all the time and expect to have their way."

"The Unseelie King doesn't want to date me, Char. He's going to *kill* me." Neither female at her sides knew all that the prophecy entailed. Not of the purpose of her heart, and not of the crown intended to sit on her head. At least, the Syren knew that the King wanted her dead, given that note he had left with Jerrek Burr's head. She thought when the best time to disclose it all might be, though when it came to such information, perhaps it was better to keep them in the dark. She didn't want that fate to alter the fragile perceptions they had of her.

"Hm," Char then mused, tapping her chin. "Fine. What if you give him exactly what he wants, but threaten *his* life, too?"

Lorrin paused, pondering the feasibility. What if she could trick the King into giving her second chance at life —a chance to defeat him? And indeed, how could he refuse, if it was only *her* heart which he needed?

"Wouldn't he just kill her anyway?" Zemir hissed. "Nothing would stand in his way even if Lorrin resisted."

"Shit," grumbled the sea creature.

"I second that too," the blonde groaned, placing her head onto the marble. The officer still speculated in light of the others' defeat. Circumstances weren't helpless —not yet. They simply hadn't looked at every angle. The guard didn't want to see her efforts be in vain. She didn't want to watch the city burn, and she didn't want to hear news of her death. Lorrin Raffe had to live —and as selfishly as she phrased it, she had to live so that Zemir could live. Lorrin had become a part of her life which she couldn't breathe easily without.

Her amber eyes lit up when she found an answer. "...Then you have to make yourself worth something," she told the assassin. "You have to become priceless."

But she wasn't of any value. The younger iman appreciated the suggestion, and understood that there was nothing a mere mortal could offer the Unseelie King. Nor the entire court. She was sure that they didn't need a jester.

Char's eyes lit up too. "He has a harem, from what I heard —"

"Absolutely not," Lorrin clipped.

"I second that," murmured the detective, her gaze down on the island. Her foot swung, lightly brushing against the blonde's. A shiver shot along her spine, but she couldn't bring herself to smile or nudge her back. It was an outrageously possessive hold that the officer had over her current thoughts. She wasn't hers, yet she expected her to remain faythful to whatever it was that they had. Yet what *was* it exactly? They hadn't spoken about it since she had apologised for sleeping with Nam-joon. Neither female would like to call it *'dating'* —and it was barely a friendship. But both knew that something kindled between them, and as much as they wanted to stifle and disregard it, it wasn't something to be ignored.

Lorrin was sure that she wanted her far more than she might want her. In what capacity, she couldn't name. She hadn't thought about it properly. Habit shackled her eagerness —and likely for good reason.

But when Zemir did things like that; made their strange relationship feel like it weighed more than it did...it made her feel sick and stupid. For wanting more than the older iman could give —and for even wanting her affection at all.

"...I will go to the Unseelie Court and stand before him as his equal," Lorrin finally sighed, before pushing off of the stool. "I will not be some demure sacrifice for his fulfilment."

The two females stared at her in intrigue as she made for the stairs.

"I need to go out," she then informed them. "There's an order to be collected." But before she could ascend to take a shower, an alarm started blaring. Very loud and unignorable. The three females exchanged looks of surprise. It wasn't the Hemmingway Estate's security system. It wasn't a car.

It was the Euradon State of Emergency siren.

CHAPTER 39

lorrin

THE SKY HAD turned red. And that part of the seafront a purple, with it. It was visible from inside of a building, but clearer from the front lawn. Arching above the capital, was the image of an all too familiar circle with thin, wavy rays and thirty four smaller circles around that. It was majik —not a hologram or some other kind of projection. It flared and pulsed with an irrefutable glow, and sparked with painful rage. The whole city could see it; fear it.

The dripping red sun.

Lorrin had always wondered why the Faery kind had made that the land's namesake all of those years ago, despite there clearly being two suns above them. But now she had to wonder if that symbol meant something else entirely. That the sun wasn't literally such, and was a stand-in for something else.

Just as Idun used it on the crest, it was a means of identification.

The siren was disorientating.

The three females stumbled out into the driveway, gaping at the phenomenon. What on earth made it an emergency? Nothing bled down on them.

"Char, is it leaking anything?" Lorrin turned to her.

The Syren's face soured and she gripped her dagger's gild handle until her knuckles blanched. "Yes. Something I've never seen before."

"Will it kill us?" Zemir hissed.

"I…I don't know," the creature struggled, faltering as she shivered and shook out her shoulders. "I feel no other effect besides the prickling of my skin."

The image remained ominous —until a few new dots flew up beside it. Lorrin squinted. They were figures like people —Maji and scholars. Bursts of brightly coloured majik flashed across the red sun. They were trying to eradicate it, but it didn't seem to be working. The symbol continued to loom, and appeared to grow a little larger with each pulse; each beat.

It was unclear as to whether they should return to the house, be it for the safety procedures or the non-fatal —as far as they knew —consequences of the symbol's radiation. No announcements were being made.

"TV," Zemir blurted, darting back inside.

They couldn't switch it on fast enough. And when they managed to, the screen displayed a jarring and slow flashing '*we interrupt this program*' panel in place of the standard EBC bulletin. The reporter was live from the Wall blockade near the border, listening in from a radio earpiece.

"*Reports and witness accounts are flooding in on the giant red sun symbol over the Idun sky; expanding with every passing second. The image was cast around ten hundred hours this morning, though it is our understanding that the alarm was just turned on. The cause has not been confirmed, but there is suspicion of activity from Gehman —the district home to the Unseelie Court.*"

"Yeah, no shit!" Char cried, throwing up her arms.

"*At present there are no instructions other than stay wherever you are, and remain calm. Majik users from the Academy are working on the scene.*"

"That's super helpful," Zemir scoffed, leaning back and folding her arms. The siren was growing louder —along with low pitched humming sound, which the assassin could mostly feel through her bones. She looked down at her hands. They trembled, vibrating with the hum. The very air suddenly seemed alive with it. Her gaze flicked to the windows. The glass was shaking. Lorrin looked at the others, but their attention was glued on the television.

The windows rattled.

How could no one hear it? It was deafening, and Lorrin was sure that blood

304

was dripping from her ears. Then it was too late —the warning never left her lips as the humming reached its crescendo, and every pane shattered. Disintegrated into pieces and fell to the sills and the floor. No shards had been projected; sheets of it simply lay there like layers of crystalised frost.

It couldn't be unnoticeable now.

Sure enough, Char and Zemir jolted at the crashes and gaped in horror. The sofa was against the furthest wall —far from the windows leading to the back gardens. They were unscathed; and simply stunned.

As bad as it was at Hemmingway Estate, it was nothing compared to the rising screams which came through the television. In a split second, Idun was plunged into chaos. Glass showered from office towers and high rise buildings; streetlights burst above the roads; helicopters spiralled —straight into skyscrapers. All the while the siren wailed, mingling unharmoniously with car alarms, the oncoming ambulance sirens and shrieking citizens. It *was* a witnessing of history; a cruel and terrifying account. And it would echo for years to come.

"Holy shit," the Syren breathed.

Lorrin shook her head, over and over. *No, no, no.*

The prophecy had spoken of disaster, but she had not fathomed something like this. The Unseelie King was proving his worth; drilling in the warning that he was not to be underestimated due to his court's small size or lack of modern weapons. Though most would argue that majik was more potent. Gehman was just getting started. And all that had happened was the breaking of glass; the crashing of small low-flying aircraft, and the reddening of the sky. She couldn't imagine the deaths.

This couldn't be happening. Not now. Not yet.

She still had one day left to live. The letter stated it. The Faery kind couldn't lie. So why was Death knocking early? The chance to save the city was slipping between her fingers like sand in an hourglass, and it was more likely that she was being called to action —to the front lines.

"*...This just in. Amidst the city-wide glass shattering, we've received a live account of Her Excellency being spotted leaving Loegon and heading for the border Wall. We have reason to believe that she wishes to talk to His Holiness* *and make a declaration of war—!"*

The broadcast was hovering between clear and static, as though another signal were interfering, despite there not needing to be that sort of signal in the first place, but everyone would hear it. Every creature would know of Nadune Madir's decision to fight the Unseelie once more.

Lorrin couldn't let that happen.

"That traitorous coward," hissed the sea creature.

"*Char*," the blonde hedged, eyeing her from the corner of her eyes.
"You don't understand," the Syren cut back. "She sent an urgent message this morning saying that if anything happened, I should gather the best assassins. That she wouldn't resort to another massacre, like her predecessors."

The imans shared a perplexed look.

"What the Hehl, you little urchin," Zemir snarled. "That's the kind of news you open up with, not blurt out at the last second!"

"Well I didn't anticipate this state of emergency!"

"And we're out of last seconds," Lorrin frowned, grabbing the burner she kept in one of her kitchen drawers. She punched in Madam G's cellphone number. It was answered immediately. "...Hello? Madam G, it's Lorrin Raffe."

"*Lorrin, oh thank the Daughter!*" the Wyche's voice cried. "*I've been waiting, thinking that you might call. Are you all right, love? Were you away from windows during the shatter?*"

"Yes, I'm okay," she insisted. "But that's not why I called. Right now, I need you to meet me on the corner of Ink and Hann as soon as possible. Bring that suit we spoke about. I can't come to pick it up after all."

There was a beat of silence in which the Favoured came to understand what was happening. This could be the last time she would hear from the girl. "*...Of course, darling. Anything you need.*"

The Syren and the guard looked on with growing fear.

"...T-Thank you, Madam G," she whispered. "I mean it."
The Wyche refused to hear any sadness. "*Gerti, you goose.*"

She did indeed feel silly —but only because she wished there was something

306

other than money to offer the seamstress. All she'd remember was beautiful works of art; brief, witty conversation and matchmaking attempts. What might the sly female think of what had become of her life? That in the end, at the front steps of death, she had uncovered a love which she could not have.

"I take it we're going to Ink and Hann, then," the detective spoke up.

Char straightened her vest top determinedly.

Lorrin quickly shook her head on her way back to the stairs. "There's no '*we*'. I'm going there alone. I'm won't endanger either of you."

"I'm not giving you a choice, girl," Zemir countered. "I'll say no goodbye. I want to be there —until the very last second."

"So do I," the Syren insisted. It was the most emotion she had ever shown on her face. And it wasn't something easy, like anger. It was desperate and it was painful. It was honest. "I joined you to see this through to the end, your Majesty."

The assassin stared at her, unsure of how to react to her sincerity. There was no doubt that it was. Instead of returning that sentiment, Lorrin offered a small smile and veer from the subject. "...You're going to have to stop calling me that."

Char grinned. "Never."

✝

Madam G was there before them, which made the iman wonder if she did in fact possess the majik needed for teleportation. It was doubtful, and the more plausible explanation was that her car was fast and she had broken several road laws.

It was worse in Loegon, and by the Wall.

Fire and smoke towered into the sky; majik flickered here and there, as the Maji and scholars had retreated momentarily to offer healing to the severely injured; and the siren rang louder still. The dripping red sun —which was still swelling —loomed like an all seeing eye. It wouldn't surprise her to know that His Holiness had launched it for precisely that purpose.

What mattered was that Madam G was there, bearing a long black clothes cover over a hanger. Swirls of purple licked about it. Not majik to attack or defend,

307

but to preserve. The Wyche teetered over as best as she could manage in high heels, meeting Lorrin halfway as she jumped from her car in grey sweatpants and a t-shirt. It was all she could pull on in a minute.

"Oh!" the Favoured exclaimed at the sight of the Syren and officer. "Extras. Who might you be? Did you finally make some friends, Raffe?"

"*Gerti*," Lorrin hedged, outraged. She snatched the hanger and returned to the safety of tinted windows. Changing clothes had never been such a tedious and hazardous endeavour. But she couldn't face the Unseelie Court without some form of protection. The assassin stripped and tugged impatiently at the zip of the slippery cover, revealing the glorious ensemble. She had called Madam G as soon as the letter from Gehman had arrived, for a quick job. It was too short notice for a new piece from scratch, so she had requested a repurposed white suit. The beautiful material was just as blinding as she wanted; just as pure. It wasn't her intention to keep it that clean —if she came back, it would be as dark and purple as the sea by the harbour.

The Wyche had likely worked sleeplessly to achieve Lorrin's vision of half a gown's skirt wrapped around the back of the trousers, as well as sewing on a large hood to the shoulders of the top —which was fashioned into a combined waistcoat and silk blouse. And to her surprise, a golden haladie knife was embroidered down along the middle of the back.

It was an homage to Selena; an echo of the Central Blades; and a symbol for every female who had been denied their power.

It all fit heavily, the weight mirroring its wearer's destiny. And it commanded attention when she stepped out of the car, sweeping the ground and draped over her head. No one would be able to tell that she still had her boots on underneath. She held her ivory dagger behind her back under the bulk of the hood.

Madam G's face and eyes lit up with an artist's pride —before she promptly remembered the mood of the occasion. Char and Zemir blinked in awe, but Lorrin's attention foolishly gravitated to the guard's reaction.

She didn't seem to know what to say. It was beautiful, but those words caught in her throat. The assassin was a sacrifice or saint —like a lamb to the slaughter;

a thing to appease a monster.

Zemir's face contorted into something resembling distress, and she neared, close enough to pull Lorrin in towards her. The Syren and the Wyche huddled by the side of the road; Char smirking as she nudged the Favoured suggestively, who looked on with barely contained excitement.

The officer dithered. "I...I should've..."

Lorrin blinked, tentatively reaching for her bare arm. "Should've what?" she asked softly. "I thought you weren't going to say goodbye."

"I'm not," Zemir rasped, frowning. "I just...you know all one's regrets rush to the forefront in times like this."

"Times like, parting?" she offered. The guard's lips were clamped shut. She wouldn't voice it. The assassin drew a breath. "So...what are these regrets?"

A bit of colour flooded the detective's cheeks, looking out of place on her stoic expression. "I should have kissed you sooner," she said, very seriously, as though the action were scheduled prayer. "I should have asked you questions before. I should have stayed away...but you invaded every aspect of my life. And it felt so natural. You've rooted yourself in it all, and it's too late to cut you out."

Lorrin wasn't breathing, unlike their audience's rapid and hushed gasps.

"You, without fail, piss me off," Zemir continued. "But I've never smiled that much. Laughed that much. And you...you've become more than what you've done. I never would have thought that I could live with someone as harmoniously as we managed. So I need you to come back, Raffe. I need you to come home."

Lorrin flinched at the caress of her hand along her frozen cheek. Before she could think of a single word with which to respond, warmth was already at her mouth, kissing it and sweeping her up within. How could she indulge in something that wasn't rage or tragedy when that was all which billowed around them? But it was in that moment that she realised she'd been feeding herself a lie. The guard didn't hold her in contempt, and she had a reason to survive.

She *had* to —there was no longer a choice.

A low rumbling forced the two apart.

The ground shuddered, jerking the unprepared Madam G onto her backside. All attention was on the large structure before them —as it was a previous culprit.

"Bloody Hehl, it's the Wall!" Char confirmed, pointing to several fractures cracking through the surface with alarming speed.

Lorrin lurched aside. "Get in the car!"

After a mad scramble, two cars raced deeper into the city towards the safety limits set out from the previous resident evacuation. It wasn't that the closest streets to the base were completely restricted —but they were empty. Not even a ghost haunted the danger zones.

"Go *faster*, oh my Goddess!" shrieked the Syren, craning her neck to look out of the window behind them. "It's breaking!"

A loud thud made the car rattle and stall. As she fought to restart the engine, more ground-shakers followed. She only stole a glance. Even that was too much. In the road they had left behind them, small chunks —in comparison to the magnitude of the Wall —had fallen down into the city.

Lorrin slammed down on the accelerator, tailing Madam G's purple Beetle down a turn in an intersection. It wasn't going to be close, but she didn't want to take chances. Not with falling debris.

There were officers by the barrier limits when they drove in, ushering citizens and the News stations away from the developing disaster. Among them was Fran Denaris, who looked unbelievably flummoxed at the odd mix of people —then enraged when she spotted Zemir coming up the rear. She flew over and grabbed her by the collar of her shirt, demanding an explanation to many things. But that was petty and trivial nonsense, when the assassin snared every curious gaze, and had cameras panning her way. She must have looked the part of a saviour, at least.

They immediately snapped back to the Wall, however, when the first sizable piece broke off. A building-wide section from the cornered middle in view from the capital offices, as far as they could see, was what was falling away.

The air stilled and the red sun paused to listen as the only thing between the Unseelie and the rest of Idun crumbled like a sandcastle beneath the tide.

CHAPTER 40

lorrin

A CLOUD OF dust settled at the base in an ash cloud.

The uproar came when it had cleared, to reveal a narrow parabolic gape in the stretch from one side of the horizon to the other. The King hadn't even knocked down the entire Wall. That was what the subsequent questions encompassed. Why on Earth would he only make a door, and what was going to come through it?

"Why are you dressed like that?" Officer Denaris finally asked the assassin.

The girl pulled the hood back up over her sunlight hair and waved her dagger. "I'm going to offer myself to His Holiness."

"Apparently Her Excellency beat you to it," one of the guards muttered. "Not the point," the Seelie clipped. Her gaze raked the length of white, unsure of what to think. "Why would you have anything to do with this?"

Something else dropped from the sky —an Elf and a Moth.

Fran reeled, startled by the pair landing from the height of the dripping red sun. Rye looked more knackered than usual, but he was relieved to see Lorrin.

"She has *everything* to do with this," he said gravely, nudging Tinnia forward to verify. The Faery nodded solemnly. "She's the one the King wants."

The onlookers were still confused.

"What's that supposed to mean?" Fran asked, stumbling back. Her wings drooped, folding together. Her voice was laced with uncertainty instead of cheek.

But the commotion was interrupted with a loud fanfare; deep and harrowing. Over the pile of rubble, a presession of Unseelie gathered. No one had to ask. They were intending to step into Loegon. The Faeries wore ancient armour, and bore long spears tipped with glinting, luminescent roughly cut precious stones. And emerging from between them, was the Unseelie King. He wasn't clear from that distance, but she could see how he towered; his enormous Drakon-like wings folded behind him, and that he was draped in black, gold and olive green. In his hand, he held the hand of a very familiar iman who was also dressed in white. The News station cameras still whirred.

His Holiness inclined his head; the girl blinked, and he and the governor were right in front of the crowd, shrouded in dark purple.

Unbridled fear flashed through Lorrin's system. But she stood in front of the guards behind her; a flimsy shield to keep the attention on her alone. She stood as the last obstacle keeping him from triumph —and in turn she felt that triumph. However prematurely, or how short-lived it would be. Zemir Kal dared to stare the Unfavoured down as well with her shoulders squared as though she might duel him; knowing he was the one taking Lorrin away from her.

"Hello," he smiled.

His voice was acid. The assassin's stare hardened into a glare. "*You.*"

Every officer drew their pistol or sword.

The King merely sighed. "Oh put your toys away. They cannot harm me —and if I witness a gun firing, my soldiers and I will kill everyone standing within my line of vision without hesitation. Including your little governor."

She could barely stand beside him. Upon closer inspection, her embellished suit was bloodied. She groaned and fell to her knees, her midsection soaked red, and a large wound above her brow bled over her face.

She was very clearly close to death.

"Your Excellency!" Fran screamed, darting forward. "What did you do, you fucking *asshole* —!"

The Unseelie held up a finger, and the Faery just froze; her muscles locked in some invisible hold. She fought against it, her wings flared and twitching as she

312

hissed curses. "But a moment," the King said. "I will give you back this fool, in exchange for *that* one." The finger lowered, and pointed to Lorrin.

The blonde went rigid.

"You look so...righteous," he mused, tilting his head to the side. His long curled hair swayed with the movement. "Like a holy maiden. So without sin."

"I suppose then you wear your sin boldly," Zemir clipped.

The assassin hated how he studied her. And grinned. "Naturally."

"Give us our governor," an officer demanded, their sword trembling. "And did you do that?" They pointed to the sky. The red sun pulsed, unmoving.

"No I did not. That was my general. Trust me when I say that it is the *last* thing about which you need to worry," the Unfavoured huffed, before throwing Nadune towards their feet. She was caught immediately so her body didn't hit the tar, and then whisked away within the crowd just as quick. He then beckoned the young iman. "Come, child. You have something of mine."

Lorrin's feet refused to move. Of the thoughts which whirled for her focus, the victor was that this moment was so final. The prophecy would now be realised, and it had led up to this. Where had the time gone? Had she lived out her last days well? She was resolved to make it to the end, to see the city heal, but the King's presence was very real. He was larger than she had pictured.

Darker.

Fran still struggled against his majik, deemed too volatile to free just yet.

"Raffe," Rye's voice then rattled her alert and awake, as he gripped her shoulder. His face was soft, and sympathetic. Even the frigid Seeyer offered her the smallest look of warmth. "It's time."

"...I know."

The Unseelie King held out a bony grey hand.

She extended a shaky arm to meet it.

But Zemir grabbed hold of her other fingers. She turned and looked back into that amber, and felt her eyes prick with heated pain. Her grip tightened, to the point where it should hurt, and rested her forehead against hers.

They couldn't say anything which they wanted here —they shouldn't have even touched. Because now it would be broadcast to all the world. And while Lorrin didn't mind, she knew that the detective's family would. They'd see her in pyjamas on television with a doomed girl holding a knife, and see how she was intertwined with a fate about which no one had known for weeks.

"Everything's going to change now," Zemir murmured.

"I...I should've been completely honest," Lorrin sighed, nodding slightly.

"What do you mean?"

"I have some regrets, too."

A throat was very rudely and impatiently cleared. "I suggest that you say farewell to your lover concisely," the Unfavoured chuckled. "For it will be the last time you see each other before Hehl."

"Uh, I wouldn't call us —" Zemir protested.

"I'm going to walk right back out of your court, Your Holiness," Lorrin firmly cut her off, unable to stomach hearing the elaboration of the sentence. "Perhaps with your head in my hand, gripping your hair."

He said nothing, and only let his dark blue eyes glint ominously.

The blonde gave the guard one last look; one which she prayed would relay her feelings; before leaning in to whisper in her ear. "...Only you." There were other things she wanted to say —words which would bind her even more, but she had to show restraint. She'd say them when she returned.

Zemir's grip lingered even as she let go and moved back towards the King.

His hand was freezing and a harsh contrast to the touch of any other living creature. Though maybe it made sense that he was cold blooded. It would make killing people as easy as sighing. He clasped her hand possessively, as though she wholly belonged to him to serve his agenda.

They turned their backs to the crowd.

"Let me go with her!" someone then shouted.

The Unseelie glanced back to see a small Syren, panting and determined, being held back by a far more grounded Wyche; elegant in her dress, though her facial expression did not reflect the same sentiment. The sea creature was seething, and also possessed a knife strapped at her hip.

"And you are?" His Holiness deadpanned.

"Her most loyal subordinate," Char hissed.

He looked her up and down, spying a fish bone with legs, but recognised the spark of rage within her. He could likely exhaust her with a few traitorous Faeries to kill. And she seemed to be of no threat to him, or of much help to her precious leader. He could tell that her majik was weak, and pathetic next to his own. If she wanted to die that badly, then he would grant that wish.

"Your loyalty amuses me, male-eater," he smirked, giving only one curl of his finger in indication of his permission. She broke away from Madam G and scurried over. Lorrin only offered her a brief glance.

The skirt fluttered out behind her, as they walked towards the threshold. "Behold," the King then addressed the apprehensive crowd; the cameras, once more as tendrils of black and purple seeped from him. "The little queen."

†

Gehman was colder by comparison.

It was summer in Idun, but the Unseelie Court seemed to exist within its own realm of physics. It was ethereal —and Lorrin didn't want to admit that, so she feigned disinterest. Though the air bit at her cheeks, the forest terrain itself was lush and diverse. The flora seemed unaffected by the temperature —and by extension, neither were the Unseelie.

Gangly lightly wrapped woodland dark Faery kind wandered and whispered among the trees, drawn by the beat of their King's wings. A Syren blinded by revenge in tow, and a self-righteous iman on his arm in a suit of snowy white. The image of a double bladed knife at her back.

How would he kill them, they must have wondered. Break them and pluck the heart from the sacrificial murderess. How might they scream?

It was all very exciting; every third Unseelie they passed flittered from branch to branch alongside them. They would walk all the way to the court, it seemed. The forest cleared after some metres into a familiar layout of houses and streets.

Faeries and Favoured by birth bustled about their lives across a town square; one not as modern as Loegon, but closer to that of the Iris District. Market stalls lined the pavements, and the people dressed about a hundred years from the past; in pinafores, long skirts, pinstripe trousers and suspenders. They all parted for their King and his entourage; soldiers marching at the rear.

He was smiling. As though he was parading and showing off a bride.

Lorrin tried not to squirm, and kept her attention on nothing but putting one foot in front of the other. She wouldn't meet the Syren's eye. She couldn't. Not after knowing that she too was walking to her own death.

Then the Unfavoured leading her steps spoke. "You're quiet," he murmured, nodding slightly at a curtseying Wyche whose teeth might have once been white long ago. "I expected some form of a fight."

She didn't reply.

"I can't tell whether you're simply taking this graciously, being spiteful, or if you have cut out your tongue."

The assassin frowned.

"...Hm," he hummed knowingly. "I see —you miss her. That dauntless iman in the pyjamas. You love her, don't you?"

It wasn't actually a question. She knew that. It was a statement plain and stark, and she gritted her teeth to show that she hated it. What good would it do to answer? He wouldn't pity her. He wouldn't spare her. In fact, he might gain some sort of sick pleasure from knowing that he was ruining that love.

"My advice would be to cling to that emotion, should it leave you docile," the Unseelie King went on. "The less you delay the proceedings the better."

Now her attention refocused. "What proceedings? And how did you lie about when I should come here?"

He chuckled lowly. "I didn't lie about a single thing. I gave you a time frame, but my soldiers got overzealous with our plans."

She stared up at him; at his sheer size, and wondered how many stabs it would take to fell him. It would be no easy feat. And using her dagger on him directly was unwise —it would only be a weapon of defence. The only way she was going to beat him was with words, and crafty ones at that.

Being the slightest bit desirable was only the first step.

"What did you do to Nadune Madir?" she then inquired. Char tilted her head as she came up at her side again, also curious.

The iman didn't expect him to answer, but he was strangely cooperative and concise. "She came to declare war. I gave her a small taste of it."

The town fell away and the streets opened up to a vast courtyard. A dark castle stood over them, menacing and overbearing, but the King looked at it with the fondness of home. The soldiers ushered them through the heavy doors, which only plunged them into darkness occasionally broken by torches on the walls. The throne room was already noisy with court members, with grating music echoing the corridors. It might have been beautiful if it didn't make her ears shrivel.

"…It's spite," Lorrin quipped, flicking her head back forwards.
The Faery had to pause to place her statement, before smirking with amusement.

It was musty in there —warm and rotting, and the blonde stood out even more from the shadows. But she held up her chin even as the King's hand finally withdrew and he left her and the Syren standing before the dais as he climbed the steps. The court was silent and still. He sprawled atop his throne fashioned from a great tree trunk; laughing and calling for wine.

"Dance," he commanded. "And be merry. The offering is in but a few short hours tonight." The dark Faery kind around the assassin and Char stared, jeering, before they echoed their ruler's distorted delight and darted off to obey. A bright pink Unseelie flittered over before climbing into his lap; barely covered in strips of fabric held by fayth and gold string. His Holiness then met Lorrin's steel gaze, and she held her knife tighter. "…Welcome to the Unseelie court."

CHAPTER 41

zemir

A SHOCK BLANKET was wrapped around her shoulders, but that wasn't what she was feeling. She tugged it around her all the same, somehow feeling chilly despite the suns being positioned midpoint in the sky. She couldn't feel the warmth of the sunslight, nor could she hear the commotion. Figures like reporters swarmed, buzzing about and submerging her head in water. All she could do was breathe into microphones, before a guard would escort her to safety.

What *was* safety?

She sat on the front steps of the precinct, preparing for questioning. Madam G was in a better condition to drive Lorrin's car to Hemmingway Estate after taking hers and ordering a Yuber back to the Wall. It was Zemir who was vacant —left a shell because of the irrational reason of fearing for someone's life. The reddened world blurred in her vision; moving without her. Living on without her.

It wasn't as though anyone had another choice, with Her Excellency in critical condition. The assassin's predicament could wait. At least that was what the more polite politicians said. Others wrote her off as dead already.

Someone then called for her. She started and glanced upwards at an Elf —the same one who had dropped from the dripping red sun with the Seeyer close behind. They both wore robes from the Hall of Excellence Academy, and looked as though they had been awake for a week.

"Zemir Kal, right?" he said gravely. "They're calling for you next."

She nodded slowly.

"I'm Rye. Raffe's friend."

She sucked on her teeth. "Of course you are."

The Favoured appeared sympathetic. "She spoke of you briefly," he went on. "I don't think either of you were friendly back then. But…you should know that it's useless to brood over it. Over her."

The guard narrowed her eyes. "Why would you say that?"

"Because she was going to kill you at *Ortus*," the Elf huffed. She froze; her brows raising. "You turned into a liability due to the work you did with The Court case," he sighed. "You see, the Ivory Blade have a creed which they live by. Never spare, never yield. She broke the biggest rule."

Zemir curled inwards and shook her head. There was something she couldn't understand. "Why…why are you telling me this?"

"Because she *spared* you," Rye articulated, so that it might sink in. "Yielded to fleeting emotion. She cast something long engrained aside…and let you live."

"No, I mean why would you tell me that I was next on her hitlist," the officer reiterated, now glaring at him. "Some friend you are."

"I don't know if she'll make it back," the Elf admitted. "So I thought that you should know. And think about whether or not you *want* her to return."

Lorrin must know something about Rye that he didn't want anyone else knowing. Things which in his eyes, were better taken to the grave, along with a supposed friend. It was no longer her place to judge, but she couldn't believe what she was hearing. Were all of Lorrin's close associates like this? People she had blackmailed into loyalty because no one would give it freely; people who would turn the other cheek at the earliest opportunity?

Zemir should be angry. That, she understood. That dagger that day had been intended for her throat, as she had held a sword to hers. Yet…there had to be some meaning in the fact that neither female had gone through with their plan. That in the end, one couldn't bear to face the harsh world without the other. Stupid infatuation had overridden instinct and vows. What a lethal, slow poison.

The iman sharply turned away from the Favoured pair and sighed into the wind. "…As I said, some friend."

"Excuse me, can I help you?" Fran Denaris' voice snapped.

"Uh —no, thank you," Rye muttered, nudging the Moth along.

The Pastel Faery clicked her tongue as she watched them leave. "…Academy folk think they're above the fucking law. Arrogant asses, the lot of them."

"Fran," Zemir scolded, levelling at her a withering look.

"Sorry," she sighed, stuffing her hands into her pockets. "They piss me off. Anyway…how are you feeling now?"

"I'm still breathing," the officer sighed. "But aren't you more concerned about your precious governor? I saw the blood; the deep wounds. She's going to be in the hospital for a long while."

"You don't care? At least you're unscathed."

"It's difficult to care right now," the iman admitted —and she never thought that she would ever find herself in a scenario related to her career where she didn't care about someone's life, whether victim or perpetrator.

"Okay what is your *problem*, Kal?" the Seelie asked, flabbergasted. "You disappear for a few days and come back a completely different person. You lied to me, galivanted with someone who *could* be a suspect, and now you don't give a shit about Her Excellency? Have you forgotten your pledge —"

"Oh for Goddess' sake, fuck the pledge!" Zemir cried. "I was never under an obligation to tell you everything. But I didn't lie to you in our phone calls. I *was* fine. I *was* at a friend's. And the only reason I've changed is because I've opened my fucking eyes, Denaris. Madir knowingly covered up the Werren Park graves. She knew about them, and it only took a little fire from the Unseelie to reveal it. Because she was never going to!"

"Wait, slow down," the Faery urged, lowering down beside her. "The graves were covered up? How did you come to that conclusion?"

"She told me," the detective insisted. "She said it my face, Fran. Like it didn't matter. Like their lives hadn't mattered to somebody."

The Faery's wings flittered in irritation. "…So what are you going to do about it? Do you want to file a formal complaint?"

"She'll deny everything," Zemir scoffed. "They all will."

"But you're a detective. Surely they can't just —"

"I'm going to resign, Fran."

Finally, she had said it. It had taken every ounce of what she thought was a traitorous body. Even after it was out in the open she felt like retching. The Guard was all she had known for too long. All she had lived for. The Seelie knew that. Which was why she was stunned, unable to find words. Zemir Kal resigning was like a fish moving onto shore. It felt unnatural.

Was it because of petty things like yearning? She wanted to believe that the decision all hinged on Nadune Madir's betrayal, and the corruption feeding out of the capital. That maybe it was mixed with fury that her family might have been right in their own twisted way. She'd never admit *that*, though.

They had left fifty calls between them already. She'd ignored every one.

Fran drew a heavy breath, and gathered her thoughts. "Zemir...this hasn't got anything to do with Lorrin Raffe, does it?"

The iman fiddled with her thumbs. "What if it does?"

The Faery started. "Kal, no, you can't throw your career because of someone. Especially her. She could be a *ki* —"

"—She *is*," the guard blurted, entirely on a whim. In hindsight, it wasn't wise to tell an officer that someone was guilty of murder. "...I know what she's done, Denaris," she sighed. "I *know*, but I —I..."

She didn't know how to say it.

Apparently, the Seelie did. "You're falling in love with her."

Zemir went rigid. A part of her didn't want to hear that. To make it real and mark it out with words. Because it couldn't be true —not like that. The assassin meant something to her, but she couldn't call it love. Love seemed weighted by ideals and guidelines which they hadn't followed. That they never would.

"Don't say it like that," she rasped. "Like I've done something unforgivable."

"Do you want me to congratulate you instead?"

The iman scoffed. "Fran —"

"No, it's time for you to listen," the Faery cut her off. "You haven't been telling me the truth, even of what you *have* told me. I'm sick of finding things out because you don't trust me. I'm here for you, damnit, and I need you to understand that. I can't lie, remember? Tell me what's going on, Kal. As much as you can. Because clearly, it's not all okay. *You're* not okay."

When had it become obvious?

She was pretty masterful at hiding her emotions. Or she had been, once. And spending time with Lorrin had unpicked at that. She was a whirlwind of doubt and uncertainty; of testing limits and finding sides of herself she hadn't known were there. She didn't want to let go of that.

"...I don't...I don't want to represent the city anymore. Not like this. I don't want to be a part of a government that lies to its people; that shuts other people out, in the name of keeping one side '*safe*'. It's like a pack fight for territory. But we could've done things differently, Fran. We could have *served*."

"We *have* served," the Seelie insisted. "The past can't be changed, or buried or erased. We vowed to protect Idun, Zemir. We have to protect the now."

"I can't," the iman said through clenched teeth. "And it's not for love. It's for me. I want to start living...for me. Whether that's out of the Guard or keeping an assassin from doing as she pleases. I can't control anything. But I can leave. I can do whatever *I* want, and it be okay. All my life, I've been trying to do what I want. I ran from what I knew for that freedom. But I've never really *been* free, have I?"

Fran looked crestfallen. Like she was losing everything. The iman wasn't her oldest friend, but she was the best. It hurt to see her go, as well as all they had built and endured. "Is this what it will take?" she asked. "To be free?"

All Zemir could do was nod. She needed this, more than anything. Time to sift through her thoughts; her fayth; her history. And she wanted to feel safe and capable of free will as she did. Then she wet her lips, attempting to make sense of something. "...Do you think the Unseelie King will succeed?"

The Faery glanced at her feet. "I don't know. I'm not going to give you any false hope. But I what I *do* know is that Lorrin Raffe is smart. She's good at what she does. If you want to ask if she'll...make it back, I can't answer that either. We will simply have to see."

The iman stared up into the sky. "…Will you arrest her, if she returns?"

The Favoured squirmed, flushing mint. "I can't lie, Kal."

That was not a clear answer. And it didn't help that she now knew the truth behind The Court murders. If she was questioned about Lorrin, she wouldn't be able to keep it a secret without looking like there was something to hide. Regret tingled at Zemir's fingertips. Prickled all over her skin.

"What if she came back a hero?"

Fran gave her a warning look. It wasn't shock. It was a strange pity. An odd understanding. Then she made a promise that was brutally unwarranted. "If that girl comes back a saviour, I'll resign with you."

Zemir jerked. "What? Wait, Denaris, you don't need to —"

"I've never seen you like this," she murmured. "With anybody. It's…it was startling, at first. But now it's almost refreshing. To see you give away a piece of yourself? That's kind of insane. I didn't think that you would ever do that. Your happiness…it's more important to me than the law. Than the Guard. You are more important than this terrible world."

The iman let a small smile slip. "I don't deserve that. And please don't make any rash decisions on my account, though I appreciate the sentiment. Matching my energy. You've always been like that. Like, I can't believe that it took me this long to understand how much you care about me."

She wanted to offer to return the favour. She *really* wanted to show the Seelie how much she cared for her too…but she didn't. Couldn't.

"Always," Fran whispered.

It was different, being in the opposite chair in an interrogation room. Alien and isolating. It almost felt as though she might have committed a crime. She wasn't going to admit what Lorrin had done before, but she couldn't hide their relations. She couldn't lie about who the iman was to her, and why she had been at the scene when she had been taken away.

She was familiar with these four grey walls; with the black table and the thin bar on the side intended for handcuffs. There was nothing restraining her —all she did was sit on her hands in pyjamas and blink away water from her eyes. These officers knew her. Not deeply, but enough to form a bias.

She'd answer as best as she could manage, but her gaze was empty and her lungs greedy. There wasn't enough air in the room.

"So, did you have any prior knowledge of the prophecy?" asked the Elf guard across from her. She knew him. He had trained and graduated in the same class at the Academy. Officer Buckley, she believed was his name. And though he didn't want to show it, his eyes gleamed with recognition behind rimless glasses.

The other guard at the door was new. She had never seen a Troll that towering before. The female stood like a brick wall; arms folded and sneer unwavering.

"Uh, no," Zemir breathed. "No, I didn't."

"And you knew Lorrin Raffe for how long?"

"Not long. About half a month and a bit."

"Okay," he sighed, setting down his pen. The Guard were trying to piece together a timeline based on what all questioned parties had recounted. Her Excellency couldn't vouch, and Char Gilligan was unable as a key witness. Knowing all of that, Officer Buckley was attempting to get something out of the blonde assassin's next closest associate: who he believed to be her lover. "Now, did she seem like the kind of person who kept secrets, Miss Kal?" the Elf continued.

It was awful —the way that they had to call her that. The question was awful too. Of course she had secrets. Everybody did. Though hers had been tangled and meticulous and deceptive, the young iman had not been under any obligation to share anything unrelated to The Court case. Apart from herself being the culprit. But that seemed redundant, now.

"...Raffe wasn't trying to deceive the city, Officer," Zemir insisted with firm exasperation. "She wants to save it. The prophecy couldn't be avoided, as I'm sure you've noticed. I think that she did us a favour. The Seeyer included. If it had been public knowledge, I think today could have been far worse."

"I don't think you're in a position to speculate that," sighed the Favoured, removing his glasses and holding the bridge of his narrow nose. "And you cannot speak for others, Kal, you *know* this —"

"Actually, she will not be saying another word," a low and chilling voice sliced into the conversation. "Libbesh, if you would."

It caused every hair on her skin rise, and drain all of the air needed for her brain. The room would begin to spin. Last night's dinner was about to reappear. She then made the mistake of turning around.

They were all there —the Kals. Her brother, Jocelyn, and her parents. Her mother stood at the forefront; her nose high and her purse on display. Beside her was a stranger —a short male in a fancy suit who vaguely resembled an aunt she had met once. He nodded respectfully, before reciting the change in proceedings according to the presence of an attorney. Apparently, that was Libbesh.

"What...what are you all doing here?" Zemir rasped.

"Is that how you greet and thank your family?" her mother snapped as she sent a glare in her direction. All protest died under that expression. At what it signified. "After what's happened today? You have a lot to say to us. Far too much to explain before you go blabbing to the Guard of Madir —you hear me?"

"How can she *not*...?" Petre muttered.

"Go on —say something," their mother hissed to her husband, lightly hitting at his chest. But he only sighed and shuffled. He didn't know what to say to the daughter they hadn't seen in years. He'd leave it to his wife, as always. When Zemir still lived at The Court, she'd been the closest to him. He had been almost sweet —tucking her in and telling her stories. Her mother was the one who gave the orders; the one who kept everyone in line. Petre was her loyal number two. Their father was merely ornamental. Complacent.

"Zemir, you need to come with us for now," Petre spoke up; somehow to their mother's slight irritation.

"I...I don't want to go anywhere with you," she told them, hating how her voice wobbled. Hating how much influence they still had. "And I don't want your Goddess-damned lawyer. At least —let me keep my dignity, you monsters."

"You are still on the family registry, idiot," her brother clipped.

"Shush, Petre. And I don't have time for your tantrums today, Zemir," their mother sighed. "You have no choice in these sorts of legal matters. It's safer to know the facts and know what's relevant. Especially after *that* display on national television. Come with us to The Court. Come home."

Zemir mustered every ounce of courage she could in order to sneer. It wasn't enough that they had simply barged in and demanded things. It wasn't enough that they willingly and repeatedly embarrassed her in front of other officers. They would no doubt talk about this for weeks. She was a grown female now —capable of making her own choices and entitled not to be treated as a child.

She drew a shaky breath. "That place has never been home."

Her mother pressed her lips into a tight, tight line. She wouldn't blow up here, however. She had at least that much pride. Instead she linked her arm with her husband and turned to leave. Though not before instructing Petre to talk to her. Alone; because stress would be bad for the baby. That prompted Jocelyn to tail.

"Um, please release Miss Kal. We'll be in touch," Libbesh then told Officer Buckley awkwardly, before following them out.

The guard sighed and waved Zemir off. "You may go."

She stumbled out of the chair, the metal suddenly feeling too cold.

"Outside," Petre hedged.

There was no choice.

Her brother had been a lesser degree of their mother, but he was completely blinded by the strive to receive her affection. She didn't offer much of it —and it had been subjective and dependant on academic and creative performance. She had taken more joy out of their awards than their existence. The fact that they were healthy, breathing and alive had never been enough for her. Even Jocelyn had not been up to her standards until she had found out where and what she had studied. And after that she had berated Petre for being in some way inferior by studying dentistry and not '*proper*' medicine. Had it mattered? Him and Jocelyn were still wealthy beyond reason.

"Come with me back to The Court," he requested bluntly by the front steps.

"Uh, no?" Zemir deadpanned. "What made you think I'd change my mind?"

"It's safer. We can protect you."

"I don't need protection."

"Not physical security," he clarified. "Legal. They're questioning you because your girlfriend willingly went to the Unseelie Court for the Daughter knows what. The prophecy might absolve you from proper involvement, but they think you're closer to her than anyone else. That you have information."

"She's not my girlfriend," Zemir murmured. "We haven't labelled it."

"But you looked very much in love on the News."

"I didn't say that I didn't care for her."

Petre's jaw clenched. "It's still dangerous."

"I am not coming back with you."

"Why not, you stubborn ass?"

She levelled at him a look that should have been self-explanatory. She could barely tolerate their presence for a minute —how was she meant to live with them again for unquantified *days*? All of those repressed memories would flood back, and she would retract into her shell. She couldn't do that. She needed to grow ever stronger and keep herself intact for the future's sake.

"…I've always wondered why you all hate me so much," she then told her brother in all seriousness. "Was me leaving not enough?"

"You ran away," he corrected. "You took the coward's way out."

"So what if I am a coward?" she said darkly. "I took the most accessible means to escape a situation in which I was suffering. To escape a Hehl."

He clicked his tongue. "Oh come on, Zemir, it wasn't that bad."

"It's that very mentality that makes me want to throw up when I see you," she hissed. "It's not a competition to see who comes out the least fucked up, Petre. It never should be. And I'm sorry that you never made it out, and turned into even more of an asshole because you couldn't stop kissing our mother's feet."

"That's not fair," he bit, his face flushing. "That's not *fair*, Zemir. I kept the peace in that house. Why can't you see that mother let you become such a wild child because I was the one picking up the slack?"

"Well, excuse me for wanting better."

"It's…it's okay to want things," he sighed, running a hand through his hair. "It's okay to want what you shouldn't have to ask for. You…you're more fragile than I am. You always have been." He glanced at her arms. "On the *inside*, if that wasn't clear. But you can't blame everyone else and keep being stuck as a victim. You have to harden now, and stop letting them get to you."

Zemir paused, finding his words difficult to swallow. It was painful to hear, and she didn't like the sour pang of shame which festered because of it. Of course she couldn't be free from accountability.

"I didn't know that you felt that way," she murmured, staring into the distance at the broken Wall. "Why didn't you tell me?"

"As if you care," he scoffed.

"I…I can pretend to," she offered, folding her arms.

He actually laughed. And it looked nearly iman.

The last time she had seen such emotion on his face was when he had married Jocelyn. He must love her for what it was worth, for him to forget momentarily that he was a tightly wound Kal. Then his amusement promptly faded on cue, and he turned back to her. "Look. I'll give you a ride to your apartment."

Only for him to pinpoint where she lived?

"The fuck you will," she said haughtily. "I have someone I can call. I'll even crash at her place if you're so worried about my safety."

"I'll call you every three hours," he warned.

"I'll answer once a day," she promised.

Petre snorted, shaking his head. Then he leisurely sauntered down the steps to walk along the street. "Of course you will. See you."

She watched him disappear around the corner, counting her lucky stars that their discussion had lasted as short of a time as it had, before her gaze snagged on a figure approaching from the other end of the bend. A tall Drakon in a plain *Nikke* t-shirt and a black, grey and yellow letterman jacket came to a halt; his dark wings flapping gently before folding in.

"Hello, I'm looking for —Oh," he said, his brows raising. "You're that female from TV. The abandoned lover, right?"

"Excuse me?"

Anger flashed through her. Had she been wrong in wanting to hold Lorrin just once more? Had it made her seem desperate and sad? That was what she felt now, at least. "Is that really what they're calling me?"

"Well...she did leave you immodest for Gehman, of all places."

It was then that Zemir remembered that she was still in her pyjamas, in shorts and a loosely buttoned shirt with the shock blanket hanging off of her shoulders. She didn't recognise him, as much as he recognised her. "Who *are* you?"

He scratched the back of his head uncertainly. "Uh, I know the girl who went with the King. I'm Lee Nam-joon."

CHAPTER 42

lorrin

THE ASSASSIN WAS hungry, but she couldn't eat a morsel.

The Syren couldn't either, but hers was a mere dietary issue. Faery food and wine were poison to those without majik. To imans. It wouldn't kill her directly —only enchant. But that effect, as Zemir Kal had once warned her, was the '*so much worse*'. By ingesting Faery delicacies, she would completely loose the function of her body. It wouldn't belong to her anymore. Her mind would wander to a faraway place and stay there, content with oblivion. She could slam repeatedly into a wall, and be unaware of the pain and blood. She could walk into a sword and laugh, because she wouldn't even know that she would die. The Unseelie King knew that. Yet he watched her carefully, standing still before him, and found it hilarious that she wouldn't join in with the festivities.

"Forgive me," she bit, "if I don't feel like celebrating my own death."

The Faery atop his lap laughed softly, making him smile at the iman's taunt. "Then forgive me," he returned, "if I shouldn't care that you starve."

"Know that your attempt at an apology is wasted," Lorrin frowned. "Because I know that it makes not a lick of difference to you."

His Holiness raised an eyebrow, fascinated by her response. She could only be so blunt and so bold because of the circumstances. Only one headed for certain death disregarded life. His pet was not so impressed.

"...She's not very stupid," the pink Unseelie whispered, directly staring with void eyes in her direction. "I thought that the common ones were untrained."

"I am not common," the assassin said before she could rein in her tongue. "I know of wealth and power. And I am not some sort of animal to whine and roar for your entertainment. The one leashed and wearing a collar is you."

The creature started. If it were possible for that pink colour to become even more saturated, it did, as she flushed out of anger and humiliation. And her cruel master did nothing to defend her. He simply rested his chin in one palm, and chuckled wickedly. As though his favourite jester had landed a joke.

That was how Lorrin felt, standing there. Like entertainment.

Char made it marginally better. Every Unseelie had their eyes on them; judged them; laughed at them. Silly little Idun citizens. Silly little iman. The music didn't fool her. The dancing was not enough to distract her eye. They all gawked and poked secret fun, like children.

"Did you know that she's called a queen?" the King then told the pink Faery. "She now runs the assassin rings in the city. Don't you think it explains her sharp, iron tongue? Her nerves of steel?"

"A queen," the creature snorted, glancing down at Lorrin before stroking her master's face. She didn't see much in the girl, though her gaze appeared to linger on her head —on her hair. "Prove it, my lord."

He smirked. "Someone bring out a fitting crown for our guest," he bellowed. "We are in the company of royalty!"

This was a disgusting joke. The Unseelie perched on his lap grinned, and ran a hand down the centre of his chest, parting the robes which covered it. Lorrin cringed at the sight of more of his grey, bony frame. But it wasn't just his body. It was more of the performance they gave; the familiarity of it. It caused her skin to crawl and her stomach to roil. This was how the council members felt when she'd sat on Zemir Kal's lap at the Central Blades Hall.

It had been her every intention, though.

Perhaps His Holiness would disturb her to death first.

A grunt suddenly tore through her throat, before she bit it down. Her knees hit the floor, as someone pushed her to kneel and tore back her hood. She knew better than to cry out or take down the culprit, so she accepted the ground as her new place of residence. Char only clenched her fists, and muttered threats.

But it was not yet the time to die.

All that happened was the placement of something of weight on her head. It had sharp jutting spines which she knew would pierce her skin if the object were pushed down any further.

"What do you think, little queen?" the King mused. "It is a small crown of gilded thorns. I thought it appropriate, all things considered."

"You wish to make a mockery of the fayth of my ancestors?" Lorrin asked.

He simply shrugged. The blonde rose slightly to meet the Unseelie's hands behind her. The thorns pressed to her skull. "...Be delicate, crown-bearer," the King warned as though he could tell. "She must be unblemished."

"I think that hair is a blemish," his pet hissed.

The Unseelie tilted his head. "Why, I think you're right. It's an eyesore. Chop it," he instructed.

Lorrin straightened, abruptly shaken. "Wait, what do you mean by —"

All she heard was the swipe of a blade. Then Char muffled a cry. The weight of the assassin's head lightened, and she instantly knew that most of her hair was now at her feet. Her mother had liked that hair; braided and brushed it, while she sang her songs. It had never been *cut*. Until now. Her eyes pricked, but there was something more pressing than that. A small line of heat bloomed at her nape. Her fingers tentatively reached for the source of pain, and felt beads of...

She took a shuddering breath as she dared to meet the dark eyes of the King while retracting. "They —they drew blood."

"Wh-what?" came the rasped protest. "My lord, she *moved* —"

Char squared her shoulders, hand flying to her dagger on instinct. The only reason she didn't draw it was because of the ruler of the court; because his gaze held the entire room in a balance...and as Lorrin had felt, in state.

"I told you she must be unblemished," His Holiness clipped in an impossibly low, cold voice. The very air chilled with each word. The Unseelie's expression turned from interest to fury in a split second. He looked at the fitful sea creature, and extended a hand. "Avenge your master."

Lorrin merely blinked and a person she had never met thudded a little way behind her. Around them, the party still raged. It was as though for a moment, the incident had been contained within a bubble. Not one eye from the audience was upon them. Only the King, guards, and his favourite pink nuisance.

"Send her to Anika," he then ordered.

A Faery with significantly more meat on their bones marched from the door closest, towards Lorrin. She was hauled to her shaky feet, but she resisted in order to make another request. "My subordinate needs water," she declared.

The pink Unseelie was pouting childishly.

The King sucked on his teeth, before tilting his head this way and that. Then a quick nod. "…Very well. I do wish to see her fight another hour."

And so Char was carted off too, in the Unseelie's other large hand; snarling and biting the air like the perfect, testy feral water beast.

It was only when they had been escorted to a corridor that the iman and the Syren exchanged a knowing glance; satisfied with the results of the ploy. Well. Almost. The assassin's hair was never meant to be touched. Now it barely brushed her shoulders. The crown of thorns should have been the object to mar her skin. But what was done was done. There was an excuse to see the court healer and leave the throne room. A holy sacrifice was never allowed to be made with an imperfect specimen.

Anika's chambers were somehow lighter than the rest of the castle. Decadent, but a refreshing change. Though the colours were not to be mistaken for warmth. The female still regarded them with indifference; bored as she pushed up from a velvet lounger. Her hands were gloved with a black substance which swirled all over the rest of her apart from her head; beneath inadequate satin. The light freely filtering through the curtains made sense. A Seelie. She had the same twisting antlers as that stag from *Moondust* —though hers were draped with creeper vines and wildflowers. Her slit almond eyes narrowed, then slitted in suspicion.

"She has a bleeding scratch at the back of her neck, which His Holiness orders you to heal," the escort explained. "And draw the Syren a bath."

The Faery scoffed; her pinned dark waves bouncing. "Typical."

They were then left under her scrutiny. She wandered around them slowly; her gaze went over every inch —every decision they had ever made. Her small black nose twitched as she made for her ornate dressing table. "…Abandon that desperation, girls. You are not leaving this place."

"How could you say that, traitor?" Char demanded.

The Deer Seelie snorted as she sifted through crystal perfume bottles. "Those are dangerously rich words, coming from an iman-eating Syren. Speaking of…why are you *her* attendant?"

"We share goals," Char clarified.

"You share foolishness."

She beckoned the blonde towards the vanity and patted the burgundy velvet stool. Lorrin lowered, her gaze locked with the creature's in the mirror and evaluating her. The Syren huffed and leaned coolly against the wall adjacent to the door, showing her teeth. She then slipped her cellphone from her pocket, and waved it around. "Damn, there really is no service," she hissed.

"…How did you end up here?" the iman asked Anika.

"I fell in love," she sighed, brushing the poorly cut hair aside to reach for her neck. "It was a scandal for the ages. I didn't care what the books said —Unseelie *can* feel; they're simply afraid of it. My Gabrial loved me for teaching him. And that asshole with the crown killed him right in front of me." She lifted her other hand, rubbing the fingers together. "…Binding glass. My security, and chains."

Lorrin's eyes didn't stray from hers in their reflection. What she needed wasn't pity. "His Holiness isn't much of a believer of love, is he?"

"I think he gave up a long time ago, when his family was executed."

Anika waved her hand across the width of her exposed shoulders; magenta light swirling between them. Even her majik was warm. Thin threads of dark pink stitched the cut closed as the Seelie kept her head in place —making it difficult to flinch —before sinking and dissolving into her skin. The pleasant heat travelled along her collar as the light misted into the air.

"Do you...want me to do something about your hair? These split ends along the curls are unforgivable. I'm going to take a wild guess —Kiilla suggested it."

"The pink bitch on the King's lap?" Char clipped. "Yeah."

"His new favourite," the Seelie sighed. "She believes herself untouchable, or even important. I hope that her rude awakening comes as soon as his previous favourite met theirs."

"So...you couldn't leave?" Lorrin concluded, dismissing the hair treatment. She didn't want it messed with any further. "Your moving to Gehman would be considered traitorous, but you could have left for greater Euradon."

"I'm a prisoner," she murmured, permitting the girl to stand up. "The only reason I am still here, alive and excused from that debauchery in the throne room, is his fascination with a prophecy. No, not yours. One which came before, about the continuation of his dreadful line. A Seelie must lay with him."

The assassin blinked rapidly. "He wants you to bear children?"

Anika drew a shallow breath and turned away. She rummaged through a chest of drawers, before producing several metal needles. "It will never get to that."

The Syren straightened, pausing whatever mobile game she had resorted to playing. "Should you...be telling us any of this?"

"I would rather die either way," the Seelie huffed. She put them back, making sure to eye the two females' ivory daggers where they had them hidden. "Now, at what temperature do you like your water, Syren?"

The Idun citizens shared a glance. They hadn't expected the Faery to be in such a predicament, but it would serve their means. They had expected a need to convince her further, but the promise to take her with them or to let her die before her prophecy could be fulfilled was perfect.

Char nodded at what she assumed to be the bathroom door. "Cold."

CHAPTER 43

zemir

SHE HAD HARDLY ever been so pissed off in her life.

The iman didn't hold it against Lorrin. She couldn't. But it was a different matter entirely to be in a *Sundeers* because of the male with whom the assassin had slept. She couldn't remember how exactly he had convinced her to join him there; to have a short chat. Looking at him boiled her blood a bit. He wasn't unattractive. He had the type of defined muscles which were maintained mainly for aesthetic purposes. His nails were too manicured to play a sport. Maybe he swam, if he was involved with any at all. And he looked quite flawless. That made it worse.

Though she had to wonder what Lorrin's type was if Nam-joon had not left a deeper impression on her. Perhaps she liked people who had more…of a character to them. Not just a pretty face.

"So…she had sex with you to forget about me?" Zemir bit out, taking a sip out of the iced coffee in front of her. "And you, to forget about your ex?"

"It didn't work, of course," the Drakon assured her hurriedly. "Well, I forgot like I wanted. But she couldn't get over you, or how she felt. And she's got it bad. Trust me —she's smitten with you."

It was stupid. It shouldn't have filled her with as much satisfaction to know that Lorrin had chosen her, and not the typical heartthrob across the table. It was childish and she was above such things like revenge…but she would gladly stoop to a position in which her passive aggression would be clear. She bit back a smile, before clearing her throat. "Okay, why were you trying to find me, boy?"

"I just…" He glanced down into his jeaned lap; shy, for some reason. And Zemir doubted that he had been so at the bar. Lorrin liked confidence. That could only mean that he didn't know how to act around the older iman. That made her curious. What did he think was going to happen?

She took a long, loud sip.

"I wanted to know if someone knew that she was okay."

Zemir blinked. "You came to the precinct to ask if she was okay?"

"I came to find *you*," he elaborated. "She told me your name, and I looked up you up online. I figured after the event this morning, you'd know a lot more than anyone else. and don't be mad at her —we're sort of friends now."

"*Oh?*"

She didn't know what to say. What on Earth *could* she say? She had no right to say that they couldn't be friends. Though she could tell Lorrin how it made her feel. She didn't want to have to keep an eye on someone over the back of her shoulder just because there was the slim chance that they could sleep together again. Besides, instinct labelled him as dangerous. No one could verify his words but Lorrin, and even if they were true, that still made his actions questionable. Why would anyone go looking for the current partner —for lack of a better word —of a past hook-up? His intentions on the surface were almost harmless. Overall he seemed kind, sweet. An odd opposite and rival to her own personality. But something wouldn't sit right with her.

"Not close friends," he tried. "You know —the kind of friend you message once a month, just to check up on? We've got our own lives. I have no intention of helping in that way again. But…you know something? She couldn't even kiss me that night. *That* was too much. The first thing people usually do in those sorts of situations, and she —*we* couldn't. I've got my reasons. And she's got you."

It was getting close to the point of pain. Even the fact that her influence had made Lorrin save a kiss for something meaningful; for hers, at the gala. She had still sought the embrace of someone else. It wasn't as though they had had a fight or anything. The assassin had done it to forget her. Banish her from her mind. It hadn't worked, but the agency had been there. It could resurface one day.

He could reassure her all he wanted, but Lorrin could easily find an excuse to do it again. Even if Zemir would never intend to leave.

No. '*Only you*'. That was what she had whispered before going with the King. Had it just been in the heat of the moment? She hated that she thought that methodically and hypothetically. She wanted to believe it blindly instead, just as people usually did. She wanted to have some fayth.

"I'm going to be honest with you, Lee," Zemir sighed. "I don't like you. Your first impression isn't great, and I won't pretend like this doesn't bother me —the being '*sort of friends*' thing and the night that started this mess. Lorrin has a tendency to run from decent things so that she won't ruin them. As if she doesn't deserve them. Do you understand? I need you not to present yourself as a solution when that happens. That aside, because I'm not outwardly petty, I also need you to see how creepy this situation is."

The Drakon faltered. "Oh. Right." It was as though he had never stopped to think it through. "…I think I get it," he admitted. "I'm sorry. I didn't mean to make this…*Shit*, this must be so weird. I had a feeling it might be, but I really wanted to know if she was fine. If you had hope that she'd come back."

"Well, why else are you here?" she got right to the point. "Don't think that I haven't missed how young you look."

Now the creature became offended. "What's that go to do with anything?"

"You tell me," Zemir quipped. "I'm sure it's occurred to you that the three of us are not quite in the same age bracket. Maybe you and Lorrin, but she's older than you by a couple of years, isn't she?"

"I'm not *that* young," he protested. "And she isn't that old."

"Did she tell you her age?"

"Yes. And I told her mine."

"Okay," the iman breathed, a little relieved. Though she was only scratching the surface. "Fair enough. Don't blame an ex-officer for asking."

"I'm in my final year at IU," he confessed. Then his eyebrows drew inwards, then out, in confusion. "…Wait, *ex*-officer? But Lorrin said —"

"Yeah, I'm resigning."

Would telling him make her more, or less trustworthy? All he had to know was that she knew her way in and around law. But she wouldn't be able to arrest him, only report. She observed him closely to watch for signs of cracking, but he just seemed nervous and hesitant. She was also growing tired of hearing Lorrin's name on his lips.

He wanted to ask her why she wanted a career change —she could tell. The Favoured was itching to piece together a story about why a Guard of Madir would quit. But it was too personal, and he was more polite than that. For now. He shifted in his seat and tugged on the sleeves of his jacket. "…I really did just want to talk to you, I swear."

Zemir twirled the straw in her clear cup. "What do you study, Lee?"

"What?"

"You heard me," she taunted. "What is your course?"

"…Uh, Physical Education."

"Oh? What aspect?"

He was floundering now. It was rather comical, and she didn't feel an ounce of shame for enjoying it. The creature glanced at the front door. The sky was still red; the sea still purple. "Wh —"

"You're speaking to someone trained as a detective, boy," she reminded him, crossing one leg over the other. "You can't fool me. So why don't you stop hiding it and tell me what you *really* study at university."

The Drakon only squirmed even more, avoiding her gaze as his story rapidly unravelled. "I…Oh Goddess, fine," he finally cracked. His wings flared a little, knocking over a chair from another table. The café was empty apart from them, since everyone was preoccupied with the morning's events. The shattered glass had already been swept up. "…I study Journalism," the Favoured admitted.

The iman raised an eyebrow, before her lips quirked at the edge of her mouth. "Were you trying to get something exclusive from me? I think there's something here not done according to the rules. Or law."

"Look, I wasn't trying to cause trouble," Nam-joon assured, holding up his hands in surrender. "I just…I wanted to score big for my thesis."

Zemir could not believe what she was hearing. "How the fuck can you even think about your thesis right now?" she hedged. "And I know for a fact that you couldn't have received permission to cover this since you had no knowledge of the prophecy either. Are you listening the words coming out of your mouth, Lee? Lorrin is in *Gehman* and you want her fate to be the subject of your final grade."

"But if she comes back a *hero* —"

Did everyone around her have a plan to exploit Lorrin based on her ability to stay alive? Did she have to come back Idun's saviour or simply make it back? She wondered why these busybodies couldn't just be satisfied with her survival. Zemir shot out of her chair, letting it rattle to the floor, and covered her ears. "Would everyone stop saying that!" she screamed. Her throat protested, breaking and cracking, like her voice. Something seared her cheeks. Something burning and wet. Her eyes widened in realisation, spilling more tears. She couldn't care less about the Drakon's shock nor of the lone barista's wary glance.

"I…Uh…" Zemir rasped, turning for the door.

"Wait," Nam-joon said, finding sympathy.

"I h-have to leave," she choked out, darting for the exit.

Fran Denaris was waiting for her, in response to her previous text message, by the iman's motorcycle. She raised a hand in greeting —but the Faery's wings twitched with unease as her friend ran recklessly. She caught her, parting her dark blue hair and starting at the sight of crying.

"Kal, I got your text," she assured. "Okay, calm down. What's —"

The iman pushed past her, shaking her head before fastening her helmet and mounting. "I need to go. But I'll call you," she promised. Then she sped off.

The walls were too tall and there was still glass all over the floors under the empty windows. Yet Hemmingway Estate was uninteresting without Lorrin.

Zemir was going to lay in the master bed, staring up at the ceiling and unable to sleep. Her eyes flicked from the sofa to the kitchen; the memories they'd made there flashing within her mind. The tears were still falling afresh. She didn't want to think of the younger iman as a necessary pawn in the victory of Idun.

She knew that she didn't even care about the city. All that mattered was living and the possible rewards she would gain from ridding Idun of the last old king. What pissed her off the most, was Her Excellency '*supporting*' her position in the criminal underworld, yet yearning for her to save her people from another war.

It seemed that no one understood. All Zemir wanted was for the assassin to return with her heart still beating. Saving the city took the furthest back seat. Of course she knew that it was insane. But surely it was common sense to value someone's life over other factors. No —that was wishful thinking. The city loved a good martyr. Especially one about whom they could speculate, since there was little information on her.

Zemir frowned. All of this time after the Wall collapse, with her attention away from television screens and the News, she didn't know what the prophecy actually entailed. Lorrin hadn't gotten the chance to tell her. She didn't want to turn the blasted thing by the sofa on either; knowing that she would bombarded by much more than she desired. Then she remembered that there was one person who might know more than they should. She didn't like it, but there was no time for her pride to get in the way. The iman made for the master suite.

Lorrin had confessed to having been given Lee Nam-joon's cellphone number on a little sticky note. Zemir tried not to think about how many times she might have called it, and picked through the jackets hanging in the wardrobe. She didn't know which one the assassin had been wearing that night. Or…perhaps she hadn't put it in the same jacket she had worn to the bar.

Her hands dug into the pockets of Lorrin's buttoned denim jacket. There was nothing in the outer ones. She felt on the inside. *There it was.* Her hand pulled out a square of paper and brought out her cellphone. The Drakon answered after a few rings —something for which she couldn't blame him.

"Um, it's the iman from the café. Zemir Kal. I…I just had to be honest. I'm sorry for running off earlier. It's just that...you reminded me of something I didn't want to think about. To me...Lorrin isn't just some hero. She...everything about her ensnares me. Keeps me. And I need her back. Saving Idun is not going to be the only thing she'll do that's of note, okay?"

The Favoured sucked on his teeth. "I think I get it. She's special to you. More so than to the city. I didn't mean to make you so upset that you cr—"

"Good," she cut him off sharply. "Forget about that now. Look, the animosity between us aside, I might need your covert journalism skills."

There was a pause, as he deliberated the amount trust he was going to put into the proposition. "...What for?"

Zemir sat down on the vanity and opened her notes app after placing the call in the background. "About the prophecy —is there anything you found out?"

CHAPTER 44

lorrin

HER HAIR WOULD regrow. But it wouldn't be the same.

Of course, she would cut the Unseelie King's dark curly hair in return. If there was one thing which she could anticipate, it was revenge. And she was aiming to exact plenty of it. The crown of thorns was a part of the prophecy, stemming from His Holiness' twisted sense of humour. All which was missing were the bodies at her feet. And there were plenty of those in the throne room.

A knock rattled the doors. Anika moved to answer.

Char Gilligan, sitting fully clothed in a brimming vintage tub, turned to Lorrin as soon as the Seelie was an adequate distance from them outside of the bathroom. "…I don't think we can trust her," she hissed.

"She's the only one in this castle who might cooperate with us, and who has proper knowledge of this place," the blonde argued.

"But she has nothing to lose by telling the King of our intentions. *We're* the ones at a disadvantage here."

"We haven't told her everything," she reminded the Syren. "And nothing that the bastard doesn't know from the top of his head. Of course we don't want to be here. It doesn't take a genius to conclude that."

Char slipped deeper in the tub and blew into the water. "…Fine."

The Seelie then called out to the pair.

Lorrin rose to get a towel, but the creature simply climbed out and held out one hand. The iman handed over her sheath. She still had a hold of her cellphone, since the Syren's pockets weren't dry. After fastening the weapon onto her hips, she simply plodded into the main bedchamber. She dripped water everywhere — Anika looked slightly horrified, but everyone seemed to subconsciously agree to ignore it. An elongated Unseelie stood in the doorway, stern and impatient.

"Are we being summoned?" the assassin asked.

The burly mosquito's gaze speared for her. Then he cleared his throat. "His Holiness has…a surprise for the sacrifice."

The iman snorted. "How charming."

He led her and the dripping Syren back to the dark throne room. The haze in the air was more prominent. The noise rang in Lorrin's ears, clanged through her bones, and didn't stop until they were halted at the foot of the dais.

"Little queen," the King grinned when he spotted her length of white. He was drunk —glittering golden Faery wine ran down his chin and chest, trailing below his shirt. Kiilla now sat giggling on his other thigh, holding a small green and yellow filigree bottle. Her master seemed alert enough to hurl subtle insults. "I have something for you," he quipped, beckoning to the sides of the room.

Three Unseelie guards walked in.

They dragged in a chained Troll, an Elf, and a Jackal Seelie. The trio were barely conscious; badly beaten and unable to move far when they were forced to kneel facing the audience, with their backs to the throne. Each one looked upwards to the girl's face, straining and desperate. Except for Hordor Fore, who stared with unbridled contempt behind quiet rage beneath his bruising. As though only embarrassed for being caught, if anything.

"Raffe!" Markus Arrium choked out, before coughing up blood. "Please —!" He was yanked backwards by the chain binding his torso and arms.

Lorrin raised an eyebrow at the sight and gingerly retreated so as not to stain her clothes. This was the last place she would have expected to see the remainder of the council. What hypocritical opportunistic pricks. Although she had driven them to that new low. For that she felt pride. If only Zemir were there to see it.

Char was composed at her side; still creating a water puddle around her feet, but pleased to see the males bound and respectful.

"We found them sneaking around the border," explained the Unseelie King. "Apparently loyalty to their wonderful city means little to them. Now, I've come to understand that they are important people to *you*. So since it's your last day alive, I thought I might extend a gracious hand and deliver them so you might say goodbye. Maybe they deserve that much."

Arrium was shamelessly the most hopeful for the girl's cooperation. Verdia Kon was reserved —so annoyingly poised that it made her blood boil. Even the Elf could muster some semblance of a reaction. The Troll knelt and stared blankly ahead as though he were ready to die.

Several snickers rippled through the onlookers. It was painfully obvious how much the dark Faery kind wished to see Lorrin in the worst iman anguish while she still had breath. Unfortunately for that crowd, she held no type of feeling for any Favoured at her feet, and had no qualms with ending them.

The assassin lifted her nose. "Goodbye."

The giggling died.

And His Holiness was surprised by her indifference, rather than seething, like his pet. Kiilla pouted in disappointment, her cruel intentions in bold all over her face. "That's all?" her master mused. "They told me that you would beg for their lives."

"They were mistaken," quipped the blonde, meeting each set of eyes. "In fact, I barely know these males at all. They're the dregs of a council I eradicated."

Arrium's eyes went wide. "Lorrin Raffe, I *swear* to the Daughter —!"

"Someone has lied to me then," the Unseelie King grumbled, lidding his eyes. "Let us see. Will the culprit reveal themselves? Do show some integrity. I won't drive anything through you."

Yet no one stepped forward.

"...My lord," Kiilla spoke, caressing his cheek. "Regardless of whose tongue slipped, we all know what happens to traitors."

"Too true," the King muttered.

"But...I think the iman should to the honours," the pink Unseelie grinned.

345

"How entertaining. Bring her a blade," he ordered.

Kiilla had to be far more simple than she presented if she thought that making the assassin execute her own superiors so publicly was a terrible thing that would haunt her forever. This hadn't been the ideal location, but she could compromise.

A short sword was handed to her from a guard, with a leather hilt.

The court now held its breath to witness some sort of traumatic resistance they were convinced would be displayed. The little Syren shifted at her side, glaring at Hordor Fore. She wanted to be the one to plunge a dagger to his heart.

Markus was wailing —a little to the iman's surprise. She had never seen him look so ugly and pitiful. Even his long fiery hair was dry, tangled and matted.

"...Perhaps I should thank you, Your Holiness," Lorrin mused, idly swinging the sword. "I had been planning on ridding myself of these bastards for a while. I was rather disappointed when you summoned me so soon after my rise, because it meant that I might not get the opportunity to dispose of them. It's very important to me, you see, not have any old members from the time before me leading at my side. I don't want to share —least of all with sexist, prejudiced males. I'll consider it a gift. You have saved me a lot of work."

The Seelie and the Elf started, recalling her words from the last time they had seen each other: that there would not be any deposing. Realising that she had so easily lied to their faces.

The Unseelie King grinned. "A gift, hm?"

"A favour, perhaps, is more appropriate," she corrected, gripping the weapon more securely. She took a step forward, and raised the blade.

"It's no fun if she's enjoying it," Kiilla hissed.

"No, but it intrigues me," was the King's reply.

Lorrin Raffe stood before Verdia Kon. There was little satisfaction in his death. She had never thought too much of him; never held him in the same reverence as the Central Blades had. He was centuries before her division, so she had always seen a walking skeleton in denial.

"Hello, Kon."

He looked up, lifting his great head. Even at this distance and on his knees, he reached eye level. She stared into that cool forest, and showed that she felt no remorse. No guilt. "Hello, Raffe," he returned.

Lorrin couldn't bring herself to ask why he had been at the border; why he had abandoned the city. She didn't care, and he had never really done anything to her directly. It was then decided that she would make his death a little quicker than the others'.

She stabbed the sword downward —from the front, in the heart and between his ribs. Markus screamed. Blood seeped from the wound, gushing over her hand. Verdia had corrected her technique when she had been training. Now he grunted, jerking in pain, but refusing to show a shred of it. His gaze did not waver, and he stared back at her with some sort of understanding.

She could have left it there.

But the assassin leaned in, pushing the blade further. She neared by his ear, and whispered something he could take to the grave. That would be her last mercy. "...I gained Her Excellency as an ally because I offered her more. I knew that you had turned traitor to the Central Blades. You fooled them all for a long time. But, so did I. The Court murders? That was me. And this will die with you."

He drew a breathless gasp —which might have contributed to his agony, as he doubled up and finally allowed his exterior to crack. It was too late though. Lorrin turned her hand, twisting the sword into him. He bit down a cry; fat tears seeping from the corners of his eyes.

She watched them glaze. "Look at me, Verdia. I'm the queen-pin now." Then she pulled out the blade, and stepped aside as he thudded to the floor.

"Marvellous!" exclaimed the drunk King. "Another, another!"

Fore was next.

Arrium's hysteria was climbing with each second she savoured leaving him for last. He was almost ignored entirely; she'd walked right past him without a pause, as if he didn't exist. Then Lorrin turned and beckoned the Syren. She wanted to show Hordor that she bothered about him so little, that she was willing to hand his death over to another. To someone with more bones to pick.

Char clenched one fist and her dagger in the other, before stalking over. There

347

was such a brilliant hatred in her olive eyes. A dazzling, burning anger. Even as they welled up and spilled with glistening tears. She'd show him no mercy. No forgiveness. *This* was part of the vengeance she had been craving.

The sea creature pointed the tip towards the Elf's throat. He said nothing. Not one word. He did not beg, but he did not kneel complacently. His gaze burned right back, but with disregard. He thought nothing of her.

"F-fuck you," Char shakily told him. "I have seen a lot of bastards in my life. A lot of sick, terrifying males. I've *eaten* them," she clarified, eyeing his frame. "But I have never met one like you. You disguised it as training and lessons, but I have bruises to say otherwise. There's a pit of flames in Hehl with only your name, Hordor Fore. This is for every *child* your whip ever cracked down upon."

Lorrin had been one of those children.

The Syren didn't leave room for any of his poisonous words. Her dagger was thrust into his neck, splattering her in red; multiple times. His eyes widened as he reached for his throat, in a feeble attempt to lessen the loss of blood. It was an unsettling echo of Jon De Polis' death. Just as she had, Char stabbed through his fingers as he choked on his blood and fell backwards.

The Jackal continued shrieking.

Then she yanked the dagger out, and wiped her cheek with the back of her hand. She knelt by the dying corpse, and stabbed his chest. It carved through his flesh, opening up the cavity to reach his heart. His limbs had stopped moving at last. Char plucked out the pumping organ, slashed the arteries which held it.

She resumed her position next to the blonde iman, dripping both blood and water, before taking a bite out of the heart like it was a soft apple.

Lorrin blinked and paled, along with many Unseelie. Markus retched, right onto the floor beside him. His Holiness still appeared thoroughly entertained.

"Hungry," the Syren reasoned, her voice muffled. "I'll take…whatever."

"Damn, all right," the iman muttered, before striding to the only thing making noise in the dark throne room aside from the Unseelie King's chilling laughter. Markus Arrium tried to shuffle back; tried to get away. But the guard kept him close and useless, even as snot joined the streams of tears. Lorrin cringed, and was tempted to turn away simply at the sight.

"You're pathetic," she sighed, swinging the sword above her head.

"N-no, *please*, Raffe," he blubbered.

"You know something, Arrium?" she quipped, still poised to decapitate him. "I actually used to enjoy our spats. It was fun. It was a refreshing break from the seriousness of the Central Blades. But now…I can't believe you sunk so low as to live up to your namesake. Standing for nothing will land you in these situations, idiot. If you act like one, you'll be treated like one. And then you'll die as one."

Metal sliced through the air.

The edge stopped just short of his neck.

He sobbed horrendously after another scream —then the stench of urine wafted through the air. The Unseelie King cackled, pointing comically. An echo of titters followed from the court. Lorrin simply raised an eyebrow. She was surprised. The Favoured was absolutely petrified of dying. His attitude had always been death or dishonour. When faced with a real imminent blade, the bravado evaporated. He was reduced to a shaking child. Did he know he was going to Hehl —if such a place existed? She hoped that he did.

Char laughed through a mouthful.

Lorrin withdrew a little to offer an explanation. "I'd like to do something, before granting you sweet release," she murmured.

The Seelie opened one cautious eye, to find the blade pointing downwards, between his spread thighs. The fear layered, and he shook his head.

"Goddess! Just *kill* me, p-please," he cried.

"No —I once told some acquaintances that I'd rather chop it off than ride it," the iman went on. "Besides —you'll have no use for it where you're going."

"*Raffe!*" he tried again. "I…I know we've had our differences. We haven't treated each other…well. B-but you don't have to —"

"Quite right," the blonde frowned, pacing before him. "I don't have to. But *you* seem to be misunderstanding something. I don't care. I wanted to make your death as disrespectful as possible. Your life and opinion means nothing to me, nor my conscience. And traitors die."

In his desperation, Arrium latched onto an opportunity. "But you're a traitor too! Y-you deceived and cheated your way…all the way to the top!"

His Holiness didn't seem to catch the detail for what it was. Perhaps to him, success was success. Even Kiilla was finally preoccupied; her face was buried in the crook of the King's neck as his hands lazily ran over her body.

Lorrin looked back down at the Seelie. "I did what you were too afraid to do."

His face fell as he realised his grave miscalculation. Then it contorted as he cried out; a sword embedded in his crotch. The pain only worsened as the assassin made a ripping motion —and the word '*rip*' was very appropriate for how she had decimated his reproductive organs.

She heard his great wails of pain mixed in with the laughter of Unseelie who thought that there was nothing funnier than castration. She heard, and felt nothing.

"You were right to be suspicious of me," the iman reluctantly offered a slither of consolation as she raised the blade again.

And then the crying was cut off, and Arrium's head landed *splat* at her hem. His body fell after. For a moment his tail twitched, before going limp.

"…He's not going to want the shameful details spread," the Syren commented from over her shoulder. "He would have wanted to die honourably."

"There was nothing honourable about him." The assassin clicked her tongue and handed the short sword over to the closest guard, before turning back to Char Gilligan. She had finished the heart, and was now licking away the blood on her hand and around her mouth.

"It's still dripping down your chin."

"But now I'm satisfied and no longer starving."

"Lucky you," she hissed, gesturing to her midsection. "I'm iman, remember?"

"…Right."

The Unseelie King started clapping slowly. Then he tugged on Kiilla's leash, and she climbed down so he could stand and descend the steps. The court went silent as the bodies were swiftly taken away for burning. It hit Lorrin then —that she had killed them. Not in the way that it should, but she acknowledged it. Those three hadn't been strangers to her. She'd *known* them.

It in no way fabricated guilt, however.

"My, what a show," His Holiness smirked, pocketing his hands. "Not what I had in mind, but definitely not a disappointment. The court doesn't usually hold such vengeful and just public executions, but perhaps we should."

"Would you like me to sit and roll over, too?" Lorrin taunted, adopting a stiff, reserved stance with her hands clasped at her stomach.

"I think he already has a dog," Char remarked.

"Quite so," the iman frowned, glancing at the pink Unseelie. This, the dark Faery did not find humorous. His expression hardened and his spine straightened —as though the alcohol had finally left his system and his duties resumed. "I'd advise you to keep a reign on your own pet, there," he said through clenched teeth. "As well as your own tongue."

"Well, if I only have a few hours left, then does it matter…?"

Kiilla tugged on his robe, and he consequently growled lowly.

"Speaking of which," Lorrin then went on, stepping forward. "I'm not on board with this whole '*sacrifice*' situation. No one has elaborated on what it means, let alone what it entails. How am I supposed to know how to act?"

"Actually, you have been acting perfectly thus far," he assured.

"I want to know what the prophecy states, word for word," she demanded. The King's ears twitched as he flapped out his wings. His face fought between surprise and amusement, before settling on a cold smile. "Are you certain, iman?"

"It concerns me, after all."

"How do you know?" he challenged. "You have your Seeyer, and I have mine. Who is to assume that they saw the same thing, in the exact same way?"

The assassin's confidence wavered. "…What do you mean?"

His lips stretched. "There are two sides to every prophecy, little queen."

CHAPTER 45

lorrin

SHE FELT COVERTLY narcissistic after hearing the dark Faery version. Although it still required her forced participation to launch, their rendition was all about peace and prosperity rather than destruction. Of course, wiping Idun off of the map was very much necessary in the King's eyes. Because they couldn't live with all of the other pesky creatures.

It still spoke of a female with a bone-white dagger and a crown of thorns — of bloodshed and ruin. Maybe slaying the remaining council accounted for that. Or maybe she'd slaughter every dark Faery on her way out.

Apparently they needed a foul heart to resurrect the Daughter.

She had to stifle laughter at the absurdity of it. Perhaps her heart was indeed that inky and dark —but why would it bring back a Goddess concerned with life and creation? Surely they truly did need a holy maiden.

"As you can tell," the King went on to explain, "our prophecies differ because of our goals. You wish to protect your insignificant city, and I wish to restore the Unseelie Court to its former glory —without imannity and the disloyal Favoured."

"Who said I wished to save Idun?" Lorrin questioned.

He blinked. "Do you not?"

"I couldn't care less about that Hehl," she sighed. "And I don't particularly care for *yours*, either. I've come to learn that I am not welcomed anywhere."

"A pity." He then turned his back to her, to go back to sitting atop his throne.

The blonde assassin dithered; the demand on the tip of her tongue but too big to fully leave. She could shout it aloud, but sound carried within Gehman. It had to reach his ear somehow. And what did she have to lose?

Char cleared her throat and leaned in slightly. "Don't be rash about this. You still don't know what to offer him," she pointed out.

"I know," Lorrin hissed back. "But...I can improvise."

Char was horrified. "No —no absolutely *not*. Why would we wager our lives on a technique of the Dramatic Arts?"

"Because I got a '*B*' for it?"

The sea creature gave her a look which was only so effective because of the blood and teeth. A look which translated to infinite second-hand embarrassment. A look which should deter the girl from making an irrevocable mistake, but didn't. She was about to stare this monster down and she wasn't even using the correct weapons. Because she hadn't yet made them.

Lorrin opened her mouth.

Char gasped. "*Don't—*"

"Your Holiness," the blonde spoke up, gathering every last ounce of courage left within her body. "I would like a make a bargain."

The Syren swore, and the King halted just short of the throne.

Court etiquette —if it could really be called such a thing —dictated that bargains were things forged by the weak, disadvantaged and mortal. All Faery kind didn't indulge in them; they had a different majik for promises between them. When it came to business deals or life debts; things for which people could be killed...the only option across species were bargains. Horrible, unfair, deceitful agreements bound by blood which could not be undone.

To make a bargain with the Unseelie ruler —him being an old king —death had to be certain to risk one's soul for merely a different kind of end.

His Holiness knew this well. He turned back around, his hair swishing over one shoulder. His expression was grave, as was Kiilla's. Haunted, almost. As if this had happened already. "...You imans are too predictable," he said tightly.

"But I do not believe that you are in a position to negotiate with me. You are set to die on an altar, and that is all that I desire. More so than your stupid city. So what could you possibly offer me that will simultaneously serve you?"

He wasn't going to stop her. He didn't stop anyone —not truly. It was every victim's right to be told that they were being a complete dumbass, but beyond that, if they wanted to go through with it, nothing could be done.

In this instance, she could propose as many bargains as she wanted, and every time she would be the only loser.

Char's face was annoyingly easy to read: infuriated.

"I want to live," Lorrin declared. "And I suppose by extension, I have to ensure Idun doesn't get obliterated. Only because it is my home."

"Those are the things I cannot change," the King frowned.

"But we can negotiate," she insisted. "Compromise."
It was difficult not to sound so fucking desperate. Because she was slipping into that despair. She simply couldn't afford to show weakness.

"How on Goddess' green Earth can you negotiate the taking and crushing of your heart?" he clipped. "You can't live without one —and you won't make it to a hospital in time to change that fact."

That was when it finally hit her. Perhaps she didn't need to beg for her heart. Maybe she could replace it.

The Syren seemed to notice her moment of epiphany.

"If you must take my heart," the iman said, "then I want another."
Gasps and cries erupted from the court as the Unseelie King showed a flicker of shock; maybe astonishment. He clearly had not thought she might suggest such a thing. How could she —it had taken her this long to think of some way to stay alive. If His Holiness had hoped she was going to accept her end without protest, he was sorely mistaken. There was no will like an iman's will.

"You want me to give you another heart after using yours?" the dark Faery reiterated. "Hm. I cannot fabricate organic material like that."

"Then give me one that already exists."

His piercing eyes slowly narrowed. "And who would be a willing donor in a place full of enemies?"

"I didn't ask for a donor," Lorrin snorted, raising a brow.

The King didn't particularly like that. His glittering teeth flashed; sharpened dangerous things designed to tear apart. Because it was a problem to force one of his subjects to give a heart, but not her. She was unimportant to him as a person with a life. Her role was their key.

All she wanted, considering the court's determination to bring their Goddess back, was to be reimbursed afterwards.

"You can't just *take* one," the Unseelie ruler hissed.

"Say that again," Char Gilligan snapped. "About *your* damn prophecy." The assassin held up a dismissing hand. "I have something to offer in return. If you give me a replacement heart, we can ensure that the Wall gets removed. That you won't be caged, and instead free. Gehman would remain untouched, and your history rewritten. Of course, you cannot reclaim the city. I know you yearn to have your kingdom restored, but it's not that simple. People live there. There's tons of infrastructure bordering it. Not much can be physically done so soon based on your demands, but you don't have to be treated continuously as you have."

If Lorrin was honest, she truly hoped that her speech would affect him and make him see some sense in not invading the city in order to gain the respect which he seemed to crave.

But he didn't.

Her words were lost on him, utterly. He held no empathy —or even sympathy —for her life or anyone who wasn't a citizen of Gehman. He likely held little feeling for his own species, too. The Unseelie clenched his jaw and sent Kiilla away with one jerk of his arm. He towered before his throne, and for the second time, the assassin felt his power emanating from that tall, lean frame.

The party had dwindled; the music cut and the fast paced dancing ground to a halt in motionless standing and hovering on wings as quiet as a honey bee's. Every court Faery stood in quiet curiosity. As entertaining as the discussion was, they wanted action. Ruthlessness. Their King would not crumble beneath such sentiment. Surely she wouldn't live much longer.

"It was never about being caged," he predictably shot down her proposal. "It was never about being ostracised —though that did play a part in it. This world has fallen to ruin without the Daughter. She is *our* saviour. *She* gave us this right. It is our nature to conquer, little queen. I thought that you might understand that."

"Don't speak to me as though you actually consider me your equal," Lorrin dared, lowering her chin to return his frigid glare. "Don't think I haven't noticed every jab of that sharp tongue —especially when you refer to me as '*little*'. I am still a queen. You've seen what I can do with a blade."

"That skill and malice would be quite useless without a heart."

"Give me one," she pressed. "Give me yours."

Char stifled a choke and vigorously wiped her face.

The Unseelie belted a startling laugh. "You're delusional, iman."

"Am I?" Lorrin taunted, arching an eyebrow. "Gehman can thrive without an old king. They can live on. Your Faeries and the Seelie are more capable than they seem. Your ancient role has been fulfilled, but is now unnecessary. The suns are finally setting on your time."

"*Blasphemy*," he growled, taking a step towards her from the short stairs.

"Not for me," she pointed out. "No religion binds me."

"I can see that," His Holiness snapped. "There was no hesitation in your kills; a sword sat so naturally in your hand; and you possess no morals."

"That last one isn't true," was her defence. "I simply refuse to believe that everything can be plainly good or evil without a doubt. There are those who show a greater concentration of one, and those who show neither at all. Isn't it more productive to govern the self, and care for things you deem worthy? Your precious possessions are different to mine —as they are to anyone else. And I defend mine to the death. We should live accordingly."

The dark Faery stroked his chin again, before tucking his long curls aside and staring down with the most unreadable visage she had ever seen.

"If we should prioritise our own interests, then why now should yours take precedence over mine?"

Lorrin often said things which backfired and shone a mirror in her face. She stiffened, ostentatiously caught in a tangle of too-clever words. And he saw it. If she was him, she *knew* that she would disregard her own words and carry on with the original plans. Nothing would stand in her way.

The King would be no different. He would be worse.

His tattered wings flapped gently, as though to shake off the dust, before he descended all the way to the lowest step. He stood too close —she could see flecks of liquid indigo streaking his dark irises. As if his majik physically and literally flowed right through every part of him.

The Syren went rigid and clutched the hilt of her dagger, but held her ground.

"Answer me, child," he crooned, reaching to take a few short strands of blonde in his palm and then letting his fingers slip back.

The girl didn't flinch, but her gaze followed the action —with repressed fury. "…That's when we succumb to compassion," she bit.

Those slightly dark lips stretched. "You fall for that weakness?"

"Sometimes my mercy is mistaken for it."

"Mercy," he slowly tasted the word between his sharp teeth. "I know her not. But you don't seem the type to know it either. Though…you're falling in love, so I suppose you are familiarising yourself with foolishness."

"Love is not giving mercy," Lorrin argued. She thought quietly about Zemir for a moment. "If anything, *they* hold you at *their* mercy."

"We know little of love here," the King sighed, leaning away and clasping his hands at his back. "The kind you choose freely every day, that is. Our love is forever, and it shackles. For Seelie as well. The bonds are hard to break, so one must be sure from the very first moment."

His words somehow seemed intended for her, personally. But no such harsh majik surged between her and Zemir. What they had was not orchestrated.

"When you make someone a priority," Lorrin said, "you'll do anything for them. For the both of you. Anything to make sure you see the next suns' rise."

"So this *is* for her."

If it had to be for anyone, yes. She wanted to live just to see Zemir again.

"Should it not be?" she asked.

His Holiness shrugged. "No matter what your reasoning might be, I doubt that I will understand."

The assassin's hands clenched into fists. The discussion had been a shot into the dark, and it looked as though she would never recover that arrow. Her skin prickled at the realisation that failure was the outcome. But she had tried.

That was all that she could do.

Char's gaze was at her feet. She couldn't offer any comfort.

The lump in Lorrin's throat and the weight in her chest were difficult to ignore, but she could be proud of her initial efforts. There was little she could do in a fight against the Unseelie. There was no majik; only her training and a sword. If the King permitted her to prove herself without immediately dismissing her as he had Fran Denaris, she might be able to wound him. If not...she didn't want to think about what would happen if she found herself frozen into submission. It would be too easy for a victory. At least that's what she hoped the ruler would think.

But, she would die with her head held high.

Then he straightened, and unexpectedly dispelled her fear.

"...Not for your speech, nor out of a speck of compassion," the King murmured, "but for the sheer audacity you flaunt before me; daring and provoking. Though do not misunderstand —you are not my equal, nor will you ever be. I simply wish to see you as part immortal, little queen. Oh the havoc you'll wreak."

The Syren's head snapped upright —shameless hope written all over her face. The assassin blinked, reigning in her boundless relief. If she dared to let her calm façade slip, she'd scream out loud. "You're...you're giving me a heart?"

"Hm." His expression didn't falter.

It wasn't an outright '*yes*', but the grunt was positive and he gave a short nod.

Though she couldn't be too sure of what would happen after the ceremony. "And you'll let me go afterwards —*unharmed?*"

"I'll set you loose," he corrected. "On Idun."

The iman swallowed. His ominous words set a chill deep within the answer. Was he going to agree to leaving the city alone...only because *she* would be its destruction? That had to be the real reason for his agreement. That the turmoil of

Faery blood would change her biology. She resolved then and there, however, that she would attempt to control any of those impulses.

"You must be aware, then," he smirked, "that such a procedure has never been done before. Not on a mortal. Consider yourself a guinea pig, Lorrin Raffe. There is little way of knowing how your iman body will react to a Faery heart. It may grant you more life beyond your set days, for as long as your body can take it. But it will not give it eternally, and I doubt that you will develop majik."

It was a hefty gamble.

But she would rather it go towards survival than to turn it down.

"I'll still take that chance," she assured. "Only because I'll die either way."

Char was far more apprehensive. "Your Majesty, but —"

"Very well," smiled the Unseelie King, completely ignoring the sea creature's short warning. "Let us go over our terms, and make this bargain official."

Lorrin stated her conditions and demands clearly; with minimal room for misinterpretation —to his apparent irritation. She couldn't afford to have this go awry. The Faery then stated his, also without loopholes. At least, so he thought. Because the two were clasping hands as she realised that he had never said that he had to be the one to rule over Gehman after the Goddess' supposed resurrection —and that she couldn't kill every court Unseelie in sight.

CHAPTER 46

lorrin

MAJIK BURNED AND stung. Not everyone's, but especially the King's. And the mark which was to permanently mar her skin —she was certain she was dying as an invisible knife carved out a flaming heart on the skin above her own.

But Char Gilligan gripped her shoulder and let her white majik mist from her palm, seeping into the iman's body and soothing the pain to something more bearable. Her face was sympathetic, but understanding. She could understand why Lorrin would choose to do this. And a part of her had to be relieved that she had managed to make that bargain, at last.

"It is done," His Holiness breathed, equally taxed. He let her hand go, and she stumbled into the Syren. The front of her chest was soaked in red. She wouldn't lose enough to bleed out —Char was there to see to that.

"The ceremony is in an hour," the King quipped as he turned, this time to exit the throne room. "You will stay with Anika until then."

A guard nodded to the opposite door to leave.

The sea creature led the wobbling girl away, ignoring the stares and whispers from the court.

The Seelie was not pleased to see the stain on Lorrin's front.

"It's not as bad as it looks," Char offered, sitting the iman down on a lounger. "I've slowed down a lot of the bleeding already."

"It's a bargain, isn't it?" she sighed wearily, lowering beside the blonde. "I can't imagine that he's already taken her heart if she's…still here."

"Not yet," Char confirmed.

"What did you give, child?" Anika asked the assassin.

Lorrin clutched at her midsection and tried to keep her breathing even. "Enough."

"Will you now live?" asked the Faery, pushing aside the deep collars of the top to get to her chest. She sucked in a breath at the sight —which wasn't much, due to the obstruction of blood. She plucked at the air for a damp cloth, and began to dab away at the wound. Lorrin flinched, gritting her teeth.

"Maybe."

"Her life hinges on her body's acceptance of majik," the Syren muttered.
Anika paused, staring at her patient in disbelief. "You are the most reckless iman I have ever had the displeasure of meeting."

"I second that," Char grumbled.

"I'll…take that as a compliment," Lorrin tried to grin.

When her skin was damp with only water, the girl stared at the mark in the mirror. Her skin reddened at the neat tears; the clear depiction of a heart above her left breast, topped with flames which stretched towards her other shoulder; just short of the column of her chest.

"Bloody Hehl," she rasped, turning this way and that as though it might reveal something else; something new and less damning. But no —she'd keep it forever. When she returned, it would be visible to everyone. They would know what she had done; what would beat within her ribcage, and no longer make her iman.

"It will knit and scar over," Anika assured. "But will never fade nor lighten underneath a scab. Consider it a raised tattoo, but you can't ever remove it."

"At least it's something I can lie about," she sighed, pulling up the sleeves back over her shoulders. It was dry due to majik, but the stain itself was stubborn.

"Will it be possible," Char then asked the Seelie, unable to stand the assassin's sureness about her future. "Will her body accept a dark Faery's heart?"

"I do not know," she answered as she beckoned tendrils of her magenta majik to heal the ruined skin. "As the creepy bastard said —this is uncharted territory.

All you can do is pray for the best."

"I don't believe in prayer," Lorrin clipped.

"Then I wish you luck," the Faery smiled with her mouth, while she frowned elsewhere. "You'll need at least that much."

The assassin didn't doubt her. Luck had been with her in spots throughout her life, and she needed it now. Her fate needed changing once more. If she had done all that she could with her own power, then she had to rely on some karma that she had surely earned. Although…maybe she had spent that good fortune. Death usually trumped sin —of that she was fairly certain. Hopeful.

If the Daughter was real, and She was as merciful as the hymns sang, would She spare Lorrin's life? Take pity on and permit her to coexist with Her precious chosen's wild blood?

Lorrin smiled bitterly. No deity would leave her so unrepentant.

✝

The sky had turned a dark magenta.

The air outside of the castle walls was filled with little balls of light which reminded her of the majik spores at the *Ortus* gala. These were just as beautiful, but Lorrin had the terrible feeling that her skin might burn if she tried to touch them. All of the alluring whimsy of the Unseelie Court shared in that effect; she wandered the ceremonial grounds in limited awe.

Strings of lanterns trapping sprites and wisps hung from tree to tree. Beeswax candles carved into figures of the Daughter —and what she believed to be Sibling Gods and even old kings —were suspended from the canopy of branches and lined along the pathways for attendees as well as the aisle to the thinly covered altar. It was an egregious thing made of iron and topped with a layer of sheer fabric that appeared both or either gold and red at different angles.

Centred on it was a stand which displayed a silver sword. Its blade was a sharp length of ruby stone; gleaming and casting the wooded offering circle in scarlet. She could already see it slicing her chest open; red on red on red.

It was like stepping into a completely new plane of existence. This didn't exist in the modern city. Even Wyches and necromancers used cleaner majik.

If she dared to stare and linger on any of it, Char was there to tug her away.

The Unseelie King had changed clothes. His golden trimmed robe was now an unnerving shade of blood red —*her* blood. He showed no inch of skin on his chest; hiding the evidence of that testy bargain; and trod the earth barefoot. On his head sat another crown —one of shards of black crystal and little branches of golden ivy fusing it together. All curiosity and humour had been banished. This wasn't about entertainment or a spectacle. This was sacred, and it was grave.

The iman and the Syren were to respect the proceedings, no matter how much they wished to resist or generally didn't agree with the fayth. It was simply basic courtesy. Which the assassin chalked up to bullshit, because as much as she was capable of keeping her mouth shut, she wouldn't have gone down quietly.

Now that she had another plan, she'd play the part of a silenced sacrifice.

Silenced, but not entirely compliant.

Her head would rise, and her fists would ball. Her dagger was close; now sheathed away in the outside of one boot. It made walking more controlled, but having it was a priority. Char openly displayed her blade —which made onlookers uneasy.

The King was planning something else. He regarded Lorrin with what seemed like pity as she wandered up the aisle. Not because he was about to kill her for his Goddess and wipe out her people, but what came afterwards. If She did descend and grace Her creation, would She approve of what they had become?

The blonde was glad that he might be pondering such questions. Perhaps it would ultimately stop him.

It was for that possibility that the girl stood and faced the Unseelie, and felt brave. Illogical and defiant. The polished crown of thorns gleamed and glinted.

"I was going to kill you, too," the dark Faery told Char. "But we will see what is to become of you depending on the rebirth of your beloved master."

The sea creature stiffened, understanding the threat.

"Blessed gathered," he began once the congregation had quietened. There had been no music, so the clearing had hummed with hushed praises and old hymns;

363

mingled with general chatter and comments on the eerie prettiness of the grounds. "We have come to fulfil the Daughter's will, given to us by the Seeyer, who spent time in prayer. The prophecy received is as follows: the wicked blood of this iman in white and gilded thorns must be spilled over the altar, and her beating heart staked with the Red Sword. Thereafter her blood may pool, and from it, Goddess will rise triumphant!"

The Unseelie and traitors cheered. Their faces were streaked red and gold and their black clothes immaculate for this occasion alone.

Lorrin's nose only rose higher.

"Behold," his tone then turned mischievous, "the Faery who will provide the iman a replacement heart!"

The blonde started, and her blood chilled. Char couldn't contain her gasp, as Anika trudged up the steps from the darkness between the trees beyond; dressed in a joke of a dress fashioned of the same fabric as the one draping the altar and held together by a length of gold twine.

The assassin communicated with her eyes. Why was she there?

His Holiness lowered his voice to a whisper in order to offer an explanation. "Seelie and Unseelie once shared blood. And I told you that there needed a willing volunteer. And she wishes to die rather than mother my future children. It will be no matter once the Daughter returns, but this is a pity, indeed."

It was *disgusting* that he thought her death a mere pity; an inconvenience. She was his court healer, if else he held her in such little regard. Did he not care? Did he not feel for even his own —forced or runaway?

"*Anika* —" Lorrin begged, reaching for her tightly clutched hands.

The Seelie shook her head and shrunk back. Tears swelled within her dark eyes. They glistened with a strange peace behind the sorrow. She *wanted* to do this, and she wanted to join her beloved in whatever existence beyond. Or simply to escape. "Let my life have agency, one last time."

The girl clenched her jaw, infinitely frustrated. For love, she'd shed a tear. She would show her iman weakness. "...I will carry you home."

"And your name will be written with ours," the Syren promised.

Anika could only bow in a show of gratitude and swallow, before she turned to step up to the iron altar as the King clicked his tongue. The Faery was made to lie down upon it, lengthwise along the left. The right was reserved for Lorrin.

Her strength had left her again. She couldn't stomach this if she knew the donor. When had she even been asked? They had been with her until it was time to leave the castle. If the King had spoken to her in the time it had taken the iman to walk to the ceremonial grounds, then the decision felt rash. Almost forceful.

Desperate, might have been the correct word.

The Seelie had seen a way out; as hastily as it had been presented; and was now gripping it with a violent determination. Perhaps death was indeed better than mothering monstrous mini monarchs.

An Unseelie youth would have sufficed —someone who had little presence and to whom she had no attachment. But Anika, in those few hours, had earned the few small petals of Lorrin's blooming ability to love. That heavy emotion made her care for things she never would have a month ago.

A stranger, and her story.

She'd tell it.

The iman decided that when she climbed back into Idun over the rubble of the Wall with the Unseelie King's head, she would make the city remember someone who had made their saviour's feat possible. Who had given her life.

Assuming that she survived the transplant at all.

But Anika couldn't die in vain. She couldn't leave this world doomed. Some things were impossible to influence for mere mortals and immortals, but the assassin would freeze Hehl to make her body accept the Seelie's heart.

The dark Faery ruler beckoned her.

Char Gilligan offered her one brief squeeze of her hand. There was a lot she suddenly thought to say. Things she couldn't communicate in a second or two, or even in one look. Neither wanted to believe that this would be the last time that they would see each other. But the Syren had seen this coming. She'd known for a while. It had truly set in after hearing the full Unseelie version of the prophecy.

And the creature had long prepared herself to remain at the iman's side until whichever last breath she took.

Lorrin filled her lungs, and made her way to the King's side. He held out a hand to help her up, but she spurned it. She climbed onto the altar herself, and laid down beside the Seelie. The gilded crown dug into her head. Her fingers found the Faery's, gripping earnestly. And the iman kept her eyes wide open. She'd see it all; drink up every detail.

Various Seelie tongues —multiple sounds and lyrics —filled the air as the chanting began. The words burrowed beneath her skin; invaded her blood. They were foreign to her, yet her being thrummed with an understanding. It was beyond explanation. And it truly sounded like a curse.

There was an awful bit of hope which bloomed at the thought that maybe her very essence was pliable to Faery majik and the languages of old. Her heartbeat took the rhythm of it, and thundered through the cold and darkness.

For the last time.

Then dark purple waves wafted above, enveloping her and the hand she held tightly, before her vision cut to black.

CHAPTER 47

his holiness

IXOR WAS CONFLICTED about whether he wanted the little iman to die or to survive. It would no doubt be entertaining to see a mortal with an immortal heart —to watch the chaos she might introduce. At the same time, he didn't want her to triumph. He didn't want her to have all that she wanted simply because she wanted it. There could only be one victor in this battle.

He was not naïve —the conflict would escalate no matter who walked back into Idun. His victory would be bloodier, but Gehman and the other districts knew that war was inevitable. In whatever form.

With the Daughter, it would last but a moment.

She would come and sweep up the mess; eradicating the imans and Favoured who had chosen to align their allegiance with the likes of Nadune Madir. He still heard her screams, even as he recited the necromancer's contract. They had been quite satisfying, but hers alone would not suffice. He needed to hear it from every pitiful creature; to see the fear in their eyes. The governor's gaze had been like Lorrin Raffe's —a long-boiling fury and confidence which only stemmed from arrogance and duty.

The only difference between them was that the blonde understood strategy and possessed patience. He would much prefer to have her as an adversary, but even at that he'd want to scoff. No one was a match for him.

Anika had been one fruit from an orchard. There would be others like her in species; others more willing and unattached to the ideals of romance. The Faery had been spared for her power and a prophecy, and now, because of '*love*' he would have to abduct a Favoured Seelie and find another healer.

Life had become an endless list of tasks and cleaning up.

Love was selfish. Love was blind.

It had stolen from him time and time again —wearing down on his fickle fayth and banishing any sentiment of soft weakness. Reality had shown itself to be a horrendous tutor for who summited and who was trampled upon. Ixor liked to believe that he had passed with distinction on those lessons. The old king had become harder, tougher and ever unmoving; equating it to wisdom and sharp wit. Never again would he fall for the trap of trust —and even *caring* at all.

All which mattered was the prosperity of his court.

He'd do anything, everything for it. Not because its citizens were precious to him, but because he had nothing else left.

Which was why he stared down at the two still females before him on the altar with contempt he chose to fiercely stomach, and grew impatient to ruin that healed skin on Lorrin Raffe's chest. To spill every drop of blood permitted, and have the satisfaction of believing her to be dead for at least a few minutes.

Once the chant had finished, Ixor Horjen reached for the Red Sword. He admired it for a moment, turning it over and watching the moons' light glint and refract through the multiple narrow faces of the length of ruby. The cut was rough and natural, and the stone had been polished and finished that way.

It was a ruthless blade handed down from king to king for ceremonies which required blood sacrifices and contracts. It hadn't seen the light of the suns since his father had been alive —a century ago. That unfortunate thought alone had him eager to cut the girl apart.

"...To You, dear Daughter, we offer a gateway back to the realm which You created," he declared, raising the sword over his head. "Take this unclean blood, and have it wash away the sins which marred us!"

The sound of the blade stabbing through was squishy and blunt and satisfying.

Cathartic. That white garment slowly turned dark red; her wonderful wickedness spreading outwardly on purity. She looked peaceful, which was the only drawback the King had about their bargain. He had hoped to see her convulsing as the life drained from her; as she looked upon the world for the last time.

Now it was as though she had fallen asleep, because of the majik needed for the procedure. But he would enjoy the sight of the blood running down towards the ground, and powering the Red Sword like it was some sort of beacon.

Carving the actual organ from her rib cage was a tricky job. He had to abandon using the sword, and use his majik instead. Scalpels made of dark purple sliced away at flesh, tearing each layer of skin and muscle until it reached bone. The simplest way to reach inside was to cut the breast bone and open the cage. Blood spilled but thankfully did not spurt, allowing the Unseelie to reveal her beating heart. It was rapid and straining in its final moments. He was tempted to let it run its course and cease, rendering her dead for a longer period of time. But he needed it to be beating; to be alive.

Anika was a similar story, though he was less careful with her. He carved each female simultaneously, and listened for the last draw of breath from the Seelie as she became entirely unconscious. Lorrin Raffe had ceased to breathe as well, but her butchering was neat.

He reached into her cavity and pulled the organ out; pumping and dripping. He placed it beside her body, permitting his majik to keep her arteries attached. The next part was delicate. He had to sever those tubes and reattach them with the Faery's within a matter of minutes.

Anika's heart beat twice as fast, but it was noticeably slowing by the second. He had to do it now.

Ixor cut off the mortal's large veins.

Char Gilligan swallowed a squeak as her body trembled. He was pleased to see her still watching. Delighted by the fact that it horrified her. It was in the paradox of her terror, when she naturally did the same to her meals in the wild. That raw anguish…that shame. The King found it to be a small consolation.

He then made quick work of the transplant.

It was an orchestra of movement —Lorrin's heart spasmed as it was squashed and pierced directly with the Red Sword, its blood flowing like a fountain. By the time the river of red had reached the grass, he had already sewn together the severed ends of her arteries to the Seelie's. Anika's blood was light and golden —and needed not to be altered for the mortal's sake. All which would change was the colour of it from dark ruby to a burnt umber. He saw the evidence of that immediately —as it seeped into her.

There was no time to study it all in detail though. He had to close her up and set her broken bones for healing. Her body would now do that on its own with traces of a healer's majik.

If only she would develop the talent, too.

Then he would never let her go.

Anika was dead when Lorrin's chest had been sewn together —then the foreign heart began to beat. It was twice as fast for her as well; accelerating the spread of mixed blood. Outwardly, nothing seemed to be happening. His Holiness was familiar with the flush of life and the will to cling to it. And the girl was gripping it tightly. The determination to see the light of day in their pitiful world was quite laughable. But she yearned for love, and he didn't doubt that she would have done absolutely anything to feel it again, with that indecent iman who had dared to look him in the eye. Glared at him, as if he had stabbed Lorrin right then and there.

The iman heart on the altar stilled, though the spell had already been cast. The blood still illuminated the sword, which in turn made it glow a brighter scarlet. Majik poured into the air, before the ground began to rumble.

The forest floor split down the middle of the aisle, as an extension of the red pool. Black mist rose from the crack, shimmering like majik but moving through the sky slowly, like smoke.

"Behold!" cried the Unseelie King, raising his hands. "She approaches!"

His subjects bellowed loud cheers, jostling for a clear view.

The world went quiet as the Red Sword shone ever brighter; let sacrificial blood and a necromancer's promise pour into the chasm.

The loyal little Syren looked on with the sole waft of anxiety and fury amongst the congregation. Her hand clung to that gold and ivory knife; hoped desperately that it would save her. Just as she hoped that her master would open her eyes and rise. Ixor was the only creature who could hear Lorrin's heartbeat. His majik still enveloped it, giving him insight as to how she was faring.

The beat itself was irregular while it attempted to reconcile her own and the Faery's —and breath was failing to return to her lungs.

Her brain was likely lacking sufficient blood and air in order to function again. Because it was not Anika directly who healed and mended, the iman's body would take its time. The golden light would coil around her bones and veins as leisurely as a constricting serpent. It could very well suffocate her. Only when her being had accepted the foreign matter, might the little queen rise.

Or maybe not. He couldn't care less.

What held his focus was the large, shadowed hand emerging from the cracked ground; its fingers then curling into a triumphant fist. All noise died. Skin marbled like milk and honey, dipped with black ink. The tips of the fingers were clouded night. A slender arm followed; then another; then a torso twisted through; the spine knobbed and visible beneath flowing burgundy drapery.

Curling golden hair framed the head, flickering up like fire. From it protruded two large iron antlers, decorated with strings of glowing stars. And a halo crowned the space behind the flames and shoulders; a rotating ring of tiny golden swords and outer circle. Then the head turned. The forehead was also dusted with soot, and at the chin was the partial tattoo of the sacred red sun symbol. The eyes too, were suns. Dripping and red. And they were filled with pain.

Blazing fury.

Ixor Horjen dared to draw a breath, something like joy bursting within his rotting heart. He had done it. His Goddess was standing right before him.

The congregation fell to their knees and held their breath, or fainted outright. Char Gilligan stayed planted and wept large tears of awe and shock; engraining the image of her Goddess to memory, too.

The Daughter tilted her head, studying the old king, then the iron altar. Two bloodied females lay side by side, with no life emanating from them. One was a

Faery, and the other without majik. Her brow drew in, and the spilling red tears gushed into rivers. Goddess said nothing, and walked on unsteady feet towards the King, down the upset aisle too narrow for Her.

The deity stumbled to the pool of blood, clawing for the Red Sword —but as the Unseelie ruler darted to Her aid, She collapsed before Lorrin Raffe.

"...My Lady," Ixor dared, knelt to the side, "This is an absolute honour. The entire Earth feels richer with Your presence. I...I pray this offering pleases You."

The Daughter did not permit him to look upon Her face and meet Her eyes twice, or give an answer. Her head remained bowed, weeping as Her gown soaked up the blood. She couldn't pull out the ruby blade. It wouldn't do any good. The organ it pierced was already decaying, and the flow of red coming to its end.

The praises rose again, but were soft and mellow. Goddess did not care for them. Her focus was mourning the wretched method which had summoned Her there. To the Hehl She had created. And Ixor dithered and frowned, unable to understand why She was not taking to the sky and hailing thunder.

Instead Her giant hand rest on the ground beside the right of the altar, feeling a faintness of majik, and the struggling beat of a Seelie heart. Her head then rose slowly, but not towards the old king. She leaned down to whisper over the dead assassin; with words which only the two of them would ever know.

A single scarlet tear bled from the corner of a closed eye, before sliding down the iman's pale temple.

CHAPTER 48

lorrin

LORRIN RAFFE HAD always thought that she had full say in her death. It had never been up to fate —she was the only master of her misfortune and demise. She had controlled it well for most of her life; the existence led by an assassin was a daily art of dodging bullets and trickery. The longer one stayed tucked away to themselves, the faster others caught on. She hadn't pulled strings secretively, so any hatred towards her had been out in the open. But it had died down when she came of age. So she wouldn't die in some jealous fit.

Her death was planned and unrelated to her perilous job.

Majik had made everything wrong.

And she hadn't counted on that.

Death's embrace was as cold as ice.

When her consciousness had slipped from her, she had never had a greater sense of that sinking feeling one got when falling. She didn't exist in a suspended state within death. It was a free fall towards an expanse of complete nothingness. What would the fayth call this? The iman knew regardless of her atheism that the truth would reveal itself, and there was nothing which she could do.

No sound escaped her mouth in breath or scream. Her descent was accepted as unflinching reality; and what she deserved. Wherever it truly was that she was going, all hope and joy and peace vanished. And all around was frigid darkness.

There was a void of sound, too —strangely deafening in its heavy silence as it crushed down on her chest. All that she could hear was *weight*; the weight of life and absence. She felt the presence of absolutely nothing at all so clearly and distinctly, that it was frightening.

She'd go mad.

There couldn't be *nothing* here —there should be something for her to touch; to feel and see. The space between life and death couldn't be profound emptiness. Loneliness. The assassin almost prayed for fire and brimstone. Anything but the vast vacuum with only herself.

Then Lorrin felt something other than falling.

It was the burning in the cavity of her chest —the burn of a lack of air. On instinct she gasped for it. Water flooded inwards; freezing and riddled with bits of ice. Her eyes might have widened in alarm, and she might have thrashed in a pain which abruptly overwhelmed her every nerve.

There was nothing to breathe.

She could only roil and drown.

And the girl felt it; the moment when her lungs might cave and she'd die back up there in the realm of the living. She experienced that dryness, that agony, and that slip of brain function. She felt it all.

But she didn't die again.

Every bit of her was still aware of each sensation.

Immortality had to be a fucking curse. Lorrin was convinced that the type of life which was repeated over and over; where the factor of living forever was that one could never stay dead; was the worst form of torment. The cruellest torture. And whether or not she deserved it, the assassin knew that *this*, was her uppermost limit. This was her greatest fear. She had been right to be scared.

Of what death was: the lack of freedom from the pain of it.

The burning spread to her skin. Still she could not cry out as she felt like being charred alive —she had never nearly drowned and the only contact she had had with fire was a first degree burn. This was twentyfold the pain; an exponential compounding of searing heat. Yet her skin did not bubble, redden, nor peel away.

Her body continued to fall and freeze and tear —but showed nothing for it.

She had to be gone from that world, then. The spell must have failed, and she hadn't accepted the Faery's heart. Anika —brave and now free, must have died, but Lorrin couldn't believe that she had joined her there in the void. If this *was* the Daughter's doing, then the Seelie had to be in paradise.

Nothing else made sense.

Then the quietest voice her ears had ever picked up pushed past the pain. It spoke in a language known to no creature; from the dawn of time nor whatever would come to exist; with such majesty that it made her joints buckle and her being useless. Yet she understood the words, without need for her mortal mind to process any sound nor form. They kept the torture at bay.

It was simply forgiveness. Mercy. Love.

And remorse.

The powerful voice had made itself small and tolerable in order to offer the iman morsels of kindness. She didn't need any fayth to know who spoke.

It hadn't all been her doing. The disasters had worked in tandem with the other prophecy. She had killed, but that was all for which she should atone. Anything else which had fallen from grace in the world was not her burden to bear. Her life would not satisfy the brokenness, and it never had to. The prophecies had been a terrible tragedy, and should never have seen the light of day. Ixor Horjen had tipped a very precarious scale, and it had not been Lorrin's duty to right it.

It wasn't all sweetness, though. The voice left instruction. There was a task of the utmost importance to be completed.

The assassin had to choose. Such was the principle of the fayth: free will. She could stay in the void, endure the pain endlessly, or she could return and endure a different pain. While the girl was sure that nothing would ever measure up to the death she had died moments prior, there had to be a cryptic catch to the offer. The pain of living took courage to face. Death was merciless, but it was predictable. Straightforward. She'd know what was to come, even if it was for eternity.

The voice then gave an incentive. To live, was to conquer fear and carve one's name into absolutely whatever might remember. To declare you had been there.

What did Lorrin Raffe have to go back for?

Royal blue and amber flashed through her memory. Even copper and scaly skin. And a gilt ivory dagger —and Ashwood, iron, bone, platinum, emerald, ruby and diamond. All of those assassins waiting for her return…and hoping that she cared enough for them. If not them, what of her aching for Zemir?

She asked the voice if the void was Hehl. She was answered with universally understood silence. Then, the revelation that she was still falling, wasn't she?

Panic clanged through her spirit. That had been *nothing*. The true punishment was further, in some direction that didn't make sense. She couldn't reconcile with the thought that she had no right to complain; no right to be forgiven, and certainly no right to return to the world above —no matter how much more difficult it might be. Lorrin Raffe was unworthy of life and its second chances.

She had cared so little for it until then; and for that of others, so she could not understand why it was being offered to her so freely.

The voice assured that no one could earn the right to live. That life was given, only, and could easily be taken. Those who clung to it found themselves paranoid, and those who faced death as a friend were met with little regret.

The girl had once thought herself well acquainted with it, but evidently she had indeed been afraid of it all along. And one could not befriend fear.

So she would choose life again. Not as a coward, villain nor as a hero, but as someone who had not yet fully lived. And when next she met the Daughter —in many years to come —maybe it would be in light, with milk and honey.

Lorrin came back to the world clawing at the air and gasping.

Her lungs had been vacant for too long. And though the darkness of the void had departed, the one of night was jarring and now somehow too bright. Somehow, the majik in the air felt tangible and the stars weren't hot enough to burn. The first face she saw was that of a giant, four times her size.

She jerked to the side, finding her fingers still gripping Anika's, and gawked at the face of God. The Daughter was crying tears that were red; that of mortal and Elven blood. She looked at the assassin as a mother would a child. And the emotion which wrenched Her heart twisted Lorrin's as well. The tears that leaked from her eyes were also bloody. But when she reached to confirm their existence, she drew back a colour closer to a rich, bronzed brown.

The Faery's blood had mixed with hers.

She could hear the rapid beat of her new heart thumping within her chest. It was fast, and made her feel further out of breath. As though she were suffering through an attack. Her rib cage and its muscles ached from being cut open, but it would be momentary. Remanent tendrils of Anika's majik would curl along it all, as would the power of the Goddess before her.

She had given her that life. Lorrin looked over Her great form; from the eyes which had given Idun its name, to the billowing bits of fabric tied to a too-thin frame. Her mind tried to whir. Could Gods starve? But...why *would* they?

Her eyes lowered to the giant hands. The edges of the deity were streaked in dusty black. It shimmered with tiny clouds of stars, but still filled the girl with pity. The deity wore anguish so well. Likely before it had been a concept.

Char Gilligan couldn't stop her feet from rushing forward —but she halted at the sound of the Unseelie King's sudden roar. It froze any living thing in its tracks. It ripped through the trees and rattled glass.

The Daughter did not flinch, nor turn Her head in that direction.

He stood, huffing and growling, as his majik rumbled into the air. "No!" he bellowed again, his manners left and his only concern being his shattered pride. "*I* am the one who should be showered in favour. *I* am the one who performed the ceremony. We're the chosen people. I am a king of old!"

His feet stomped the ground and his unused, tattered wings unfurled to their impressive span. Like Night Unleashed, Ixor Horjen then ignited as a violet torch. Majik flurried about him in a whirling storm, and consumed. His sapphire eyes flickered electric with the surge. "It is my right, *mine*!" he shrieked.

Lorrin exchanged a brief glance with the Daughter. She shook Her great head. Goddess would deal with him.

She settled on Her knees, the swirls of white and gold moving in liquid fluidity as Her limbs stretched and remembered the constraints of physical movement. She looked upon the King again, pity taking the place of brute fury. He had no rights. Nothing divine could be earned.

Ixor's majik moved —an arm of it speared into the crowd, and stole away a creature. His victim flailed. Lorrin's eyes went wide as she realised that it wasn't an Unseelie wrapped in black. It was a small Syren in a Phoenixes vest.

"Grant me my favour," he demanded, the harsh twister of purple calming long enough to keep Char where she was; feet off of the ground and her throat in his hold. "Grant it to me, or I'll end this insignificant cretin right here!"

Threats and unwarranted force were unfavourable to the Daughter. His rage had clouded any semblance of sense.

The sea creature struggled, and furiously kicked her legs, before he put a stop to it. All movement halted, and the same spell which had locked Fran Denaris' muscles held hers. Her olive green eyes widened and her mouth fell open —but now no sound; no breath was drawn or exhaled from her lungs.

Lorrin thought about crying out as she willed her body to respond again. But her legs were stiff and she fumbled upon the iron surface, only managing to ball her hands into shaking fists. She couldn't let him harm her. But if she rushed for them, wouldn't it hasten the King's response?

The congregation had not dared to shift. All which they could do was kneel, watch and weep. They would share in Goddess' internal torment. And the deity said nothing to Ixor. She offered him no advice, no promise of some grace —and most importantly, no acceptance. There was no need for Her to plead for the Syren's life. No interest. The Daughter was a young God —full of mistakes and childish whims. The world to Her was but a painting; a work of art to be admired and not touched, which had now simply been smudged. She certainly wouldn't prioritise one life unless it was destined for some sort of great purpose.

It was then clear that Char Gilligan had no such fate.

But that did not mean that she had to die. Not here, and for nothing. "S-stop," Lorrin ground out, hauling herself upwards to sit somewhat. Her voice felt...new.

Foreign. "Leave the Syren out of this. It is not her fight."

Ixor Horjen stared at the blonde with such burning fury that he couldn't stop himself from glaring at the deity as well. "See how this iman mocks me! She has forgotten my power."

"*You*…you never had any," the assassin went on, straightening. "And you can no longer call me entirely iman."

His Holiness bared his sharp teeth as he slid the dagger at the sea creature's side out of its sheath. Char could do nothing; barely even squirm, as fear and rage flooded her scaled face, while her own gold and ivory blade pressed to the taut skin of her neck. It didn't pierce —not yet.

"Is this…how you beg for favour?" Lorrin frowned. Her whole demeanour had shifted from desperate and enraged to an icier regard. Almost as indifferent as Goddess before her. They appeared like a mirror of sorts; one a reflection of the other; or perhaps more accurately, the mortal resembled a strung puppet.

"I do not beg," the dark Faery said through his teeth. "It was promised to me."

"…**And so it can be taken away**," the Daughter finally spoke aloud for the first time. Her voice shook the ground and trees, and swept up the hills. It felt neither feminine nor masculine; and the pitch neither high nor low —it was utterly unclassified. Unheard of. In a language which all could comprehend.

Even Ixor paused, his dark eyes widening. The sound was enough to render him stunned. The divinity unleashed almost righted his irrationality…almost.

"We brought You back," he murmured. His fast grip on Char was unrelenting. "The sacrifice…all of this. It was to restore Your glory."

Goddess' form rumbled as She moved to rise. "**You were not asked**."

A flush invaded his grey skin; sudden and harsh. The congregation were just as swiftly unsettled with confusion. Of course, only their Goddess could humiliate and shame him so —and he not lash out in offence. Because before Her, all were insignificant. All were unworthy. And favour was indeed not a right.

"**You are presented with a choice, Ixor**," the Daughter said. "**As are all. Your existence was once celebrated because it met a need which arose. But you have fulfilled that purpose. There is nothing more which you can do for**

379

My people. This is where your story draws to its end, little king."

It was the most that She had spoken at once to them, and it split a mountain at the far border of Gehman to the rest of the country. Evidently, these words had been necessary. She wouldn't have said them otherwise. And the Unseelie ruler would not have accepted them from anyone else either.

But simply because his Goddess had put him in his place, it did not mean that he would heed Her judgement. He didn't have to bow and surrender. She was after all, inadvertently telling him to fuck off and die. No king would do that. The pride and greed had consumed him; taken up residence in the place where love had withered, and he was never going to kneel.

The congregation were beginning to pale and become restless.

The Daughter did nothing. There was nothing more for Her to say. All that had needed to be done was informing Ixor of his fate —of his expired purpose, and that it would do him no good to seek destruction. The conclusion to the matter of his heir was likely as a result of this revelation.

Above all, free will.

"Let the Syren go," Lorrin bit.
Perhaps it was the worst thing she could have done at the worst possible time, because that embarrassment flared and his hand took to his rash retaliation. He growled as he refocused. There wasn't even a scream. The King's hand moved — and Char's head lolled sideways, partly sliced off.

"*NO!*"

A voice broke as it shrieked. Lorrin couldn't hear herself screaming. But she gathered up every speck of strength and wrath to channel through her burning body and her twice-as-fast heart. She leapt up from the iron altar, and plunged her quickly drawn dagger into Ixor Horjen's throat.

CHAPTER 49

lorrin

SHE KNEW WHY he had done it.

Why he had been so humiliated by the Goddess' instruction, and why all that he could do in petty response was to kill her…friend. That was right. Char had been her *friend*. That image of the Syren's hidden agenda revealing itself had been proven false already, and should have faded. Char had cared for the girl. She knew of her pain. She had supported her in vengeance, and done every single thing that had been asked of her. And she had been happy to do so. Proud to.

And she had gotten her own taste of revenge, at the very least. She had slain Hordor Fore, and said her piece. Murder was never justified, but would Goddess take pity on the Syren and take the creature to paradise after all of the years she had suffered upon Her tainted Earth? No other scenario was fair.

But the Daughter's voice did not assure Lorrin of such a thing.

A real, loyal friend —something of which Rye had fallen short. Char Gilligan had died as her friend.

Ixor Horjen had done it for the sole reason that he could.

His shackles were gold and could have been kind if he had let them. It was only because Lorrin Raffe had opened her mouth and ordered the sparing of her *friend*, that he thought it fair to cause her misery and kill the Syren anyway. He had had nothing left to lose. But Goddess' new favourite had much, much more.

But Char had also died because Lorrin had been unable to do anything. She had not mustered the will to use her muscles and fight. She had lain there, weak and dizzy. The only reason she had been able to launch herself was a surge of adrenaline that had not kicked in until what she felt was rage, not fear.

It surged violently through her rehabilitating system; pulsing with heat and anger and thirst. Nothing on Earth could quench it, but His Holiness' life would come close. It was majik she channelled; only majik made her a physical match for the King. Anika was still aiding her after death —though Lorrin's nature was twisting healing into destruction. Her eyes took Seelie likeness and were washed completely bronze, glowing like the Daughter's. And her short hair stood on end, flaring in Her image too: the mixture of divinity from Her life-giving mercy in the void. Even if it wasn't the mortal girl who processed all that was happening at that moment, this was what Ixor had meant. *This* was the terrible power which would be loosed. And it was intoxicating.

She could kill without a single tremor of hesitation. Violence would crawl and burrow itself beneath her skin. And this was only with one enemy; the mightiest Unseelie. What could she do to an iman army? To a Favoured?

Would she ever…belong to herself again?

The rage and foreign majik crippled rationality like paper to a flame.

Lorrin Raffe became something else entirely.

She'd never forgive herself. But her voice rang through the clearing as she gave the King no chance to orientate himself. The dagger went in and out, again and again as he staggered backwards into a tree and let the sea creature's body go. His majik curled around Lorrin's neck in defence as his wings flared outwards and hit candles and ornaments —before he thudded against the ground. Flames licked along the grass. But she hardly saw the fire.

"I CURSE YOU. YOU WILL REMEMBER HER NAME!" she still roared despite the constricting wisps at her throat. Hot tears of blood streamed down her cheeks as she delt a stab for each word into his neck. "HERS, ANIKA'S AND MINE. EVERY SOUL. *ALL* OF THEM!"

Purple splattered out onto her already stained suit, and his dark majik engulfed them. Now the ceremony erupted into chaos. Unseelie fled the scene; terrified of what was to come when their King was dead, when Goddess returned and the partial iman still craved blood. The flames rose, and quickly ate at the trees.

Something gently touched Lorrin's shoulder.

Her body straightened; went rigid as her erratic movements ceased, and then set ablaze. It wasn't the heat of fire. The burn was from within, along her straining nerves, heart and ripping muscles. She hadn't even noticed that her insides were rupturing. Blood forced its way up her own throat, causing her to heave and jerk from astride the King. The possession had ended, and the majik had settled. A purple haze continued to fog the fire, but she knew that the Daughter was still there. Her scarlet eyes still wept in the dark.

Ixor wasn't moving. She might as well have decapitated him. His eyes were wide and glazed; bloodshot and skyward even though that was hardly his final destination. She felt no pity for him, knowing that he was falling now —spiralling into an abyss and experiencing that death over and over. Lorrin started shaking.

She had truly done it.

She had killed the Unseelie King. With just a knife, too.

Her hands dropped the dagger as though it wasn't hers, or as if she needed to get away from it. The ivory blade was hardly visible beneath the dripping violet. Bile rose up with the blood. Her hands then went for her neck and chest. She couldn't breathe. This sort of response was alien. The urge to hurl and the lack of air had never gripped her gut. Every time that the girl had killed, no feeling lingered. Any feeling hindered the ability to live on. Her gaze flicked to the deity's.

Those red eyes illuminated the shadow; pierced through the flame, and looked down at Lorrin with a mixture of pity and disappointment. She shouldn't have felled the King. His life —not his head —had not been hers to claim. Despite his actions and despite his final choice. Despite the unreconciled fury.

She was hardly better.

Lorrin's vision blurred as her face screwed up. She could barely cry —it was something closer to gasping for breath. Then her body curled, and she gave up a large splatter of what had been in her stomach. It didn't help. Now she could feel the tearing within her clearly. And she couldn't scream.

Goddess didn't seem to be in any sort of hurry. But it would be an utter waste if Lorrin were to die again, after all she had bargained for. She was in no position to beg or plead with the world's Creator, but She had to see the desperation in her jade eyes. She had to see the terror.

And then She did.

Her giant finger tapped the top of her small head. The burning changed —it didn't sear, and instead it soothed the sharp sensations. No longer was the girl's new heart struggling to keep her going; her muscles and bones hardened, fortified, and her blood pumped steadily. Her lungs then expanded again, alleviating the crushing weight on her chest.

She breathed. Or tried to. Though the impure air came back in splutters, she inhaled it greedily —before coughing violently again. The fire still raged around her, and its smoke was rising. Choking. Ordinarily, she would fall unconscious. But something iniman was keeping her awake. The Daughter looked to the sky, mouthed something unrecognisable, and then outstretched Her great arms.

A droplet hit Lorrin squarely in the centre of her forehead.

Then her nose.

Then her lips.

Rain poured abruptly and with force —such an impact that the assassin needed to pull her hood over her head and bow down. The water pinged melodiously off of the sturdy gilded crown of thorns; something that she had forgotten she was wearing. It did not grace her head —it was cold and binding, as though it had been wedged there deep into her skull.

When it had begun to cease, the deity turned back towards her. There was no need for an elaboration. It was time to fulfil her end of the deal.

"Go," Goddess told her, lifting Her hand to point towards the castle. "**You will find it deep under the ground. Garner patience when you do.**"

The girl rose, pulling back the hood and grabbing for the dagger. She ignored the wobble of her fingers, and forced them into a fist around the cold, bloody and bejewelled handle. Her gaze landed on Char's body laying against the foot of the altar. Her eyes were still open, too —seeing nothing. She wouldn't know that they had won. Or, at least dealt with one evil.

'*My friend*' was what her gravestone was going to say.

The assassin's chest tightened as she willed herself to turn away.

✝

Lorrin Raffe dragged mud and dark blood into the polished stone palace.

She had a hunch about where she was meant to go. The only things that were under the ground were the prison cells and cellars. The Daughter had instructed her to find something lost —not to Her, but the world. To Idun. Something which should have been found long before, if not for the Unseelie King's obsession.

Something which could save them, or start a war.

The blonde didn't want to deliver the city only to then raze it. Not now. Or even before. Her conscience —which was working in overdrive —warned of sleepless nights due to guilt. This was no longer something about which to be indifferent or selfish. The destruction wouldn't be by her own hand, but she would hold responsibility. And the final choice was not hers to make either —whatever it was down there would be passed the baton. Ever since she had died and come back, the prophecy's fate was no longer concerned with her.

She hoped for the sake of her own sanity that the lost saviour or villain had a speck of emotional capacity, unlike those who'd come before it.

Maybe it's a creature that faded into some sort of obscurity, Lorrin thought as she followed the hallways downwards to stairwells. A thing now in fairytales, hidden for centuries by the Unfavoured and their lawless practices when it came to imprisoning…frankly, anything. Maybe it had great wings that Ixor had clipped; or a scaled tail and terrifying limits to oxygen from the shore.

Truthfully, it could be a bloody unicorn and she would still have to free it.

The air was dry and thin, which did nothing for her recovering lungs. There was a scent on it that drifted between blood and sewer water. Her nose wrinkled, and she mourned not having a mask.

Her gaze caught a large shield of polished silver hung on the wall. She paused, straightening and lifting her chin. All of that blood; red, violet and bronze…she resembled the girl from the horror novel Karrie. Even with the golden thorns.

A pair of heavy footsteps thudded along the stone; methodically, like a routine watchperson's march. Her pale hand curled tighter on the dagger, and she drew it to her chest. There was little pain in the bargain's mark now, and the edges of the torn and hardening skin scratched against the narrow collars of the white suit. She could feel it —the constant reminder of that consequence.

But she was alive. She was here.

Other matters could wait.

The footsteps neared. It was at times like this where she wished she'd brought a gun along. Though bullets did not kill the Faery kind, it did wound. It would have made for an adequate distraction from the slicing of a knife.

"Who goes there?" a gruff voice sneered —about two feet ahead.

She couldn't simply slip past. Whatever guard it was needed disposing of, as they were blocking her route. So she strode right over.

Akin to most of the guards she had seen, this one was muscled and sour; the former a trait uncommon in Unseelie. They were hunched and fuzzy like a bumble bee, with two pairs of matching wings. She couldn't help wondering if the creature came complete with a stinger, too. But Lorrin had dealt with targets a few times her size. Her approach was silent. Calculated. The Faery wouldn't know that she was there until they got a visual.

The white blade flashed in the mounted torch's light.

The guard could only let out a grunt as the girl pushed them into the wall and plunged her dagger into the neck, before swiping. The creature fell to their knees, gurgled on the inky black blood gushing from the deep wound over their grasping hands, before falling forward onto the stone. The wings drooped, turning lifeless and flimsy over the corpse.

Lorrin sidestepped the body and spreading pool, supressing a repulsion that should be intrinsically moral.

She then wandered on further into the looming shadows, thinking that it would be cumbersome to carry a light. Her feet hesitated, recalling the sleek object on her person. The blonde produced a cellphone —the one she had been keeping safe for Char. Her heartbeat echoed within her ears. She couldn't —it felt disrespectful to use the device after what had happened. Wrong and stomach-churning.

But, it was just the torch function.

Surely there were worse things she could do.

Her shaky finger was sliding the control centre down from the top of the screen before any action even registered. A clear purple print was left on the glass. She couldn't wipe it off on her trousers fast enough. The white torch icon stared back at her, stark and judging. Long shadows in the halls danced around the flickering flames. They were coming in closer.

The sudden beam of light was startling.

Lorrin held the coral blue cellphone up ahead of her, casting harsh white onto the stones and trembling enough to create jerking dark monsters on her own. Her feet pushed on. It was almost as if she was being led. Although she was guided by the Daughter's words and a tug, Char Gilligan was with her in the light.

Tears rolled down her cheeks again; this time made of water.

She was going to carry the Syren's body all the way back to the capital in her arms and bury her herself. *My friend.* No one would forget her name.

From there, she wasn't sure how many flights of stairs she descended. All she could hear was the shuffling of her feet and the dripping. The frigid temperature also dropped dramatically, going from cool Autumn to the onset of Winter. A still wind clung to the air, indicating a quick exit of some kind.

The assassin blinked the blurriness away in time to locate another guard, now closer to the cells. She wouldn't know that off of the top of her head —Goddess had planted that hunch. The cellphone was then slipped back into her inner pocket as the lining of flame torches returned.

An arrow shot and studded the wall an inch from her ear.

"Intruder," the guard snarled, hefting their crossbow.

This Unseelie was tall and slender, like a tree. Rough bark patched with moss and mushrooms armoured their limbs —or was perhaps a part of them already.

The creature's bug-like eyes widened. "Wait. Is that…His Holiness' *blood*?" they rasped, the green draining from their face. The strategy was to cower and to shake, as though the crossbow was not a tactical advantage. "…There's so *much*! Oh Goddess. Y-you slew…a king of old. You *monster*!"

They were petrified.

"Your King is dead," she stated bluntly, her voice still gravelly and odd. "He died very foolishly, might I add. This will go down in history as a sorry attempt. Now," Lorrin sighed. "There is a matter of the victor's spoils. I heard that Ixor was keeping a tight grip on a rare treasure. You…know what's down here, don't you?" the girl mused, feigning a degree of nonchalance. Her dagger gleamed in the fire as she twirled it for good measure. "Tell me."

"*Never*. And you —you'll never get away with this!" the Faery shrieked.

She didn't bother with a retaliation. The blade was embedded in their narrow dominant shoulder before they could fire another arrow. A wild scream pierced the night; boiled the cold; and curdled the assassin's blood. She made quick work of slashing the Unseelie's unprotected throat after they'd been forced to drop their weapon; feeling momentarily satisfied with the *thud* of the body.

That satisfaction was only an echo of its predecessor, and she felt her stomach twist once more. The assassin bent down to swipe the ring of keys, knowing that she was in no shape to break anything out. Her feet then marched onwards.

The prison cells themselves finally came into view.

Iron and Ashwood bars half rotted as they separated each cubicle —a space very similar to the dimensions and feared uncleanliness of a public restroom. The air was laced with the smells of decay and misery, even though it still breezed in and out; cool enough to be sickeningly cold in prolonged thin clothing. Every cell she passed was either empty or littered with bony remains.

Only one emitted light —the one at the end on the right, slightly larger than the others. That warm glow was snuffed out at the nearing of Lorrin's footsteps. That was the one. Her newly squeamish gut told her so.

These bars were better maintained by comparison, and reinforced. Whatever it was —it was far more dangerous that the prisoners who frequented the place.

Without that brief light, all the girl could see was darkness when she halted to peer inside. There was no sound, either.

Then she jumped from her skin at the appearance of a pair of eyes.

Lorrin had encountered many different types of gazes all throughout the years. Large ones, small ones, narrow ones, square ones, diamond, slit-pupiled or void. Nothing could unsettle her anymore. Or so she had thought.

The eyes which stared at her ripped apart all that she was worth. There was nothing special about the colour or shape, but they glowed in the shadow and did not blink. Round and silvery and gold, with the bright luminescence swirling those colours periodically like the lights in a nightclub. The pupils were not those of an animal either —irises ringed shrinking pools of nothing.

They didn't squint or tilt for a better view. The lack of light was not a bother, and they could make out the tall, soaked murderess and her knife just fine.

A shiver shot up her spine.

That unease about the dark which she had carried with her…it resurfaced once again. The assessing gaze tormented the feeling; magnified it. A realisation drew all of the warm from within her, out.

Unlike hers, these eyes could see in the dark.

The glow then began to grow. The prisoner neared, slowly, with caution. All she saw was a bony grey hand grip and curl along one bar. Lorrin knew that her heart was still beating, but in that second she couldn't be certain.

"…Who are you?" a deep voice long unused, rasped.

It was a demand, not to be repeated.

Her brain tried to sift through information. Nothing seemed right. But it came to one answer which might appease. One which might be understood.

"The bloody queen. Slayer of the last old king."

CHAPTER 50

lorrin

IT WAS A person, not a thing.

"Slayer," they tasted the word—almost savouring its brutality. The fingers tapped the bar around which they'd curled. "…You killed him?"

"H-he killed my friend," the girl justified, but she had to wonder why she felt compelled to do so. They did not know each other. Evidently what loomed before her was capable of intelligent consciousness, but it didn't mean she could unload her experience in a conversation. There was no time for that.

"It was in…revenge?"

They seemed disappointed.

So Lorrin bared a little more of herself. "I refused to let him live on, knowing he had taken people I knew from this world, without remorse."

The prisoner tilted their head; only noticeable in the alignment of those eyes. "I have waited here with pained patience for many years, dreaming of the day I would finally drive a sword through Ixor Horjen. And now…you mean to tell me that a mortal abomination has stolen my prize —just like that?"

The assassin dithered. "You…you're *not* here against your will?"

"Don't you know who I am," they purred, grabbing hold of another bar. "Who do you think you are to be asking me such a thing?"

She blinked, fear dissipating into dumbfounded confusion.

The Daughter had not misled her. She certainly did need to have patience to deal with what sounded like an immortal being from a time so long ago that they had forgotten the way of the world. The voice oozed arrogance and entitlement —a type that only befit the rich and noble.

"I am the saviour of the land of the dripping red sun," Lorrin stated clearly, decided that placing herself on equal footing might encourage some respect. "I do not know who you are, but I was sent to free you by your God —"

"I do feel the presence of divinity," the creature cut her off. "I wondered for only a moment why I heard a mountain crack. However, that majik is with you as well as outside. It flows in your impure blood."

The girl clenched her fists. "She saved me."

"Then you must be quite something, for the Daughter to spare a second of Her time and a kernel of Her power on the likes of an iman."

"It was a prophecy," she clipped.

"Pesky things," the prisoner clicked their tongue in complete mock sympathy. "To devote one's life to them is the most foolish endeavour."

"Do you want to get out of here or not?" the blonde frowned, jiggling the ring of keys. "I have other places to be."

She was answered with lengthy silence, and then a sigh. She wasn't sure as to how much of this back and forth she could take in her state —or ever. Maybe she hadn't been the right person for this task. What was needed here was a willing ear to listen, and some empathy. Her reserves were low on both. How could she bring herself to comfort anything which had insulted her, and resented her role in a story of which she had never wanted to be a part?

Lorrin had never given much thought to it before, but she didn't have room for pity and goodwill. Life had been plagued with one disaster after another — from the very moment her parents had fallen in love; years and years before her birth. As someone who had grown used to the blows that existence had swung; the relentless battering which refused to pause even for breath; the space to heal had never been granted, and she was incapable of giving it to others.

It wasn't that she couldn't recognise trauma in others, or her direct infliction

391

of it. She simply hadn't worked through her own.

"…It would appear that the world has forgotten me," the creature then mused. "I had wanted to become legend, but time has turned me into myth."

She didn't know what to say to that.

"What is your name?" she did finally ask.

The answer had to be retrieved from long fading memory. Grey fingers scratched the chipping rust. "…Ciaran Hawkthorne. I used to be a prince."

Lorrin started. Her own fingers dug into her palms. She had to reassure herself that it was coincidence that his name was pronounced the same way as 'Syren'. It couldn't be karmic punishment. It couldn't be retribution. She forced the acidic thought down and focused on the other information she had gleaned.

"You were royalty? When was the last time you were outside?"

Royalty still existed in the modern age, but the way this male spoke sounded closer to the Victorous era.

"1867, if I am not mistaken," he answered, unsure. "But I have occasionally been informed of what occurs beyond Gehman since."

That confirmed her theories.

"*Fuck* —you waited one and a half centuries to kill the Unseelie King."

Ciaran belted a sudden and dry laugh. "Is that what he called himself?"

"Is that not what he was?"

He laughed again. "I knew that bastard was a narcissistic prick, but I had no idea he had crowned himself in all seriousness. I thought it a jest when the guards forced me to bow to an egregious crown of iron. Now I know he had clung to a power long lost with dear, pathetic life."

At least the two shared a hatred for their captor.

"If it is any consolation," Lorrin quipped, "I can give you his head."

"It's not," was the curt response. "It means nothing if I did not kill him."

"Well, gosh —sorry for not exercising self-control in my fit of revenge," the assassin clipped sarcastically. "Clearly I should have known that there was a lost prince in the castle prison who was destined to slay my friend's murderer."

One hundred and fifty years had worn his sense of humour.

"Indeed you should have," he agreed, sighing wearily.

"Unbelievable."

She wanted to turn around and storm. The temptation to abandon the insufferable supposed prince was reaching its pinnacle. But the Daughter would know if she had fulfilled her promise or not. If she wanted to live and not return to that void of pre-Hehl, she needed to swallow her opinions and coax him out. She couldn't give back the satisfaction of Ixor's death, so another plan had to be devised.

"...Now that he is dead, Gehman is lacking both a leader and a direction," Lorrin said carefully. "Perhaps you could —"

"The throne of the dark Faery kind is not mine to take," he swiftly interjected. His eyes narrowed in the warning of anger.

"So your only purpose was to end Ixor?"

"At the time," Ciaran admitted. "It was to be the catalyst of an ugly dispute concerning Seelie and Unseelie. I failed to meet that deadline, getting caught for my plot, and was set to be executed. But something made that madmale spare my life, and imprison me instead. He never explained why. I simply saw it as a new method to drag out the torture. It was clear that his objective was to keep me alive, at least, despite the way in which the other prisoners were treated. Did you know that the bare minimum to keep an immortal alive is foul water and stale bread so hard that it could break your teeth? I had to suck it down."

"That's sick," Lorrin cringed.

"So you *do* in fact possess empathy," he mused, and she could tell that he was smiling even without the confirmation of gleaming teeth. "I was worried that my dear saviour did not care at all."

"I am not your saviour," corrected the girl. "I am your key."

It was at those words that something snapped within the creature. His stubborn and prideful amusement melted away, before the sound of movement bounced about the cell. He staggered onto his feet; the eyes rising to indicate his height to be comparable to that of the Moth Seeyer. She spied his torso first —a plane of toned muscle despite the starving, with black tattooed feathers and a large marking spanning from his right side around to his back. It was intricate and a white that

393

almost glowed on his skin. The swirls looked familiar in the dimness, but she couldn't quite place from where. His arms followed a similar trend of toned skin and bone —though not to extent that it should be, because of whatever type of Favoured he was. His trousers and loose suspenders were as aged as his sentence, and his once polished shoes now sported holes and scratches.

Ciaran certainly had the face of a prince; angular, stubbled —with a perfected almost-smile. His hair stood up, in the most curious shade of strawberry platinum blond, while his ears were pointed like a Faery's. Full illumination helped his eyes to stand out less, but the colours only swirled ever clearer.

He stared down at her as though he knew, and finally stepped forward into the flickering light. Two dark things flared out behind him. Lorrin couldn't disguise her audible gasp. Black feathered wings like that of a bird of prey sprouted from his back, flapping as he flexed and rolled his shoulders.

If he had been the King's captured enemy, that meant Ciaran Hawkthorne was a Seelie. *The* Seelie Prince who had disappeared and been presumed dead. At least that was what their history books accounted. She might have recalled his name before if she hadn't been so fixated on its sound.

"Your Highness," she blurted. Suddenly she didn't know how to behave.

His face pinched, but he didn't actually say anything to indicate his irritation. "...My key," he smiled slightly, meeting her gaze. She couldn't look away from his —from that silver and gold even as it made her dizzy. "Somehow, I believe that means something to me. I've been here for too long, so my memory is fogged, but I recall those words. That they mean something tied to fate."

"You can ask the Goddess outside."

The Faery drew a deep breath. There was a hairline scar over his left shoulder; in a jagged bolt. "I am prepared," he said. "To see what the world has become."

"Uh...it's chaos right now," she coughed, before beginning to flick through the metal keys. They all resembled each other —except a far slender one in a dirty gold; its head three small, triangulating melded rings. She slid that one into the lock, and turned. It clicked open. The door swung outwards, and Ciaran had to duck and tuck his wings in to walk out onto what was arguably cleaner floors.

The Seelie shook out his wings —which flittered dust everywhere —before cracking his neck and knuckles. The muscles seemed to swell and fill out. Lorrin wondered if he might have been bred specifically for the purpose of war.

"Do you…know a faster way out of here, your Highness?" she asked.

"Oh don't you go calling me that, too," he bit. "Hawkthorne will suffice." Lorrin Raffe had been taught that there were certain positions which did not allow any form of casual address, no matter the circumstances. She stared at him, utterly flabbergasted. What sort of royal would ask to be called by their name only? The blonde held her dagger aside and shook her head. "I couldn't possibly —"

"Say it with me," he instructed. "Hawk-thorne."

The girl frowned, adamant. "I am not calling you that. I was brought up to respect titles that high. Even if your kingdom no longer exists, I can't drop formalities."

"*Hawkthorne*." He raised one eyebrow. He was as stubborn as she was.

Lorrin tried. "…Ha-Hawk…th-thorn."

"Now put them together."

Her tongue refused to cooperate. And her frustration only pooled and overboiled. "You know what —how about I call you Hawk?" she suggested, hanging the keys on a hook by the furthest back wall.

When she turned back he was a lot closer —his broad chest the only thing in her line of sight. It rose and fell with breath; damp and grey. And that tattoo…the leaves and branches matched the pattern which decorated every map of the city. Lorrin stiffened, and stumbled into the wall. Had Idun been his kingdom? Was the place she called home rightfully his to rule? The possibility wouldn't settle in the pit of her stomach. His form shadowed her entirely —she only came up to the base of his neck. Ciaran then leaned forward, bending slightly at the knees in order to be level with her souring face as she brought her still-dripping ivory blade up towards her chest in defence.

"You want to shorten it further?" he chuckled, spotted feathers ruffling. "Now where did those unshakable principles concerning respect go?"

The assassin swallowed her discomfort and folded her arms. She wasn't going to budge an inch for this male. "It's Hawk or your Highness."

His eyes trailed over the blood once more. She could add more stains to that white, and claim his head too, if she so wished to. His muscles flexed as his mind drifted to a place where it shouldn't. "...Hawk it is."

He thankfully whirled away, giving Lorrin the chance to hiss out a breath and click her tongue. She hated that he was good-looking —hated that he had the sort of natural charm and enchantment which made her guard lower. Which meant that he was immeasurably dangerous.

Zemir...Zemir was waiting for her to come home.

"We need to get out of here," the girl insisted after clearing her throat. "There are people expecting me back. I have to return to the city."

"Hm," Ciaran grunted, but he strode ahead and began to lead them out. He appeared to know precisely where he was going —back up one set of stairs, before a sharp veer to the left towards the breeze. That made Lorrin suspicious.

"By the way," she then tilted her head, glancing back towards the cells. "Why haven't you ever broken out before? You seem to have this place mapped."

"How do you know I have not tried?"

The assassin's jade eyes narrowed. "...Initially I thought it was because you were biding your time, but now I realise that you definitely would have shattered those bars sooner rather than later, and faced Ixor Horjen as equals. Either you did try in the past, or have never stopped."

The Seelie nodded slowly. "You're a fine sleuth, bloody queen."

"Raffe. Lorrin Raffe." He'd hear of her name eventually, anyway.

"*Raffe*," he smirked. Then his amusement faded into a pained frown. "...If it had been possible for me to escape, I would have done so and slain that dark lord. Ashwood weakens majik of the Faery kind, and can be poison in concentration and frequency. I was unable to draw any ability while in that cage."

A satisfactory answer. And in truth, the blonde was more offended than she allowed her face to show. Never in her life had she thought herself a detective — or even a person of rational thought and judgement. And being a key was not all which she was good for. He seemed to have forgotten the blood painting her suit very suddenly. She was not the hero, and she wouldn't pretend.

She also didn't like the way he had tasted her surname in his mouth —having the second syllable linger in a strange disbelief.

"The guards' entrance is just through this door," Ciaran murmured after some distance along Lorrin's original route. She hadn't been able to see, so her fingers clung to his bare arm. His skin was ice. "You *have* killed them all, yes?"

"Only the ones who stood in my way," she clarified, extending her knife. "I wouldn't know of the ones stationed outside."

"Do watch where you point that thing," the Faery hissed.

She proceeded to wave it around haphazardly —simply because she could. "I assumed that everyone was attending the ceremony, but be prepared. I only ran into a couple of guards —though we may also meet angry villagers."

He laughed. "Is pissing people of a habit of yours?"

"A way of life," she grinned, before gripping her blade knuckles-out.
The foggy streams of dawn flooded the hallway as Hawk pushed the door open. It wasn't that heavy, but his strength was still replenishing. He didn't look ready for a fight, however. And that was a good thing, because the land was deserted. The fog was light and thin, spreading lowly among the tree roots and shrubbery. But it hid no Unseelie. No traitorous Favoured.

"Looks like we're in luck," whispered the girl, lowering her dagger.

"I wouldn't be too sure," Ciaran murmured. His wings flared out to their full breadth —a more impressive span than Nam-joon's —and majik the colour of the sunrise whispered at his fingertips. "Maybe the guards are elsewhere, but it's not like the common Unseelie to confront in the open. Look between the leaves."

She followed his pointing hand. The wind rustled through the branches, the same way it moved in the castle, and the light made something catch the corner of her eye which she wouldn't have noticed. A child —she could tell not by short stature, but the glance she caught of its small face —darted away into the thick.

"…They looked like a dandelion."

An afro of white seeds like a full clock; skin a shade of mint green; eyes large with a luminous white ring around little pupils almost as deeply unsettling as the Seelie's. They'd pierced right into her being, and engrained her visage to memory.

"I bet I know her father." Hawk narrowed his gaze. "A spineless idiot, but keen senses. A sufficient soldier. But that child is far more skilled and conniving than he. Clever and self-serving —aside from her devotion. She will not stop simply because her King is dead. What a vicious Unseelie."

"I didn't…I didn't run into a dandelion before," Lorrin quipped.
"Still alive then," he ground out through his teeth, before those wings tucked in tight. The echo of the thud travelled on the wind. "Keep your eyes open until we reach the Daughter. Our safety is not assured until we reach Her."

"Are you asking me to duck and cower?" she huffed, raising her dagger again. "I'm insulted. Once upon a time, I was Idun's end."

He cast her a straight, sidelong glance; that swirling colour grounding her and her rage. "I'm asking you…to humour her, End-Bringer."

CHAPTER 51

lorrin

THE AIR WAS even crisper and more brisk at dawn.

It kept her stiff and shivering. She knew by the dryness of her nose that it would run as soon as she was back in the capital. Ciaran Hawkthorne didn't appear to mind the cold. Lorrin had been almost certain that frost would gather there on his exposed grey chest. Yet he breathed the air as though it was all he'd ever known, and trod the earth as though he'd once worked it.

It proved a mission to keep pace with him.

But that could not be her concern. All on which her mind focused was a little dandelion weed. She wouldn't kill the Faery. Lorrin Raffe was a lot of things, but she was not the sort of villain to stare a young child in the face and take their life.

The thought rippled, and brought the memory of the first false accusations to the forefront. That iman had been a child, too. *Almost* in her jurisdiction, but the fact of the matter was they hadn't come of age. And she had taken that life.

All for her own gain.

I was different then. Cruel, she insisted, stomping after Hawk. The breath left her lungs in a way that was haggard and heavy —a most basic rule that every assassin had drummed into them to manage: never give away your position.

Her attention scattered.

She had killed a child. There was nothing which she could do to take it back.

And she could justify it all she liked; that someone with no family left would not be missed, rendering them insignificant. But it wouldn't be the truth. That was the very lie she had fed herself in order to take that blade across the iman's neck in the first place. She had felt nothing then. What…did she feel now?

A shiver shot up the assassin's spine at the sound of a snapping twig.

The Seelie ahead didn't pause, implying the sound to be inconsequential. An unease still lingered with her, urging her to be careful. It was foolish for her to slip into such a state of trust with Hawk.

Fucking *Hawk*.

Had she seriously given the unpredictable key to the city's fate a *nickname*? He had been right to be surprised. Offended. For him not to correct her etiquette —he must truly have abandoned and hated royal life. Or at least the stiff and stuffy formalities of it. He wasn't as uptight as she had thought that he might be. No pole resided up his ass, but it didn't change the fact that he was a Seelie prince.

The Faery kind lived and saw the world differently to that of other creatures. Even those twisted by forbidden majik, malignant curses or the thirst for blood. Seelie and Unseelie shared common things which tied their ancestors together. One of them was power. Every Faery with the ability to wield majik had an innate kill switch. Anything could be the trigger. And nothing could stop the firing.

The Unseelie had embraced that. Their cousins had supressed it.

It was the shamelessness of the Unfavoured which had let to a division. But in Lorrin's humble opinion, the Seelie were not *better*, but rather, self-righteous. They saw the darkness as evil and malice; anything that the light did not touch as impure. The dark Faery kind were not justified nor correct, but subjecting them to that oppression had not been the answer. Some things were wild and needed no understanding. All vengeance stemmed from abuse inflicted by someone who had been blinded by majik, their own trauma, or greed.

Faery politics were messy and troublesome, and had never caught Lorrin's attention. She'd killed any for money, though. But that didn't mean that she had gotten herself into their feuds; their wars.

Now they were making it everyone's Goddess-damned problem.

Whether Hawk liked it or not, he carried that title and power. He answered to no one, and would be worshipped as a God. Lorrin glanced at his side profile. Gaunt and deathly. Her lips twitched in a small smile.

He was definitely going to hate it.

The thudding of feet, this time she heard.

Her gaze flicked to her right, and her breath stilled. The bushes were quiet, but not silent. The child was not hiding. Her concealment was part of her plan. Then she emerged. A soft dress and pinafore covered cracked, muddy feet. She was brave —the little dandelion. She approached the pair as though they had already lost, and had walked into a trap. In her trembling hands, she held out a long metal needle. Ones like Anika had in her dresser. In her eyes there burned a complicated tangle of anger and valour; easily mistaken for pitiful desperation.

"Traitors," she bit. "Murderers."

Lorrin glanced down at the ever-present bloodstains.

"No, we're not on the same side," Ciaran sighed, straightening. "But that does not mean that one of us in the right."

"*I* am," she insisted, gripping the needle tighter. Her white eyes gleamed with bloodlust. "I've been told how dangerous you are, Seelie Prince. You tried to kill the King, but luckily you were caught. They had to put Ashwood in your bars so you wouldn't be able to use your majik."

Hawk smirked, and brought up one hand. Mist rose from his bony fingers.

The child's eyes widened, and one foot shuffled backwards.

"You're frightening her," Lorrin hissed.

"Ugh, hardly," the Faery sneered.

"And *you*," the Unseelie said shakily, redirecting the needle. "You're the one who actually slew the King. During a sacred ritual, no less!"

"...He killed me first," the assassin deadpanned.

"We are nothing without him!" she shrieked fiercely.

Lorrin raised a brow, rather taken aback. Judging by Hawk's expression, so was he. Ixor Horjen had made himself Gehman's saviour. Their only hope. He'd been so desperate to hold onto the throne that he had actively undermined his citizens' ability to live without a monarchy or leader. They had given up their identities to root them in the old king. The court truly was directionless.

"It is not a ruler's place nor right to become all his people are," Hawk ground out. "They should never be that dependant."

"His Holiness was the only one who could lift us up again," huffed the little dandelion. "He was our chance to beat our enemies. To destroy the city, instead of keeping on suffering under it."

"My bargain aids with that," Lorrin assured, nodding vigorously. "There will be no more Wall. There will be no more discrimination."

Both Faeries stared at her in bewilderment.

"Are you that stupid?" Ciaran asked genuinely.

The blonde flinched. "Excuse me?"

"You must be, if you think that bringing down the Wall will just fix everything. That it will change the opinions and presumptions of the citizens to dissuade them from harming any Unseelie. If anything, your preposterous and rash thinking will only fuel the flames. You will present extremists with an easier opportunity."

The assassin curled away.

All which she felt aside from the humiliation and reproach was a bitter and heavy guilt. She had not been thinking. It wasn't just her ignorance —it seemed that she had no knowledge of true conflict. She hadn't lived through a war; had never known the lowest poverty; had never cared for the government nor for her dark city. Lorrin Raffe didn't give a shit about morality or welfare. When had that changed? What gave her the impression that her suggestions concerning Gehman would be of help. That *she* could be of help?

This was not her fight. Intervention was beyond her.

Still her face flushed to match the red splatters on her suit as she gritted her teeth, and her hand gripped her dagger so tightly as it shook. It didn't matter that she was wrong. But it was way that Hawk had said it —how he had made her look like a foolish, nosy, righteous busybody. Someone blinded by their goodwill.

So she would bury that emergence of pathetic compassion and well-meaning intent, deep down in the darkness still brewing in her chest.

Ciaran simply shook his head and sighed when she dared to turn back, as if some good friend had deeply disappointed him. As if she had said something so unforgivable. His jaw clenched with contempt. "…You cannot stitch the rift of a canyon by filling it up with sand."

His words hurt in a way she didn't want to understand.

"Hmph," grunted the child, momentarily lowering her guard and the needle. "We can actually agree on something."

Majik then flared into the air, mixing with the fog. Hawk's mood appeared to have been permanently affected. His icy gaze turned to the Unseelie, and it alone caused her to shiver in a flood of fear.

"Little girl, I would run back home now if I were you," he warned. "It is not safe in Gehman. A lot of things are going to change. Including to whom you bow."

"What? No, I came to get justice!" she countered.

"On whose authority?"

The dandelion dithered for a split second. "The Daughter's."

Lorrin scoffed. And it was one hundred percent petty. "Strange, seeing as She is the One who sent me to find and free this male."

"You have to be wrong," she insisted, nodding importantly. "Why would She favour a Seelie or show an iman mercy?"

"Who are you to question Her mercy?" Hawk clipped. "And perhaps you are unable to sense the strange majik in this female, but she has Goddess' chosen favour. You will respect that, should you not wish to meet your King's end."

Lorrin would have elbowed and shamed him for threatening a child. But all she felt now was disinterest. If he wanted to kill her, she would not stand in his way. It would keep blood from her hands, and the churn away from her stomach. That had to be the reason why she was suddenly disgusted by death: because she was doing the killing knowing precisely where the victims were going.

The little Faery flushed a darker green. "You're really terrible. I pray you'll be haunted by this, and remember my name. All of our names."

"You never stated your name," Ciaran interjected.

She glared up at him, that fury regathering. "…Klok."

403

That was all she left them with, before she turned to dart through the trees and disappear into the lifting fog. Above the crumbling of society; above the escape of a forgotten prince…life was precious. In the end, she too, feared death.

The villainous hero was not shaken by the confrontation in the slightest. This seemed normal. He ran a hand through his short hair. "We must keep moving."

"She didn't give us a surname," Lorrin murmured.

The Seelie's wings then flapped slowly, dispersing the cloud, before he continued along the path she could not see. The suns rose on their left. "…Common Unseelie do not have family names. They cannot afford one."

†

Goddess had not moved from where the assassin had left Her.

The deity still stood by the altar, staring down at the body of Ixor Horjen, with an expression so blank that it appeared unconcerned. Her head turned as Lorrin Raffe and Ciaran Hawkthorne approached, with the girl darting for Char Gilligan.

The Daughter regarded the Faery with what turned into expectant irritation. Her dark brows knitted, and the blood still streaked. "**Boy**."

Hawk shifted on his feet, and glanced elsewhere. "Grandaunt."

Lorrin spluttered. "He…he's Godborn?"

Offspring wrought of incomparable strength to mortal mothers —hidden away for their safety and immense power. Once myth, now before her very eyes.

"Mm," the Seelie hummed. "Did you not know that?"

"*No!*" Lorrin cried, glancing between the two immortals. Neither met her gaze as she grumbled. "…This day keeps slamming into me like waves of water."

"My Grandfather," Hawk then coughed. "He lords over another world. I have not seen Him for centuries. My grandmother was a Seelie queen who wanted to meet God. She, uh…called the wrong one. You can guess what happened after."

"Ew," the assassin couldn't help remarking.

"Rude," he scoffed.

"*Enough*," Goddess silenced the pair. She had to lower Her voice to a whisper, yet it still shook the trees. Her gaze settled on Lorrin. **"You have done what was required of you to live again. But your role does not end here."**

The blonde straightened, her heart pounding to a new speed.

"You intend for her to *guide* me?" Hawk raised his voice. "Please reconsider. She is but an unexperienced girl, ignorant to politics and majik."

"You are to guide *each other*," the Daughter corrected —almost sneering. **"The two of you are in need of a friend as much as ever. Fight together. Dine together. Laugh together. Weep together. Lean onto one another. Be to each other as brother and sister, since neither of you know of that bond."**

For the first time, Ciaran and Lorrin were on the same page.

There was no way in high Hehl that the part iman had gone through all that she had only to babysit. She failed to see the logic behind placing the Prince in her care, under her watch —which was about to be become extremely busy — when his lineage was what it was. He didn't need her. And she didn't need him. Those sorts of things could not be imposed, either.

"Surely You jest," begged the Faery.

"I don't need a brother," the assassin insisted. "And I have friends."

"Had," dared the Daughter. **"You have lost loved ones to the prophecy. Ciaran lost his to time and battle. Another looms, more complicated than the last. It will need the both of you. Try to get along in the meantime."**

Lorrin gaped, hugging the Syren's body to her.

This...the ripping in her chest was what the old king had felt at Her far more hurtful words. She hadn't thought much of the deity's insult before, but now that one had been directed at herself, it was intolerable. Should the Gods have flaws, then They couldn't parade around feigning perfection.

What right did the Daughter have to press on the wound of losing Char and Anika? To remind the girl of her failure to recognise and keep such relationships?

Two dead bodies bled beside her. Two friends.

"Their souls are already gone," Goddess assured.

Lorrin was dying again. "...I don't suppose...You'd tell me where they went?"

The answer was silence.

405

"But I didn't ask for this. For Idun to fall," the blonde continued to protest. "I didn't ask for the prophecy, and I didn't ask for responsibility. I don't care for my city, and I certainly lack the capacity to care for *this male*. The only other thing which holds my affection is back over that Wall, waiting."

The Daughter raised an eyebrow. "**I did not advise you to transfer your capacity from one to another. Your detective is not a hindrance nor a part of this arrangement. Love her as you wish. And you will come to find that you and Ciaran have a lot more in common than you think.**"

"Was this Grandfather's idea?" Ciaran bit. His wings stood open and stiff; the spotted feathers resembling sharpened daggers. She didn't answer him. Not even a fake smile of pity. The God in question was older than Her. Only such a dynamic would allow Her to push this, and provide the most flimsy explanations. That was likely all which the Seelie needed to come to his own conclusion.

"…Why me," Lorrin demanded.

It was a question which needed no further additions. Goddess knew why she asked it, and what answers she sought. But they were apparently not Hers to give. The flow of bloody tears ceased, and She turned to the crack opening the ground in the middle of the aisle before the altar.

"**Things will only grow worse. Learn what is most important.**"

"Wha —what do You mean —?"

Hawk's enormous wings were then blocking her field of vision; arced above them in order to shield her gaze from the deity departing. He knelt at her side, almost as if he might embrace her, too, but thank goodness he didn't have a stomach for that either. Even through the solid thickness of the dark things, the golden light behind them was enough to make her snap her eyes shut. It was a piercing burst; bright enough to be seen through a space satellite. And then it was gone, and the world was cool and still.

The earth beneath her was damp yet crumbly. Whatever warmth that had been with her was now gone. Without the giant of shadow and milk and honey on the horizon, Gehman was as icy as the snows of the Northern Pole. Hot tears hit pale, scaled skin. Char's body wasn't cold, or heavy enough. She fought to reach with a shaking hand and gently close her eyelids. The head still partly lolled off to the side. Lorrin's fingers retracted as though she had been electrocuted.

"Your High —*Hawk*," she rasped, her breath visible. "Can you fix this?"

The Faery paled even further. "Bring her back? No."

"No. Her…her neck," the assassin could barely get the words out. "I…"

But it was all right. He understood.

He pinched his thumb and forefinger together, before pulling a thread of majik from the air. With an invisible needle, he guided the light to the slit along Char's neck. It moved with the sewing of his wrist, stitching up the wound. It was an indescribable relief to see the sea creature's head roll back naturally; as if part of the weight had been eased from Lorrin's shoulders.

She managed a sob.

Ciaran glanced at the other bodies. For the Seelie he patched up her chest — and for the old king, he severed his head entirely. He knew that the girl wouldn't be able to carry both of her friends and the Unseelie's head, so he gripped that curtain of curled raven hair and tied it into a sling.

Lorrin stood; lifting the Syren into her arms after sheathing her dagger. She was far too light. Hawk then slung Ixor's hair over her shoulder, the head hanging like a morbid handbag. It still bled purple. In truth, the assassin didn't want any little part of the old king in such close proximity to Char, but she was left without choice. They needed to get out of the district, and there was only the two of them.

She glanced up him —at the person she was now meant to call family. Or eventually. He took Anika's body in his arms, mindful of her antlers, and began to walk south. They were silent for a long time; the only exchange a few heavy breaths. The forest was eerie without Unseelie in it; without life. The King's head would deter any Faery from approaching and raising a weapon to the Prince and the Slayer. Rather, no one would dare try anything against Ciaran. But they would watch, and they would remember.

It was only when they neared the threshold —the crumble of Wall, that Lorrin Raffe spoke again. Loegon was just ahead, and early birdsong felt misplaced in the slowly warming quiet. "…What now?"

The suns' rays shone through between the glass skyscrapers. Had they always looked that imposing? Had the city always appeared this wealthy and unconcerned with what lay beyond the Wall. Beyond, into Euradon?

It was a new dawn; a new day. But the girl wept.

No one knew what had happened in that castle; in that district —and all that the News would focus on would be her hollow victory and the return of a Seelie prince. A new hero.

The dripping red sun was gone from the sky, and Ixor's head kept bumping into the side of her calf. She tried not to flinch at every instance —but the fury in its expression was difficult to block out. Hawk's answer then took her by surprise, even though she was staring blankly ahead and had in fact, asked for one.

"I'm your brother, Barbee."

A bit of life flickered in her jade eyes, though they still streamed searing tears. It wasn't funny. She didn't deserve to laugh. "…Fuck off."

"I thought I would give you a nickname too."

What silly, easy humour.

Nothing was ever going to be as simple. There would be a lot to discuss, organise and explain. And she was unsure if she could do it. One of the Faery's wings then brushed against her shoulder, causing her to shrink.

But his smile was small and warm.

CHAPTER 52

lorrin

IT WAS OVERCAST, but not raining at the funeral.

The clouds were too full and stubborn. Lorrin Raffe's eyes did not follow the same sentiment. Her vision was so blurred with the flow of tears that she couldn't finish reading out her speech; she couldn't look anyone in the eye, and she couldn't bury her friends alone. She had laid them in their caskets —and insisted on changing their clothes, brushing their hair and cleaning their wounds. No one else was permitted to touch them directly. Except Anika's family, who she had met with the day before after returning to the capital.

Sherry and Mykel had lived their lives with very little hope that their daughter had still been alive after being captured by Ixor Horjen. Her death now hit them like the glass shattering —suddenly, loudly and sharply. One part to mourn her disappearance, and then her sacrifice.

She had died with a hero's honours.

The fact that her heart beat within a mortal female was far more of a struggle to understand. But they listened to every bit of the girl's story. To their daughter's story. They all did. And called her the Saviour.

It was different with Char. Her few friends arrived from the coast, bringing the scent of salt along with them. Giselle was among them in a seashell decorated wheelchair, with a bouquet of seaweed and coral. The Mer hadn't said that much to Lorrin, but she knew how hard it was to find the words. But she managed to express Char's wishes. She had wanted to be cremated, and then scattered into the Lois Sea. Lorrin decided that her dagger was to be placed with the legacies before her, in the heart of the Central Blades Hall —in the Gold Corridor.

The only way in which the assassin was coping was having Zemir Kal at her side, holding her trembling form. Their reunion hadn't been at all as either had expected. Lorrin hadn't gathered the courage to say that she was in love with her, and the News stations had gotten in the way of a proper embrace as soon as she set one foot into Loegon. But the older iman hadn't been shy with the recount of the whirlwind event.

She had appeared before the press, misting the dawn; splattered in red, black and purple. The King's head at her leg. Beside her was a Seelie with the wings of a dark eagle —a small, dead Faery gathered in his arms. Zemir had recognised Char Gilligan, and tears for Lorrin's sake had sprung from her eyes.

A crown of gilded thorns glinted in the sunslight, a bargain marred her chest, and majik flowed through her. A Faery heart replaced her own. And she spoke of starved marble giants weeping blood, speaking in a language which didn't exist. Lorrin Raffe had met God —had died and lived and killed and avenged.

The Seelie at her side had been freed from the Unseelie King's dungeons, and was indebted to the assassin. His gaze had the effect of freezing people in their tracks, whether in reverence or fear. It was only a few hours later that he revealed himself to be lost royalty —but not Godborn. Ciaran Hawkthorne had not said it aloud, and had urged Lorrin not to say it either.

And for whatever reason, he was under the Saviour's care.

Zemir had at least been informed that the two were to be siblings. Which she insisted had not been the greatest worry. The girl could have returned married and pregnant, yet all that would take precedence was the flow of breath in her lungs.

The blonde was familiar with the signs of jealousy relief, though.

It had been nearly sixty-eight hours since she had returned, and the city was desperately trying to regain some normalcy. Contrary to her instruction, the Wall was undergoing repairs. The only reason she hadn't stormed to Nadune Madir's office was because she was well aware of what Gehman would think, what the rest of Idun would think —and of what Hawk had said.

She forced herself not to care. To turn the other cheek. Bargain be damned —
Ixor Horjen was *dead*. They were no longer her concern. Not for a while, anyway.

Instead, the girl had accepted medical care, fussed over funeral arrangements
and sat through interviews. Those had been the hardest part. They asked questions
too simple and inconsequential to the experience she had had. Her answers hadn't
reflected that, obviously, but they had chalked up the choking on tears to grieving.
Which wasn't inaccurate. Merely an understatement.

One black marble gravestone was engraved with, '*My friend, worthy daughter
of the Daughter*'. Char Lilybeth Gilligan. Giselle was to thank, once again. Lorrin
hadn't known that the Syren had a middle name. She'd never asked.

"She met God too, you know," Lorrin whispered, her head against Zemir's
shoulder. "Char. She looked upon Goddess' face, at least once."

"She's with Her now," the iman whispered, before tightening the wrap of her
arm around her waist. "At peace, knowing she is honoured."

She couldn't bring herself to even give voice to her doubt.

Hawk stood to her other side, stiff and solemn in a new suit. He was there
only for her sake —besides the fact that he had nowhere else to be —and had
helped her with the planning and execution of a proper Hero's Farewell. But he
couldn't be sure of the sea creature's final destination either.

Anika's grave proclaimed her to be the saviour of the Saviour, a knower of
true love, and her parents' precious little Faery.

Lorrin's heart —*her* heart —had raced as if some part of her lingered in the
world of the living, and was present for her body's burial. It was rather surreal.
The speeches hadn't lasted long enough, and she had only blinked to find herself
outside, overlooking the white caskets draped with the Euradon flag. Guests had
brought umbrellas, wanting to be prepared. But the girl had had a feeling that no
rain would fall. As if she had such authority over the elements.

She had left the uttering of the send-off she had altered to someone else, too.
Every part of her had wanted to…but they each refused to cooperate. So she stood
and leaned into the more put-together detective, hoping that the females heard.

411

"There, I see gathered at the Daughter's feet are Her beloved," read the priest. "You have earned that place, all worthy and heroic. All who fall in Her name are blessed; remembered and welcomed with ardent cries. We hear them. May they resound beyond your journey home. Rest, now. The battle is over. Herein are you forever immortalised: warriors. Sisters. Daughters. Friends."

The clouds rumbled and the breeze smelled of the sea.

When it came to the lowering Anika's coffin, she could no longer bear it. She couldn't watch, and couldn't think about how the Seelie would one day be nothing but a skeleton. Char's casket was only for the ceremony, and her body would be turned into ashes. She couldn't not decide which one was worse.

Ciaran flapped a wing in front her half-heartedly, but it had been Zemir who had hugged her into her chest. She was wearing her ceremonial Guard of Madir uniform for the last time, and the gold buttons, tassels, pads and braiding scratched her face. But she clung tightly for dear, dear life.

When she had regained the nerve to pull away, her gaze met Valerie's.

The Syren hadn't bothered with black attire —or formal wear of any sort; in fishnet, jeans and leather. But dark circles ringed her bloodshot eyes, and her complexion was as pale as death. She hadn't come to sit and sniffle through the proceedings. No flowers were on her person. She came to say goodbye and hello.

"I'll be right back," Lorrin told Zemir, turning so that she could march over. The iman glanced in that direction, sceptical. "I know her," the blonde assured. Zemir huffed, but pressed her warm lips to the girl's freezing temple.

The walk over was painful and too quick. But standing before the Syren, she found that she didn't know what to say. Not even a simple greeting. Did she even have the right to offer her condolences?

Valerie was not someone who indulged idle chitchat. She stared at the mortal, with such disdain that it was as though she knew that it had been the assassin's fault. "...She wouldn't have wanted your rich shit funeral, you know."

Lorrin held her tongue. It was an utter slap to the face. "Char deserves only the best I can offer her," she rasped. "But it's not about me. I just wanted to give her a Hero's Farewell. Anika, too."

"Damn right it's not," the Syren bit, baring her teeth. "...But do you honestly think that Char would've wanted her death paraded for the cameras? That she'd yearn for the spotlight when she's only know darkness for so long?"

"I don't care about the media, Valerie," Lorrin insisted. "I've pushed them away the entire time. I only wanted to do right by my friends."

"Too late for that," she spat. "And wow, I can't believe you're calling Char a friend after what she told me of your little agreement at the assassin rings, you unfeeling bitch. You sure these just aren't pity point —?"

"*Stop*," Lorrin begged, her voice cracking. "P-please. Don't..."

Valerie watched her struggle for breath as a fresh wave of tears flooded down her pale face. It was clear that she would disapprove of all that she did, whether to soothe her own conscience or truly repent. Nothing was good enough, because as she was concerned, Lorrin had made a fool of *her* friend. "Do you even know that she didn't want to be buried?"

"The casket isn't even in the fucking ground," the girl said tightly. "And yes, I know that she wants to rest at home. In the harbour. But I wanted a grave, only to show how I thought of her, but never got the chance to say. And yes, it's my fault she's gone. Maybe...I want to earn a slither of her forgiveness. But it's not about money or showing someone up. It's about love."

The sea creature huffed, then shook her head. "...I hate you. A lot. And I'm not going to have anything to do with your underground fan-club. I think that's a fitting consequence for failing to bring *my* friend back, alive."

Lorrin pressed her lips into a tight line, her shoulders still quaking as she wept. She couldn't open her mouth. She couldn't retaliate, nor could she defend herself. Because Valerie was right. She had failed.

So she turned around sharply, and marched back on pieces of broken glass to the funeral. Before her crying could become ugly and audible.

She was a ghost at the reception back at Hemmingway Estate.

Hawk leaned against the wall next to her, watching the guests and pissed off as appropriately as his name. He hadn't gotten much out of her about the bitter confrontation with the meat market Syren, but it seemed as though he could go on a lot based on the scent which lingered. He was taking their predicament far more seriously than she —and her guess was that it had something to do with his mighty Grandfather. He jumped along with Lorrin when Rye came up to them, alone. He had fished out an old suit he had worn for some Court member's wedding, and still wasn't getting enough sleep.

"Raffe," he murmured, briefly glancing upwards at the towering Seelie and gulping. "Um…we haven't had a chance to talk since you made it back."

The blonde shifted on her chair, shakily adjusting the skirt of her fitted dress. "…I haven't had anything to say," she responded truthfully.

"I'm glad you made it back," he offered.

Was he? Really? She was tempted to blow up right there and then, and tell him to shove his pleasantries up his ass. That they could no longer be friends and associate as they had before. He hadn't betrayed her, nor she him, but it felt that way. There was an uneasy disconnect that she couldn't see a way of mending.

Her lips parted.

"Lorrin."

Her head turned. Zemir halted before the three, with a plate of grey looking finger sandwiches filled with chicken mayonnaise, cucumber salad, and cheese. In her other hand was a hot Sundeers gingerbread mocha. Her gaze raked the Elf, and her nose wrinkled at the suit.

"Detective…Kal, right?" he smiled nervously.

"Just Ms Kal. I quit," she clipped, parking on the chair next to the assassin. Her cold gaze remained on the dithering Favoured, even as she held the plate and coffee out to the reluctant girl. "Open for me," Zemir whispered, turning towards her. She placed a small triangle inside her obediently unhinged jaw.

Rye looked to Hawk, but he was ostentatiously staring out into the gardens through the newly replaced windows. So the display was regular and welcome. He cleared his throat —to Zemir's irritation and withering patience.

"Do you want something?" she asked him, making it abundantly clear that he was intruding. "You're just standing there. I'm busy, in case you hadn't noticed."

"I…I actually wanted to speak with Raffe."

"Good to see your manners still intact," the iman huffed. Then she held up the coffee cup to Lorrin's lips. It was only after she had taken several sips that Zemir turned back to their audience. "...Ask her, then."

The assassin looked at Rye with swollen eyes and a large lump in her throat, unsure if she'd be able to speak as much as he needed her to.

"Raffe, I know that I...that the way I saw you off wasn't very...uh, anyway. I wanted to apologise for not having sufficient fayth in you. I should've known better after all of these years. I really am happy to see you back, Saviour —"

Lorrin clutched onto Zemir's shoulder. "I think I'm going to be sick."

She hated the title, utterly. She hadn't saved *shit*. Her stomach would churn at the mere mention, but for some reason, when hearing it now specifically from Rye —from the same person who had dubbed her '*End-Bringer*' —the sick was very real and rapidly charging.

"Excuse us," the older iman hissed, guiding the blonde to her unsteady feet to help her hobble to the bathroom.

"You're rather terrible at this..." Lorrin heard Hawk remark.

Zemir knelt down, patting her back after making it in the nick of time, before adjusting the hairpins holding her short waves in place. She stared up at her, trying to decipher her expression. Her golden eyes flicked down to meet her gaze, only compounding the harshness of her emotionlessness. The silence was absolutely deafening. Neither broke eye contact even as she stood and offered her hands. Lorrin slid her palms along hers, then let herself be pulled up. Then her mouth suddenly started working. "...I feel like I have a hangover but without any of the fun, fuzzy memories. Instead it's a jarring nightmare."

She looked down at her leather boots.

The first night back had been spent alone in the hospital. When she had been discharged the next afternoon, she told Zemir of the terrors she had experienced. It had been the first time she had slept in fifty hours. And all her brain processed were fragments of death and slaughter. She'd woken up screaming at the estate. The detective had managed to calm her down, and given her pain medication for her still unpredictable heart. Lorrin had never been affected by work. Ever. It had to be that organ in her chest, or the strange mercy of the Daughter which softened her adamant walls and opened the floodgates of bottled trauma.

"Hey," Zemir quipped, lifting her chin to make her look her in the eye. "I'm right here. Don't you dare think for a single moment that you'll annoy me to the point where I would walk away."

Lorrin didn't deserve that.

It wasn't the same as caring for recovering veterans. She hadn't served her country or her city, and she certainly hadn't made herself worthy of anyone's devotion or adoration. Least of all from the person she did love.

She pushed away to rinse her mouth at the sink.

"I'm serious," Zemir insisted.

The assassin forced herself to straighten, her fingers curling on the pale porcelain. "...Your reassurance, though warm and welcome, does absolutely nothing. I hear it, feel its certainty, but...I can't retain the feeling. I can't...believe..."

"I'll keep bloody saying it," she promised. "Until it sinks in, or you're sick of it. But I won't be sick of you."

"You will be," Lorrin bit, viciously. "One day you're going to look at me and see what I see every time that I look in the mirror. And you'll be immeasurably disappointed. Perhaps confused."

Zemir took her by the shoulders and made her meet her eyes again. "Never."

Her face crumpled, and her vision blurred afresh. "Ze —"

"Pushing people away is not what you need, girl," she insisted. "And I'm not asking you to be satisfied with me. I'm not asking you to forge more friendships. I'm asking you to accept the fact that there are those who care, and won't stop. Those whose hearts twist and wrench at your pain. No matter how much you kick and scream. Because we all grieve, break and heal differently."

Her dark fingers were wiping away the quickening flow of tears before Lorrin could register anything else. She leaned into the touch, feeling like nothing existed beyond it. Surely no one had ever carefully wiped away her sorrow. Having the officer do it was thing that she could get used to. When she opened her eyes, Zemir had that unnerving look again. Of a warring mind.

Then she spoke. "Do you think that some things are just so deeply engrained in fate that nothing can stop them?"

Lorrin paused. "What do you mean?"

"Everything," she breathed, her eyes flicking back and forth. "Nothing at all. From smallest, insignificant thing, to the largest explosion. Gehman's court. The truth. Love. You making it back. The feeling of home."

Suddenly she understood what the question was about. Zemir couldn't say it directly, but she wanted to express relief. That there was not a third body being buried at the Hall of Sacrifice cemetery. She was selfishly elated that the part iman had come back to her. That they had been granted that chance.

It was the flood and irrationality of hope.

Lorrin blinked. "If there are multiple versions of our reality...then there are worlds where we made it, and ones where we didn't. Infinite possibilities for us to have met, and just as many where we didn't."

It wasn't worth her restless worry.

The detective's eyes caught the light overhead. "Then...on behalf of all the Zemirs who know of this feeling, I'm grateful that we live in this one."

Lorrin was shamelessly staring at her lips. "What feeling?"

"I have the faintest suspicion that you are actually fully aware, but you really want to hear me to say it."

The girl's eyelids fluttered. "...Maybe."

But Zemir didn't. Wouldn't. There were certain things which people found easy to say, that others gathered the greatest courage to even fathom. In the case of the detective, she would take mere action over words. She needed her words to mean the world should she ever voice it, but for now, Lorrin would accept stolen glances and the lacing of fingers. This was new for her too. She had been prepared to dive in, while Zemir dithered at the shallows. At least she was at the pool.

Lorrin wanted to kiss her, desperately.

Despite this not being the time nor place, her face was too close and the room was too small. There were a whole other host of reasons why she couldn't do it now, but one of the most prominent ones was that she found herself tentative at the edge by the diving boards now she stood at their height. There was something which gnawed at her, especially since she was back home.

"I...I'm not the same," Lorrin whispered, clutching onto Zemir's shoulders. "Not just physically. I came back changed, Kal. I...I died. I need the time to reconcile with that. So please...take this slowly. Be patient with me. I hardly understand what's wrong with me, but I think I'm trying to make sense of what happened in Gehman. It won't be quick, or easy." Her fingers clenched the regal jacket tighter. "...But I'll be okay. We...we'll be okay."

"We?" The detective's voice was delicate and honest, not taunting.

The girl's cheeks flushed slightly. "Are we not...is this not a '*we*'...?"

"I...I don't know."

Lorrin drew a sharp breath as Zemir leaned in to rest her forehead on hers, even though it was hot and damp. She firmly gripped her waist and held her close against to her front, preventing her from stumbling. She didn't need to say a single word. Everything was in that amber. In jade.

Was this it? What she'd avoided all her life in order never to feel devastation and regret? Those risks didn't disappear, by any means, but there had to be a peace made with the possibility that would always remain. She had to understand that one day, Zemir might find it tiresome. That love wouldn't be enough.

Lorrin was the first to look away; overwhelmed and giddy. "...Would now be a bad time to say that I don't think I can do this anymore?" she murmured. "The reception. I want to go upstairs...and sleep."

Zemir softened, as though that was perfectly okay.

CHAPTER 53

lorrin

THIS NEEDED TO happen.

She couldn't contain her apprehension as she stood outside of Her Excellency's soaring Loegon office. Most walls were entirely glass. The girl clenched her fists and stared up at the two crowning towers as though they would eat her alive. But the frames stayed in place; the windows did not glint with life; and the large steel doors were shut, revealing no long carpet tongue and wooden teeth.

But this *needed* to happen.

She had to face the governor —her work would now be never-ending and the support which had been assured still needed to stand.

The assassin was physically recovering, and so was Idun. Though she couldn't yet say the same mentally, things were improving. The terrors were down to two nights a week. She had stopped crying herself to exhaustion every time she visited Char's grave. And Hawk was finally exploring his options on what he wanted to do in the twenty-first century: another education. Because of his status, aside from his association with Lorrin, he had been invited to study at the Hall of Excellence. She was happy for him. It would keep him out of her house, and unchain him from history. From his own story.

Lee Nam-joon had apparently finished his thesis on the prophecy and her role in it, and was set to graduate in the coming month. She hadn't read it —she wasn't in the space to relive it again —but she wanted to one day.

The past wasn't going to stop her from living on.

With an abundance of free time, Lorrin had taken up a hobby: scrapbooking. She was going to document every detail of the life she'd live to the fullest. The first addition to it had been Zemir's signed badge of the city's coat of arms. The iman had burned almost everything; save for the few good quality garments which Madam G had promised to alter.

However, when Zemir finally resigned, Fran Denaris resigned from the Guard of Madir with her. She refused to tell anyone why, but she assured them all that she would be fine, and had taken up security personnel gigs in a variety of sectors —which only made Lorrin all the more nervous. She couldn't imagine bumping into the sour Faery on a wild night out. Or anything remotely fun.

She hadn't made proper friends with the rest of Faecide and Homicide. A part of her was afraid, and another worried that they would find out what she truly did for a living. For now they were people she knew, to whom she could offer a smile and have a couple of drinks with. Being the head of the Central Blades didn't bode well for staying friendly with law enforcement without Zemir as a part of it. But they wouldn't come to know of the crimes that she had committed since killing Jon De Polis. If the older iman's word was to be trusted.

The only other positive she saw from it was that since she was struggling to pick up her blade, she could give orders without being expected to kill anyone. It did make other admin tasks more difficult, but she had chosen the subordinate leaders with great care. And she vowed to put a little more trust in them.

Their respect for her now was carried down or shallow. What she had for the city had had an impact on things she had not even anticipated. She wasn't going to be cruel like those who'd come before her, but she couldn't have her assassins thinking of her as some righteous saviour.

Her bloodied crown was that way for a reason.

The golden thorns had become a symbol —one with which she was also slowly learning to reconcile. But she could deal with the stains and thorns. They were no longer bringing on the most awful memories; they didn't force her to rush to nearest bathroom. She could breathe.

She wanted to get better.

She wanted to live.

Her Excellency did not harbour the same wariness of her growing reputation. She wouldn't kneel in submission at Lorrin's feet. In the ideal scenario, the females were equals. Two powerful leaders with as much to benefit as to lose. Of course, that wasn't the case here. The governor was superior in position and influence. The blonde's only leverage was the criminal underbelly. Her people could dispose of hers —very messily, but not impossibly.

Nadune Madir was as grave as ever. Near death had only hardened her further. She sat impatient in the room intended to receive guests in the north tower. Thirty floors down, Zemir had implored Lorrin to be quick. They planned to get bubble waffles afterwards. Her mind whirred helplessly. It had all of the signs of a date, but the iman would never call it that.

Her Excellency cleared her throat and gestured for Lorrin to take a seat. Two Trolls in suits which seemed a touch too small for them guarded the doors. A sprite the size of her hand flitted about the room, from one monitor mounted the wall to another. An assortment of tea, coffee and cakes were spread on the low table before the governor.

"My eyes and ears," Nadune spoke, picking up a cup. "Ira."

"Ah."

She sunk down onto the opposite narrow sofa; the white arms sculpted into alpha Drakon. But it was still far too clean cut and monotone. Not a splash of colour or any other show of personality. Real personality —not heritage and public image. Although dismal grey said quite a fair amount about a person already.

"Can I offer you something?" the iman then asked, before taking a long sip. Her spine was not so straight, and her skin not so pale. "I can call my personal assistant if you require something not on the table."

"Oh, no thank you."

"Hm." Her voice reverberated with an odd disappointment. "Well, then. Let's keep this brief. I'm sure you lead a very busy life now, as do I."

"I appreciate that, Your Excellency," Lorrin said truthfully.

"So…how is your rehabilitation going? I trust that you have been resting well. Have you yet returned to the Central Blades Hall?"

That was what she wanted to discuss. The girl's wellbeing was in the light of the city's problems, almost trivial. Things of importance were the delicate little agreement she held with Nadune, and the falling in line of the assassin rings. The governor had to be absolutely certain that it was worth colluding with the rancid underbelly now that Lorrin had actually returned alive.

The part iman was no fool. She understood that it was merely business. Her Excellency didn't particularly hate her. She simply had to wary of potential threat and protect her citizens. The assassin who sat before now; tentative and damaged; had no intentions of betrayal or searching for loopholes. She certainly wouldn't trust the government blindly, no —but she would strive to make their arrangement worthwhile. They needed each other for the time being.

"I am set to return to office from next week," she answered. "I was advised not to be hasty in anything strenuous or directly linked to the incident."

"Oh, of course, of course," Her Excellency quipped, setting her cup down and picking up a piece of shortbread. "I am not trying to rush you, your Majesty. I just need to take stock of all my assets."

Lorrin started. So that was her true place.

Nadune looked her dead in the eye, even as she leaned back. "You *do* plan on being an asset to me, don't you? To the city."

She didn't have a fucking choice. If she didn't want the rings to face the law, which could very easily be arranged, then cooperation was not to be treated as an option. It was the condition of support. Now was not the time to strike. The girl's eyes lowered from those dark and slitted ones, like some sort of defeated animal.

"O-Of course, Your Excellency."

The governor knew of her power and how to wield it. Lorrin would have to relearn. She had been too eager before. Fear was effective, but she didn't want to lead with that. She needed loyalty. Friends.

"Good," Nadune almost purred, reaching for her cup again. "Now, the other thing. I've been asked to arrange a portrait sitting of you. It will only go up when you…pass on, but it needs to painted now, while your triumph is fresh. When are you available to sit? I may need several dates."

The girl struggled to swallow.

It felt wrong to have her portrait done at all.

Her priorities had shifted since that ambitious little assassin had vowed to carve her name into the stars. It now seemed nonsensical; inane and grossly villainous. It was not her who deserved to have her face hanging from the walls of the Hall of Legacy. It would linger even after she'd finally be gone. Her head, fat with self-importance and a business smile masking the city's fiercely tucked away corruption. Joining the ranks of the more noble and deserving honoured there made all of her shortcomings and sins come to light.

And no amount of guilt felt appropriate.

"…The weekends work best," she said anyway. She'd swallow it down. Her greed and ambition was still greater than conscience.

"Fantastic," the iman then smiled with her mouth only. "I'll book the next two. Then, that concludes that, seeing as you're not back at work. Be sure to book a meeting once you have your little office in order."

The blonde slowly rose to feet. "Oh yes, will do."

Like Hehl she was going to find herself answering to anyone. She stalked out, leaving Nadune Madir with her tea and cakes. And frowning out at the Harbour.

The breeze was harsh on Lorrin's blue jeans and oversized t-shirt —of which she tied the hem into a knot just above her navel. It was the light colour of the dawn; something that she had come to appreciate.

She raked her hair back with a pair of round white rimmed sunglasses, gripped her leather backpack and gestured to Zemir —who was too engrossed in a novel called '*Full Deck*'. The iman stood leaning on one hip with her free hand tugging through her blue hair; perhaps the picture of cool.

"I'm done," Lorrin announced.

The older iman glanced aside and fished for the keys to her motorcycle in the pockets of her wide-leg tan linen shorts. It wasn't with irritation. Zemir was most likely amused. She gently fanned herself with collar of her loose cotton blouse, before sauntering to the parking spot where her most prized possession waited.

Lorrin had been on the bike a total of two times. The first hadn't been an actual drive, and the second was a secret she was never going to tell —that she'd gone for a joyride on her own. It had only been for a few minutes, and she had returned in mint condition. But the feeling had been irreplaceable. Untethered, and free. Powerful. That was where Zemir got all of that gall.

There was nothing like it.

To the iman's knowledge, Lorrin had never ridden her motorcycle before.

She tossed her a helmet. "Bubble waffles, here we come."

"You've got to try the '*summer fruits parfait*' this time," urged the girl, fastening the strap securely and mounting behind the driver. She wrapped her arms around her midsection and let out an exclamation as they sped off.

There was a different freedom as the wind bit at them.

She had had control when driving her own car, and the fun had come in the form of pushing limits. On the back of Zemir's motorcycle, she had no control. All which she could do was hang on and enjoy the interlude from the heat of the suns. There was a peace she felt; with her eyes closed, her head skyward, all while Zemir laughed and revved the engine.

They couldn't get to *Hansel & Gretel* fast enough.

The line wasn't very long. Still, Lorrin couldn't help feeling as though all eyes were on them. The two females stood out distinctively, especially when together. Having her face up on billboards didn't help, either. Overnight she had turned into some sort of celebrity —a whole host of companies clamoured for advertisements and endorsement. But that wasn't what she wanted. What she needed. She needed this life to be quiet and slow. Savoured.

Once they had gotten their waffles —one banana and pecan, the other inspired by the Victorous sponge since the summer fruits had been sold out —they sat on a wooden bench on the pier, overlooking the sea to the southeast as they ate. Gulls and sprites swooped down to try their luck, but most glided high through the air like the colourful kites soaring in the sky.

She remembered something then.

When she had still believed in the fairytales about which she'd read, sprites and wisps gathered in abundance. They had led her to wild roses and the traces of castles. Ruins that had left their impression on the world. There had been no magic keys or lost princes, but there had always been stories.

The suns warmed her face through the breeze. And for the first time in a while, her skin didn't feel like it was ice cold.

"It *was* a date," Lorrin quipped, before dotting Zemir's nose with icing sugar. "That time we first came to the beach. Even though neither of us said it."

"What," she deadpanned, hurriedly wiping at it.

Her revenge was ice cream; a smear from her chin up to her opposite cheek. And the assassin was about to protest —until she felt her tongue swipe it up in one fluid movement. She went rigid. Zemir lingered, figuring out what exact shade of jade her eyes were. Then she leaned into what she actually wanted. Lorrin arched into the deepening kiss, tugging the older iman in closer with her free hand. Her open hand reached for the girl's neck. She swore that she felt love in it. Something that wasn't casual, and something selfish. It was the kind of embrace that was too sweet and sickening for the public. But she didn't ever want it to end. The taste of ice cream and nuts had never been so delicious.

Zemir watched her blink rapidly when she slowly pulled away. She was never going to grow used to the way her eyes roared with flame in the sunlight. How she spoke with them, when certain words evaded her. The iman then offered her a few of those morsels intended to avoid. "…I know."

Lorrin's heart picked up its pace. "Does that mean —?"

Something abruptly vibrated.

It was Zemir's cellphone. "Shit, another twenty," she hissed.

"Another what?" Lorrin leaned closer. "…Oh my Goddess, are you seriously *complaining* about Instantgram follow requests?"

Zemir lightly scoffed. "Look, when you told me about social media, I figured it made sense for you. You're an integral part of our history now. But I'm…I'm still just me. So unimportant next to you."

"Excuse me? Who told you that?"

She shifted nervously. "...I didn't do anything in the end. After you had left, everyone just pitied me. And I didn't even have the nerve to file a complaint when I quit. I feel...like my fame is something of an accessory."

Lorrin couldn't believe that she was hearing. *The* great Zemir Kal was having thoughts of inadequacy. She was feeling horribly, wrongfully spotlighted. The most talented and dedicated detective to ever work for the Guard of Madir. There was nothing that Lorrin could offer to make her discard those thoughts, but just as she had for her, she could provide unrelenting reassurance.

Pale fingers inched towards bronze. "I once read somewhere that blessed are those who live for fayth and city," she murmured. "We are our own people in our own rights, and deserve celebration. And the prophecy...that was something that I had to do. Alone. It tested me, challenged me —and I am better for it."

Zemir started, before giving into the smile forcing its way onto her face. She gripped those hesitant fingers on the bench, leaned back and took a bite out of her coned waffle. Then she tilted her head and gave the blonde a quizzical look. "That was too sentimental. Even for you."

"Guilty," Lorrin heartily admitted, getting back into her own cone. "But one hundred percent serious. Don't ever think someone else makes you special."

Zemir sighed and glanced back at her cellphone. "I can't understand how I keep getting requests when my profile is utterly empty."

The assassin sat upright. Despite not having any semblance of a smartphone, even she had managed to post from her tablet with a good Wi-Fi connection. "No, no, no. I have pictures with you on my feed. You need them too." She plucked it from her hand and opened the camera.

"Wait, what —?"

"Smile for me." She grinned and gently grabbed the iman's face, pinching in her cheeks, and made her look ahead. She varied her expressions of happiness — and then pulled away to start typing something. Zemir tried to grab for the device, but Lorrin held it out of her reach, insisting that she wait for her to finish.

When she had, she jumped up from the bench. Her short hair still billowed in the breeze. "It's good to be home."

426

Zemir just stared at her, a smile growing. Then her curiosity piqued. She opened the app and went to her profile. There was now a post. Several slides of Lorrin grinning, laughing —while her own face had remained pouty before she had given a playful snarl and turned aside. And below that, in the caption, were the three words '*grumpy x sunshine*'.

Every time that she felt Zemir's body against hers, it was as if they'd been apart for an ungodly amount of time. Days. Months. Years. Impossible, but rationality had never been with her —ever since she had set foot in *Slow Poison*.

They stood before one another, carefully undoing every zip and button with meticulous leisure. Instead of the fumble of desperation, there was a heat in the slowness; a pleasure in patience. This way, she could concentrate and memorise every part of herself that the iman touched. Her arms. Her waist. Each breast, and its peak. Her thighs. Her spine. The healing mark on her chest.

The vulnerability of having Zemir look at her and see everything in such clear light was enough to make her blush. Bearing one's soul, if they did indeed have such things, in that moment was nothing. What the eyes drank in was what should spark fear. Was what made one weak.

Each kiss was slow and thought out, as if it had been planned. Lorrin was restless despite her enjoyment of the pace. Her muscles fought to betray her and *do* something —to grip that blue hair and rake through it furiously. Her mouth shouldn't be that warm, that gentle. It'd break her apart, utterly.

But then mercy was granted, and Zemir retreated to lead her towards the bed. Not even the setting suns would rush them; rush this. Every time their gazes locked, Lorrin found herself a little at the mercy of gravity. She had known of breath once, she thought, as blood continued to rush to the surface of her face. Such vital things were somehow no longer innate and uncomplicated. Everything was an effort. About which she didn't dare to complain.

There was a slither of mirror on the left side of the bed. They sat facing it, and

Lorrin sat between her legs. She turned her head to ask for an elaboration. Zemir softly kissed her nape, before taking one of her legs and lifting it up over her own. Now she sat open to the length of silver —and to exploring fingers. "You said that you wanted to know my kinky secrets, Raffe," she murmured.

"Oh. I…" The assassin's spine arced as she threw back her head. But Zemir took hold of her neck and made her look down at the mirror again. Those amber eyes didn't stray from hers in the reflection.

"I want you to see what I do to you," she said along the curve of her reddened ear. "I want you to see what *I* see."

Lorrin gasped out a breath.

Zemir's hands burned and left their warmth on her arms and stomach. Lower. They wandered everywhere as she planted her mouth on Lorrin's quivering shoulders and her neck. Fingers grazed the inside of her flexed thighs. The tips taunted her without the slightest hurry. Zemir bit down on her skin when she felt out the extent of her arousal. Then the fingers disappeared within her, and she watched their descent. Her body jolted, desperate.

It was all fire. It had been from the start. And she was gulping for air through the flames; though willing to burn among them. Her hands clawed for something to hold her down in reality, lest she find herself lost. And the tears she cried were ones of bliss, not pain or sadness.

Zemir still licked them from her temple. Lorrin began to writhe at the sudden onslaught of sensations; her hips rolled, following the movements of that hand, and yielding to it. It mounted and tore at her far too quickly.

But she wouldn't forget it —the image she stared at in the mirror of herself so desired and near satisfied. Yet not fully. She shifted to swivel and face the older iman, holding onto her shoulders as hers still heaved.

"Unbelievable," she whispered. "…Give me more."

"Say please."

"Oh my Goddess —"

Her body was drawn closer, so that their lungs shared the air between. It was the slightest touch, that kiss. It set off fluttering things in the pit of her stomach. She had never realised how much she'd wanted this. Wanted the two of them together burning in something close to love, for however long they would be granted.

Zemir then gripped her thighs and pulled them down onto the mattress.

"Ride," she instructed.

Lorrin raised an eyebrow. So she wasn't the only one who wanted to throw self-control out of the window. Zemir wouldn't admit it aloud, but the slight flush to her face and the breathlessness of her lungs made it obvious.

The blonde sat up, aligned herself accordingly, before lifting one of Zemir's legs up over her thigh and grinding forwards. Both of them shivered at the feeling, and dug their fingers into each other as the fire only raged.

What a sight —if it had been the older iman's goal to savour the look on her face as she'd moaned and come undone in her arms, then she would seize this opportunity to stare down at her bronze face. The way she bit her lip; bit down her sounds of pleasure. The way in which she wasn't nearly overwhelmed enough to close her eyes. She could make out slitted gold, intense and determined.

"*Faster,*" Zemir demanded through clenched teeth, her short, black-painted nails scraping. But it sounded a lot more like a beg.

In the cool of the next dawn, Lorrin Raffe leaned out against the balcony in the wrinkled t-shirt she'd worn the day before. A long cigarette burned between her lips, billowing smoke as she absentmindedly went over the past month while staring at the blue sea. Flashes of purple flickered in her vision, but did not hurt as intensely as they once had.

The bites and scratches trailing her legs stung in the open air.

The sky and its clouds were melancholic before the suns fully peaked over the horizon, but she liked the grey. For a moment, all the world was unrighteous. She would like to think that the Gehman ordeal hadn't stolen as much as it had from her, but there was no other way to reconcile herself with existing here again.

For how much longer would she feel the disconnect?

"Hey."

As usual, Zemir's voice grounded her a little.

She leaned with her, as she had come to do, with pyjama shorts and the cotton shirt over her shoulders. "Couldn't sleep?"

Lorrin shook her head.

It hadn't always been the cause of nightmares. Sometimes, her body simply refused to rest. She was sure that that took its toll, but no evidence of it showed itself outwardly. It didn't make her tired or unalert. Maybe, it made her numb.

"...I thought that you were going to die," Zemir eventually murmured. She had never garnered the courage to say it aloud so starkly. Not even when she had offered words of comfort before Lorrin had gone to the Unseelie Court. She hadn't allowed herself to damn the situation.

Lorrin took a drag. "I did die," she reminded her.

Solemnity turned to pain. "You know that's not what I meant."

The blonde sighed. "You know, technically, we could die at any moment. Any hour of the day. That inevitability might not be the same as when you know that the path you walk is to your end, but the fact is we don't all live forever. We have to accept that. And...one day you'll have to say goodbye to m —"

"Please don't finish that," begged Zemir. "Don't do that now."

She couldn't bear to stomach the fact that because of that Seelie heart, Lorrin would die long after her and bury her, too. She didn't want the girl's life to turn out that way, thought she had no choice. An existence where she would come to bury those she had known.

Lorrin's lips clamped the cigarette, before she exhaled.

"...Maybe we should wash up," Zemir then suggested, turning away slightly.

"Kal," the assassin breathed. "Death makes things mean something, don't you think? Because we're so finite, we pursue things just as fleeting. But I'd like to think that there are certain things which flourish in spite of consequence."

Like love.

The iman paused, but didn't move away. "Sometimes, you terrify me, Raffe."

"Then let's terrify each other."

430

Her dark lips lifted at the corners. She didn't look so scared now. No. Not all. Then she laughed. "Is this flirting, girl?"

For some reason, Lorrin couldn't answer. Not now. Would she hate her for it? Would she dodge the topic as usual?

Zemir's eyes lowered to the ground far below them, before she looked out at the harbour as though she might see precisely what Lorrin saw —and asked her the most casual question she had ever heard. "…Stay beside me?"

This was the sinking into the pool of which she had been so afraid. The deep end was just ahead, but feeling the water lap against them was enough.

The suns were turning the blue-grey into hues of deep orange. But the rest of the world disappeared at those fragile words.

"Yeah?" Lorrin murmured.

"Yeah."

ACKNOWLEDGEMENT

'*There's a Dagger in Your Back*' began as a passion project
to put some of my friends into one book. From strings of unwoven
ideas, it was stitched into the intricate novel it is today.
Thank you to every single one of those flatmates; Lauren, Charlotte,
Ryan, Johnny, Sid, George, Jack and Harry, for providing
the inspiration and motivation.

Thank you to Shyanne Taylor, for being a great friend
—who I met very fittingly because of this project. I loved
fangirling and exchanging sneak peeks with you.

Thank you to every single one of my Street Team
members and early readers
—for encouraging me every step of the way.